A MAD
AND MINDLESS
NIGHT

ALSO BY ELIZABETH COLE

Honor & Roses

Choose the Sky

Raven's Rise

Peregrine's Call

A Heartless Design

A Reckless Soul

A Shameless Angel

The Lady Dauntless

Beneath Sleepless Stars

Daisy and the Duke

Heather and the Highlander

Rose and the Rogue

Poppy and the Pirate

A MAD AND MINDLESS NIGHT

Elizabeth Cole

SKYSPARK BOOKS

PHILADELPHIA, PENNSYLVANIA

SkySpark Books
Philadelphia, Pennsylvania
skysparkbooks.com
inquiry@skysparkbooks.com

Publisher's Note: This is a work of fiction. Names, characters, places, and incidents are a product of the author's imagination. Locales and public names are sometimes used for atmospheric purposes. Any resemblance to actual people, living or dead, or to businesses, companies, events, institutions, or locales is completely coincidental.

Ordering Information:
Quantity sales. Special discounts are available on quantity purchases by corporations, associations, and others. For details, contact the "Special Sales Department" at the address above.

A MAD AND MINDLESS NIGHT / Cole, Elizabeth. – 1st ed.
ISBN-10: 1-942316-20-8
ISBN-13: 978-1-942316-20-6

Chapter 1

1810

"Tell me the truth, Reggie. How do I look?"

Ashley Allander already knew the answer. He looked like a perfect devil.

The woman he called Reggie surveyed him with knowing eyes, saying, "You'll do for an evening in Town."

So would she. The yellow silk of her dress glowed in the candlelight, contrasting with Ash's dark blue jacket. Together, they'd draw more attention than any other couple in London.

That was how Ash liked it.

The lady in gold was Regina Fox, one of the most sought-after courtesans in the whole city. To have an affair with her ensured a man notoriety for years. To keep her attention was a more difficult task. Ash was one of the very few who had. Though their relationship was now one of friendship rather than passion, all the years between hadn't dulled his appreciation of her.

"Shall we go?" he asked, offering an arm to Reggie.

She slipped her hand into the crook of his elbow. "Yes,

indeed. I wouldn't want to be late."

"You still refuse to tell me what this mysterious event is?" Ash asked. "Not even a hint?"

"Some things ought to be surprising," Reggie said, "or the world would be too dull." She yawned then, to punctuate her comment. "I can't stand dullness."

Ash knew exactly what she meant. He lived for excitement, for conflict, for anything that could keep his mind from turning inward. Luckily, he had Reggie to keep him from the doldrums.

Her proposal of an evening on the Town, capped with a promise of an unusual encounter, was just what he needed. Lately, Ash had been too much at home, too inclined to fall into the melancholy he hated, too tempted by the chemical diversions he often ached to be free of.

"Where to first?" he asked.

Reggie named a favorite gaming house, and Ash told the carriage driver where to go. Then he sat opposite Reg and settled back for the ride. "Can I guess?" he asked.

"Certainly," Reggie said, with an impish smile.

Ash mentally ran through the possibilities, but whenever he was about to guess one, Reggie's expression made him hesitate. She looked far too excited and too pleased with herself. This had to be something singular.

"Have I missed my birthday?" he asked suddenly. "Or something else?"

"Your birthday is in January," Reggie said, "and it's now July, so I should hope I haven't neglected you *that* badly."

"Well, you have been occupied," Ash noted, delicately referencing her profession.

"I am presently at leisure," Reg said cheerfully. "Lord Spalding and I have parted ways... most amicably, of course."

Ash was surprised to hear it. The man had been an ardent patron.

"His wife wants to go to Italy for a year," Reggie explained, "and she insisted on his company."

"Ah, marriage. It does impose some constraints."

Ash had never been constrained by marriage himself. As one of the more disreputable rakes in London, his experience was confined to other people's marriages...in particular the rich, bored wives of inattentive husbands. Such ladies sought out more interesting company. Ash was actually quite discreet, but despite all his efforts, he did occasionally have to show up for a duel with an annoyed husband.

Fortunately, Ash was skilled with both a sword and a pistol, and this fact was well known. It helped limit the number of duels he was requested to engage in.

Reggie laughed softly. "Another world," she said. "Domestic bliss. I suppose we'll never know anything about it firsthand." Her voice was a little wistful.

Ash didn't like to think of anything making Reggie sad, so he said, "What could be better than our world, Reg? We do what we like, with whomever we like, whenever we like. The city's ours till dawn, and we never have to rise before noon."

Reggie nodded. "True. Oh! Speaking of rising, I have encountered a slight inconvenience. Now that my arrangement with Lord Spalding is concluded, he will no longer provide for my lodgings, and..."

"You know you don't have to ask," Ash interjected. "You're a guest at my house for as long as you like. I insist."

"Thank you. It should only be a matter of a few weeks."

"I expect so," he said, with a laugh. "How long have

you ever been without a patron?"

"Not very long. Though there's something to be said for autonomy. I'm looking forward to tonight…my first night in a long time without a patron to please. It's good to be with a friend." She reached forward and took Ash's hand, squeezing it briefly. "I'm so glad you wanted to join me."

"Any time," he said, again catching a hint of somberness in Reg. "Especially when you've promised a surprise."

Her expression grew secretive again. "Just you wait."

Reggie seemed bound to make the most of her evening. She and Ash hit half a dozen favorite haunts, from private salons to gaming hells, all populated by wealthy guests eager to play in London's underworld. Everywhere they went, they ran into old acquaintances and new admirers. And everywhere, they were noticed— the Woman in Gold and the Fallen Angel.

Ash heard the nickname murmured around him, not just tonight, but for years, ever since he'd come to London. The name was now part of his identity, almost a calling card. Secretly, he hated it.

Reggie noticed his reaction to it one time that night, and whispered, "Ignore them. The name means nothing."

"Have you just come to London?" Ash returned, with gentle sarcasm. "A name means everything."

"And yours is well known," Reggie said. "In your way, you're more influential than your brother, who must content himself with the title of Lord Forester."

Ash snorted. "May it bring him joy."

"You envy him."

"Envy *him*? You're joking. I've never wanted the title."

"Not the title, but the life he has now. A home, a role,

a wife. A *purpose*," she added, with a certain edge to her voice.

"That life?" Ash asked incredulously. "My brother is the perfect model of a perfect Englishman. Committed to serving his country and king, living the quiet family life in the country. I'd die of boredom within a month."

"What of his other activities?" Reggie murmured, while she waved coquettishly to an acquaintance across the room.

Ash stumbled half a step before recovering. "We agreed not to talk about his other activities."

It had come as a shock when he learned his brother Bruce was a spy. It wasn't the sort of thing one expected to hear about a straight-laced, dull as mud, comfortably placed viscount. But it was true. Some time ago, Bruce had come to Ash for help getting information from a very shady place, and Ash rose to the occasion. Of course, he demanded to know why Bruce needed such assistance. Bruce revealed himself as a member of a clandestine organization dedicated to protecting crown and country against all enemies. He even shared the name: Zodiac.

"Why are you telling me all this?" Ash had asked, suddenly uncertain of the stability of his world.

"Because," Bruce had explained, reasonably enough, "it's quite possible one of my assignments won't end well."

"Meaning you'll be killed."

"Yes. In which case, you inherit everything. If you become viscount, rattling around Old Harrow, at least you'll know why. Whatever the official story is, at least you'll understand."

Ash had barely spoken with his brother for over a decade, yet the idea of losing him—even for some glorious patriotic cause—made Ash turn cold. "God knows I don't want to rejoin respectable society, and respectable society doesn't want me to rejoin either. So don't die, Bruce. As a favor to me."

Bruce had smiled, saying, "I'll do my best. Don't ever speak of this, of course."

Ash rolled his eyes. "I do know the meaning of the word *clandestine*."

"You can talk to Miss Fox about it," Bruce amended. "She knows."

"What?" Ash was actually offended by that. "You told *Reggie* before me?"

"It was a matter of necessity," Bruce said. "She happened to wander into one of my assignments, and I had to ensure she didn't expose me. Besides, why should you be surprised when you're not informed, Ash? You made it clear that you were done with the family."

"If that's so, why'd you ask me for help?" Ash had retorted.

"Desperation," Bruce had said. "It won't happen again."

That was the last time Ash spoke to his brother, on that topic or any other.

It wasn't the last time he thought of it, though. Ash and Reggie discussed it once or twice, before Ash declared the topic verboten.

Yet now Reggie had to hint at it again. "I confess to a lingering curiosity," she said. "You don't?"

God, yes, he did. But he'd rather die than admit to it. "It's not my affair," he said, affecting a lack of concern. "I've got enough affairs of my own anyway."

"Do you?" Reggie asked. "You haven't engaged in a duel for months. I remember most of your affairs ending at dawn when a husband or father got wind of it."

He acknowledged that with, "I'm a little out of practice."

"Well, another chance will emerge," Reggie said. "We wouldn't want you to get rusty. It would upset the rumors that the Fallen Angel wins all his duels because the Devil protects his own."

"Rubbish." Ash laughed, feeling better at hearing the absurd story.

"I only report what I hear." Reggie smiled at him, and leaned a little closer. "In truth," she added, conspiratorially, "I don't like your dueling. I always worry till I hear the news that you're safe."

"I'm in no danger." Indeed, Ash couldn't remember a time in his adult life when he risked himself for anything. He didn't consider dueling a risk.

"It's time," Reggie announced, interrupting his thoughts. "Follow me."

Ash followed Reggie to a private room of the club she insisted they visit tonight.

Standing there was someone Ash wouldn't have guessed in a thousand years. Bruce Allander. Lord Forester. His older brother.

"Hello, Ashley."

Ash stared, unprepared for this juxtaposition of his upright, boring brother sitting here in one of London's darkest and most debauched corners. "What the hell are you doing here?" he asked.

"We need to talk."

Chapter 2

ASH CAST AN ACCUSING GLANCE toward Reggie. "Well, you win. I'm surprised."

"I thought you wouldn't meet him if you knew." Reggie looked apologetic, but still determined.

"You were right." Ash turned back to his brother. "Nothing for it now. What do you want from me?"

"First, to ask you how you're doing. It's been some time." Bruce was in full form, all serious expression and stiff upper lip and spine straight as a lance.

"I'm still alive," he said. "Sorry to disappoint."

"Oh, Ash." Regina shook her head. Then she smiled at Bruce, her deep brown eyes snapping. "A pleasure to see you, my lord. How is your wife?"

"Very well," Bruce said. His expression changed for a moment, becoming almost...*tender?* Ash couldn't believe it.

"You're looking well too, Miss Fox," Bruce said, after a moment. Most men needed a moment after seeing Regina at close quarters. "Vibrant, as always."

"Of course she does," Ash returned in his most insolent tone. "Thanks to the company she keeps." He let the insinuation linger.

His brother stood still for a moment, obviously fighting off the urge to reprimand Ash for his scandalous ways.

"I need your help," Bruce finally said.

"Again?" Ash said. "I can't imagine what it must have cost you to say those words."

"You're not making this easy, Ash."

"Why should I?" Ash stood to his full height, which was still several inches shy of Bruce's towering stature. Yet another way Ash would never measure up.

Bruce looked at him for a moment, then deliberately sat down on one of the upholstered chairs by the fireplace. "Can we put enmity aside for one moment? Do you think I would have come here if the matter wasn't vital?"

"No," Ash replied quietly. "I guess not. This is one of *those* things, isn't it?"

"As you say," Bruce confirmed with a half-smile, "one of those things." He meant the assignments that so frequently took him into danger, all for the sake of the Crown. "How did you guess?"

"Why else would you bother coming all the way to this less than elite venue, in secret, just to talk to me? If this was legitimate business, you'd be Lord Forester, summoning me to a meeting in one of your lofty domains."

"Can't argue with that logic," Bruce admitted.

"You once promised you'd never ask for my help again." Ash crossed his arms. "Yet here you are. So what is it? Another delve into some bookmaker's files? Or do you need me to threaten a lady with ruin so you can ferret some secret out of her family?"

"No," Bruce said, "it's nothing so immoral."

"Pity. I suppose you'd better explain what you want

done. Though I can't imagine how I can help. I have no military training, nor spycraft, nor the overbearing love of the king and country your circle seems to have in spades."

"No. What you have is a highly developed sense of skepticism and a willingness to go happily into situations that would destroy other men's reputations."

"Ah, so we get to the point. I have no reputation to save, and therefore am ideal?"

"You're far from ideal," his brother said. "But there's no one else to use right now."

"Use for what, exactly?"

"There's a man named Albert Morrison. He contacted the government over a year ago, explaining he and a colleague developed a new method of communication that could assist our side in the war against France. To be very brief, he struck a deal with the military and was given funds to continue his work—and a promise of compensation at the end, with the understanding that once it was ready, he would hand everything over to the British government."

"So?"

"His contacts in the War Department haven't heard a word out of him for many months."

"He absconded with the funds." Ash shrugged. "Too bad, but hardly surprising. What's it got to do with your group?"

"According to those who knew him, Albert Morrison was a loyal subject and a patriot. Stealing the money would be out of character. So is the lack of communication, for that matter. The concern is that something has happened to him. Perhaps he's being blackmailed, or coerced to keep silent."

"Even if he is, you said no one can find him."

"Actually, that's just changed. We know his location."

"Where? If you think I'm gallivanting off to the continent to chase wild geese, you're much mistaken."

"You only have to go to the town of Worthing. Well, near it. A place called Grasmere House, right on the coast."

Ash grimaced. "That's worse."

"I need you to go to the house, meet with Morrison, and observe the situation. Essentially, reaffirm his cooperation with the government, or return with a report about why it ended. You could hardly ask for a simpler quest."

"For a quest, it doesn't feel particularly heroic. There's not even a damsel in distress to save."

"Just as well," Bruce said drily. "Considering you tend to ruin ladies rather than save them."

Ash glared at his brother. "Not interested. Sorry to waste your time." He turned to go.

"Wait, Ash," said Reggie, putting up a hand. "Your brother didn't mean to say that."

"Of course he did," Ash said, turning back to Bruce. "Regardless, I don't see why you'd need any sort of secret agent to go. Sounds like a job for a normal clerk."

"A normal clerk wouldn't have the intelligence to observe the place, or Morrison's methods. Nor would a normal clerk be likely to learn if Morrison is facing some unusual obstacles—such as blackmail or coercion. You've seen both of those factors at work."

"Even so, you think he'll tell *me* if he's in trouble?" Ash asked. "I'm not exactly an obvious choice."

Bruce spread his hands out. "Not as Ashley Allander. *You* are a deviant, disaffected rake. You flout society and associate with the worst sort of people on a lark."

"Something to do," Ash said, not sure if he managed to hide the hurt that unexpectedly welled up after hearing his own brother assess him just as everybody else did.

"You're also well-read, intelligent, a keen observer... and you have a gift for getting people's confidence, whether that's in their interest or not," Bruce went on. "To get past any risk of your reputation preceding you, I've created a new persona for you to use. No concern that anyone will recognize your real identity...and once this assignment is over, you can go back to your usual diversion. If that's what you want."

Bruce handed Ash a slim dossier.

Ash flipped it open, reading over the life of a Mr Ashley *Allen*. Government clerk. Etonian. Distinguished service record. Spoke French, German, and Latin. Never married, no siblings.

"Sounds like my extraordinarily dull long-lost twin," Ash commented. "You think anyone will believe this?"

"All you have to do is behave." Bruce frowned. "You're after a little information. No need to draw attention, make a scene, or draw anyone into your personal maelstrom."

"How boring."

"Think of it as a puzzle. Learn why we lost communication. Learn why Morrison moved from London to Worthing, and what the status of his work is. Ask for a demonstration, and learn whatever else you can. You can pay him directly if it's a matter of funds."

"Hold a moment," Ash said. "I have a limited budget."

"Yes, I know," Bruce said, so matter-of-factly that Ash wondered just how much information his brother had on his life. "You're good at appearing to be far more extravagant than you really are."

"Thank you...I think."

"The Zodiac can advance you some money. Enough to convince Morrison you're a legitimate agent who can fund his work, if needed."

Ash frowned. "I can see a number of ways for this to go horribly wrong."

"I wouldn't have asked you if I didn't think you were capable."

Capable. In this context, that was either a compliment or an insult, and Ash had been so disconnected from his brother for so many years that he didn't know which it was. "So, just to reiterate, you want me to go to an isolated country house, and skulk around until I find something useful. Why don't *you* go?"

"I've done that sort of thing before," said Bruce, "but in fact, I've got somewhere else to be. An assignment I can't talk about."

"Then why not send another of your colleagues?"

"We're stretched thin. A few, ah, vacancies have arisen."

Ash frowned. "Do I even want to guess what causes a vacancy in a ring of spies?" He didn't think of himself as a coward, but Ash also enjoyed breathing.

"There's always a risk," Bruce admitted, which wasn't at all reassuring.

"How long will this take?"

"I can't be certain. A week?" Bruce guessed. "Perhaps two. Anyway, it's summer and there's no reason to linger in London during the summer."

"That's true enough. So a few weeks at the seaside, is it? Very well."

"You won't be completely adrift," Bruce promised. "I'll arrange for a valet to join you."

"I have a valet. Sullivan has been with me for years."

"Leave him in London. The man who will accompany you has certain…talents. And he'll be able to get in contact with the Zodiac, if needed."

"It'll hurt Sullivan's feelings," Ash warned cheekily.

"Do you take anything seriously?"

"I suppose you're about to find out."

"If you don't—"

"I'll do it," Ash interrupted, right before he wondered why he'd passed up a perfectly good chance to bow out. "How difficult could it possibly be?"

"Thank you."

"Well, that's it, then. I'd say I'm looking forward to it, but that would be a lie."

"Spare me, Ash."

"Give my regards to your wife. What's her name again?" Ash knew her name, but he couldn't resist goading Bruce about it.

"Sophie," he ground out.

"Oh, yes. Someday I'll meet her. I'm sure the name would come more easily to me if I ever had occasion to visit the old estate."

"You were always welcome at home, Ash."

"Ah, *no*, I wasn't," Ash reminded him.

Bruce only shook his head. "Point taken. You're welcome *again,* now that I'm Forester."

"If I survive this odd little assignment, perhaps I'll come for a visit."

Bruce nodded, evidently pleased, to judge by the flash in his eyes. "The Zodiac will set things in motion."

Ash escorted Reggie out of the room, not willing to think too hard about what he'd just agreed to.

"It's different, at least," Reggie said as they walked. "You're always saying you're bored. And we both know what can happen when you get bored."

"Don't," Ash said. "Haven't I told you? I've been free of any need for laudanum for a long time now." It was true, he told himself. He didn't *need* the drug. He simply wanted it occasionally.

"I'm glad to hear it. Aren't you intrigued?" she asked, turning back to the subject.

"A little," he admitted. "Though I do wish there was a lady to save."

Reggie smiled. "You never know."

Chapter 3

NO ONE ELSE WAS GOING to save Nora, so she resolved to save herself.

In general, it was not the thing for ladies to climb out of a window, run over a roof, scale a trellis down to the ground, and then run off into the night. However, Nora didn't regret her actions for a moment.

She did regret she didn't have something warmer on. She wore only a thin summer dress, which would have hardly protected her from a draft inside the house she just escaped from. Although it was summer, the wind rushing in from the sea was misty and cold. Goosebumps prickled her bare arms.

Nora spent a few precious moments running down the main drive from the house, the one that led to the Worthing road. She pressed her feet hard into the slightly muddy surface, leaving clear footprints behind.

Then she turned off the drive. She moved carefully over rough grass, leaving no prints at all. Circling back to the house, she descended the narrow stairs of the cliff to the beach below.

Once at the base, she moved as fast as she could, stepping over the wide, flat shore. The ground beneath her bare feet was partly rocks and partly sand. All of it was damp, with clumps of seaweed or flotsam pushed into treacherous ridges by the tides.

In the distance, a slender tower rose above a spit of land that jutted into the sea—an abandoned lighthouse. The sea appeared black, as did the sky. No boats or ships could be seen.

Nora kept a steady pace, her eyes fixed on the ground before her. She couldn't afford to trip or hurt herself. Ahead of her, another steep cliff rose up at least a hundred feet. At the top was a narrow track, which would eventually lead her to a tiny village, where she might beg for some proper clothing from a local woman, if she could do so unseen.

From there, she'd find a way to travel to the next town, where she could give a false name and work till she could afford to journey to London. Once in London, she could begin to search for her brother. Eventually, she'd discover where he was. Most importantly, when she returned to London, she'd never have to look at the ocean shore again. She'd be back with her family, safe, warm, and out of the trap she'd been pulled into.

Nora had planned this latest escape attempt as carefully as she could, considering her meager resources—no money, no supplies, no friends, no idea if she'd succeed.

She only hoped that her disappearance would not be noticed immediately, and when it was noticed, that her pursuers would be led off on the false trail she left for them. They should assume Nora was making for the main road and Worthing. Instead, Nora aimed for the longer, more dangerous path over the beach. She would risk the longer route if it meant she had a better chance of reaching civilization.

She paused to catch her breath and peeked over her shoulder. In the distance, at the top of the cliff to the south, she saw several windows of the place known as Grasmere House glowing brightly—too much light for this hour of the night. Drat. They must know she was gone.

Nora cursed the cold sea wind and continued on, but only for a moment. A new sound made her stop in her tracks. She turned her head halfway, listening intently. There it was again…the baying of a hound.

"Oh, no." The hunting dog wouldn't be tricked by false clues. Her scent would lead any pursuers directly to her, no matter how much Nora stumbled through puddles and rivulets across the beach. She had to hurry.

"Elanora!" a voice boomed out, ricocheting off the rocky shore until it seemed to come from everywhere at once. "Elanooooraaaa!"

The call was almost cheerful, as if this was just a game of hide and seek, instead of Nora's desperate bid for freedom.

The voice was still far away, but it would soon get closer. If she could reach the cliffs, she could climb high enough to be safe from the snapping jaws of that cursed hunting dog. She only needed a little more time…

Then Nora stepped on a patch of rotting, slippery seaweed. Her foot slid beneath her and she fell. Her hands shot out to break the fall, and the rough surface of the rocks scraped her palms. Her ankle was twisted under her leg, and she whimpered once in pain.

"No, no, no," she muttered. "Get up."

She scrambled to her knees, looking around to see if the cliff face had magically moved closer to her. Unfortunately, it looked further away than ever.

"I can make it," she said, trying to rally her spirit.

Instead, the sharp barking of the hound put more fear into her heart. That dog obeyed only one person in the world, and it wasn't Nora. The thing would pounce on her, bite her, clamp down on her arm or her neck and there was nothing she could do…

Just before the panic completely shut her mind down, Nora saw movement behind her. She instantly moved the opposite direction, crawling on hands and knees as fast as she could, all her careful planning ruined.

"Stop right there, woman!"

The booming voice cut through her brain. Nora halted, her breath coming fast and shallow.

The sound of growling made her look behind her. The dog was terrifyingly close, lunging for her. Only the leash held by its master kept it at bay.

"Heel, Tippo. Sit. Stay."

The dog obeyed, though its growl still filled the air.

Another shape moved toward her.

"There's my darling wife," the man said. He loomed over her, hands on his hips. He stood over six feet tall, with blond hair now dark with rain, his beard also darkened with mist. His eyes normally looked blue; tonight, they were hardly more than black pits, a match to the dog's angry gaze. It was a face many found pleasant, with a strong jaw and a ready smile. Though he was smiling now, Nora had no illusions. He was furious with her. "I wondered where you had got to."

"I'm not your wife," she said. The wind tore the words away, and in any case, there was no one around to hear the protest.

"Oh, sweet Elanora." The big man shook his head. "It pains me to see the madness overtake you again. Of course you're my wife. It's my duty to watch over you."

"You mean imprison me."

He sighed. "Another delusion. You're safe in the house. You're not safe out here. Look, you've fallen already and hurt yourself. What other proof do you need that you're not able to go out on your own?"

He reached down to her, his hand like a descending cloud.

"Let me go," she begged. "Please. Let me go."

He didn't even bother to answer her. Instead, he curled a meaty hand around her arm and dragged her up. "Come on, come on. You'll die of exposure."

Nora chose not to bring up the fact that he was responsible for her scanty wardrobe.

She cried out in pain when he made her take a step toward the house. Her ankle was already swelling.

Cursing, the man swung her around and picked her up. Being twice her size, it was an easy feat, though he complained the whole way.

"You look a mess," he said. "As if you've just escaped Bedlam."

She winced.

"Don't care for that thought, do you? Well, if you want to stay out of Bedlam, you'll behave yourself from now on. I can put you away with just a word. A single *word*, Elanora. That's a husband's right."

She closed her eyes, knowing it was true.

He went on, "Your room is far more comfortable than what you'd have in an asylum. I feed you, I clothe you. You've got servants and you've got plenty to keep you busy."

"Until you finish your testing," she muttered. "What then?"

"Don't irritate me further, Elanora. You're fortunate I even went after you. What was your plan?"

He grunted as he navigated a patch of wet, jagged rocks. Tippo trotted alongside, alert but no longer barking.

"You were going to beg for meals?" he guessed. "For

a place to sleep? Do you have any idea what would happen to a woman alone? If a man sees you, you'd be put to work, all right. But nothing a woman of your class would endure."

"I didn't have a plan," she said, hoping to placate him.

"That's clear enough. I thought we were through with this nonsense!" he said. "What attempt is this? The eighth? Tenth? Tell me. Don't claim you don't remember!"

"Tenth," she whispered.

"Well, there won't be an eleventh. You don't get the freedom of the house anymore. You'll be locked in your room unless I let you out. You'll work during the testing, and you'll be on your best behavior. Understand?"

"I understand."

When they returned to the house, Nora was taken directly into the parlor, where another woman was sitting. She wore an exquisite, rather ostentatious gown. She rose upon seeing them, her lovely, expressive green eyes now narrowed. "What is this?" she asked. Her voice was sweet, but there was menace in it.

"My bride has returned from her evening walk," the man proclaimed with that false heartiness Nora hated so much.

He directed Nora to a long chaise, and she sat, sagging in exhaustion.

Then he turned to the door. "I'm going to call for Mrs Lloyd. Keep an eye on her, will you, Isabelle darling?"

As he left, the other woman approached, standing over Nora.

"I think he meant 'keep an eye' in a figurative sense," Nora said wearily. "There's no need to loom over me."

The woman reached out and took Nora's long braid of strawberry blonde hair in her hand, tugging it once. "Shut your mouth. Your sense of humor is as diseased as your mind."

"My mind is far sharper than yours, Mrs Kingfisher."

The lady sneered. "Insolent. Should I have Mrs Lloyd cut your hair off? That's what they do in asylums, you know. Keeps the inmates tidy, and keeps the lice down."

"No, please."

"A little vanity about that, eh?" She tugged the braid once more, making Nora wince, then let it go. "Next time you try anything, it's the hair you'll lose first. *I'll* see to that if Mr Morrison won't. Understand?"

"Yes." Nora knew it was true. Morrison was utterly enthralled by his mistress.

Morrison returned with a maid on his heels. She was a middle-aged woman with grey hair and a stolid expression.

"Before Mrs Lloyd takes you upstairs," he told Nora, "you will explain how you left the house and what your intention was."

"I left the house through the front door." Nora hadn't, of course, but it would be folly to reveal how she actually got around.

"Nonsense." Isabelle glared at her. "We would have seen you."

"I'm very quiet," she murmured.

"The door was locked," Morrison said.

"No, it wasn't." Nora looked him in the face, keeping her gaze clear and unblinking. "I tried the knob, just to see, really. And it turned. So I slipped out."

Morrison snorted, but looked as if he might have believed her. "So you ran off to the beach? Why not go directly to Worthing? I saw your tracks. If it hadn't been for Tippo leaving the track, I'd have been riding along the road at this very moment looking for you!"

"My head was muddled," Nora said.

"She's lying," Isabelle said. "She must have had some goal down on that beach."

Nora looked over at the other woman with very real disdain. "What should I have done? There's no boat. And the swim to the French coast is a bit far for me."

"Don't be clever," the other woman warned.

"You were the one implying I had some grand plan."

Isabelle took a deep breath. "I told you she's trouble. Send her away!"

"Now, now. That's my privilege, Isabelle," he said, "as her husband."

Morrison looked to Nora, weighing his options. Then he sighed. "Once this is over, Elanora, you can go anywhere you like. A few months more is all we need."

"You said that in spring."

"There have been…complications. We're doing great work, Elanora. You know that. And in the end, we can all be very proud. But until then, you need to behave."

She nodded, not daring to look at him.

He gestured to the maid. "Tuck her into bed, Mrs Lloyd. I think my Elanora is getting a little too excitable lately. You know what to do."

"Yes, Mr Morrison," the maid said. "She won't slip out again."

"See that she doesn't."

He turned to Nora once more, putting a big hand on her neck. "Behave. *Remember* that, wife."

Nora bit her lip and kept silent. Nothing she could say would move him now.

Mrs Lloyd hurried her all the way up to the attic, where she had lived as a virtual prisoner for the last year. She was put to bed as if she was a child.

Nora heard the bolt slide shut after Mrs Lloyd closed

the door.

Locked up once again. She took a few unsteady breaths. She fought the feeling of despair welling up. She would not give up.

She needed a better plan of escape if she wanted to succeed. Time was running short. The testing had been delayed, but soon enough, the others would have what they needed, and Nora's skills would be redundant.

What she needed was a distraction. Something unexpected. And no matter what plan she made, she had to escape alone. No one else could be trusted.

Nora turned onto her side. She wasn't sure how much strength she had left. One more escape attempt, perhaps. Not two.

"I'll think of something," she whispered into the night. "Something has to change."

Chapter 4

ALL TOO SOON, ASH WAS ready to leave London on his mysterious assignment. As promised, Bruce arranged for a valet with special talents. The man who arrived on Ash's doorstep a day later did look the part.

He was perhaps five or so years younger than Ash, and was dressed in practical clothing made of sturdy wool cloth in dull colors—the universal mark of the serving class. He was short, but had such good posture that he looked taller than he was. Stick-straight brown hair was held back in a queue, an old-fashioned look that neverthe-less suited him. Light blue eyes darted quickly over Ash and then everything in the room, missing nothing.

"Name's Crewe, sir," he announced himself to Ash. "Timothy Crewe, but I'm called Crewe. I'm to be your valet for the journey."

Ash never enjoyed lying all that much, so he decided to have it all out with the servant immediately. "Sit down, Crewe." He gestured to a chair by the window.

Crewe sat, managing to make the movement look more like work than relaxation.

Ash said, "I don't particularly stand on ceremony. If

you're to be my valet, you'll need to be…adaptable to my circumstances."

"Yes, sir."

Those blue eyes looked at him, guileless eyes that didn't betray a hint of knowledge about Ash's true goal for this journey.

"Look, Crewe, I understand that this is all confidential. And clandestine. And whatever other c-words you care to add to the list. But I need to be able to talk with you honestly if something comes up. I can't do that if we're dancing around who and what you are. If you can't drop the act in private, I'd rather go alone."

"Don't want that, sir," Crewe said easily. "The Zodiac was quite clear you needed a helping hand. That's what the Disreputables are for."

"What?"

"Oh, I'm a Disreputable, sir," Crewe explained. "Your brother didn't mention it? It's the collective name for all the servants and such who assist the Zodiac. So I think I'll fit in quite well as your valet, you being rather disreputable yourself."

"So you were told about me?"

"Full details of the assignment and the agent. Not that it took long to learn about the assignment. We don't know much, do we?"

"We do not," Ash agreed. "Possibly my brother is just using this so-called assignment as an excuse to get rid of me. Wants me to stumble off a picturesque cliff or something. Is it your job to see that done?"

Crewe shook his head. "My orders are to do everything I can to keep you alive. Your brother was most insistent about it—told me that if you died, I wouldn't be far behind. He can be somewhat intimidating."

Ash laughed. His brother was a tall, unloveable hulk

of a man, who also happened to be a peer. Bruce could use his fists or his rank to win a fight. Yet Crewe merely rated him "somewhat" intimidating. "What exactly were you before you became a valet?" Ash asked him.

"Bit of this, bit of that."

"Expand."

"Well, when I was a lad, Mum sent me out to the streets everyday. I got no supper if I hadn't got something worth getting. So I learned to pickpocket, and later to nap a peter if I thought I could carry it—"

"Nap a what?"

"Oh, that's when you cut luggage off a coach, sir. Just slice the leather strap or the rope, and boom, there's your prize. Falls right into the street and you just grab it and run. Good odds, because there's always something to fence in a traveling trunk."

"What went wrong?"

"Nabbed one night," Crewe said. "I wasn't quick enough and this young bobby snagged me right off the street. Convicted, of course. But since I was only twelve and so short, the beak took pity on me and kept me from the gallows."

"Beak?"

"The judge. Most of 'em are heartless, but sometimes you get lucky. Anyway, spent two years in Old Bailey, and when they turned me loose, Mum was dead. I had to go back to thieving—what else could I do? But I chanced on a gang, and started jumping houses with them. I was a good cracksman, too. Real fast, and no noise! But it turned out that the gang I took up with weren't the most faithful friends."

"Imagine that," Ash murmured.

"When the law got hot on them, they set me up for the fall. Abandoned me in the middle of a jump and let the law drag me off while they got clean away with the haul."

"Back to prison, then?"

"Gallows, for certain. Funny thing, though. While I sitting in gaol, waiting for my turn in front of the beak, I saw someone who I knew from the old days. 'Burnett,' I say to him, 'you done for, too?' Because I knew what was coming this time.

"And he just smiles at me, and says, 'Crewe, I'm only in here due to a misunderstanding. Just you wait and see.' So we sat there, talking about everything that happened to both of us since we last saw each other as boys. A few hours later, a lady shows up at the cell door. A *real* lady, I mean. Pretty and clean and in a getup that cost more than I stole in my whole life. She looks through those bars and says, 'Burnett, I hurried over as soon as I could. They're going to let you out now.'

"This lady knew Burnett! And then Burnett says, 'Milady, Crewe here needs out, too. Could you please? He's got no one else.'

"She looks at me, then Burnett, then me again. I tell you, I never knew what Judgment Day meant before that lady looked me in the eye. But then she says, 'If Burnett vouches for you, I'll try.'"

Ash raised an eyebrow. "The lady must have succeeded, because you're still alive."

"She did. Don't know how she convinced the gaolers to let me go—bribe, probably. But I left the place with Burnett and this lady, feeling like I sneaked out of hell. Turned out, he was a Disreputable. So now I am too. Learned to put my skills to better use than I had before, because when you get a chance to cheat the gallows, you take it." Crewe brushed his hands together, as if ridding them of dirt. "That's my tale."

"And after all that, you're going to press my shirts?"

Ash asked.

"Along with whatever else the job requires."

Crewe rode with him on the journey from London, a journey that grew increasingly uncomfortable as the roads turned narrower, less traveled, and more desolate.

They reached their destination around twilight the second day. At least, it seemed to be twilight. All the fog coming in from the water, combined with low, heavy clouds, conspired to make the very air murky.

Ash stepped out of the carriage and took a moment to stretch. The last few miles were the worst, the road being hardly more than a dirt track riddled with cobbles. He looked around, taking in the scene.

Grasmere House was impressive for its size alone. The stone walls stretched in either direction from the entry-way, and soon became lost in the misty gloom. Ash looked up, wondering if the roof would also be lost in the dense fog rolling in from the sea.

He didn't see the upper roofline, but a flash of white caught his eye. Then he blinked, wondering if he was see-ing things.

The white shape was a woman. She stood on the pro-truding roof of the first story of the house, leaning against the side of a dormer. The white he'd noticed was her gown—a filmy, flimsy excuse of a dress with a high waist and no sleeves to speak of. Women's fashion had of late completely disavowed practicality, a trend Ash approved of until this moment.

She must be freezing, Ash thought, and irrationally wondered if he ought to toss up a jacket of some sort.

Her light-colored hair was loose and writhed in the breeze as if it had a life of its own. Ash didn't believe in ghosts, but the woman was making a strong case for the phenomenon.

Then the woman realized she'd been spotted. She crouched down and took a step back, using the dormer to hide. Ash still stared at her, though, too surprised to do anything else.

The woman caught his gaze and put a finger to her lips, an expressive plea for silence—one a ghost presumably wouldn't bother to do.

"Sir?" Crewe asked, looking curiously at Ash. "Something wrong?"

Ash quickly shifted his attention to Crewe, who'd taken his valise in hand. "Nothing wrong. Let's get inside before this mist soaks into our bones."

Crewe nodded agreement and went ahead of Ash to the doorway. Ash chanced a last look up at the place where the woman in white had been, but now nothing was there but a swirl of thicker mist pushed in by the ocean breeze.

"God damn," Ash muttered. "What did I get myself into?"

Chapter 5

WHO IS HE? NORA WONDERED, looking down at the new-comer. *And why is he here?*

Over a week had passed since her doomed escape attempt, and when the light was fading she had ventured out onto the roof again largely because being cooped up in the house was abhorrent to her. Given the options to either metaphorically climb the wall or literally climb the roof, the choice was clear.

She didn't go with an escape plan in mind, but just to be unobserved and free for a while. When she caught sight of a carriage approaching Grasmere House, she almost didn't believe it. But it kept coming, with no sign of the driver hesitating. This house was the intended destination.

The man who got out was a stranger. Nora was certain she'd never seen him before. She remembered everything, but even without her knack for memory, she'd certainly remember him. Even a brief glimpse left her with an impression of uncommon, well, beauty. *Almost angelic*, she thought, with a fancifulness she didn't often experience.

Then he looked up and saw her.

Nora reacted like a cornered animal. She wasn't fast enough, for he kept looking, and there was no way he could mistake what he saw.

Don't, she thought frantically, and put her finger to her lips in an instinctive move.

He raised one eyebrow, but then was distracted by his servant, allowing Nora to slip into the growing shadows.

Nora climbed through the unfastened window of an empty room, and made her way through the rambling house to the second floor, to a room just above the parlor. She knelt by the fireplace. The house was constructed in such a way that the flues were connected. By keeping quiet, she could hear a conversation in a lower room almost as clearly as if she was standing in it.

The visitor must have been unexpected to everyone, because Morrison wasn't waiting for him and had to be tracked down by a servant. But Nora heard the faint sounds of a person in the room below. Footsteps pacing. Not nervous, but with energy.

Who was this man?

A door squeaked open. "Good evening, sir," Morrison's voice boomed. "How can I help you? Lost your way, have you? We should be able to put you back on the right track."

"I'm where I intend to be," the stranger said. "You are Mr Morrison."

"Yes," Morrison said, after a pause. "And you?"

"The name is Allen. Do you remember me from the meetings?"

"Ahhh..."

"No matter," Mr Allen said smoothly. "I've been sent to see how you're getting on. Your updates must have gone astray."

"Updates," Morrison echoed.

"Yes. The updates promised in exchange for the funding. We're all quite interested, naturally."

"Of course." Nora could hear the strain in Morrison's voice. He was not at all prepared for an observer, particularly not an official one! And how did this man, Mr Allen, find them anyway? Nora knew that Morrison chose this house precisely because it was isolated, with no chance of being spied on.

Nora leaned closer to the empty fireplace. Morrison was speaking.

"So. You made it from London in one piece. How did you hear of this house?"

The stranger only said, "Don't suppose you've got some brandy warmed up for a guest?"

The tone was relaxed, even familiar. Nora wasn't sure if the man thought he was expected, somehow, or if he was merely used to dropping in at remote houses.

In either case, Morrison responded in a lower voice, as if he too had been calmed. "Certainly. Rather, we'll have some ready in a moment. You've caught us a bit off guard, Mr Allen. We're not used to guests here. All work and no play."

"So you're progressing," Allen said. "Can you give me specifics?"

"Of course, of course…but you'll want supper first. Settle in. After all, you can hardly just turn around and leave again, after a journey down from London!"

Despite the banality of the words, Nora was a bit surprised that Morrison even offered supper, or suggested that the stranger should stay. Didn't Morrison want the man gone?

For her part, Nora didn't want him to leave! Not yet, anyway. The stranger came in his own carriage and brought his own luggage. Nora might be able to make use of those things, given enough time to decide how. She despised thievery, but she was desperate.

No matter what, Nora needed the stranger to remain at the house for at least a few nights. Morrison should understand the need to act naturally so as not to arouse suspicions. Then again, she knew all too well that Morrison couldn't be trusted.

The conversation moved away from the fireplace, as Morrison escorted the guest back to the foyer, where he'd be shown to a bedroom.

Drat! Nora had to move quickly, or she'd be spotted. That was one thing she couldn't afford to have happen just now.

She crept through the hallways and upper rooms of the old house. Fortunately, she was well acquainted with all the house's foibles. She remembered the location of every squeaky floorboard and rusting hinge, so she could move through the house making less noise than a ghost.

In her attic room, Nora hurriedly checked her appearance in the cracked mirror. She looked odd, she acknowledged sadly. Morrison deliberately provided her with clothing that was mismatched and ill-fitting. Anyone looking at her would conclude that her mind wasn't all there. More significantly, following her fourth escape attempt, he forbade Nora to have any clothing for the outdoors. She possessed no pelisse or jacket, no shoes suitable for walking outside, and certainly nothing that would keep her warm. Thus, even if she escaped, she faced the twin difficulties of convincing people she wasn't mad, and trying to survive out of doors in poor weather.

Nora was more resilient than Morrison could have dreamed, and she tried to train herself to endure cold and damp through her rooftop excursions. However, surviving several nights or weeks was another matter entirely.

That stranger had been quite well dressed. She could probably pinch a few pieces from his luggage and he wouldn't notice. Armed with a man's coat, she could likely sleep outside for a few nights.

It was worth a try. Of course, that meant she'd have to get into the stranger's room, before she lost her opportunity or her nerve.

She'd go tonight, late, after the man was asleep. He'd never even know she was there.

Chapter 6

FOR ALL THE PROTESTATIONS OF surprise at a guest's appearance, Morrison's household adapted very efficiently. Ash's luggage was brought up to the guest room immediately. The carriage was wheeled away by a young boy who promised to feed and care for the horses. Dinner was to be at eight o'clock, leaving Ash time to brood at the window while Crewe unpacked and readied the essentials.

"This was a mistake," he muttered, staring outside. The view faced not out toward sea, but rather toward the track they had ridden in on. The land rolled in gentle hills and valleys to the north. Little of civilization could be seen, and nothing to hint of the Channel just outside the south face of the house.

"Would you like another room, sir?" Crewe asked. "I can inform them."

"It's not the room, and you know it."

"Too early to surrender, sir," Crewe said cheerfully, moving around the room as he worked. "At least find out if Morrison has a good cook."

Ash smiled at the comment. "Or a good wine cellar."

"That's the spirit, sir."

Crewe made a perfect valet, and just before the chime sounded, Ash stood dressed for dinner. His jacket had been brushed, his clothing pressed, his shoes polished. No one could have guessed that all those items had been crushed in a trunk an hour before.

"Well done, Crewe."

"All in a day's work," the valet commented. "Have you any special instructions for me while you're at dinner?"

"Take a walk through the house," Ash said. "I want to know how many people are here, and what sort. Particularly any women."

Crewe raised one eyebrow.

"I'm not reverting to type," Ash said testily. "I thought I saw a lady when we arrived. She was trying not to be noticed. I want to know who she is. If it helps, she was dressed all in white."

"Doubtless you'll meet her at dinner."

"Perhaps. In any case, learn about the household—and the house—so you can tell me later. What if we have to leave quickly?"

Crewe gave a crisp nod. "Consider it done. Enjoy your meal." As the servant of a visitor, Crewe would eat in the kitchen with the other servants, where he'd begin his own investigation.

Ash descended the massive central staircase to the ground floor, where he was led to the dining room by the laughter of a woman. It was not the woman in white. Ash was disappointed, even though the lady he saw now was gorgeous by any measure.

She stood only five feet or so, a tiny figure to have such a large presence. But she dominated the room with her personality. She had a wealth of hair the color of copper piled on her head, large green eyes set deep, and a mouth that was made for laughing…or kissing. Or other things. Sensuality radiated from her, particularly when she noticed Ash's entrance and looked him over.

He had to remind himself to not react as he would if he were himself in London. As the Fallen Angel, he'd return her look with one just as appraising, and then likely issue an invitation to some secluded spot.

As the clerk Mr Allen, he was supposed to behave… which meant *not* sparking an affair with a woman he didn't know a thing about on the very first night he arrived. Anyway, her attention was actually rather off-putting. Despite her beauty, there was something mercenary and even cold in her gaze. Ash associated that look with prostitutes of the underworld as they selected new clients for the evening. It was not a flattering comparison.

By then, Morrison also noticed Ash, and strode up to him.

"Come in, come in. No need for formality, when we're such a small company!" Morrison turned to the lady. "Mrs Kingfisher, may I introduce Mr Allen to you?"

The lady assented with a smile.

Ash was introduced as an agent of the government, and he recited his false credentials and history to the lady he learned was Mrs Isabelle Kingfisher.

He'd memorized everything Bruce had given him, so he could talk without thinking too hard about the answers he was supposed to give. A drink was offered, then another. Ash wondered if they intended to get him drunk before the first course.

"Are we waiting for anyone else?" he asked politely, when Morrison gestured to the table itself.

"No, no. As I said, guests are a rarity."

So who was the woman in white?

The discussion remained superficial throughout the

meal. Ash knew better than to press for details too soon. He had to let Morrison get used to his presence. So they talked of general news, the ongoing war with France, and the area around Grasmere House. Ash learned that Worthing was the nearest town of any size.

"Have you never been?" the lady asked. "You simply must go into Worthing while you stay here, Mr Allen. It's so charming and quaint compared to London. But of course it is still appealing to the better sort. Why, the Princess Amelia spends much time there, bathing in the sea for her health."

Considering that the king's youngest daughter had been doing poorly for years, Ash wondering if there was any benefit at all for the princess. But he nodded. "If it will do for a princess, it must be worth visiting."

"The king himself comes from time to time," she went on. "He's most interested in his daughter's progress. He was here only last week."

"Do you go there often?" he asked. "Is that why you're staying in this house, where Worthing is close enough to visit?"

"I go when the mood suits me."

"That's how she does everything," Morrison added, looking at the lady as if rapt. "Mrs Kingfisher takes orders from no one!"

Ash smiled politely. "So you are not here to assist Mr Morrison with his work, then," he guessed.

Mrs Kingfisher's smile went brittle for a moment. "Mr Morrison's work is quite beyond me," she said. "I'm a lady, and not trained to fiddle about with glass and flames and all those codes!"

At the mention of codes, Ash perked up. But he didn't want to appear too eager. "I can't imagine much is beyond you, Mrs Kingfisher."

She shot him a look filled with promise, a promise he didn't particularly want to fulfill.

Dinner was followed by drinks in the parlor, and entertainment provided by Mrs Kingfisher, who was quite competent at pianoforte. Still, Ash couldn't say he enjoyed the little concert. Time spent listening to music was time not spent discovering what Morrison's problem was.

Bruce had been convinced that Albert Morrison was somehow prevented from communicating with the government. But that wasn't the impression Mr Morrison gave—he appeared to be fully in charge and able to work. So what was the problem? Why had he dropped out of society, save for the company of Isabelle Kingfisher? The next obvious question was the location of *Mr* Kingfisher…who would likely not be pleased to see his wife flirting shamelessly with other men.

On his way back up to his room, Ash swayed as if he was drunk. The minuscule amount of alcohol he imbibed didn't leave a mark, but he was skilled at pretending to drink far more than he did. He looked around, going slowly. He hoped to catch a glimpse of the woman in white. The upper floors of the house felt strangely deserted, and candlelight was minimal. Dark patches of shadow seemed to writhe as he passed them with his held candlestick. The house echoed with every step. Why the hell had Morrison chosen this rambling, ruinous pile when he didn't need all the space? How many people truly lived here? Was the woman in white real, or had he imagined her?

Ash pushed open the door of his bedroom, glad to see Crewe there. The valet was the closest thing he had to an ally.

"I survived dinner, and more importantly, the conversation at dinner. How was your evening?" he asked Crewe.

The valet made a noncommittal noise. "The servants are an odd lot. I wouldn't call them friendly."

"Did you manage to learn anything?"

"A few items of interest. They're all new to Grasmere House, though most are locals. Morrison hired them all about a year ago, when he came down from his London home. They say you're the first visitor, excepting Mrs Kingfisher. She's not quite a visitor, since she shows no sign of leaving."

"And any news of a woman dressed all in white?"

Crewe snorted. "I did get an answer to that, of a sort."

"Go on."

"The butler, Mr Lloyd, was quick to tell me that there are a few stories of ghosts in any old house. Here, it's a young woman who cries and leaves wet footprints on the stairs. A drowning victim from a hundred years ago. Some say they've seen her, usually at night. She's dressed in white, of course."

"A barefoot ghost. How charming," Ash said. "I would have thought they would have a better lie prepared. If the ghost has been haunting the shore for a hundred years, why was she dressed in a modern gown?"

Crewe nodded in agreement. "They weren't pleased to hear my inquiry, certainly. But no one else said a word—Lloyd was the one they all looked to for the answer."

"So he runs the place."

"That's my guess. The servants seem a little scared of him."

"The master is a bit off too," Ash muttered. "And the one other guest is notable in her own way."

"Mrs Isabelle Kingfisher? The servants said she's been here for months. I gathered she's Morrison's mistress."

"I think so," Ash said slowly.

"You're not certain? Isn't that the sort of thing you

ought to know…"

"…as the reprehensible rake I am?" Ash shrugged out of his jacket. "Yes. I can usually tell with half a glance. Isabelle Kingfisher is undoubtedly his mistress. However, I suspect that's not *all* she is."

"Must she be more than that?"

"She protested a little too much when I suggested she was involved in Morrison's work. Why should she distance herself from it? The project is *for* the British government. There's no need to hide an interest."

"Perhaps Morrison doesn't like to admit he needs assistance? From a woman, at that."

Ash pondered. "Maybe. Either way, I'm not much closer to an answer than I was when we arrived."

"It's only the first day," Crewe reminded him, sounding a bit perplexed. "Just how quickly did you think you'd get to the bottom of it?"

Ash was used to learning everything quickly. As a child, he'd stampeded though the same lessons that his older brother was studying. Ash picked up languages like they were playthings. Puzzles which confounded his tutors appeared simple to him. When he grew older, he applied the same skills to reading people and situations, discovering that the challenge was only marginally greater. In short, it had been a while since he ran into anything that he couldn't think his way around. Yet this house and the people in it were enough to make him doubt his own intellect.

Having seen to everything before Ash retired to bed, Crewe said from the doorway, "I'll be going now, sir. If you hear or see anything a bit off, no doubt it's just a few restless spirits."

"The only spirits I believe in come out of a bottle."

The valet rolled his eyes. "Good night, sir."

The door shut firmly, separating Ash from the rest of the world.

He was anything but sleepy, and he sat on the edge of the bed, thinking. Anyone looking at him would see only the calm, urbane personality he always showed. Inside, he felt like he was falling. What had he got himself into? What had Bruce been thinking, asking Ash to do this? Why had he said yes?

To please his brother.

Ash swallowed. Lord, he was stupid. He was so desperate for his brother's approval that he agreed to this mad plan where he pretended to be someone he wasn't, to accomplish a thing he didn't even care about.

The thoughts circled inside, over and over. Ash couldn't shake them, couldn't argue against them. Whenever this happened in London, he'd just go out. He'd lose himself among the pleasures and diversions of the city. Or he'd find a friend, talk until dawn colored the sky and he was too tired to think. If he could, he'd find Reggie. Reg would listen, as she always had.

Reg got him into this, his thoughts reminded him darkly.

She had good intentions, Ash countered himself. Reg always wanted Bruce and Ash to reconcile. It wasn't her fault that Ash was now lost in a mess of his own making.

Without a conscious plan, Ash moved through the room. He found himself staring down at the small wooden box he'd packed.

I shouldn't have brought this, he thought.

He opened the lid.

I should put this away. Now.

He pulled out the contents.

I should stop.

He didn't stop.

A quarter of an hour later, Ash lay prone on his bed, lost in a drug-induced haze, one that smothered all his thoughts and left him numb. It was all he wanted…an escape, even for a little while.

Chapter 7

NORA WAITED PATIENTLY, ONE EYE on the moon outside, and one eye on her bedroom door. Mrs Lloyd brought up dinner on a tray. The maid didn't say a word about a guest in the house, but she reminded Nora that she was to remain quiet and meek…"for your health."

Nora stifled a most unladylike snort. It wasn't her health that concerned the household. It was the chance that someone would raise awkward questions if Nora was seen. That meant Morrison didn't trust the newcomer—or he hadn't thought to bribe him yet. *How interesting*, she thought. Perhaps the enemy of her enemy was her friend?

"You're to take your medicine tonight," Mrs Lloyd announced. She held out a large bottle of golden brown liquid, along with a tiny cup. "No excuses."

Nora bit her lip, and reached for a handkerchief on a nearby table. "Must I? I've been very well this past week." She'd been *docile*.

"Mr Morrison was quite clear in his instruction."

She made a show of disliking the notion, but she dutifully sipped the nasty liquid Mrs Lloyd poured into the cup. The medicine was laudanum—opium blended with strong alcohol. The stuff was burning, sickly sweet, and guaranteed to send her into slumber…

…if she actually drank it.

Nora waited until Mrs Lloyd turned her back. Then she spat out most of the medicine into the handkerchief wadded up in her palm.

By the time Mrs Lloyd finished putting the medicine away, Nora had hidden the soaked handkerchief and climbed into the bed.

"Ah," the maid said. "There's a good girl."

"Is there another blanket?" Nora asked, in her sweetest voice. "I was cold last night. It's so chilly by the sea."

Mrs Lloyd nodded. "I'll fetch it for you." The maid was always more genteel when Nora acted biddable and weak. But Mrs Lloyd was firmly in Morrison's control, and would never help Nora escape.

So Nora would have to look for assistance from another quarter. The gentleman who arrived earlier that day had occupied her mind since she first sighted the carriage. He'd seen her on the roof, but he hadn't said a word to Morrison. If he'd mentioned it, Morrison would have stormed into Nora's room a minute later and made his displeasure known.

Nora watched Mrs Lloyd leave the room, then waited. She continued to measure the moon's progress across the sky by looking at the increasingly shortened patch of light on the floor. When she judged the time to be around one in the morning, she slid out of the bed and went to her bedroom door, which was of course bolted from the other side.

However, she had a method for unbolting it, and a moment later she was free.

She moved through the halls until she reached the bedroom where the stranger was staying. She eased the door open—it wasn't locked. She slipped through, and then closed the door as silently as she had opened it.

Her eyes were adjusted to the darkness, but she spent a long moment surveying the room.

At the moment, it seemed quite tidy. The panels of the canopy bed were open, and the man was sleeping, the covers pulled up over him so that his body was little more than a vague shape. He seemed utterly lost to the world. He didn't even twitch when a gust of air from the open window stirred the curtains of the bed.

Nora smiled, pleased to find someone else who also liked an open window—she was so often told that night air was unhealthy.

Assured he was asleep, she took a few steps toward the clothes press, where the man's belongings would be stored. She opened the heavy wooden door of the press, dismayed when it squeaked slightly. She glanced back to the bed, but saw no movement.

The darkness meant that she had to use touch more than sight to discover the contents of the press. She quickly found a plain shirt and pants, which she might use to disguise herself. Putting them aside on a shelf, she kept looking, then encountered a flat, heavy wooden box. She pulled it out and raised the lid.

The dull gleam of metal glinted out at her. The box contained two matching pistols, with silvery barrels and grips of highly polished ebony wood. The metal was covered in delicate etching. The weapons looked both elegant and deadly, more works of art than tools. Nora lowered the lid carefully, noting an inscription carved on the inner side, and put the box back in the clothes press. He surely didn't expect to go hunting with that style of gun. Did he have some other reason for traveling armed? Perhaps it was merely for safety, she told herself, though the pistols looked distinctly showy. They were designed to be noticed.

In any case, the guns didn't concern her. She continued her search, hoping for some clue of the man's purpose, or something useful for her escape.

She found a small packet of papers. She glanced over at the sleeping form again, but the shadows of the canopy obscured him.

Unfolding the papers, she scanned the writing, searching for clues. The poor light made reading difficult, but Nora had a special knack. Soon enough she folded the papers back up, putting them in exactly the same place where she'd found them. Thoughts swirled in her brain, but she'd sort through them later, once she was safely back in her room.

Beneath the letters, she found something more—a stack of folded bank notes. A *large* stack, far too much for an ordinary person to carry about him on a trip. What was Allen doing here? Nora bit her lip, considering her options.

Temptation struck her hard. That much money could get her very far indeed, with no questions asked.

No. It was one thing to filch a few old pieces of clothing. It was quite another to willfully steal money, a *lot* of money. Nora shoved the stack of banknotes back where she'd found it.

"Have you come to haunt me?"

Nora whirled around and froze. Her heart dropped.

The man was awake, his upper body propped up on both elbows. He gazed at Nora calmly, as if it was perfectly normal for him to find strange women in his bedroom at night.

She had no idea what to say. She simply stared at him, wondering if he was going to rise from the bed and seize her, with the intent of bringing her to Morrison. Or worse.

"Well?" he prompted. "Is this your usual practice, to hover over guests and decide whether or not to haunt them? Are you a good ghost, or a bad ghost? Or have I mistaken you?"

As he spoke, he slipped out from under the bedclothes and took a few steps toward her. By the time Nora realized the danger, it was too late—an arm flashed out and a strong hand took her by the wrist, not allowing her to run away.

Not that it mattered. Nora was still too dumbfounded to move. She felt as if she were underwater, or perhaps stuck in stone.

The reason for her distraction was simple enough. He wasn't dressed. At all.

Nora had limited experience with men, but she could say with complete confidence that this man was the most attractive one she'd ever seen or expected to see. Nora instinctively wanted to touch him, to add to her knowledge...and also for the pure pleasure of touching something so gorgeous. She blamed the night, which must also be responsible for her thinking that his eyes glowed a bit, with a warmth that she was surely just imagining.

"Do I meet your approval?" he asked, almost lazily.

"What?" Nora asked. She had no idea how long she'd been staring at him, whether it was seconds or minutes— long enough for him to think the worst of her morals. "Oh! I...I'm sorry. I didn't mean... That's not what I... I need to leave."

"Not quite yet," he said, in that same calm tone. "You just arrived."

"No, I..."

"My name is Ash," he said, looking her over curiously. "And yours?"

"Nora," she whispered, keeping her eyes fixed on his face.

"That wasn't too difficult, was it? Why don't you tell me what brought you here tonight, Miss Nora?" Ash smiled at her.

Something inside Nora woke up, a spark of energy she'd almost forgotten she possessed. "You didn't tell anyone you saw me earlier."

"You asked me not to." Ash mimicked her gesture from earlier, with a finger over his mouth. She found herself entranced by the curve of his lower lip.

Eventually, she remembered to speak. "Thank you. He'd be furious if he knew I was out on the roof."

"Who?"

"Mr Morrison."

"Who is he to you?" Ash asked. At that moment, he reached out, grabbing a long dressing robe hanging from a nearby chair. Nora expected him to put it on, hiding his naked form. Instead, he draped it over her shoulders. "You really ought to acquire a better wardrobe, Miss Nora. So far, you've been rather underdressed for conditions."

"And what about you?"

"Don't criticize my sleeping habits," he said, still sounding as if such a topic was not at all absurd to be having with a stranger in the dead of night. "I'll get dressed… if you promise not to run away while I'm occupied."

"Very well," she whispered.

Ash gave her another smile that did nothing to calm her nerves, but he did walk over to the clothes press and pull out a few items. He moved leisurely, as if he was caught in a dream.

Nora turned her head to follow his movements. She told herself it was to make sure he didn't notice any subtle changes in the order of the contents of the press. The result was that she got a scandalously good view of him from the rear. She turned her head quickly, lest he catch her peeking.

After a moment, he walked back to her, now dressed.

"There. We're both quite respectable...well, slightly respectable. I'd still counsel you to invest in a few more warm pieces."

Nora pulled the fabric of the robe tighter around her body. "He doesn't let me have warm clothes. He doesn't let me out."

"Out of the house?"

"Out of the attic."

Ash's eyes narrowed then, either in suspicion or flat-out disbelief. "He confines you to the attic?"

"He tries. This house is rather, um, porous, though. One can move about if one is motivated."

"You're motivated, I take it. Specifically, you're motivated to stroll along the edge of the roof."

"Yes. It's a way to...be free." Oh, why was she telling a stranger all this?

"And you're what relation to the man who keeps you confined in the attic?" Ash pressed.

"I'd rather not say, and if I did tell, you wouldn't believe me."

"You're a most unusual ghost."

"I'm not a ghost."

He put a hand on her waist, then slid it around to her lower back, and gently pulled her close to him. "No, you don't feel like a ghost," he murmured.

Nora caught her breath. "As I told you."

"So you did...but I like to verify. Can't just take your word for it. Experimentation and all that." He bent his head, and now his words came closer, his breath warm against her cheek.

"Experimentation?" she echoed.

"Just to be absolutely certain."

His eyes were extraordinarily dark, she saw. His pupils were dilated, as if he were drugged.

"Mr Allen," she began to say.

"Call me Ash, please."

"Ash."

"Sounds sweet when you say it," he noted, his mouth hovering over her own.

Then he kissed her, his lips grazing hers till she sighed against him, a need long forgotten now rekindling with this unexpected touch.

Ash heard her, and held her a little tighter against him. He deepened the kiss, slowly, as if he had all night to explore her.

Nora was so flummoxed by the strangeness of this situation that she simply accepted it for the moment. She hadn't been touched like this in ages, and certainly never by a stranger.

Memories welled up in her, fighting the present moment.

Her first kiss, from a third cousin, stolen in a garden in high summer. Exciting as it was amateur.

A later kiss, on her wedding night. More loving, more ardent.

A kiss on a spring morning, blown cheerfully into the air toward a retreating figure she assumed she'd see again…how much more fiercely she would have kissed him if she'd known…

But then the memories lost their hold in the face of the present moment. Nora focused on the man in front of her. Her hands swept up his chest, noting every detail. She inhaled when he ran the tip of his tongue along her lip, unexpectedly feeling the desire to throw her arms around him, to tell him everything.

For all the audacity of his actions, he didn't do a thing more than kiss her. Nora sensed no urgency in him, just a profound pleasure in the moment. It was as if time ceased to matter.

But time moved anyway. A few moments later, he drew away, slowly ending the kiss. He didn't release his hold on her, though. He surveyed her for a long moment, a smile hovering on his mouth. He seemed immensely pleased with her.

"Well," he murmured. "You must be a dream. Though you're lovelier by far than any others I can recall lately."

Nora took a deep breath. "I assure you I'm a real person. You're holding me, in case you hadn't noticed."

"Do you mind?"

"Being held?" Nora paused. "I…I don't mind."

"Good. Because I rather like how you feel."

"Oh." Nora's cheeks went warmer still. She didn't say that she rather liked being held *by* him. Even though he was a stranger.

Her good sense reasserted itself. Nora shook her head once and pushed at him slightly.

He released her in an instant, allowing her to step away.

Nora looked back at the closed door. "I must go. If Morrison sees me out of my room…"

"He should be asleep by now."

"All the same, I must get back in case he checks on me and finds me gone."

"Back to the attic?"

"Yes." Nora took another step, and this time he mirrored her action.

"Nora," he said, "you are confusing as hell, and I'm not letting you waft into my bedroom in the middle of the night and then simply waft out again after spouting a lot of nonsense. If you want to get back to your attic prison, you're going in my company."

"You don't believe me."

"I'm withholding judgment." Ash moved to the door.

"Be careful!" Nora whispered. "Don't let anyone see you."

"Yes, I caught that part." He gave her a conspiratorial smile, but then peeked out of the door with every appearance that he took her seriously.

He held out a hand, indicating she should join him. Nora put her hand in his, just as he pulled the door open and drew her through.

"Show me," he breathed by her ear.

Nora led him through the hallway and the narrow back stairwell, up the flights to her attic door. Ash followed closely. He continued to hold her hand, and Nora actually felt better for it.

When she reached her door, she tugged her hand free. "This is my room."

"Show me," he repeated.

She opened the door. She went through and Ash followed, surveying the space.

"Nora, what's going—"

"I can't explain now, and you can't stay here." Her gaze fell on a watercolor she'd made recently. Nora grabbed the little painting, folded it up, and pushed it into Ash's hand. "Look at this. That's what all this is about, why you're here. You need to go now. Don't let anyone know we've spoken. I don't exist."

Ash closed his hand around the paper. "What the hell am I supposed to do—"

The creak of a floorboard somewhere below sent panic up her spine. "Did you hear that? It could be him. He could come up here any second. *Please* go."

"I'll see you again," Ash said.

"Yes," she said, something wild beating in her chest. Hope? "I'll find a way to meet you again…when it's safe. You must not look for me. Understand?"

Ash nodded, and then left, looking back over his shoulder one last time. Perhaps he expected her to dissolve into mist, like a doorway to fairyland.

After she closed the door behind him, fixing the bolt, she moved to the bed, unconsciously sliding off the dressing robe. She froze halfway through the motion. She was still wearing *his* robe! If anyone saw it, she'd be done for. Nora pulled it back onto her shoulders and dove into the bed, pulling the covers up to her neck. God help her if either Morrison or Mrs Lloyd came up to check on her and adjusted the blanket, or decided to rouse her.

Then, to make matters worse, she heard footsteps on the floor immediately below. Ash had moved almost as silently as she did, so it was unlikely to be him. But what if someone else saw him wandering the halls?

She strained her ears, dreading the sound of Morrison's voice, raised in alarm or accusation.

Nothing.

It seemed Ash managed to remain unseen.

Still, someone was coming up to the attic.

Nora took a few deep breaths to steady her heart. She needed to appear deep in slumber.

She closed her eyes. Footsteps were approaching, and then the doorknob turned. A glow against her eyelids meant someone carried a lantern.

Nora kept her breathing slow and even, careful to not react to the people now in her room. It was Morrison and Mrs Lloyd. Morrison moved heavily, stomping even when he tried to be stealthy. Mrs Lloyd was much lighter on her feet, and Nora relied on the rustle of her skirts to tell where she was.

"Any trouble today?" he asked.

"Not that I noticed. She opened a window earlier, but on the seaside, and only to let the mist in, the fool girl. She once told me she talks to the weather."

"That's thanks to the medicine, I'm sure." He sounded unconcerned. "Looks as if the medicine worked tonight. I was worried that the man would see or hear something, but…"

"She's lost to the world," Mrs Lloyd agreed. "I told you, sir, that I doubled the dose. She might not wake till noon." Nora felt a hand smooth the blankets by her feet.

"Good," he grunted. "Keep to that regimen until the guest leaves. Last thing I need now is Elanora mucking up our situation. We don't want this man to start asking questions."

"Is that Mr Allen here for long?"

"Not sure. In any case, if he knew she was in the house, it would complicate things. See that Elanora's under control for the duration."

"Yes, sir." Mrs Lloyd picked up the lantern again, and the light flashed against Nora's eyelids.

She gave a little moan, like that of a disturbed slumberer.

"Let's go," the maid urged.

Moments later, the bolt was slid shut, and both sets of footsteps faded down the hall.

Nora sighed in relief. She'd taken too great of a risk. She never should have gone to Ash's room. She should have fled the moment he saw her. She shouldn't have promised to meet him again.

She certainly shouldn't have kissed him.

Why had she done those things?

Why was she still wearing his dressing gown?

Nora curled up on her side, pulling the gown around her body. The scent clinging to the silk lining was unfamiliar, but comforting. She breathed deeply, trying to identify all the elements of the smell: sandalwood at the base, then something greener, perhaps sage. And hovering over that, a dry, dark aroma, like coffee or raw cocoa.

Nora would remember the complex scent forever, especially because the circumstances were so odd. She'd have to hide the robe before she fell asleep. It was incriminating on so many levels. How to explain how a strange man's dressing robe found its way into Nora's room? The very notion implied something sordid, a suggestion of illicit meetings for the basest of purposes.

Nora was no stranger to what happened at that sort of meeting. She'd been married, quite happily so. Her husband had come to her room most nights at the beginning of the marriage. Still, she'd never been tempted to curl up in his dressing gown, inhaling the smell of it as if it could transport her somewhere.

Nora sighed. She'd been confined so long that interaction with anyone made her dizzy. She was extremely fortunate that this man chose not to betray her already, though he could still do so at any time. For all her efforts, she was still trapped. And she didn't even have the clothes she had intended to nab! She'd been forced to leave them in his room. Bother.

I'll see you again was what he had said. She hoped so, and she prayed that it would be as an ally, not an enemy.

Chapter 8

ASH DREAMED STRANGE, VIVID DREAMS that night. He wandered endless hallways in search of a mysterious woman in white. Several times he was sure he found her, and could reach out and touch her, but then she faded again, leaving him alone.

He kept walking, despite his growing exhaustion. The hallways never ended, but shadows kept thickening until he seemed to be walking through a grey fog. Then he realized he was awake, in his own bed, staring up at the top of the canopy bed in the grey, featureless light of early dawn.

Rolling over, he groaned in frustration. This was exactly why he shouldn't have indulged in his vice before bed last night. That brief period of peaceful slumber inevitably gave way to tortured dreams later on, and a miserable following day.

However, this time had been different, in that his dreams weren't usually so singular. The quest for the woman in white occupied him the whole night, the same dream lasting for hours. Normally, his dreams grew fractured and jumbled, putting him in a dozen different places, with a cast of dozens of people from his waking life.

Instead, he dreamed only of Nora.

Ash blinked, then sat up. Why did he call her that? Why was he so certain of her name?

Nora. The instant he thought her name, the memory of her face suddenly bloomed in the front of his mind, along with an unmistakable arousal.

That was unexpected.

Ash had to wake himself up fully. He had to shake off the lingering effects of the drug and then never, never take any opiate again.

Just as he'd promised himself last time.

He grimaced. His intentions were always so good... until the need to lose himself in the forgetful haze of the drug emerged again.

"Nora," he said out loud. Such a specific detail to dream up. Actually, everything about her had been strangely specific. The strawberry blonde hair in the messy braid, the dimple in her cheek, the way she sighed when he held her...

...and the journey up to the top floor, where she told him she lived. He could retrace his steps by day, prove to himself if his memories were real or not.

Ash stood up, intent on doing just that, when he remembered her last demand. He wasn't to look for her. She would find him.

Madness. It had to be a dream. There was simply no way he could stumble into such strangeness the first evening he arrived, no matter how out of his depth he was.

He'd almost convinced himself when he saw a small piece of paper lying on the bed under his pillow. That was the paper she'd given him last night. It had to be real.

Ash pulled the paper out and looked it over. In the

light of morning, he could see it clearly. It was a painting. A small watercolor to be precise, not much larger than his hand. It depicted the shoreline, with Grasmere House at one edge and a slender tower at the other. It must be a lighthouse. This was what Nora declared to be so important?

He reached for his dressing gown, and realized it wasn't there. Damn, she still had it. Didn't matter how pretty she was, she'd both disturbed his equilibrium and made off with his clothing.

"Unacceptable!" Ash said softly, parodying a stuffy lord. Then he smiled. Now he had another reason to see her again.

His gaze drifted back to the watercolor. Though simple, it was well executed. The image was surprisingly detailed, even to the point that the flotsam along the high tideline had been carefully rendered. This was not a dreamy vision of an ideal shore. This was exactly what the artist saw, the same shoreline as the one right outside this house.

He looked closer, sure he was missing something. Why had Nora considered this paper so very important? After a moment, he noticed something around the border of the image—very faint dashes and shapes. It would be easy to dismiss them as mistakes, or strokes of the brush to get rid of excess water. However, there was some regularity to the pattern. Ash had no idea what it meant, but Nora could explain, whenever she materialized again.

In the meantime, he had spying to do.

After telling Crewe his plan as the valet helped him dress for the day, Ash saddled a horse for himself and headed off along the seaside track. It was not yet mid-morning, and he avoided meeting all the other inhabitants. The last thing he wanted was to explain his interest in the lighthouse to Albert Morrison.

Ash rode along the top of the cliff toward the distant lighthouse. The path was well away from the cliff edge, a fact that reassured Ash. He hated heights. Just the thought of looking down at an expanse of empty air made him queasy. As a child, he'd always watched enviously when Bruce climbed a particular tree on their family estate, a towering oak whose branches grew sparse and spindly at the top. Bruce always yelled down at him to follow, to climb even halfway up to see the view. Ash refused, determined to keep his feet on the ground. As an adult, he followed the same practice.

Yet, when he reached the tower of the lighthouse, there was nowhere to go but up. He'd tethered the horse and walked around the property already. The cottage where the keeper must have once lived was now abandoned and crumbling. The tower was a separate structure, and appeared to be more solidly constructed.

"It's all inside," Ash told himself. "It's perfectly safe."

He didn't believe it was perfectly safe, but the image of Bruce calling out to him from the top of that tree so many years ago came back to him. He'd taken on this whole business to silence memories like that one. All he had to do was discover something of what Morrison was up to, and then he could report back to Bruce. Mission accomplished. Then the memories would fade.

The door to the tower was new, despite the fact that the place was no longer functioning. Odd. He opened it and went in. Wooden stairs spiraled up around the inner walls. Ash tried the first few, which were solid. He went up, putting a hand on the higher treads whenever a stair creaked beneath his feet. There was no railing to grasp, and nothing to stop him from tumbling downward should he slip.

"Stop thinking," he muttered, hoping to banish the scenarios his overactive brain presented him.

Eventually, he reached the top, emerging through a sort of hatchway to clamber into the chamber where the light once beamed out to sea.

The light was dormant now. However, there were plenty of signs of recent activity. The floor was swept clear of debris, and the open windows—only the light itself was glassed in—let in a breeze from the ocean. In one sheltered corner, something sat concealed under heavy canvas.

Ash pulled the canvas aside and saw a stash of strange objects. Lanterns of varying styles and quality were packed into crates. There were candles (somewhat nibbled by mice attracted to the tallow), rectangular metal plates of many sizes, several hooks, and a length of rope coiled up. But most remarkably, there was glass. A lot of glass.

Panels of glass were carefully packed into a crate of their own. Some pieces were about the size of his hand, some were the size of a broadside. Some were thin, some were thick. The glass rippled on one panel, while another was convex like a magnifying lens.

Lens. Ash picked up one piece of glass. That's what these must be. Lenses of some sort, intended to magnify or focus light.

Since the main light was not operative, Ash decided that the smaller lanterns were the tools being used. He held up one of the glass panels to a lantern's side, trying to decide what effect it would have. He didn't want to actually create a light, and in any case the bright sunlight would obscure any manmade flame.

Sunlight. Inspired, Ash held up a glass panel to the east window. He was rewarded with an intensely bright spot on the floor, proving that the glass worked as a magnifying lens. How far away could such a light be seen? Was that what Morrison was testing? And if so, why was it taking so long?

After testing a few more of the lenses, Ash packed everything away just as he found it, then peered out through all the windows that circled this upper room. He could see the Channel sparkling in the sunlight. Various fishing boats and a few larger ships sailed by, some close to shore, some barely visible. Ash could also see the bulk of Grasmere House, far down along the cliff, on the other side of a long strand of beach. Moving along, he could just glimpse a town he presumed to be Worthing.

Building up his courage, Ash stepped up to the window edge itself, and leaned over a bit. He managed one look down at the ground below before pushing back hard on the sill to propel himself into the center of the room.

"Christ," he breathed. The vertigo threatened to overwhelm him. "Why did I do that?"

He sat on the floor at the base of the big light until he recovered. He wanted desperately to get back to firm ground, but to do so he had to climb those steps downward.

It was a dizzying journey for him, moving carefully, step by step. He winced every time a board creaked, but he reached the bottom.

"Never again," he muttered, as he left the tower. He was never so happy to see a horse. He mounted up and rode away as fast as he could. Glancing back, he swore, "Never going up into a tower again. *Ever.*"

He found a winding path down to the beach, and took it until the horse's hooves hit hard packed sand. Ash rode along the beach at the tideline, noting how well it matched Nora's watercolor. She must have been let out of the house to paint, for there was no way anyone could have depicted such a scene from memory. Perhaps she was exaggerating when she said Morrison kept her locked up.

Ash returned to the house a few hours after he left, and that evening was invited to join Morrison for dinner. Mrs Kingfisher was nowhere to be seen.

He asked again about the invention. He already had a rudimentary account of what it was intended to do, since Morrison had described it to the government when he asked for funds. "So this invention that will improve military communications—does it have a name yet?" he asked, easing into it.

"Not a final one. We—I call it light signaling, for the most part."

"And its exact configuration?"

Morrison looked surprised. "It's like semaphore…only more so."

"How, specifically?"

"Well, lights."

"Instead of flags," Ash guessed. "To be seen at night."

The other man looked relieved. "Exactly!"

"How far is it visible at night? How accurate is it?"

"That's what I'm working on," Morrison said testily.

"Can you offer any hints so far? You've had well over a year," Ash reminded him.

"I'm…defining the parameters."

The way Morrison said the phrase made Ash pause. It was as if he was parroting someone else. In fact, it seemed he didn't understand the process any better than Ash did, despite being the inventor of it.

"Excuse me," Ash said, "but have you been ill lately?"

"Ill? Why?"

"You seem a bit out of sorts when it comes to discussing your invention. I wondered if you suffered an illness that's slowed your progress."

Morrison looked uncertain whether to seize on this explanation—or not, if it would lead to a revocation of funding. "The project will be completed. I just need a little more time."

"How much more?"

"A few months. I'll conclude it by autumn, surely. I have to keep ordering new glass plates from the local glassmaker, and they often break. And the glassmakers don't know what they're for, obviously, so they get confused…"

Not surprising, if it was Morrison giving the orders. The man was confounding, just like everything else in this house.

"And my demonstration?"

"Tomorrow night, weather permitting," Morrison promised. "I'd do it tonight but I'll need Mrs Kingfisher to assist and she's not here."

"I remember her saying she had no involvement in your work," Ash said.

Morrison frowned, remembering the exchange as well. "She doesn't. I just meant that I'll need an assistant. The demonstration needs a sender and a receiver."

So what did he do for an assistant under normal circumstances? Ash wondered. But all he said was, "That makes sense. I look forward to seeing how it works."

"And then you can be off the next morning!" Morrison said, with far too much enthusiasm.

A contrary streak gave Ash his next words before he even knew he was going to say them. "Afraid not, old fellow."

Morrison's face fell. "What's that? Why not?"

Fortunately, Ash was good at making things up. Thinking fast, he said, "I've actually booked passage on a ship sailing from Portsmouth in about ten days. But who wants to hang about, just waiting for a ship to sail? You won't mind if I remain here, will you? Of course not. That's true hospitality, and I won't forget it when I report back." He offered a smile to Morrison, knowing full well that the man wouldn't dare try to hurry him out, not with the implied threat that a lack of cooperation would mean a negative report.

"Certainly…" Morrison replied, looking anything but pleased.

"Excellent. That's sorted, then." Ash turned his attention to the meal. He'd have plenty of time to unravel the various secrets at Grasmere House.

Following dinner, Ash retired to his room as soon as politeness allowed. He wasn't sleepy, but he lay down on top of the bedcovers. If Nora kept her word to meet him again, it wasn't likely to happen until later, when the household quieted down.

Crewe came in while Ash lay staring up at the canopy of his bed.

"Are you well, sir?" the valet asked worriedly.

"Perfectly," Ash assured him. "I'm just resting in anticipation of more reconnoitering, or sallying forth, or forging ahead…whatever this sort of activity is called."

"Did you have a particular aim for your reconnoitering, sir? Or is it a more casual sallying forth?"

"Is that mockery I hear?" Ash raised his head to see Crewe's expression, which was the picture of innocent concern.

"Well-intentioned inquiry, sir. If you told me what you hope to accomplish, perhaps I could assist."

"I don't think I need assistance tonight," Ash said. "Tomorrow, I'd like you to go into town and find the glassworks." Ash explained a bit of what he'd found at the lighthouse. "I want to know if Morrison truly keeps ordering more glass to be made, and if so how often, and how much he's spending. When I spoke to him at dinner, he betrayed a rather vague understanding of what his process required…despite him being the author of it."

The valet nodded in comprehension. "I can manage that."

"Be careful," Ash warned. "Don't put yourself in danger."

"I'll avoid broken glass," Crewe said drily. "I do know what I'm doing, sir."

"Well, that makes one of us."

"You're doing quite well so far."

"Stumbling around in the dark."

"A man must walk before he can run. Did you want anything before bed?"

"No, thank you. I plan to read for a while. I'll ring for you if you're needed."

Crewe fussed about for a few minutes more, looking for something he didn't seem to find. Then he left.

Ash pulled out a book he'd brought along and read by candlelight, until he grew absorbed in the text and forgot what brought him here.

"Excuse me," came a soft voice.

Startled, Ash looked up to see Nora standing at the foot of his bed. She had moved as silently as a ghost, and was dressed in the same summery white gown. This time, however, she was smiling at him, the dimple appearing in her cheek. In the candlelight, her eyes were a deep, vivid blue. It was the first time he saw her in enough light to be sure.

He just looked at her for a moment, delighted by what he saw. "You came back."

Chapter 9

"I TOLD YOU I WOULD," Nora said. She'd debated it, but in the end the opportunity to speak to someone who wanted to speak to her was irresistible.

"I wasn't sure if I dreamed you or not. Hold on a moment." Ash found a thin ribbon among the wrinkles of the bedspread and marked his place in the book he'd been reading.

Nora noticed how carefully he put the book to the side of his bed. "What are you reading?" she asked.

"Kant."

"The German philosopher?"

"Yes. Critik a der reinen Vernunft. In English it would be Critique of Pure Reason."

"But you read it in German?"

"There's no English translation. Anyway, language changes meaning, sometimes. And with Kant, precision is important. It's one of my favorite books," he added, as if it were a dark secret.

"Oh." She didn't expect that at all—not that she knew anything about his reading habits. Or any of his other habits. "Did you study philosophy?"

"Yes, among other things." Ash's response was a little curt. Perhaps she should not have asked.

Then he rose from the bed. When he reached her, Ash gave her a sober look. "Nora. I've got to get one thing out of the way."

"Yes?" she asked, nervousness spiking through her.

"Last night…did I kiss you?"

"Oh! You did." That wasn't what she thought he would ask.

"Ah. Wasn't sure if I dreamed it. Apologies. I…wasn't quite myself."

"No need to apologize." She paused, then said, "You didn't shock me, if that's what's worrying you. I'm a widow."

"You are?" He sounded surprised. "I'm sorry. For your loss, that is."

She nodded once. "Thank you."

"I'll behave in the future."

"Considering the situation, you were a gentleman. Thank you."

"Speaking of the situation, what *was* your reason for coming here last night?" Ash asked.

"I wanted to find out more about you."

"You were going to snoop, you mean."

Nora felt heat creeping into her cheeks. "It sounds rather undignified when you put it like that."

"But I'm correct?"

"Well, yes. But Mr Morrison didn't put me up to it," she added.

"You've made it clear that you two aren't on the same side. Which brings me to my next question. What is your relationship?"

"It's…complicated."

"Use small words then, so even I can understand."

"Let's just say he sometimes finds me useful for his work."

"How so?" He pulled out the watercolor and unrolled it. "I went to the lighthouse today. I saw the equipment stored at the top. But what do the images on the border of the page mean?"

"You noticed," she said, pleased with him. "They represent the code flashed from the signal to the viewing point."

"What?"

Now she was puzzled. "You don't know about the signaling?"

"Not enough. Morrison discussed it a little, though he didn't explain it very well."

She stifled a snort. "No, he wouldn't."

"So, can you? Assume I'm very stupid and explain it to me from the beginning."

Nora wrinkled her nose in thought. "Instead of telling you, I can show you. Follow me."

Once again, Nora led Ash through the twisting hallways of the house until they reached the top floor. Ash shadowed her every move, and made no noise as he walked. *Very skilled at that for a clerk in some government office*, she thought.

She lit a candle, then turned to find Ash leaning against the wall. He looked quite at home, and he surveyed the room with interest.

"So this is your domain. Easier to see with some light. By the way, you stole my robe," he said, affecting a stern look.

Nora said, "I didn't realize until you had already gone. I hid it last night so Mrs Lloyd wouldn't notice. Shall I retrieve it for you?"

"No hurry, so long as it's well hidden. I wouldn't want

you to get into trouble on my account."

This man was likely to bring her nothing but trouble, unless she handled him carefully in order to use him to escape.

"Why were you the one to come down here?" she asked, hoping to learn more about him. "Did you meet Mr Morrison in London before?"

"Not as such," Ash replied. "I'm just here because no one else could come. Bit short-staffed, you understand."

"Short-staffed? With a war going on?"

There was something distinctly evasive in his shrug. "I'm not the one who makes the decisions. I was told to see how Albert Morrison was getting on with His Majesty's money, and that's about it. Morrison worried some folks when he stopped communicating. Why was that?"

Nora paused, thinking how to answer. Everything depended on whether she trusted this man. She'd be foolish to do so. So a lie would have to suffice. She said, "He wanted to come to this house so he could perform more tests. The sea and the lighthouse are ideal."

She watched Ash's expression carefully, trying to judge whether he accepted such an incomplete explanation.

He didn't.

"But why just up and move? Why not inform anyone of where he was going?" Ash looked her over. "Were you with him the whole time? Before the move here? When did you meet Albert Morrison?"

So many questions. Nora didn't have a good answer to any of them. Well, there was the truth. Could she tell a little truth to satisfy him? "I first met Albert Morrison about four years ago. We found a common interest in some amateur scientific endeavors."

"You mean you're the one who assists him…not that Kingfisher woman."

"More or less," Nora said. In fact, Morrison was the assistant to *her*, but Nora didn't think Ash would believe that.

"If it was a common interest, then why are you locked in a room now?" he asked, with far too much logic.

"I can't tell you. Why should it matter? You only want to know about the invention."

"Why should it *matter*?" he repeated. "Nora, you can't tell someone you've been confined against your will and then expect them not to care!"

"It's not your concern," she said.

"I'm making it my concern."

"It can't possibly be in the scope of your work. Which is what, exactly?"

The cagey look was back. "I'm just a minor functionary. It's quite dull."

"Not as dull as being trapped in a house for a year, I'll wager. Tell me more about what *you* do."

"First tell me more about being trapped." Ash walked to the door, examining it with a keen eye. "Are you really confined under lock and key?"

"I'm confined all too often. Particularly since you came. They don't want you to see me."

"Yet you manage to get out when you need to. How?"

"I pilfered a spare key months ago, during one of the periods when I was less supervised."

"Even if you have a key, there's a bolt on the outside of this door. Surely he uses it."

Nora smiled. "The bolt is iron."

"I expect so," Ash said. Then he paused, looking speculative. "The wooden door isn't that thick. A very strong magnet could affect the bolt from your side."

Nora was impressed. He must have studied more than philosophy. She pointed to a large rock on a shelf. "I found that on the beach. It's magnetized. I noticed how the sand patterns around it were affected."

"They let you take it home?"

"I didn't announce that it was magnetized." She rolled her eyes.

"If you're that resourceful, how is it that you haven't escaped long ago?"

She sighed. "No money, no friends, no supplies. I have tried, but I've yet to succeed."

"Why not ask for help?" Ash asked. "Ask me, for instance."

"I don't know who you are or what you are. You certainly don't seem to be the sort to toil away in an office. You were raised to read Kant, and everything about you suggests much better blood than the average government worker. So what are you?"

Ash's eyes narrowed. "Believe me, Nora, I'm nowhere near a center of power. Nor am I important. I'm just a second son…a distant second."

"You have a brother?" she asked, suddenly interested.

"Yes, though we hardly talk. Why do you ask?"

"I have a brother. I'd give anything to see him again."

"Why can't you?" Ash asked.

"He's in India, or he was the last I heard. I've no way to get in contact with him."

"Leaving you alone with Morrison," Ash concluded, bringing the conversation back around to the beginning. "Well, if you won't tell me about you or him, tell me about this light signaling. How is it done?"

Nora nearly sighed in relief. That was a relatively safe topic.

"I can explain the process," she said. "You know

about semaphores, I trust?"

Ash nodded. "I couldn't read a message, but yes, I understand the principle. Flags held at different positions, that sort of thing. So sailors can communicate with another ship at sea."

"Yes, though it's used on land as well. The process has been refined, too. During the last war, signal towers were built for the same purpose, staffed by signalers to pass messages over long distances. This isn't from one ship to a second ship and done. With the towers, one can pass a message from Deal to London in a little over an hour."

Ash nodded in understanding. "That would be useful in a war."

"The initial idea was to be able to warn of an invasion. But any message can be sent."

"So long as you don't mind everyone who can read it being able to see it."

"Precisely," said Nora. "So our idea was to take the concept of the signal towers and try to make it more useful. For one thing, signal flags or structures are designed for daytime use only. They're essentially silent all night."

"But with light, darkness is actually helpful," Ash said. "You use lanterns to flash messages made of light."

"Yes." She paused for a moment, thinking of how to put it. "Morrison has been working on various methods to see what lights shine brightest, and which lanterns can be fitted with flaps or covered to show or hide the light as needed to spell out the messages."

"Is that the reason for all the different glass panels I saw in the lighthouse?"

"Yes. It's trickier than it sounds to get the balance of brightness and sharpness. If the glass is correctly made, you have brightness without losing precision. Bends in the glass can create uncertainty of location. We've been working on defining—"

"—the parameters," Ash finished, his eyes bright.

Nora nodded. "If the system is to work, it needs to be standardized. All the equipment and distances and practices need to be the same. The signal is communicated via lantern and mirrors. Several prototypes of lantern were tried, each one improving on the previous. The ones we're using now are probably the best anyone could hope for. They're bright, sturdy, and easy to carry."

"Lanterns aren't exactly new inventions. Why so many tries to get it right?"

"To signal the correct patterns of light, a special casing was required, so that the signaler can open and close the lantern very quickly, and slide the front panel in a few different ways in order to show the correct pattern of light. Also, ship captains are wary of flame, so the lantern has to be movable without being fragile, or allowing the fuel inside to spill."

Ash looked intrigued. "I think I understand the basics. So you've got a big lantern somewhere tall and visible. Someone signals, and the other records the message. How long does it take?"

"Depends on the message," Nora said. "It's much slower than speaking, obviously. But I've never seen a signal exchange go on for more than a quarter hour."

"Is the time pre-arranged?" he asked.

"For the way we do our testing, yes. One person in the lighthouse and one at Grasmere House, on the seaside, each with a timekeeping device. One could arrange to have a signaler and receiver constantly on duty, though. Say in a war, where there are men who could take shifts, just watching for any signal at all. Then a message could be sent whenever it's needed. The receivers would relay it up the line of command, and those in charge can react accordingly."

"Very useful."

"People need to learn the code, naturally," Nora went on, heartened by Ash's genuine interest in the process. "It's a little bit like another language, because each letter's light position must be memorized."

"Light position?"

"Yes. Each letter of the alphabet is assigned a unique pattern." Nora picked up a small book and a candlestick.

"Imagine this is a lantern." Nora held the book a foot in front of the candlestick. "The flame is covered now. If I expose the top third"—she pulled the book lower— "a viewer would see a bar of light at the top. That's the letter A."

"The top of the lantern? Isn't that hard to tell at a distance?"

"Well, that's one of the challenges," Nora said, frustrated. "And one of the things the different glass configurations could help clarify. Convex lens brighten the light, so you can see it from further away. But it distorts the light too—so it's harder to be sure of the pattern. I've tried several different methods…I'm not trained in this sort of thing though, so it's slow. But at least I can remember the full code. It takes Morrison forever to spell a message out," she added in a grumble.

"*You* came up with the code, didn't you?" Ash asked.

Nora wondered if she'd said too much. "I helped."

"You came up with it," he repeated, with a little smile. "You're ten times more clever than Morrison is. I can tell that already."

"Twenty times," Nora corrected, even as she felt a little glow in her core. Even if he was just spouting flattery to keep her talking, it felt good.

"He doesn't want a woman taking credit?" Ash went

on. "Is that why he pretends the idea is all his?"

Nora bit her lip. "Partly. He certainly wants the money that comes with the credit."

"What do you want?"

"Just for it to be over," she said. "Once it's done, he'll let me alone."

Ash stepped up to her, taking the book and the candle away. He set them on the table and turned back to her. "Nora, do you believe that?"

"He said so."

"Do you believe it?" he pressed.

No. She didn't believe it for a moment, not after what Morrison had done to her previously. But this man would never take her side after hearing her story. He seemed sympathetic now, but he wanted something from her. Once he got what he wanted, he'd be gone.

If only she didn't *want* to tell Ash the truth. Something in his eyes encouraged her to do just that, to spill out her heart and soul and let him deal with the pieces. But who did that? This man didn't really want to hear about what happened to Nora. He wouldn't believe the truth if she told it to him. He certainly wouldn't believe the truth about Morrison.

"Nora?" Ash prompted, when she didn't speak. "What's wrong?"

The gentleness in his tone nearly undid her. Nearly.

"Nothing is wrong," she said. "You should go. If you want to help me, you'll pretend I don't exist."

✳ ✳ ✳ ✳

In the few days since Ashley Allen came to the house, Nora had grown bold. Even though he brought complications of his own, she found that with him close by, she could think again. Perhaps the mere possibility of change was enough to wake her from her months-long stupor. Morrison nearly broke her, but now Nora's mind was her own again.

In particular, she thought about escape. Her idea of stealing clothes from Ash no longer appealed to her. It would be rather difficult for her to travel as a boy anyway. But that didn't mean she couldn't improve her wardrobe. Instead of the flimsy, ridiculous dresses that Morrison permitted her, she'd sneak into Mrs Kingfisher's room and take one of *her* dresses. The lady had so many, she couldn't possibly notice if one went missing, especially if Nora took one of the plainest gowns.

She waited until a day when Mrs Kingfisher traveled to Worthing, as the lady did so often—usually when there was news that someone from the royal family had come to town. Nora considered Mrs Kingfisher an irredeemable snob, desperate for the reflected glory of being near a princess or some other figure. What did the woman think? That Princess Amelia would see her across the lobby of the hotel and invite Mrs Kingfisher to tea?

Possibly she would. Nora didn't know much about the habits of princesses, but Isabelle Kingfisher *was* a beautiful, haughty, well-dressed lady. Exactly the sort that a princess might know. Perhaps she'd even enjoy Mrs Kingfisher's conversation. Nora always found her vapid…though it wasn't Nora the woman strove to impress. Morrison certainly found her fascinating. Likely that had more to do with Mrs Kingfisher's physical charms, which were hard to ignore. The way she cinched up her stays actually made Nora laugh, but Morrison appreciated it. Nora wondered if Ash did too. *Stop that*, she told herself. She had to focus on getting into the room.

Unfortunately, when Nora tried to get in that day, the

lady's room was being tidied by a maid, and Nora couldn't afford to be seen anywhere near the door. She retreated. She'd have to try again later, perhaps during supper, when the others would be downstairs and the upper floors quiet.

So she waited, agonizing, until dark fell.

After sneaking into Mrs Kingfisher's room, Nora delved through the clothes press, past yards of silks and satins in vivid colors. It was like touching a rainbow. Unfortunately, Nora didn't need a rainbow.

"Doesn't this woman own anything dull?" she muttered.

Finally, on the bottom shelf, Nora discovered a light grey gown. It was a very fine linen, but the cut was plain, and she should be able to pass unremarked in most situations in such an outfit—provided she could also get her hands on the proper accoutrements. She needed shoes, and some undergarments, a pelisse or cloak of some sort, and gloves, and a hat... Missing any single item might attract attention. Ladies required so much to appear proper. Yet another reason Morrison avoided giving her a suitable wardrobe.

Nora kept searching the room for suitable items. She pulled out a pair of kid gloves dyed black when something else fell from the same shelf.

Curious, Nora picked up a bundle of letters tied with a pale blue ribbon. She unfolded the first and scanned it. Nora's French was passable at best, but from what she could tell, this was a letter from a lover. The others were all written in the same hand. Nora didn't like to think of going through such things, so she packed the bundle away again.

She gathered the gown and gloves and other items in her arms. She leaned over the candlestick on the writing desk, ready to blow out the light.

There was a piece of paper on the desk, with the words *GET HER SON TOOL SOON FIREBIRD FLY NORTH* all written in a column. Nora whispered them out loud. She'd seen these words before, since she had watched them flash from the lighthouse during the last round of testing. Morrison's messages had turned incomprehensible lately, just these strings of random words. But why was the message in Isabelle's room? Had the woman been watching the test from somewhere in the house?

Or was it just that Morrison left this list on his mistress's desk? The block letters left no clue as to who wrote them.

Then she just caught a glimpse of a partially written letter in beautiful feminine handwriting. It was in French. Mrs Kingfisher must have begun it before going down to dinner.

Nora read the name at the top. The same name of the lover whose letters were so carefully preserved.

Mrs Kingfisher maintained that correspondence despite being Morrison's mistress, and married to the absent Mr Kingfisher? Nora wrinkled her nose at the thought. She wasn't a moralist, but the idea of a woman keeping two lovers while married to a third man struck her as deceitful beyond reason…not to mention difficult and exhausting.

She read what she could of the letter before she could stop herself, and that meant the candle glow betrayed her.

The door swung open, and Morrison's bulky form filled the opening. "What the hell do you think you're doing?"

Nora spun around, clutching the bundled clothing to her chest. "I can explain!"

Morrison saw the clothes, and his eyes narrowed. He

lunged forward to grab Nora.

She ducked by instinct, dashing to the right, hoping to get by him and through the door.

Nora didn't have a chance.

Morrison snapped his arm out to the side, and his balled fist caught Nora square in the face.

She didn't even cry out. The pain was so sudden that she just stood there.

The clothing lay in a pile at her feet, knocked clean out of her arms.

Morrison stepped to the side, once again blocking her path. Though his eyes were narrowed, he seemed equally surprised. He hadn't meant to strike her. But as he looked over the pilfered clothing, any potential remorse for his action evaporated.

"I was going to ask why you were in this room, but now I see that you were stealing."

"No," she said, a patent lie.

"You're a thief," he spat. "How did you even get out of your attic?"

Nora stared at him. He couldn't ever guess the truth. She had to tell him something. "Mrs…Mrs Lloyd. Didn't bolt it after giving me my dinner tray." She put her hand to her face, feeling the heat where he'd hit her. "You hurt me."

"It was your fault," he growled. "You're the one who tried to run away when you were caught!"

He reached out again, this time grabbing her shoulder. "We won't have that happen again. Come with me. And don't you dare say a word," he added.

Would Ash find her if she screamed? Nora doubted it. Even if he did, Morrison was bigger and taller and meaner.

She allowed Morrison to steer her back up to her attic

room. He pushed her in roughly, not following.

"Explain yourself. Quickly."

"I…"

"Speak!"

"I wanted a dress," she whispered. "I'm cold up here."

"You've a blanket and a fireplace."

"I want a dress. She has so many. I have none."

"You don't deserve one, Elanora. Madwomen don't get a new gown every season. Because they're not in society, are they? They only need enough to cover themselves. Do you understand?"

"Yes."

"You're just agreeing with me."

"Would you be less angry if I said no?"

He took half a step toward her and Nora shrank down to her knees, fearful that he'd lose all restraint.

Morrison apparently reconsidered. "I'll come back when I've decided a suitable punishment. Until then, you can contemplate what you've done. And when I do return, Elanora…" Morrison didn't even finish his statement.

He pulled the door shut. Nora heard the bolt snap. She remained kneeling on the floor, pain and misery washing over her. She'd taken a foolish risk, and she got caught. If only she hadn't ever spoken to Ash! She'd got excited, believing she might change her fate.

Instead, she enraged her captor and endangered herself. Nora raised her hand to her face again, wincing when she touched the skin. Tears filled her eyes and dripped down, stinging when the salt crossed the bruise.

Nora didn't look in the mirror, afraid of what she would see. Instead, she simply broke down and cried.

Chapter 10

AFTER SUPPER, ASH WENT TO his room and waited for Nora to appear. But minutes ticked by, became an hour, then two, and she never came. So he decided to go to her.

The house was quiet as he made his way to the top floor.

He tapped once, paused, then once again. "Nora? It's Ash. I'm alone." He saw the bolt and slid it to the open position.

There was a long pause.

"Come in." He barely heard the command before he was inside.

Nora stood in the middle of the room, once again in the long, simple white gown he'd first seen her in. It seemed to be the only one she had. She was facing away from him.

"You shouldn't be here," she mumbled. "What if they find you?"

"What happened?" Worried at her defeated tone, Ash took a step closer.

Nora turned halfway. She was holding a hand to her face. Then Nora dropped her hand, revealing an already purpling bruise on her cheek, just under her eye.

"God damn it," he said. Ash wasn't a violent person, but at the moment he wanted to hunt Morrison down and do something very violent.

"It was an accident," she said.

"He accidentally struck you in the face?" Ash asked, incredulous.

"It doesn't matter. It will heal."

"You're cut," he said, seeing a line of crusted red where the skin had broken. "We need to clean it. When did it happen?"

"During supper. He came upstairs and found me."

"He excused himself to get something he was going to show me. I wondered why it took so long for him to return."

Ash gestured for her to sit, and poured out clean water from the pitcher at her wash stand. He soaked a cloth and knelt in front of Nora. "This might sting."

She closed her eyes, submitting to his aid. Ash cleaned the cut as carefully as he could. Nora sucked in a breath once, flinching.

"I'm sorry," he said.

"*You* shouldn't apologize," she whispered, her eyes still closed.

"Morrison should, though. Want me to call him out?" Ash offered. "I prefer to avoid duels, but I'll make an exception for you."

Nora smiled. It was just a flicker, but it was the reaction he was hoping for. "Don't be silly. You can't do that, because you don't know I exist."

"I can find a way around that detail if you give me a moment." Ash found another cloth and gently patted the wound dry. "There. Have you got any gauze to dress it?"

Nora nodded and stood up. "I'll do it."

Ash watched her move about the room. "We've got to

get you out of here," he said once she was finished covering the wound with a patch of clean, loose-woven linen.

"We?" Nora asked. "You have your own agenda, do you not?"

"Forget agendas, Nora. He hit you." Ash took her hand and led her to the side of the bed. "Has that happened before?"

"Not like this." She put a hand to her head. "I'm actually a bit dizzy when I stand."

"Lie down, then," Ash said.

Nora obeyed, curling up on her side so the bruise wouldn't touch the pillow.

He unfolded the blanket at the foot of the bed. But instead of simply covering her, Ash lay on the bed next to her before spreading the blanket over them both.

"What are you doing?" Nora whispered.

"Keeping you company." Ash shifted until he lay on his side facing Nora. "You didn't think I'd just dash off, did you?"

"I don't know what to think about you, Mr Allen."

"So formal," Ash said, "especially considering our present circumstances."

"Just because we're in bed together doesn't mean you should take liberties," Nora said primly, though there was a hint of laughter in her voice.

Ash caught her gaze. "Do you want me to leave?"

"It was a joke."

"Sometimes making light of something is the only way to resist it," he said. "I don't want to scare you, Nora, especially after what he did. If you'd prefer to be alone…"

"No!" Nora looked a bit alarmed at her outburst, but then said, "It's better with you here. Though I shouldn't ask you to stay. He could come up any time."

"I'll hear him and hide," Ash said reasonably. "You've got a dark shadowy corner over there. He won't notice."

"You're far too confident. Do you hide in other people's rooms very often?"

"When necessary." Ash certainly had some experience in leaving ladies' homes via unconventional means. Strange how a rake's skills overlapped with those of spying. "Anyway," he went on, "why don't you tell me something I don't know."

"Such as what?"

"How about a childhood memory?"

Nora stiffened. "A memory? Why do you say that?"

"Because you must have a few. Tell me a good one." Ash wanted to distract her, both from the pain of her wound and the dire situation she was trapped in.

"A good memory," she said, pondering.

"Anything you like. Close your eyes, and think about a time that you were so happy you couldn't speak. You'll feel better when you have. Trust me."

Nora dutifully closed her eyes, and her face slowly relaxed as one memory took her away.

Ash noticed it, delighting in it with a kind of hunger. God, *this* was his weakness. Not the scandals or competition or the wild life of London's underworld. It was this, his desire to be good. To do good. To listen to the secrets and take away the pain.

This was exactly what got him into trouble in the first place, all those years ago. When he was a naive, eager boy, anxious to please. Strange how he recognized the feeling, and still ignored the warning signs.

"Once, when I was nine," Nora began, "and Daniel was twelve—"

"Daniel?"

"My older brother. We stayed at a house in the Lake

District. One of the aunts or a great aunt…I don't know who invited us. But we stayed the whole summer, and so many days we simply roamed. I suppose we didn't go far. Distances always seem further when you're young. But every day we had a lunch packed, and a blanket, and we'd climb the highest hill we could find, and try to go all round the shore of a pond or a lake, unless mud turned us back."

"Mud stopped *you*?" Ash asked. Nora didn't seem the fastidious type.

"Not me, so much. I just hitched my skirts up. But Daniel would complain so…" She smiled. "One afternoon, we put the blanket down and just lay there, watching the sky. The clouds always change there…every minute. Daniel tried to make shapes out of the clouds and I tried to count one hundred birds, but I always lost count around sixty-three. My dress was green, with lace flounces in five rows along the bottom hem. I felt so grown up to have five rows of lace. And one slipper was smaller than the other because I stepped in water and the leather shrank…"

As Nora spoke, Ash fell into the story. It was so vividly rendered. He could picture her as clearly as if he stood there himself, so many years ago. He wished he had been, because the idea of meeting Nora when she wasn't burdened by all the madness going on in the house was incredibly appealing. Nora was meant to be joyful. Why the hell would someone be born with a dimple in her cheek if she wasn't meant to have a happy life?

She was finishing her story. "…and Daniel said in parts of Asia they eat crickets and I didn't believe him, and the whole afternoon it was sunny and cloudy all at once, just shadowed till I got almost too cool and sunny till I got almost too warm, over and over, and I wished it would be like that forever."

Nora sighed. "That's it. That's my happiest memory. Just an afternoon with my older brother. How silly."

"Not at all." Ash wished he had a memory like that with his own older brother. But all his memories of Bruce were tinged with darkness. They all occurred in the dreary halls of their rambling family estate, with their father's disapproving gaze finding them at the worst times. "It sounds lovely."

"What's your happiest memory?" she asked, inevitably.

He shook his head. "I don't know."

"Yes, you do," Nora said.

The day he heard his father died, Ash drank a bottle of champagne, took Reggie to a gambling hell, and won over a thousand pounds in three hours at cards. He couldn't play a bad hand that night. His heart was racing the whole time, he couldn't stop laughing, and he had the most ravishing woman in England on his arm.

He'd take Nora's picnic over that any day.

She was waiting for his response. Ash said, "Nothing comes to mind."

"Something must. You don't seem like a man whose life is misery or drudgery."

"Don't I?"

"Your life must be exciting."

"Not from where I'm watching it…other than the moments when I discover mysterious women in remote houses, of course."

"Oh, there are other times this has happened to you?"

"I assure you this situation is unique." He paused. "Do you feel any better?"

"Yes, actually. Thanks to you. It's helpful to know there are still good people in the world."

She clearly thought him a different sort of man than he actually was. Ash normally didn't care a bit what anyone thought of him…but then, that was easy, because most people thought the worst of him. The experience of being considered good was so novel that Ash wasn't sure what to do with the feeling. So he did what he normally did—he tucked it away in his mind to worry about later.

"Ash?"

"Yes?"

Nora didn't look at him when she said, in a rush, "Could you kiss me? Like you did before?"

"Nora."

"Unless you don't want to," she added, speaking so quickly the words piled onto each other.

"It's got nothing to do with what I want," he said. "You've just been hurt, and you're not feeling quite like yourself…"

"How would you know?" she asked, a challenge in her voice.

"I meant that I shouldn't take advantage of the situation."

"Yes, but I'm asking, so you'd just be responding to a lady's request, which is perfectly acceptable for a gentleman to do."

"You've mistaken me for a gentleman. I'm not."

"Then prove it by taking advantage. Either way, gentleman or not, you've got to kiss me."

Ash had no intention of proving just how far from a gentleman he was, but he was curious to find out if his hazy dream of kissing Nora would hold up to reality. So he kissed her.

Nora's mouth was warm, her lips soft. She leaned closer, her hand sliding up his arm as if to make sure he wouldn't escape.

He didn't want to escape. He slid one hand to the back to her neck, mindful of the bandage on her cheek. He kept the kiss light, worrying that he'd inadvertently hurt her. But a light kiss wasn't the same as a restrained kiss.

Ash teased her lower lip with his tongue, then moved to her chin, and then her neck, keeping his touch light, using his breath more than his mouth to elicit a reaction from her.

Her reaction was as rewarding as it was maddening. She gave little sighs of satisfaction that made Ash want to stay with her all night, because he wanted to hear that sound over and over, as a result of the many things he wanted to do with her.

Her hands had found his shoulders and she tightened her grip every time he moved to a new place along her throat, relaxing again when he took a breath. The natural sensuality of her touch was enough to get his mind racing.

His fingers accidentally brushed against the edge of the gauze bandage, and he abruptly remembered the situation.

"This may be a bad idea," he murmured.

Nora leaned back against the pillow, a smile hovering on her lips. "I didn't mind at all."

"Nora," he said softly. "Do you believe me now?"

"About what?" she asked.

"About not being a gentleman." Ash shifted slightly, reluctantly pulling away from her so that certain parts of his anatomy would stop reacting quite so much to Nora's body.

"The term *gentleman* is meaningless in any case," Nora said. "True nobility can't be found in a title. Morrison dreams of attaining some sort of rank. Baronet, or knight at the very least. Some reward for giving the invention over to the government. Yet even if he were made a duke, he'd still be the same foul person inside."

"You know," Ash raised himself up, propping his head on one elbow. "Part of me still can't believe Albert Morrison actually struck you. It doesn't match anything I've been told about him. He was described as a loyal, reliable sort of man."

A dark look crossed her face. "After all this, you still don't know the truth, do you?"

"The truth about what?"

"The truth about Albert Morrison." The expression in her eyes was unlike any he'd seen before. This Nora was fierce.

Ash put his hand out, inviting her to take it. "What do you know about him? You know something no one else does. Tell me."

She bit her lip, looking down, once again the meek lady. "I shouldn't have said… Never mind."

"Nora, please. You've got to trust me, at least a little bit."

She breathed deeply, once, twice. Ash stayed quiet, waiting. Then her slender fingers touched his offered hand.

"The truth is," she said very slowly, her eyes fixed on him, "the man in this house, the one you're calling Albert Morrison…he's *not* Albert Morrison."

Chapter 11

NORA REGRETTED THE WORDS AS soon as they came out. But she couldn't stop herself. Her heart was still racing from his kisses, from how he'd been lying so close to her on the bed. She'd never been so aware of her body's reactions—and her body certainly reacted to Ash.

His attentions took her breath away, and made her want far more. She hadn't experienced real desire for so long—she almost begged him to go on, to be bolder, to prove he wasn't a gentleman. But he was, and he didn't lose his composure for a moment. Perhaps that was why she confided in him.

The secret had been building up inside her, and she simply couldn't keep it bottled up any longer. Still, it had been a mistake. Ash would never believe the full truth. Indeed, to judge by his expression now, he could hardly understand the words she'd just said.

"He's not Albert Morrison?" Ash asked, speaking very distinctly, as if they might not be using the same language.

"No," Nora said. "He's an imposter."

"And you know this because…?"

"My full name is Elanora Wells Morrison. I married Albert Morrison nearly four years ago. The man downstairs is Albert's twin. Edmund."

"Twin," Ash echoed. It was unclear whether he believed her or not.

"Yes. He's the twin brother of my late husband."

"And you're living here because Edmund is your guardian in some way?"

"No." Nora had to spell this out clearly. "I'm living here because he impersonated my late husband for the purpose of kidnapping me and stealing my invention for light communication. He wants the money from selling the final product to the government. More than that, he wants to *become* Albert Morrison. He's always been jealous of his brother."

She waited for him to recoil, or call her unhinged, or laugh, or simply to give up on her in disgust.

But he didn't do any of those things. He just waited for her to continue. When she didn't, he said, very quietly, "Tell me."

"Tell you what? Where should I start?"

"How about when you first met your future husband?"

Nora remembered that day, as she remembered all days. "It was on Twelfth Night. A party at the home of one my brother's good friends. Albert Morrison was a dabbler. He was always looking for new innovations, new technologies. He was particularly interested in what had come out of the war, and through some social connections with a few retired officers who talked about their experiences, he developed an interest in communications. He thought that there was a place for better, faster methods. It was his main interest at the time we met, and so he spoke of it to me. I think he was rather surprised when it caught my interest, too."

"Go on," Ash said.

"He called on me the next day, and then escorted me to some lectures and to other parties. My brother liked him—I think he was even more pleased than I was when Albert proposed. It meant someone would take care of me when Daniel sailed for India."

"So you married."

"Yes. I was very happy. Albert provided for me, and we lived quietly. We associated with his friends, mostly. Mine had already married and scattered. But it didn't matter. I was content, until…"

"You met Edmund?"

"I never actually met him. He wasn't invited to the wedding, if that's any indication. Albert told me they had been close as boys. But Edmund was wild, reckless. He got into scrapes, and squandered his money, and eventually fell into debt. Albert refused to give him any funds, since he knew where that would lead. He and Edmund barely spoke for years."

Ash nodded grimly. "That I understand. But please go back to the invention. It *was* Albert who approached the government for funding, wasn't it?"

"Yes. We had several ideas, but to test them properly we needed some capital. Albert wanted to be able to sell the product or the process to the government anyway, because he assumed its primary use would be for long distance communication. So, through an acquaintance, he received a contract with the War Department. An initial investment, plus a promise of more upon the achievement of the final version. We had just begun the work when…" Nora trailed off.

"What happened?"

Nora shuddered, the memory of the day surging upward with such clarity that it might have happened yesterday.

"Edmund contacted him out of the clear blue. Said he wanted to start over, begged his brother to help him. Albert couldn't say no, not to his brother. I think he wanted to bring Edmund in on the project in some way. He must have written to him with details, and then he visited Edmund somewhere in London. The last time I saw him was when he got in the coach.

"Albert wrote to me nearly every day while he was gone. The initial letters were full of hope for reconciliation with his brother, and for Edmund's return to good society. He'd given his word that he'd turned over a new leaf. And Albert, good-hearted but rather naive, had believed him."

Nora continued to explain to Ash what happened.

In a later letter, Albert expressed some disappointment and trepidation in his brother's behavior, but he remained determined to make up with him. He hoped to come home soon.

The next letter had quite a different tone. It was brusque and alarming. In it, Albert requested that she come to the address as quickly as possible. He'd fallen ill and needed her. Naturally, Nora followed the instructions and found her way down to the address he'd given.

At the house in London, however, it was Edmund who met her at the door. Immediately, his eerie physical similarity to Albert disturbed her, like a looking-glass gone wrong. And then, before she could properly understand what was happening, Nora became trapped in a nightmare.

"Elanora," Edmund said. "I'm glad you came."

"Where is Albert?" she'd asked, anxiously. "He said he was feeling ill."

"I'm much better, thank you."

"I don't care about your health. I'm asking after my husband."

"I am your husband."

Nora shook her head, sure she'd misheard. "Where is Albert?"

"Right in front of you."

She whirled around, as if she'd see him standing there. In the mirror on the wall, she caught Edmund's reflection. The man was chuckling.

"This isn't funny," she said.

"No, it's quite serious," he agreed. "I am Albert Morrison, you're my wife, and any dissent on that point will end quite badly for you."

Nora instantly protested—Edmund had to be *mad*, she said. He cut off her words only by physically restraining her, and then threatening her with more dire consequences. "The law will believe me, Elanora. Who have you got on your side? I heard all about your life. You don't have any close friends. You live more or less alone, fiddling around with your little inventions."

Nora had gone still.

"Oh yes, I know about those. He told me everything. Told me that you're very clever. Also told me that there's money to be made…so it's fortunate that I, Albert Morrison, am here to collect that money."

"You're not Al—"

He twisted her arm slightly. He was stronger than his brother was. "Let's practice that response. Call me Albert."

"No, don't be absurd! Albert would never let you do this. Where is he? I want to see him! Bring me to him."

Edmund laughed then. "I'll show you what you need to see."

Nora fell silent. Picturing the scene, with her darling Albert lying on the bed, choked her up. Her mind simply stopped working.

"Nora? Nora." A hand covered hers. Ash. "What did you see?"

Nora told him the rest, in words no louder than a whisper. Ash listened without interruption.

She concluded, "When the undertakers came, they were told it was the body of Edmund Morrison. That's the name he was buried with. That's what Edmund's creditors were told. And the only person who could ruin his charade was me. But I was easy enough to deal with—he contacted a doctor, gave his own story, and asked for a diagnosis. The doctor declared me mad, and Morrison generously took on my care. The doctor complimented him for keeping me!"

"Why didn't he send you away to an asylum?"

"It wouldn't have fit with his plans. First, asylums cost money. Second, I might have talked and convinced someone else of my story—unlikely, but possible. And finally, he needed me close to him because he wanted to get the details of the work Albert and I had been pursuing."

Ash nodded slowly. "So he took you to this house, where you're both still working on the process?"

"Yes," she said. "And before you ask, I did try to leave! But no one would help me. All the servants in this house were hired after Edmund took me. I tried to tell them the truth at first, but they believed exactly what he told them, because he was a man."

"And the one paying them," Ash added, musingly. "So he substitutes his dead brother for himself, thus throwing off his own past, as well as getting his creditors off his back. He slips into his brother's life to make a fresh start."

"Mostly to make money," Nora corrected. "Once this

whole business is concluded, he'll take the reward and run. Leaving me behind for good. Which will suit me! I'll find my way back to London and perhaps learn where my brother is."

Ash's brow was furrowed. "Not to alarm you, but what makes you think Edmund will let you go peacefully? If I were him, I might well think you were a…liability."

Nora shook her head. "He's not that depraved."

"He benefited financially from your husband's death. Why would he balk at killing you too?"

"But he didn't kill Albert!" she protested. "Albert's death was natural!"

"How do you know?"

Nora paused, then said uncertainly, "Albert's face looked very peaceful. I saw the body lying there. There was no violence done. And he'd been complaining he felt unwell in his last letter."

"Poison would probably make someone feel unwell," Ash pointed out. "And you already said Edmund was envious of Albert's life."

"I…don't believe he could have actually *killed* Albert. They were brothers!"

"Ah, well. You must be right. I can't think of a single famous example of a brother killing his brother out of jealousy."

"Oh, stop it," Nora said, disturbed by the inference. "You weren't there."

"Neither were you," he reminded her. "I'm just inquiring about the possibility. If Edmund is capable of theft and kidnapping, why not murder?"

Nora looked at Ash more carefully. "You're discussing this as if you take it seriously. You haven't yet told me I'm crazy. Or asked me if I'm sane."

"It's not a useful question," Ash replied. "The only

answer anyone can give is *yes*. A sane person says yes because that's the truth, and a mad person says yes because they can't see the truth."

"But surely you have an opinion on the topic of my sanity."

Ash looked at her for a long time, then said, "This may be an odd question, but how did you *know* that the Morrison who met you in London wasn't your husband?"

"The same way you know your reflection isn't yourself when you look in a mirror. Edmund Morrison is nothing like his brother. To me, they look entirely different," Nora said. "They're identical twins, but not exact copies. Albert had a birthmark on his left arm, but Edmund has it on his right. Their hair parts differently. Edmund is a bully. Albert was kind."

"Did he know you knew?"

"Yes, of course, but he didn't care. What could I say? No matter who I told, they believed I was mad because Edmund said I was. No matter what argument I made, the conclusion was the same: mad."

"After Edmund Morrison took on the role of Albert Morrison," Ash asked carefully, "did he expect you to be his wife in practice as well as in name?"

Nora was confused for a moment, wondering exactly what he was asking. Then she understood the expression on his face, a combination of embarrassment and distaste and even anger.

"Oh!" she gasped. "No. Never. He was only interested in my ideas. He never saw me as a woman, just as a way to wealth. He'd much rather have Isabelle. Why?"

"Just trying to ascertain his motives," Ash muttered, though he looked relieved.

"Is that part of your assignment? Would that matter to a minor clerk sent to check on the status of a project?"

Nora was getting a little sick of Ash's evasiveness regarding his profession, and she definitely wanted to change the subject.

"You've become part of the assignment," he said, unexpectedly. "No one mentioned you at all, yet here you are."

"Yes I am," she agreed, bitterly.

"If I were you," Ash said, "I'd want justice for what's been done to you."

"You haven't been listening, have you?"

"I have, Nora. Sounds to me as if I'm the only one listening to you."

"What sort of justice could I expect?" she asked. "Should I inform the government of what truly happened?" Nora said sarcastically. "Because what a group of highly placed gentlemen who've already invested heavily want to hear is that they've been tricked, and it's too late to do anything about it. Besides, eventually Edmund Morrison will deliver the process, which works. So what does it matter to them whose name is on it? Will they replace his name with mine, a woman's? Not likely."

"Is that what you want? To have your name and work be public?" he asked.

"I don't care about fame. I just don't want him to win."

"Then help me," Ash said. "Give me the details of the process. Show me how it started, how it works. I'll make sure the right people know who's responsible. Then Edmund can be detained and face the consequences he deserves. He'll be imprisoned or transported. Either way, he won't bother you again. You'll be free."

Nora took a deep breath, considering. She didn't know if she could trust Ash. He was hiding a lot, and for all she knew, he intended to learn all she told him and then run

the ocean and told me to start swimming. Nothing here is what it was supposed to be."

"Not a particularly well-informed organization," Nora said, with a little smirk.

"If they knew all the answers, they wouldn't send people to find them, I expect."

"That's true enough. How long have you been working for this group?"

If Ash told her it was his first—and only—assignment, she'd never trust him. "I'm afraid I can't tell you," he hedged.

"Then tell me about the group."

"I can't do that either."

"You're not offering much," Nora said, with a warning in her voice.

"I wish I could tell you more, but I can't."

"What's the group's name?"

He sighed. "Also secret."

"Mr Allen!"

"Call me Ash."

Her eyes narrowed. "Is that even your name?"

"Yes. Ash is short for Ashley." And Allen was short for Allander, but the last thing he needed was for this woman to ever hear his full name. That would eventually lead her to his full reputation.

"But you can't tell me the name of the group?" Nora went on, blessedly passing over the issue of his name.

"What good would it do you? It's clandestine by definition. No one would ever recognize it, or admit it if they did know of it."

"Perhaps, but I would like to know. Call it a show of good faith."

Ah, what did it matter? Though it pained him to think so cynically, he had to acknowledge that Nora wasn't exactly a threat. As she already pointed out, once someone was declared mad, nothing she said would be listened to.

"You can't tell anyone," he prefaced.

Nora shot him a withering glance. "Who would I tell?"

Edmund Morrison, perhaps. Ash briefly considered the notion that this was some sort of elaborate ploy that Nora and Edmund were working together on, in order to expose him. Then he dismissed it. The two weren't allies. The bandage on Nora's face was all the evidence he needed for that.

"The group calls itself the Zodiac," he said.

"Why?"

Ash blinked. "Who knows? Who cares? It's just a name."

"You're a member of this group and you don't even know why that's the name?"

He wasn't a member, but again, he couldn't tell Nora that. It would destroy the tiny amount of confidence she had in him.

"What's important is that I'm here," he said. "Now you can take advantage of that or not. Your choice. But if I leave, how many more chances do you think you'll have?"

Nora swallowed nervously. "None," she murmured.

"Let me help you," Ash said. "You haven't been able to change your situation on your own. Now I'm here. Why not take advantage of me?"

She raised one eyebrow. "Take advantage of you?"

He smiled, acknowledging the innuendo. "Of my presence, I meant."

Nora rolled her eyes, but he caught the tinge of pink in her face. The innuendo hadn't been lost on her. In any case, since she'd already begged a kiss from him, Nora couldn't claim to be uninterested.

He didn't know much about convincing reluctant witnesses to speak to him, but he definitely knew how to talk to women. "Nora," he said, keeping her hand in his, subtly running his thumb along the top of her hand, just where he'd want to kiss her again, if the situation had been different. "You can trust me."

"You're rather persuasive," she muttered. "Is that something they teach you?"

He learned that skill in an entirely different setting, one he never wanted to talk about with Nora or anyone else. "I just want to help you," he said, avoiding the question.

"Because it's to your benefit," she said. "You're taking advantage of me."

"No, I'm discussing an alliance. The benefit is mutual. I complete the task assigned to me, and you get your liberty back."

"Ah." The little sigh that escaped her lips was barely audible, but it told him everything he needed to know. *That* was what Nora wanted. Freedom. That was what she wanted more than anything else.

"Are we allies?" he asked, keeping the eagerness out of his voice. The decision had to be hers.

Nora sat there for what seemed a terribly long time. Ash was patient. He could feel her thinking, almost hear the flood of thoughts inside her. All he did was hold her hand. What he wanted to do, he realized, was hold all of her. He wanted to keep her very close, in his arms, and keep everything else out.

Ash wasn't used to that sort of feeling. He didn't generally feel inspired to protect the women he was with. Granted, the sort of women he associated with didn't need protection, or want it. Certainly not from him. Nora was different.

She sighed, clearly having made her choice. Ash awaited, unexpectedly tense.

"We can be allies," she said.

Relief washed through him. He raised Nora's hand to his lips and kissed it, without really planning to.

She looked surprised, then her eyes narrowed. "I said allies. Not friends. Or anything else."

"Understood," Ash said. "I'm just glad you agreed."

Nora's skeptical look slowly softened. Then she smiled back, rather cautiously. "I…I'm glad you asked." Then she glanced around the room, as if she'd forgotten where they were. "You should go now, though. For this to work, we absolutely can't be found together."

Ash stood up, promising discretion. He left Nora's room in a state of combined exhaustion and exhilaration. He'd learned more in the last few hours than he'd known since the very beginning of this whole misadventure. Yet he felt as if he was just falling deeper into an ocean that might not have a bottom.

Nora's story was unbelievable. Still, he believed her. She was a surprisingly cool and convincing witness, with an answer for nearly every question Ash had thrown at her.

Then there was the way she looked at him, as if he was a hero instead of a villain. It should be more difficult to earn the status of hero, he reflected. Especially for him.

Safe in his own room, he looked at the little box that held his supply of the drug he relied on. At the moment, he didn't feel an urge for it. His need for it was always greater when he was bored, or feeling anxious.

He certainly wasn't bored now. Though he felt a bit on edge, he wasn't experiencing the overwhelming anxiety that usually sent him to the drug in order to lose himself in the haze. Relieved, he put the box back.

He fell asleep pondering all he'd learned, and dreaming of Nora as a medieval lady imprisoned by a dragon. The threads got tangled in his exhausted brain, until he found himself arguing in his sleep with a dream-image of his brother, who insisted that spies didn't need suits of armor. Ash pled his case, telling Bruce he'd feel differently if he'd seen the lady or the dragon. Bruce said that Ash lacked the training to be a true knight. The dragon would eat him.

He woke from his strange, uneasy sleep when Crewe entered the room. "Morning, sir. Sleep well?"

"No," Ash said, the image of a fire-breathing dragon still in his brain. "Perhaps some sun will help wake me up."

"No luck there. Dreary outside, worse than the day we arrived."

"Blast." Ash sat up and swung himself out of bed.

"Sir, I'm sorry to say that your dressing robe has gone missing," Crewe said, sounding upset. "I've looked everywhere, and I can't find it."

"Oh, sorry, Crewe. Not your fault. There was an incident the first night."

"An incident? Did you spill something on it?"

"No. A ghost stole it."

To Crewe's credit, his only outward reaction to Ash's comment was to deliver a silent stare lasting exactly two seconds before saying, "Is that so, sir? How unfortunate."

Ash would have to tell his brother that whoever was training these criminals-turned-servants was doing an excellent job.

Of course, now he'd have to explain everything to Crewe. So as he washed and dressed for the day, he told what happened, starting with Nora's sudden appearance on the roof and later in his bedroom, on to the events of last night—well, most of the events. He left out the kiss, and the fact that he'd lain in her bed. He did relate what she'd said about the Morrison brothers.

"If I may say, sir," Crewe noted after considering the whole revelation, "she doesn't seem precisely reliable."

"Interesting observation. What did you say your previous professions were again?"

The valet said with wounded dignity, "I wasn't operating from behind the walls of an asylum!"

"Perhaps you would have been, if the circumstances of your life had been a little different. What if you were born rich, with a family willing to pay to put you away somewhere rather than endure a scandal? What if you were a woman, with no ability to contradict a husband when he announces his wife is mad? What if the world wasn't fair, and sometimes the wrong people ended up in small rooms with bars on the windows, while the people who should be locked up are free to walk the streets?"

"See your point, sir," Crewe said. "But I'd feel better if you knew a bit more about her story."

"I can't ask Morrison anything about it, not without risking her safety. And Lloyd and his missus are either in on it, or will accidentally reveal that I know of Nora. I can't even contact the brother, because Nora doesn't know where he's living—also, though she's quite confident in their eventual happy reunion, I wonder for a moment if he benefited from marrying his sister off. I'm a bit trapped here."

"Good thing you've got me." Crewe grinned. "I'll send a request to the Disreputables. They'll be able to hunt down some facts about the lady."

"How fast can they do that?"

"Don't know, but the sooner I ask, the sooner they'll

get on it. I can post something from town. That way no one here will get wind of it."

From the way Crewe spoke, Ash knew he was far more skeptical about Nora's story. Once he spoke with her, Crewe would be convinced.

But if the Disreputables uncovered something that contradicted her story, what would Ash do then? He'd already put himself on the line. He told Nora the name of the Zodiac, which all on its own was more than he should have committed.

If she turned out to be mentally unbalanced, that would certainly end any possibility of the Zodiac listening to him. And it would be the last straw for Bruce, who was probably already looking for a reason to recall Ash from this assignment.

Yet Ash did believe Nora. Despite all the outward strangeness—the running about on rooftops, the claim of identical twins, the admission that a doctor called her mad—there was something fundamentally convincing in her story. Or perhaps he was inclined to look beyond the surface. After all, he had plenty of experience being judged for what others said about him, rather than his own actions. Nora didn't deserve the same thing happening to her. No one did.

Then there was Nora herself. Ash couldn't stop thinking about her. His reactions to her were so out of the ordinary for him. And not simply because she had appeared in his room one night. He often had women in his bedroom, but always because he invited them there. Nora was the opposite. She wasn't looking for diversion. She was seeking escape.

Ash would help her do that. The first step was learning everything he could about Nora's invention, and about the man calling himself Albert Morrison.

Chapter 13

THE NEXT NIGHT, JUST BEFORE midnight, Ash once again crept up to Nora's attic, knocking softly on the door. "Nora?" He didn't say his name. There was no need.

"Yes," she said from her side.

He slid the bolt and opened the door, leaning in. "May I come in?"

"You're being rather formal, aren't you?" Nora smiled at him.

"Well, one shouldn't throw off all the rules of courtesy just because the situation is uncivilized. It is polite to ask to enter a lady's room."

"You may enter," she said, clearly amused.

He did. "I had a quiet day. Edmund was out and about —mostly because I tried to ask him some questions at breakfast, I think. And that Mrs Kingfisher has been gone all day, again."

"She traveled to Worthing," Nora said. "I saw her leave in the open carriage. I can see all the traffic on the road from the north window. Edmund rode out too, probably to join her."

"She goes to town frequently?"

"Yes. I'm surprised she tolerates this house at all. She

obviously prefers the city to the country. But a mistress must make concessions, I suppose."

"You disapprove of her?" Ash asked.

Nora said, "I know I'm supposed to be appalled at the notion just on moral principle, but I confess I'm not. *Mr* Kingfisher would have an opinion, I imagine, but she's been here for months, and her husband hasn't come looking for her. So who am I to judge?"

"Very open-minded of you," Ash said. "Well, let's get on to a better topic. You said you would demonstrate how to do the actual messaging tonight."

"Yes." She held up a lantern and some colored glass panels, then put them into a sack. "Midnight is usually when we test, so this will be a good time to show you—the conditions will be the same. Come along up."

"Come along up where?" Ash asked. "We're already on the top floor."

Nora pointed to the window. "Though there. We have to go out onto the roof."

"Is that necessary?"

She looked at him curiously. "Are you afraid of heights?"

Ash grimaced. "No, I'm afraid of falling from them."

"Just follow my lead. I've never had a problem."

"Something tells me you've had more practice at this than I." Ash took a deep breath, even as he felt his skin crawl. But he could do this. If Nora could run about on rooftops, so could he. He hoped.

He made it though the window and onto a narrow ledge. "Oh, Christ."

"Don't look down!" Nora said, from ahead of him.

"Too late," Ash muttered.

Nora scrambled over the sloping surface, moving with perfect confidence, despite having the sack slung across her shoulder. Ash was wildly jealous.

She looked back. "It would be best if you did exactly as I do. See where I put my hands and feet. Not all the tiles can be trusted."

"Can any of them be trusted?" he asked. But when she resumed her ascent, he followed along, heeding her advice.

A few moments later, she brought them to the edge of the roof, where the various wings of the house parted. Beyond the gap, there was a small flat space that covered a peak above some part of the house.

"We're above the servants' quarters," Nora explained. "The servants rarely go to bed before one in the morning, and when they do finally reach their beds, they sleep soundly.

"We're going over there, that flat part. Just a little jump to get over," she said.

"Jump? You said nothing about a jump."

She offered her hand to him. "We'll go together. It's easy."

He almost took it, then shook his head. "If I fall, I'll just drag you down with me. You go first."

She did, then turned back. She was only about five feet away, yet it felt like she was in another world.

"Your turn."

He took a breath. Then another. And another.

"You really should jump over *tonight*," Nora said then.

Ash stepped back. "Don't do that! It breaks my concentration."

"You don't need to concentrate. You need to jump. Now."

"Give me a moment."

"You've had a moment! Jump," she needled him. "It's hardly more than a step. I did it, so can you." She reached her hand out to him once more. "Take hold. There, and…"

He jumped. A little jump, true. But it was nonetheless a jump over dead, empty, black night.

"Well," he said after a few seconds of blank-minded shock at what he'd just done, "that was the first time in a long time I've felt any urge to pray."

"We're quite safe up here," Nora said.

Ash threw her a skeptical look. "Compared to what?"

"Compared to being in Edmund's presence, for instance," Nora retorted. "Now, if you're done assessing the state of your soul, I can show you what you've come here for."

Nora motioned for him to stand facing the coastline. She stood beside him, pulling the lantern and other items from the bag she'd slung over her back.

She lit the candle, but then shuttered the lantern quickly so no light escaped.

"Always start from dark, from nothing," she said. "That way, the receiver of the signal won't be confused by extraneous light. Now, according to my system, the signaler begins any message with two long green flashes. That means I'm about to send."

"Like that over there?" Ash asked.

He pointed all the way over the beach, to where the lighthouse stood. A flash of green just caught his eye.

"What?" Nora frowned. "No one is supposed to be there! We're not scheduled to test tonight!"

"Someone is there all the same. Edmund? Could he have mistaken the night?"

"No. He would have told me. Should I—"

At sea, there was a triple flash of green.

"Do you see that?" Nora prodded him hard in the side.

"Ow, yes." Ash caught her hand in his and held it. "No need to jab me."

"I got excited," Nora said. "That was the sign that the receiver is ready to watch for the message! They're not signaling to Grasmere House, they're signaling to a ship! Now keep looking."

He saw flash after flash. There were subtle differences, but in truth, he couldn't quite describe what all the variations were.

"Is this a test?" he murmured.

"Hush," Nora said, her gaze fixed on the distant point.

"It's light, not sound…"

"I'm concentrating," she whispered.

Ash fell silent. He could do nothing but wait. He had only passing knowledge of Nora's system, so he couldn't be confident that he was even noting each flash pattern correctly. The ones using colored glass were the easiest to discern. One flash was decipherable: red light in the top of the rectangle. A brief feeling of accomplishment faded when he saw another flash, this one different. He began to see what Nora was talking about when she discussed the shortcomings of the process. The patterns needed to be studied and memorized if someone wanted to work at any speed to send a message. And receiving a message meant that a person needed to write down the message painstakingly, letter by letter.

It occurred to him then that Nora wasn't writing anything down. Of course, they hadn't expected to see a transmission. This was a happy accident. However, Nora's intense focus suggested she was mentally recording each flash.

So he watched her, captured by her expression. Her mouth had fallen open a little, and her eyes were wide, so as not to miss a thing. The wind from the sea whipped her hair loose from its binds, sending it in tendrils across her face. She blinked rapidly, tugging it away from her eyes.

Well, he could be a little helpful, at least.

He stepped behind her and reached up, gathering her hair up in his hands, catching the loose strands and tucking them into her braid.

Nora stiffened for a moment, then understood what he was doing. She returned her full attention to the lights, leaving him to hold her hair from her face and wait patiently until the messaging concluded.

Quite naturally, Ash stepped closer to her and put his free arm about her waist. He had no tactical reason for that. He simply liked to be near her.

The flashes continued for several minutes, not that Ash was complaining. It seemed Nora was correct about needing to speed up the process. It was one thing to watch the display on a fine summer night—especially with such a lovely companion—but it would be another matter to do this sort of work in rainy or freezing weather.

Finally, the flashes stopped. Nora didn't say anything for a moment. Then she took a deep breath, as if waking up from slumber.

"Interesting," she commented, her voice distant.

Ash was just about to ask what the message had been when he caught another flash, this time out at sea again.

"Nora," he said, in warning.

"I see it."

They watched again, but this time the message was far shorter. Within a few minutes, all was blackness out on the ocean.

"Who was out there?" Nora asked, clearly bewildered.

"This isn't typical?"

"No! There's never been a ship involved. It's always been Edmund at the lighthouse and me here at the main house. No one outside this house even knows about it. That was his whole point." She sounded frustrated, even angry.

Ash pulled her a little closer, releasing her hair as he slid his hand down her back, hoping to soothe her. "There must be an explanation. Why would he bring someone else in? Were you discussing the role of a ship, maybe? Did you need to field test the lights onboard?"

Nora shook her head, her hair tickling his skin. "I mentioned it once in passing, but Edmund didn't ever say he wanted to perform a test like this one. It's too early, anyway! We're still working out the wrinkles in the code."

"Speaking of that, what was the message? Remember I'm not fluent."

"It's another odd one."

"Odd? What do you usually use?"

"I started out with quotations from Shakespeare, lines of poetry, simple sayings—*Brevity is the soul of wit*, that sort of thing. Phrases we didn't have to think about too much. Then, several weeks ago, Edmund started telling me to use other phrases, just random words together. He said he didn't want us to rely on guessing the next word, which in all honesty is probably the most intelligent observation he's brought to the process."

"So what was this message?"

"The one sent out was *SHIP GO EMPTY BIRD STAY TWO MISS ONE*." Nora sounded puzzled, quite understandably.

"You read all those flashes and remembered each letter, and you don't even have to look?"

Nora stiffened for a moment, but then said, "I've had practice."

"I'm still impressed."

"Oh…thank you."

"What was the reply?"

"Just *RECEIVED, ALLY*. They may have misspelled that last word. It looked like *ALLE*."

"Who does Edmund know with a boat?"

"That was a ship," Nora corrected. "Did you see how high above the waterline that flash came from? This wasn't a local fishing boat. It was a larger vessel."

"And you say he doesn't usually conduct tests without you."

"Never. I'm better at it, and he lacks patience. You saw how long that took. He's probably riding off to the nearest public house for a drink. Or a game of cards." Nora spun so she was facing him. "What if he suspects? Is that why he didn't tell me? What if he's guessed we met, and he just wants to be sure he doesn't need me for further work—"

"Nora," Ash said, putting his hand on her shoulders, "Calm down. I'm certain no one in Grasmere House knows that we've met. Well, Crewe knows. My valet."

"You told your *valet*?"

"He's with me," Ash explained. "And besides, I had to tell him where the dressing robe had gone."

Nora's eyes widened in disbelief for a moment. "Are you joking? You exposed me over the whereabouts of a robe?"

"Crewe takes his job very seriously." Ash saw that she still looked stunned. "Nora, I trust him."

"I don't," she muttered. "He could turn on you or me at any moment. All it would take is a few words."

"You've got to have more faith in people."

"Why should I?" she asked bluntly. "People are interested in their own advancement more than anything else. You should know that. You're here out of self-interest too, aren't you? You're just carrying out an order."

"I prefer to think of it as doing a favor for someone."

"You're a very odd spy."

"Am I? How many have you met?"

"None that I know of," she admitted.

Ash looked her in the eye. "Nora, you've been treated badly. But not everyone is like Edmund Morrison, and you are *not* alone. I'll do everything I can to help you get your life back."

"Why? What's in it for you?"

"Occasionally I do the right thing. If only to confuse people."

Nora smiled a little, and that was worth it. Then she glanced around. "We should go in. You've seen what you need to. Much more than I expected, actually."

Ash had been avoiding thinking about the descent. "I don't suppose there's another way down?"

"Well, there's the quick way," Nora said, gesturing meaningfully to the edge, "but you can only use it once."

Ash shuddered at the thought. "No, thank you."

"Follow me. Do what I do and you'll be perfectly safe."

"Give me a moment," he said, staring at the distant ground with trepidation.

Nora said, "Or you could stay for a while. It's actually quite lovely up here."

"You must be mad if you consider this lovely weather."

Her expression shuttered. "I get over-exuberant when I'm out of doors."

"Wait," Ash said. "Forgive me. It was just an expression. You're obviously not mad. You're intelligent and observant, if a little eccentric in your habits. Which is charming, by the way."

She gave him a skeptical look. "You're just saying that because you need help getting down off the roof."

"I'm saying it because you are charming." Ash drew her closer. "And if you want to stay up here, I'll see that you're not bored."

"Is this how you cover up your fear of heights?"

"Is it working?" he asked.

"No," said Nora. "I think you're desperate to hold on to anything…including me. Now follow. I'll see you get down alive."

Chapter 14

NORA LED ASH OFF THE roof and back into the relative safety of her attic. She briefly wondered if the man was putting on his fear of heights—how could a spy be afraid of anything?—yet the expression on his face, and the way he'd reacted to the idea of the jump, convinced her that his fear was genuine. She helped pull him through the window. "Safe now," she told him.

"Thank Christ."

"You shouldn't take the Lord's name in vain."

"Believe me, I wasn't."

"You believe in God, then?"

"From time to time," Ash said. "God doesn't particularly believe in me though, if past experience is a guide."

"What past experience?"

"The experience of literally my whole past." Ash offered the glib explanation with a laugh. It was clear that he had no intention of discussing it further.

"And your fear of heights? Is that from your past as well?"

He shook his head. "If it is I don't remember it. It's just that my insides turn to ice every time I look over a ledge."

"You went on the roof."

"I had to, didn't I? You were there."

Nora wished his comment was more about her than what she knew. Still, it was pleasant to think of. The way he'd held her up there…Nora could swear she still felt the warmth of him next to her. His hands in her hair, around her waist…it should have been distracting, but instead it had bolstered her, letting her concentrate wholly on deciphering the message. Well, his breath on her neck had been a little distracting. And delightful.

"I should go," Ash was saying. "Unless you've got any more to teach me?"

Nora gave him a look, thinking of exactly how subtle and seductive he'd been. "I'm not sure there's very much I could teach you."

"If you think of anything, I'm your very willing student."

His smile took her breath away, but she said, "Go downstairs, Ash. You're excused."

He left then, though his presence remained, an unmistakable weight in Nora's mind. So did the words that had flashed across the dark. SHIP GO EMPTY BIRD STAY TWO MISS ONE. It was nonsense, yet there was a hint of meaning. Or was she trying to make sense of random words? A child might write a message like that…so the significance might be as childishly pointless, someone playing at language. Yet she couldn't quite put it aside. Instead, Nora put it away with all the other messages, into her mind, where she would never lose it.

* * * *

The next morning, Edmund came to Nora's room. In most of their interactions, he treated her as either a difficult child or some exotic specimen—hoping to wheedle out more from her brain, as if she knew all the answers and was merely withholding them out of spite. She told him over and over that the soul of science and invention was experimentation. Trying. Failing. Trying again. He still thought of it as a magic trick or a ritual, where understanding was not required.

This time was different. Edmund was distraught, though initially he tried to hide it. "We've got to work faster. This is taking far too long," he said.

Nora didn't have much sympathy. "The work would go faster if you let me be free. Then I could go to the lighthouse and to the glassworks, and we wouldn't need to wait for the dark of night to test. Like last night."

"Couldn't test last night," he grumbled. "I was busy."

Nora stared at him, trying to decide if he was lying. If he didn't flash the message, who did? "Who knows what we're up to here?"

"Too many," he said.

"How many is that? You, me…Mrs Kingfisher?" Nora was feeling mischievous, so she needled him, "Or do you refer to the people Albert told? The ones who gave him the initial funding?"

Edmund grimaced. "May bureaucrats rot in hell! Apparently, I slipped up somewhere. They've sent a representative."

"The government?" she asked.

"The department funding the project. He's here now, this clerk. Asking all sorts of questions, and he wants a demonstration. I can't use you, obviously, so Mrs Kingfisher will have to help, and she doesn't know the codes like you do."

"You *can* use me," Nora said. "I'll signal from here, and you can take him to the lighthouse and show him your side of the demonstration. If he asks who the other signaler is, tell him it's Mrs Kingfisher."

Edmund sighed in relief. "That's true! Why didn't I think of that?"

Because I'm the brains, Nora thought. "It doesn't matter. Just keep him close to you at the lighthouse."

"I should, and then throw him out the window."

Nora got sick to her stomach. Would Edmund be that desperate? She had to get the notion out of his head. "Don't even dream that," she said. "The *last* thing you need is more attention. If this clerk doesn't file his report, or whatever it is he needs to do, there will be more questions. More clerks. Eventually, one might even find me."

Edmund glared at her. "Don't you dare attract attention, Elanora. This man doesn't know you exist and I aim to keep it that way."

Nora stifled a laugh. *He's lain in my bed.* But all she said was, "The demonstration will mollify him, won't it?"

"Maybe," Edmund said doubtfully. "He plans on staying here for at least a week! What if he wants to see more? What should I show him? What will convince him to keep the project on the books? Something I can do myself?"

It was ironic that he had to beg Nora for an idea of how to show off her invention without including her. She sighed. "If he wants to see more after the main demonstration, you could set up some instruments in the parlor downstairs—show how the light and the glass panels work. You could show the chart of symbols and offer to transcribe a message of his choosing."

"Sounds complicated."

"Perhaps you should have thought of that before you stole my invention and impersonated your brother."

"Never say that, Elanora." He loomed over her. "Never speak those words out loud, or I'll drag *you* up to that lighthouse."

"You need me," she said, trying to sound confident. However, she also remembered something Ash said before, when he suggested Edmund killed Albert. Was the man actually capable of such an act? Nora was no longer certain. "You won't complete the project without me."

Edmund turned away abruptly. "One problem at a time. I'm going to Worthing to get some supplies," he said. "I'll return tomorrow, and until you see me again, you are not to stir. Don't make a sound. Don't bother Mrs Lloyd. And above all, don't do anything to alert our guest that you're here."

"I understand," Nora said meekly.

Edmund nodded and left.

Nora understood everything he said. She just had no intention of obeying.

As the day went on, the sky grew grayer. Clouds billowed up thick and angry along the coast, and then, just around sunset, the rain began. Nora watched from her windows.

The rain hit the panes, rattling constantly. The roof also pattered with rain. The wind whistled under the eaves. In short, the weather was dreadful.

Mrs Lloyd hurried in with Nora's meal tray. On the occasions when Edmund was gone, the housekeeper gave Nora the bare minimum of attention. Nora knew that there was little risk of anyone coming to check on her before morning.

Anyone, that was, but Ash.

He slipped in around midnight and closed the door behind him. "Do you mind that I came up tonight? I know we can't perform a terrifying climb to the roof again. Thank God."

"True. But there are still many things about the

process you can learn, and we can discuss them here in this room."

"It's safe?" he asked. "Edmund rushed off somewhere today. Said it was urgent business, but something tells me he's avoiding any opportunity to talk about the light signaling."

"You're quite correct."

"Well, I can't say I mind," Ash noted. "Despite being stuck in this house in the middle of nowhere." He looked around. "How do you manage though, day after day? You must be climbing the walls!"

"Or the roof," she said, with a smile.

Ash frowned, unamused. "Whatever else happens, we have to find some way for you to leave Edmund's influence."

She agreed, though it would prove difficult, especially if Edmund pressed his claim as being Nora's husband Albert. A husband had many rights over his wife in terms of the law, especially if the wife was found to be mentally incompetent.

When she mentioned that to Ash, though, he brushed it away. "I can't believe any judge could speak to you and think you're less than brilliant, not to mention perfectly sane."

"According to you. But is a spy a good witness?"

"We'll worry about that issue when you have an appointment with a judge."

"Well, first things first," Nora said. "You know about the light signaling now. How else can I help? What do you need to know?"

"I'm no expert," he said. "So whatever you tell me will help."

"Very well, I'll begin at the beginning. Mankind has always known how to use certain tools for sending information over long distances. Primitive cultures used fire, whether that meant a large pyre on a hilltop or smoke emitted in patterns. Later, people got clever and made things like flags, or eventually the semaphore, which allowed for more complex messages, as you know. A sailor uses two flags and various arm positions. A semaphore tower has movable, foldable wooden arms that accomplish the same task."

Nora stood up, her arms held straight out to her sides and her hands pointed down. "This position represents E." She then tilted her arms so her left pointed down to the floor and the right toward the ceiling. "This is F." She tilted the other way. "D."

"I see."

She relaxed her stance. "There are twenty-six letters in the English alphabet, so there are twenty-six positions to memorize. A semaphore operator manipulates various levers and ropes to change the position of the wooden semaphore apparatus. As I've mentioned before, it's effective—but not subtle. The semaphores are fixed in place. Everyone knows where a tower is and can easily watch it. Even when the messages are coded, you still risk someone discovering the code and reading all your mail."

"Hence the idea of using light," Ash said.

"Yes. You can communicate at night, as well as day, as long as it's not too bright to obscure the flashes. You can move around a bit. Yes, it helps to have height, but there are many spots one might use—a bell tower or a church steeple, or the top of a hill, or a cliff..."

"Or a lighthouse," Ash said.

"Yes. The lighthouse used to be functional, but a more modern one was built several miles to the east, and this one was decommissioned."

"Leaving him free to use it when he likes."

Nora nodded. "As he's done for nearly a year."

"Why so long? Surely the testing could be done in a matter of weeks."

"We don't test every night. Edmund fears that someone would notice."

"On this stretch of nowhere? Who would even be around?" he asked.

"There are more people around here than you'd guess. Farmers and tradesman and travelers. It only takes one set of curious eyes…"

"Like mine?" Ash said.

"I wouldn't describe your eyes as curious." In fact, Ash's brown eyes were rather beguiling, but she didn't say that, since it would only get her into trouble.

"Then what?" Ash asked. He gave her a smile that suggested he knew exactly what she hadn't said.

"It doesn't matter," said Nora. She'd got off topic. "The point is that Edmund is very concerned about secrecy. When I have a new idea, such as the colored panes—"

"You're responsible for that?"

"Oh. Yes. Let me show you."

Nora was truly excited to share her idea, especially because she'd had no one to share it with for so long. But Ash did seem genuinely interested in what she was doing. Nora knew why—his task was to learn all he could. But he asked intelligent questions and never drifted off. Edmund often did, since he had no interest in the idea beyond the money he thought it was worth. Ash clearly liked the lanterns and glass and the light, to judge by how he played with them.

"So to send a message, I need not just any lantern," he was saying, "but a particular style, with glass panels of different colors."

"Yes, at least if you want to use my method. I'm sure

it can be improved, but this is what I have. Now pay attention," she began as she pointed to the lantern. "As I showed you, every letter of the alphabet can be rendered as a flash pattern on one panel of the lantern. The most common letter is E, so that's a simple one: the clear glass panel fully exposed for one second."

Ash nodded, fiddling with the lantern he held. "Easy enough."

Nora moved her lantern to cover half the panel vertically, so only a narrow strip could emit light. "This is S. Still simple, yes?"

"So far."

Nora demonstrated each letter by covering the appropriate part of the panel with a metal flap and using the correct color of glass. D looked like E, but the flash was green instead of clear. The vowels were all clear. "That way, the receiver at least knows a letter is a vowel, and if they work backwards from the other symbols, they should be able to guess at a word even if they only wrote down the consonants."

"Interesting," Ash murmured. "A bit like Hebrew."

"You're familiar with Hebrew?" she asked, startled.

"Only the rudiments. I learned a bit in the course of my studies."

"And you read German. What sort of philosophy did you study?"

Ash looked uncomfortable. "Theology, actually."

"You did?"

"Yes."

"To be a spy?"

"I never intended to become a spy," Ash said. "I certainly didn't train for that."

"What were you training for, then? The church?"

"Yes."

She waited for another sly grin, a hint that he was joking. Nothing changed in Ash's expression, which was both earnest and slightly defensive.

"You were going to join the church," she repeated.

"Did I not tell you I was merely a second son? I had to do something."

"Why not study law?"

"I don't particularly like arguing."

"But you enjoyed praying?"

He shook his head. "It doesn't matter. Life took a different turn."

"Perhaps the Lord didn't want you to serve in that capacity," she joked.

Ash didn't smile. "Definitely not."

She sensed pain behind those words, something far more complicated than a change in vocation. Whatever happened, he obviously didn't intend to talk about it.

"Well," she said, returning to a less controversial topic, "once you've memorized all the letters, you need to practice words. You must learn how to hold the lantern and flip the panels open and closed."

He looked profoundly grateful that she'd returned to the signaling. "Can we practice? Send me a message and I'll try to read what it is. I don't suppose you've got the key written down?"

"Edmund is adamant that nothing is written down, lest it be stolen. I keep it in my head."

"How long did it take you to memorize all the letters?"

"Not long," she said, "but then, I invented it."

"Very well. Send a short message." He walked to the far corner of the room. Nora blew out the main lamp that had illuminated the space, leaving only her signaling lantern lit.

She flashed a one-word message, going slowly.

Ash narrated what he saw. "Red, lower half exposed. Clear, upper half exposed. Red, all exposed…"

Soon, she finished her message. "Well?"

"I'm not sure," Ash said, from where he stood. "Six letters, with two vowels…"

"The first letter is L."

"Lo…" he murmured. "Lo…"

Nora opened the panel to give light to see by as she walked over to him.

"London," she announced when she reached him.

He said, "I see how it works, at least."

"The problem I'm working on now is that what you can see clearly from across a room is much harder to see from a mile away," Nora said. "That's why I introduced colored glass. Using only clear meant that the receiver couldn't tell if the whole upper half was exposed, or just a slit…that sort of thing. Similarly, the receiver must have good eyesight. Very good eyesight, actually."

"For military use, that shouldn't be too much of a barrier," Ash said. "There are enough young men with good eyes."

Nora nodded, but said, "I just wish I could refine the system to be more foolproof. I've tried several different ideas…this is the best I've done."

"It's far more than most people could achieve," Ash said. "You should be proud."

"Someday…when I can tell someone."

"Besides me, you mean." In the dim light of the room, Ash found her hand and held it. "Don't despair, Nora. I will get you out of here."

"You'll pray for me?" she quipped.

"No chance of that," he said instantly. "The one thing I learned from my time as a student is that the only person you can rely on is yourself."

"That's not the usual message promoted by theologians," Nora noted. "You'll have to tell me how you learned that lesson."

Ash shook his head, and let go of her hand. "It's not a pretty story," he said.

"It can't be *that* bad."

"That, my dear, is where you are wrong." Before she could reply, he went on, "I should go while the house is quiet. No sense pressing our luck."

"Will you come back?" Nora asked, a nervous flutter in her belly. What if he simply left the house now? "You don't have to, after all. You've got the fundamentals of the process."

"It's not the process I'm interested in," he said. "It's the people around it. Of course I'll come back, Nora."

She nodded, even as he left the room and bolted the door after him.

Once she was alone, all the familiar doubts rushed up, and she anticipated a sleepless night, sure she'd never see him again.

Chapter 15

ASH RETURNED TO HIS ROOM. He tried to write down what he remembered of Nora's code—he only recalled a few letters.

What he *wanted* was to take more of the laudanum. His nerves were on edge, the old anger welling up in him. He worked to forget his past. Speaking to Nora brought it up to the surface again. He shouldn't have said anything—he should have come up with a quick and easy lie for her. But he didn't want to lie to Nora. Of course, he couldn't tell her the truth, either. So that left him in the awkward position of being unnecessarily mysterious.

He muttered, not for the first time, "Why did I agree to this?"

To erase the scandal that defined him.

If the scandal were a painting, he could recreate it blindfolded. That's how vivid his memory of it was, and how furious he still got upon thinking of it.

He'd been nearing the end of his studies, eager to advance into a career in the church and eventually settle somewhere, with a little parish and a lot of time to himself, when he could read to his heart's content, and contemplate the sorts of things that intrigued him—which were, invariably, lofty and intellectual and far from the everyday concerns of most people.

No one would believe it now, but Ash had been a very shy and studious boy. He spent most of his days with books, not with people. Girls were more of an abstract concept than a reality to him. There were housemaids and such in the great building he grew up in, but young Ash regarded them as entirely separate creatures. He saw their starched white aprons, and scarcely comprehended that a person was behind the uniform. Maids were a method to make food appear and dust disappear. All Ash asked of them was not to disturb his books while they cleaned.

By the time he actually met a young woman and recognized the appeal, he was serving as the assistant to an elderly curate. It was Ash's duty to visit any parishioners who could not attend church regularly. One such woman was Mrs Goulding, and she had a daughter who was a few years younger than Ash.

Mrs Goulding unsettled him. She was married, but her husband was far away on some military campaign, leaving her to her own devices. She drifted about her estate, often complaining of some obscure malady that prevented her from going out and instead trapped her in the sumptuous rooms of her husband's house. She also had a few gentlemen who called on her with regularity, and when they appeared in the house, she invariably glowed with pleasure and made them stay to entertain her, sometimes way beyond customary visiting hours.

Ash always got nervous when she looked at him. It reminded him of the way a cat looked at a mouse. The older woman's eyes were calculating and predatory. Even when she laughed, her eyes didn't.

However, he felt entirely different about the daughter. Her name was Susan. Susan was sweet and delightful, with long gold hair that ended in fat curls. Her big brown eyes seemed to find the humor in things, and her body was all suggestive curves, though at the time, Ash barely understood why he was so attracted to those curves.

Susan sat in the parlor with her mother when Ash came to call. She poured the tea and served out little plates of sandwiches and biscuits—Mrs Goulding was too frail to perform the task, she always claimed, with a languid wave of her hand. Susan was quick to answer questions and keep the conversation going. Within a few weeks, Mrs Goulding allowed the "youngsters" to walk unchaperoned on the estate.

Every time Ash saw or spoke with Susan, he fell a little more under her spell. He didn't fully realize what he wanted, other than that he wanted to be near her, and to hear her voice, and have her smile at him. Susan seemed to return the affection, for she always talked to him, and asked him about this or that problem. Ash enjoyed solving problems, not just for Susan, but for everyone in the parish. For a few months, he was astonishingly happy with his life.

One afternoon while they were walking, they passed into some trees that hid them from the view of others. Susan stopped and looked at him.

"Would you like to kiss me?" she asked, with a coquettish look.

"I'm not...it wouldn't be proper..."

"I didn't ask if it would be proper," she countered, leaning closer. "I asked if you *want* to."

He did, so he kissed her. Clumsily, to be sure, though she seemed pleased, and kissed him back. On the way back to the house, Ash was dizzy with love and a new-found desire.

He never dared transgress further than a kiss, because Ash was deeply worried about sin. Beyond that, he wanted to focus on his calling. A career in the church would confer a very safe, if modest, income. He intended to marry one day, of course, but until he was settled and ready to provide for a wife, he wouldn't seriously contemplate courting. Susan was a charming young woman, with many callers and friends, and likely some who considered themselves suitors. Ash never spoke a word about marriage, fearful of locking either of them into an agreement they weren't ready for.

Then, one day, Susan pulled him into an unoccupied room in her house, and kissed him as soon as she closed the door. He returned it at first—every second alone with Susan was a pleasure to him—but when she pressed herself closer, he felt a sense of panic, and pushed her back.

"What's come over you?" he asked, half aroused and half terrified.

"I've seen you look at me," Susan purred. "Aren't you curious? Come here to the couch. We can do whatever we like."

"I'd like to leave," Ash said.

"*No!*" Susan's voice rose sharply. "Don't you dare!"

Instantly, the door flew open, and Mrs Goulding stormed in. She took in the scene of Ash and Susan, and looked puzzled more than shocked, as if she expected something else.

"What is going on here?" she asked finally.

"Mama," Susan said, "you remember Mr Allander." As if they were at tea!

Ash was totally confused at this point, and offered apologies for...he wasn't sure, actually. Words just kept pouring out of him.

Mrs Goulding cut him short. "Were you in this room alone with my daughter?"

"Yes. Technically. For half a minute. Nothing happened…"

"No? Then why has my Susan confessed she is with child?"

Time seemed to stop for Ash. "What?"

"Mama, no!" Susan sounded angry. "That's not…you arrived too soon!"

"You shouted!"

"Yes, but…" Susan glanced at Ash, and he saw a flash of guilt in her eyes.

All became clear. He blithely walked into the trap without even knowing a trap could exist. Susan had done something she shouldn't have, and now she trying to use Ash to get out of it.

"I never did anything to Susan," he said.

"You kissed me," Susan retorted.

"Nothing more."

"But you cannot *prove* that," Mrs Goulding said. "So if my daughter is with child, you might be responsible."

"You cannot prove anything either," Ash said, his anger rising quickly. "I will not take the blame for any of this. If Miss Goulding needs a husband, she should consult the father of her child…if she knows who it is," he added, hoping to hurt.

Susan gasped and turned red.

"How dare you! The son of a viscount should have better manners." However, Mrs Goulding gave him a slow satisfied smile. Snakes probably smiled like that after ingesting a mouse. "You are so very angelic looking—I suppose you've heard that before. Not hard for someone to believe that you use your looks to advantage. Perhaps by visiting a lonely wife and her sweet, innocent daughter over and over again…when there is no one to say what goes on in the house.”

“Nothing untoward ever happened. I’ll tell everyone that.”

“Don’t think you can walk out of here!” Mrs Goulding snapped.

Ash shook his head. “I will walk out, and I will never set foot on this property again. I will never speak to or communicate with either of you again. And I’ll tell the world the truth about your natures.” He turned and stormed out of the room.

“Ash, wait!” Susan cried. She had followed him, and now put a hand on his arm.

He shrugged it off. “Don’t ever touch me,” he said, disgusted. “I can’t believe you tried that…trick.”

“It was Mama’s idea,” Susan whispered. “I’m so sorry, I didn’t want to do it like this. But she thought…you’re the son of Lord Forester, and that would be a better marriage. And you do have affection for me.”

“I *did* have affection for you,” he corrected. “As a friend for a friend. Clearly, there’s someone else you have *more* affection for.”

“Don’t hate me! I’m weak, I know that. Not like you. I just didn’t know what to do…”

“Stop playing innocent,” he said, still walking. “You’re obviously anything *but* innocent. When I go out the front door, I will never look back, understand?”

“At least don’t speak of it! Don’t shame me further, I beg you!”

He shot her a look. The last thing he wanted to do was speak of it. He sighed. “For the sake of the person I thought you were, I won’t say anything.”

“Oh, you are an angel!” Susan smiled though her tears.

"You wouldn't know an angel if you saw one." With that pronouncement, Ash left the house, determined to forget all that happened and never think of it again.

He didn't speak of the incident to anyone. He felt like a fool for getting so close to a scandal. It seemed that the Goulding women's hasty scheme had unraveled as quickly as they put it together. They had no way to prove Ash was in any way responsible for Susan's pregnancy, and no leverage to force a marriage, not when Ash was of the aristocracy and the Gouldings were not. Without Mr Goulding in the country, there was not even a male relative to take up the cause. No, Ash told himself it was over.

He was wrong.

While Ash returned to his daily life, his study, and his work, Mrs Goulding had decided to push his father to agree to what Ash had already refused. A desperate act of a desperate woman, because Mrs Goulding must have been under the impression that Lord Forester cared one whit about Ash or his reputation. She had apparently threatened the viscount with scandal, but she did not know how ruthless the Viscount Forester was.

He *destroyed* her. He learned more of the situation than Mrs Goulding wanted to tell, for it turned out that *both* Mrs Goulding and her daughter were pregnant. He learned this detail from the misguided Mrs Goulding herself, who probably hoped it would gain his sympathy. Instead, he gleefully made the news public. She retaliated the only way she could—by smearing the viscount's son. As the stories began to circulate throughout the county, in hushed and horrified tones, Ash was blamed for both Susan's and Mrs Goulding's pregnancy.

Ash, buried in his studies, was actually one of the last to hear of the rumors, and by then it was far too late to mount a defense. People believed what they heard. Ash denied the stories, but no one listened. Why should they? The truth was boring.

The rumors continued to spread, with embellishments making Ash out to be a cold-hearted, calculating predator who destroyed the two ladies' reputations for the pure pleasure of it. Ash was told to leave by his school and his church. No one believed him, no one supported him. He was told to beg forgiveness.

Instead, Ash vowed that he'd go to hell before he asked forgiveness. He had done nothing he regretted.

He left school, but he couldn't go home.

His own mother had been shocked to the core by the stories. Ash never knew exactly who had told her—his mother lived a very sheltered life, and that sort of gossip wasn't the kind of thing she'd hear over tea. Yet hear it she did, and the result was that she never contacted Ash again. She died less than a year later. Logically, Ash knew the consumption that killed her had likely been festering in her lungs for a long time before his scandal. But the added pain and stress must have worsened her illness and sped up her death.

His father's reaction to the whole fiasco was to laugh. Forester told Ash that if he was stupid enough to let a woman threaten him, then he deserved to lose everything. He threw Ash a sum of money and told him to get lost.

Bruce was no help, of course. He was abroad, and anyway, Bruce was always so proper and upright that Ash could predict his response. It didn't even occur to Ash to try to convince his brother of the truth.

So Ash went to London, in the hope of getting lost and forgotten amid the crowds. He failed at that spectacularly, because he wasn't willing to change his identity, and thus all the rumors followed him.

He found a little comfort in gambling. Casting everything on one chance, where nothing was known…he relished the instant before the reveal, when all things seemed possible. Of course, he quickly learned that not all things were equally possible, and he soon taught himself the tricks of counting cards, judging probabilities, and—most importantly—learning when to quit. He liked to quit, actually. There was an incredible power in walking away from a gambling table when one could stay.

He walked away one night, only to run into a stunning woman in a gold gown, who had obviously been watching the game, and him in particular.

"Sixty pounds?" she asked.

Ash did a mental calculation of the money in his pocket. "More or less," he admitted, expecting that the woman would suggest how he might spend it…on her.

But she merely tilted her head up a bit, a motion of approval. "You are wise to stop when you did. Most men don't have the gift."

"I'm not most men," he said.

"No, Mr Allander, you are not." Her smile deepened, as if they shared a secret.

"You know me?" he asked, a feeling of disappointment creeping up on him.

"Only by reputation."

"I see."

"Reputations are interesting little creatures," she said. "I have one myself. I am Regina Fox."

Ash recognized the name. He'd heard it several times in passing, among casual acquaintances in gaming hells, or drinking companions intent on sharing all the latest gossip.

He looked the woman over, a little surprised. She was not what he expected the most expensive courtesan in London to look like. She was beautiful, no question, though she didn't flaunt her physical charms in the same way many of her competitors did. She didn't need to, not with the knowing look in her eyes. But she was also a little older than he would have guessed, and had some quality about her that he couldn't name yet. "Miss Fox," he said finally, "how do you do."

"I wonder, Mr Allander, if you would care for a late supper. I'm hungry myself, but I hate to dine alone."

"You surely have a number of men who would be pleased to escort you."

"I do," she said, "but I'm asking you."

"Why?" he asked bluntly.

She raised one eyebrow. "Take me to supper, and I'll tell you, Mr Allander. After all, our conversation must begin somewhere."

So Ash took her to supper. He then took her home, and spent days, and weeks, and months in her company. She was Miss Fox, then Regina, then Reggie and Reg to him. She was his lover, his teacher, his friend, and his sole confidante.

Without Regina, he had no idea what his fate would have been. She claimed him as a novelty, but soon they found a connection neither had ever known before. For some reason, Regina decided that Ash needed to be molded, and she would do the molding. She knew the world like no one else. She knew how to spin a scandal to one's favor. She knew how to excite and how to cool passions. She knew how to live on other people's money.

She taught Ash nearly everything she knew, and he was a good student. Together, they'd had their run of London's darker side, and Ash never regretted becoming what the rumors said he was. He was determined that no one would ever trick him again, and that no one would ever have such a hold on his heart that he'd lose his head.

He kept the first part of his vow. He kept the second part as well…at least until Nora swept into his life. Nora, who was as contradictory and unexpected as Regina had been so many years earlier. Though the two women were completely different, they had that in common.

Now, the recollection of his past mistakes, and the endless work of forgetting every subsequent decision that mired him further in the life he'd made for himself, destroyed Ash's nerves. He found the box with the precious laudanum. He had pretended to hide it far back in the clothes press, so he'd be able to ignore it, but he knew where it was every moment. The feel of the wood grain was comforting, familiar. He lifted the lid to see the little glass container that held the laudanum. Beside it, there was also a small, paper-wrapped cake of pure opium. Ash regarded that as a talisman. He never needed to eat the opium, and he told himself that meant he was in control. The laudanum was weaker, so how bad could his habit be?

"Shouldn't do this," he muttered, even as he began to pull out the bottle. He'd stop once he returned to London. As soon as this madness was over.

He sneered at the empty promise. He'd told himself the same sort of thing before, over and over. He never kept the promise.

How could he make a promise to Nora then, when he couldn't even hold himself to a simple edict to stay away from a drug he didn't even like half the time?

Ash's hands shook. He felt a curious sensation then, as if he'd stepped outside his own body and was looking down on his double, a man who was caught at a crossroads. He could either take the drug, as he always did, or he could put it away, just this once.

He waited, curious, as if he wasn't actually the one

making the decision.

Then, with some astonishment, he watched as he put the glass container back into the wooden box. His own hand did it, yet Ash felt completely disconnected from the act. Had he really done that? Had he refused the one thing he always turned to?

Why?

Because Nora wouldn't like it.

Ash could barely believe the thought. What did he care if Nora approved of his little habit? She hardly knew him.

But he did want her to trust him, and if she knew he could lose hours and days to a substance like this, she'd never rely on him for anything, let alone something as important as her liberty.

No one would rely on him again, if they knew. Bruce would cut him off for good. Reggie would be horribly disappointed in him. He could practically see her face now, her efforts to hide the contempt she'd feel.

Ash lowered the lid.

Then he crawled into his bed and tried to sleep like a normal person, without resorting to substances to cloud his brain. Every time he thought of his past, he deliberately summoned an image of Nora's coded letters. It helped, largely because he then thought of Nora, who was independent of everything that brought him here.

He finally fell asleep, the image for the letter N in his mind, a bright red flash of light against his eyelids.

Chapter 16

DESPITE HOURS OF DEAD SLEEP, Ash rose in the morning feeling even more on edge. His brain felt thick and groggy. He cursed Bruce for tricking him into leaving London at all, and cursed him again for getting him into this mess.

He went downstairs in search of some coffee. He found an empty carafe at the sideboard, which did him no good at all.

"God hates me," he muttered.

"What was that?"

He turned to see Mrs Kingfisher standing nearby, in a casual morning dress that showed off her attributes.

"I was lamenting the lack of coffee," he explained, holding up the carafe. "Though what I'd actually like is a bowl of *cafe au lait*," Ash confessed.

"Easily solved, Mr Allen," she said with a smile.

She rang the bell to call a servant, and a maid entered. "Yes, ma'am?"

"Our guest would like a *ca*—" She stopped short. "What did you say again?"

"*Cafe au lait*. Half coffee, half warm milk."

The maid nodded and left.

"You have continental tastes, Mr Allen. Have you been abroad?"

"A few times," he said, "but my tastes were set early. I had a rather French tutor of French. He had an opinion on everything, mostly to the effect that the French version of anything was superior. On the matter of coffee, I'm willing to concede his point."

The maid returned just then, and set down a steaming bowl that smelled good enough to banish the worst of his fog. "*Vous êtes un sauveur. Merci.*"

The maid blushed and withdrew from the room.

"How charming," Mrs Kingfisher said. "Such a lovely sounding language. Unfortunately, I don't speak a word of French."

"Never too late to learn," he said after taking a sip of his drink. It was perfect.

"Perhaps one day," she said. "Tell me, Mr Allen, what do you intend to do with the rest of your time here? Have you a plan?"

He did: find out all he could about Edmund Morrison and then decide how to spirit Nora to safety. "I've no plans," Ash lied. "After I'm satisfied here, I go to Portsmouth. When I return from that errand, I'll give my report."

"To whom?"

"My superiors in London," he said, deliberately being obtuse.

She smiled at him. "It must be terribly exciting to live in the hustle and bustle of the city. And working for His Majesty's government directly! How very noble."

"It's kind of you to say so, but it's not all it's painted to be."

"Ah, you are modest."

He smiled. *Modest* had never been a word associated

with Ashley Allander. "Am I?" he asked.

"Or you know how to keep a secret," she said.

Ash wasn't modest, but he was discreet when he needed to be. "Certainly. I have a host of secrets."

Her eyes sparkled. "You must share one."

"Mrs Kingfisher, that is the one thing I must not do."

She pouted but then said, "Very well done, Mr Allen. A man of his word. That is refreshing, in a world where so many people cannot be trusted."

Ash blinked, wondering at the turn of this conversation.

But Mrs Kingfisher kept talking. "Well, until you're off for Portsmouth, you need a diversion. May I suggest a trip to Worthing? It's quite civilized, and you'll find much there to amuse you. Of course there is the sea, and one can bathe for health. But there are other options. Mr Morrison often meets companions for cards. Are you fond of cards?"

"As much as the next man," Ash hedged.

"You should go to Worthing. Stay the night! The hotel is more than acceptable. The king himself has a suite there, did you know?"

"Quite an endorsement." The woman was practically ordering him out of the house. Had Edmund put her up to it, because it would sound suspicious coming from him? In any case, playing Edmund at cards might be a good way to glean more information. Perhaps spying wasn't that difficult after all. Ash gave her a smile. "It's an excellent idea. I'll go tomorrow."

* * * *

For Nora, the night came on slowly. She watched the clock far too much, and fretted alone until nearly midnight.

Ash came in, shutting the door before saying, "Hello."

"Hello." Nora was thrilled to see him. Apparently it didn't take much to delight her, after being cloistered away for so long. "Did you need to know more? I'm not sure what else I can tell you of the process."

"I didn't come up for that," Ash said. "I wanted to see you. I made an excuse to remain here mostly because I don't like the idea of leaving you behind so soon. Are you quite sure you'll be safe?"

"He needs me alive and alert," Nora said. "At least until he's paid in full."

"What if I persuade the Zodiac to help me come back to retrieve you when Edmund Morrison gets detained by the more legitimate authorities?"

"You mustn't worry about me. I'm not your concern."

"That's where you're wrong. I do worry, and you are my concern. If for no other reason than that you're the key to this invention."

"But you have all the information to duplicate it. You don't need me."

"What if you've got some other secret hidden away?"

She stiffened, thinking of what she hadn't told him yet, her real secret of memory. "Am I just a well of knowledge, then? Something for you to draw from till I'm dry?"

He frowned. "Nora, you *are* cynical. I came up here tonight just to see that you're well—physically, that is— and to tell you that I'm off to Worthing tomorrow. Likely staying over too. But I'll be back. I didn't want you to think I've abandoned you." He smiled. "You watch all the comings and goings from your lookout tower here, don't you? If you saw me leaving, you'd think the worst of me."

She might if he hadn't told her first. Of course, perhaps he was just telling a story now, to make her think there was hope, but in fact he was off to London to take credit for the invention and perhaps he wasn't even working for the government at all…

"Nora?" Ash was looking at her with concern in his eyes. "What's wrong?"

"Nothing," she said, stifling a sense of paranoia, something that had plagued her since Edmund Morrison took her. "What are you going to do in Worthing?"

"Quiz Morrison, if I can. He plays cards in town. I want to join in a game or two, to get some questions answered while he's distracted."

"Don't lend him any money," Nora warned. "He loses—quickly and often. He gets into debt, and he hasn't the means to pay it back. He'll welcome you to the table if only because he'll think you're a new source of loans. He's running out of cronies who will advance him anything."

"How do you know that?"

"Oh, he's rather talkative with me, because he presumes I'll never be able to share it. Anyway, his pecuniary situation is…untenable. That's one of the reasons he's been so anxious about getting paid for Albert's contract."

"So he can repay his debts?"

"Edmund won't pay a penny to his creditors. He just wants enough to leave the country with his mistress."

"He could sell this house and land, if needful."

Nora laughed. "He doesn't own this property. He rented it, and you can trust that he wants to be gone before the next quarterly payment. The servants will be left high and dry too. He'll be in Paris by then."

"Why Paris?"

"Because Mrs Kingfisher is always hounding him

about it. There's no better place than France," she mimicked, her hand in a gesture remarkably similar to Mrs Kingfisher's affected manner.

"She's that enamored of Paris? She told me she doesn't speak a word of French."

Nora shook her head. "You must have misunderstood her. She's talked about it. And I've seen a letter in her own hand, written in French. So if she reads and writes it, she certainly speaks it."

"What was the letter about?" Ash asked.

"Some love note. I didn't keep reading it." She added, "Granted, when I saw it was the exact moment Edmund came into the room and that's how I ended up with a black eye. But even if he hadn't, I wouldn't have read it." All Nora had to do was close her eyes to see the letter again. But the idea of examining another woman's private correspondence to a lover seemed prurient.

"To someone other than Edmund?" Ash pressed.

"Yes. Why would she write to Edmund in French? In fact, why would she write to him at all? They're in the same house!"

"So she wrote to a distant lover. Not her husband?"

"I don't think she's written to her husband since she arrived here."

"So she's got a husband, and an English lover, and a French lover. Must keep her occupied."

"What she does is of no interest to me," Nora said. "She can have Edmund if she likes. I just want to be left alone."

"Haven't you got sick of being alone, yet?" Ash asked, his voice more curious now.

"It would be different. It would be my choice. Alone doesn't have to mean lonely."

"It often does, though."

"How would you know? Are you lonely?"

An odd expression crossed his face, but then he shrugged. "From time to time. Who isn't? Other than those who don't think at all." His opinion of those people was obvious. "My point, Nora, is that I would prefer to know that you're happy, wherever you are."

"You want to ensure that?" she asked. "Then do whatever you must to see that Edmund Morrison is punished for all he's done and all he's planning to do."

Ash smiled. "You may rely on me."

A few moments later, after checking on the progress of her wound, which was healing rapidly, Ash gave her a kiss on the cheek and left. Nora felt as if he'd done far more. Her nerves tingled at the idea of asking him to stay. She didn't have the words to do it though.

"Please come back," was what she said.

"Count on it."

* * * *

In the morning, Ash prepared to head to Worthing, and Edmund Morrison was coming along. Ash ensured it with the mention of a card game. The two rode in Ash's carriage, leaving Grasmere House in the mid-morning.

Isabelle Kingfisher saw them off, standing at the front door with a smile on her face. "Enjoy yourselves, gentlemen! I'll be desolate until you return." The understanding was that the men would likely stay in Worthing overnight, since a night of cards could go very late indeed. Ash had a bag packed with all his essentials.

It wasn't a long journey to town, but it felt like another world. Even a short time at Grasmere House made Ash realize how isolated it was. Worthing was bustling, with men and women of all classes in the streets. There were public houses, there were newspapers, there was a coffee house. In short, civilization. Ash could get the latest news and hear the latest gossip. The buzz of conversation was exciting, and it made him long for London.

Edmund was eager to start playing and pointed out his favorite spot. Ash told him to go on. He'd join him in an hour or so. "Need to stretch my legs first," he said.

Edmund disappeared into the building, leaving Ash truly alone and free for the first time in a while. Crewe, who'd driven, announced that he was taking the carriage around to the nearest public livery to wait. "Just send word if you need to, sir."

Ash nodded, and then walked down the main thoroughfare. There was the hotel where the Princess Amelia was said to stay, and where the king himself stayed when he visited. There were the advertisements for the "cure," showing illustrations of gentlemen and ladies neck deep in the sea, supposedly being washed clean of all that ailed them.

After Ash had paced most of the town, which took a little over an hour, he went into the building where Edmund was playing cards. Ash prepared himself for a long afternoon and evening of sitting, talking about inconsequential things, and staring down his opponent. He'd learn more about Edmund Morrison at a card table than he'd learned at Grasmere House. Nothing brought out a man's personality like winning and losing money.

As it turned out, Edmund's talent for losing money far exceeded any talent for cards. Ash watched as the man got deeper and deeper into a hole, cursing his luck until a brief rally made him ecstatic once again. Ash himself played even more conservatively than he usually did. He was here as an observer, not to make a fool of anyone.

Once, around four in the afternoon, he lent Edmund

twenty pounds to keep him in the game, and he saw the expression on the other man's face: a mix of greed, gratitude, and desperate calculation.

"Won't forget this, I promise," Edmund vowed. "I'm a man of my word! I'll pay you back later tonight, should fortune smile on me."

Fortune smiled for a brief time, and then Edmund began to lose again.

Ash suggested a break. "Supper, perhaps. You could clear your head."

Edmund shook his head. "No, no. Must not give up! It's here, you know. It's all about being in the right place, at the right time. If it's not me, another man would get my draw and walk away with the winnings! Can't let that happen."

"Morrison, you're not using your brain. It's not all chance. You need to think," Ash began to say.

"I've got my methods, Mr Allen," Edmund almost snarled. "I'll see this through."

Ash sighed, recognizing the signs of obsession. He'd seen it often over the past ten years.

Then, over the next few moments, there was a sudden rise in the level of conversation throughout the room. Ash looked around, alert to the shift in mood. "Something's happened," he said quietly, putting his cards face down on the table.

"You can't leave the game. You'll forfeit," another player warned him.

Ash just waved it off, rising to his feet. He flagged one of attendants over, one who'd just entered the room. The boy came quickly.

"What's going on outside?" Ash asked him.

"Fire, sir!" the boy returned excitedly.

"Oh, Lord, fire here in the town?" The player who'd

just warned Ash about leaving the table mid-game now did exactly the same thing. He dashed off toward the front door, undoubtedly frantic about his own family or possessions or both.

"Not in town," the boy announced to everyone in general. "But it's a huge fire. Lighting up the sky. Looks as if the old lighthouse on the point has gone up in flames!"

Ash glanced over at Edmund, who had lost all the color in his face. The top of the lighthouse held a large number of the lenses and lanterns, surely worth a few hundred pounds on their own, not to mention all the time it had taken to develop them.

"It can't be on fire," Edmund said. "It's stone!"

"The inside is wood frame," Ash pointed out. "So is the keeper's house at the base." The tower would act as a flue, drawing the flames and increasing the damage.

"But no one lives there now!" Edmund protested. "How could a fire even begin? Unless…" He trailed off.

Ash understood what the man was thinking. Nora tried yet again to escape while she thought she had an opportunity. Perhaps she had, and she reached the lighthouse. Perhaps she lit one of the lanterns, and there was an accident. The fire got out of control. Nora would be revealed to the world if people rushed to the fire and saw her there.

"I need to go," Edmund muttered.

"We'll use my carriage," Ash said. There was no way he'd let Edmund Morrison near Nora without him to keep her safe, assuming she was involved. Ash couldn't stop himself from thinking of the worst—Nora dying in the flames. "I need to see this."

The other man nodded. "Let's go then."

Within moments, Crewe was ready to drive them back. It didn't take long to reach the narrow track leading to the lighthouse, and Crewe guided the vehicle over the ruts and stones until the carriage came to an abrupt halt near the blaze.

"Dear God!" Edmund gasped, seeing the destruction. The heat of the fire made it hard to breathe from where they stood. Anyone inside the lighthouse would be dead.

"All the equipment. All that time..." Edmund said, in a dazed voice. "How could this happen?"

"Could someone be here?" Ash asked him. He hated that he couldn't say Nora's name—but he was still not supposed to be aware of her existence. "Should we look?"

Edmund's eyes widened. Forgetting all care, he turned toward the blaze, howling, "Elanora! Isabelle? Elanora! Anyone? Anyone!"

Ash watched the other man try to step closer to the fire, but the heat was simply too much. He was just about to suggest walking around the fire, when Crewe grabbed him by the shoulder.

"Sir!" Crewe said. "Look!"

Ash turned to follow Crewe's outstretched finger. There was another light on the far side of the long beach that sat below this cliff. Grasmere House was alight. But the light wasn't just coming from the windows. Ash's heart dropped.

"The house is on fire too." *Nora.* If she wasn't here, she was still in the house. Still locked in on the top floor. "We have to go, Crewe."

The Disreputable nodded once, already bounding for the driver's seat on the carriage.

"Morrison!" Ash yelled. "There's no one left to save. Get over here! We need to get to Grasmere House before it's too late!"

Edmund turned, saw the first hints of the fire in Grasmere House and screamed "No!"

"Come on, Morrison," Ash repeated. "Or I'll leave

without you."

Edmund rushed to the carriage. "Dear God, *go*. I need to find them! What in hell is going on?"

Ash had no answers. He needed to see Nora safe again, and if he found her otherwise, he would make punishing Edmund Morrison his vocation for the rest of his days.

The carriage sped toward Grasmere House. But with every passing moment, the distant fire grew larger.

Chapter 17

THE SAME MORNING, NORA WATCHED from her attic room as Ash and Edmund climbed into the carriage. It rolled away down the long drive, and then turned onto the Worthing road, which followed the coastline to the east.

The house felt hollow without Ash there, and she couldn't wait for him to return. Of course, Edmund and Isabelle frequently left on various errands or diversions, and since Nora was so often confined on the top floor, with no company, she sensed the great number of empty, silent rooms in the rambling mansion.

It was a long, dull day. Nora kept glancing out to the drive, hoping against all hope that Ash might choose to return early. Or, even better, bring a brace of soldiers with him, Morrison in irons between them. Alas, the drive remained empty.

At least, it did until she saw Isabelle ride out on horseback, shortly before sunset. The woman was riding hard, which was unlike her usual practice, when she rode the horse barely faster than a walk, fearful that the resulting wind might disturb her appearance.

She evidently didn't care about that now. She was

riding east, though not on the track to Worthing, but much closer to the coast. She was heading for the lighthouse.

"Meeting her French lover, perhaps," Nora said out loud. She was still thinking of what Ash had said before, about Isabelle claiming not to speak French.

How ridiculous. Nora could close her eyes and see the letter, with all its heated, immature declarations: "Keep watch for an inferno. I will set it for you! The secret will be ours. For when you see the fire, know that it means I am done with the others…"

Nora huffed, the sound loud in the quiet room. Who ever loved like that outside of a book? So passionate and over the top? Not her! Nora knew what love was. It was the gentle warmth of knowing a true companion, someone who was steady and forthright, someone who calmed. Someone who put out fires, not started them! She and Albert had that for a brief few years together—a quiet sort of friendship, with the added intimacy of being husband and wife.

Why would Mrs Kingfisher seek out more tempestuous affairs if she had that sort of companion? Why would she want an inferno?

Nora didn't want an inferno. She wanted peace, on her own terms. She was sure Ash would agree with her. He seemed to hold himself apart from intense emotional fires, as if he'd been burned before, and learned from it.

Still, he wasn't devoid of passion. He'd shown that in the few days he'd known her. He might not offer flowery declarations, but she could imagine him sharing some deep secret, spoken in a low voice just for her, with heat that was undeniable.

Nora got rather caught up in imagining that scenario, and more, so that she forced herself to laugh out loud to stop her overactive brain. That was the trouble with isolation. She had far too much time to think. She ought to move. Should she risk a rooftop excursion? It was twilight now.

She slid off her slippers and climbed halfway onto the windowsill. That was when she saw it.

A light flared far down the beach—not a flash from a signal lantern, as she first thought, but a flame. Had someone started a bonfire on the headland?

No. She watched for a little while, and realized it was not bonfire. It was bigger than that...and growing. The lighthouse was ablaze. The flames ate at the wooden parts of the structure, and grew brighter every passing moment.

"*Inferno*," she muttered.

Nora remained on the windowsill, watching the lighthouse be consumed. Flames licked the sides of the ruins, and the tower itself looked to be in danger.

What seemed to her to be some overly dramatic expression of love—or a poor translation on her part—now took on a much more sinister air. If Mrs Kingfisher set that fire, she had a reason. Was it a signal to some unseen partner? If it was, then the other half of her words were probably just as literal: "I am done with the others and they will be only ashes by morning."

No. Wasn't that madness? To think something so fanciful? Yet it all made sense to Nora. Isabelle Kingfisher could be returning to the house right now. She was planning something, and if she got to carry her whole plan out, Nora was going to fall victim to it.

Shouts echoed from below. The household had noticed the distant fire as well, and they were undoubtedly all flocking to the cliff side to see the spectacle.

Nora couldn't waste a moment. She got off the windowsill, and dashed down the stairs to the second story. Mrs Lloyd had just exited one of the bedrooms, a bucket of water in each hand.

"Hey! What are you doing out? Get back to your room!" The housekeeper dropped the bucket to the floor, water splashing everywhere. Then she lunged toward Nora while screaming for assistance.

Nora skidded to a stop. The way to the ground floor was blocked now, and in any case, others would soon be swarming upward. Nora aimed for Ash's bedroom and got in just as Mrs Lloyd reached the doorway. Nora slammed the door shut.

She didn't have a key, but she might block the door with something heavy. She seized onto the nearest thing, a short bookcase, and dragged it to the door just as someone pounded on the heavy wood.

"You can't escape, you little wretch!" Mrs Lloyd called. "You're trapped!"

Nora looked to the window. She wasn't trapped at all. But she did need to pack for her journey.

Into one of the travel cases Ash brought, Nora dumped his book, the bank notes, and pistols. She looked around and grabbed anything else seeming useful or important.

She pushed open the window sash and looked out. No one was about in the yard. They were probably all gathering inside the corridor to break the door down, or they were on the other side of the house, gawking at the burning lighthouse.

Nora leaned over and dropped the case over the ledge all the way to the ground. She waited a moment, wondering if anyone heard the thump.

Then she flung her legs over the sill and prepared to step outside onto the narrow edge. The jump to the ground was further than she liked, but what choice did she have?

Nora jumped from the upper story and landed in a graceless heap. She got up quickly, happy she hadn't hurt herself. Then she seized the bag and walked away from the house. She sniffed, smelling smoke. It was too strong to be drifting from the lighthouse fire, and anyway, the wind was wrong. She glanced back, and saw blackish plumes rising from the roof. "Oh, no." The house itself was ablaze. There was nothing she could do about it.

Nora ran to the stables. She had never touched a horse that hadn't been saddled already—it represented a total void in her skills. But she could hardly call a stableboy over, so she took a deep breath and tried to puzzle out the mystery of how to saddle a horse. The horse in the first stall was no help, shying away every time Nora attempted to pat it.

"I hope you're not using my absence to escape on your own."

Nora jumped in alarm at the voice. She spun about. "Ash! What are you doing here?"

He frowned at her. "More to the point, what are you doing here? The whole house is blazing, and it looks very much like you intend to ride off into the night alone." Ash walked into the stable, the valet he called Crewe at his heels.

"Yes! I was."

"Setting a fire was little extreme, don't you think?"

Nora gasped. "I didn't set any fire! How could you think I'd be that reckless?"

"So you're just using it to your advantage?" He looked angry. "The first chance you had, you head off on your own. Didn't wait for me. I suppose with only Mrs Kingfisher here, you felt—"

"She's not Mrs Kingfisher!" Nora shouted.

"What?"

Crewe gave his employer a look Nora knew all too well.

"Don't do that!" she said to the valet. "I'm not insane!"

"When you have to make a point of it, ma'am..." Crewe began.

"I meant Mrs Kingfisher isn't who she says she is. Please, Ash, believe me."

"Who is she, then?" Ash asked.

"I don't know!"

Ash's skepticism now mirrored Crewe's.

Nora took a deep breath. Excessive emotion would make her seem off balance. Unfortunately, all her emotions were running to excess now. "You saw the lighthouse on fire, didn't you?"

"Of course, that's why we left town to come back here. Didn't stop to help put it out, on account of no one lives there, and we saw the fire starting here. I thought you were going to be trapped in the attic."

"I think Mrs Kingfisher set both fires—I saw her riding to the lighthouse earlier. In a letter she wrote, she said something about an inferno. I read it—the one in French, that she denies she speaks..." Nora explained her theory as quickly as she could, sometimes jumbling her words in her haste.

Ash let her speak, though he still wore an expression she interpreted as disapproving. "You were going to leave without me. You weren't going to try to find me later either."

She grimaced. "I thought you were out of danger. But she's come back here to finish what she started. The house, the fires...think of it! She must be after the process and the code—Edmund must have told her how much more it was worth. And she wants to be the only one who knows about it, so she burned everything to hide what's been done. We have to go. Now."

"Sir?" Crewe asked, very quietly.

"What is it, Crewe?"

Nora despaired. The men must think she had well and truly lost her mind.

"We ought to take the carriage, and go *now*."

Ash nodded. "I agree."

Nora blinked. "You believe me?"

"I believe it's safer for all of us to get away from here," Ash said.

Crewe took that comment as an order and ran back to the carriage he'd driven from Worthing. Ash moved in the opposite direction and opened all the stall doors.

"What are you doing? The horses will wander out."

"Precisely."

Then she understood what he meant. If none of the other horses were accessible, it would be more difficult for anyone to follow them.

Ash looked at the line of animals now moving outside. "Let's go."

Nora pointed to the bag at her feet. "You'll want this."

Ash picked it up, exclaiming at the weight. "My God. What did you pack?"

"Everything I could manage to fit."

"Evidently." Ash heaved the bag onto the carriage. "All right then, we'd better be off."

He offered a hand to help her in, a gesture that was so civilized and so out of place considering the situation, that hysterical giggles began to bubble up.

Ash saw what was happening and took her hand very firmly. "Take a breath, Nora. And get in."

The threat of hysteria was quelled for a moment. Nora climbed into the carriage, followed by Ash. Crewe had the contraption rolling away from the house seconds later.

"With luck," Ash said, "everyone will be too busy

with the fire—"

A tremendous shout came from the direction of the house.

Ash poked his head out of the window. "So much for luck. Sounds as if Morrison noticed our going."

"Oh, dear lord," Nora said. "He'll chase me down."

"He'll have to calm a horse down enough to ride it first. We've got a good head start."

A bang came from behind them.

"You've got to be joking," Ash muttered. Then he yelled, "Crewe! Keep low!"

"What's happening? What was that?"

"Gunshot," Ash said laconically.

"He's shooting at Crewe?" Nora gasped. The carriage lurched forward as the horses put on a new burst of speed.

"He's shooting at all of us. Don't worry. We'll soon be out of range." He sank back in the seat. "The sooner we can reach any outpost of civilization, the better. Morrison can't attack a whole town to get to us. And that other woman…"

"Not Mrs Kingfisher, whoever she is."

Ash was seated opposite her, facing the receding house. His expression was anything but pleased. "Bad timing," he muttered.

"How so?"

He shook his head. "Doesn't matter. I wanted to… never mind. At least we're both alive. That's something."

"What's wrong?" she pressed. "What can I do?"

"Nothing. The goal now is to get somewhere reasonably safe, where Edmund Morrison won't be able to get to us without our knowing." Ash's face was now closed off, unreadable. "Just sit back, Nora. Not all of us are genius inventors like you. But Crewe knows how to drive a carriage…and I know how to sit in one."

"How reassuring!"

"I'll get us to London," he said hotly. "Though I'm not sure if anyone will be pleased to see either of us once we do arrive."

So Nora sat back, keeping a wary eye on Ash as the carriage sped through the darkness.

Chapter 18

AFTER THE CARRIAGE GOT AWAY from Grasmere House, Ash slowly calmed down from the nervous, physical tension that drove him during the initial discovery of the fire, unexpectedly finding Nora in the stables, and their subsequent escape. They were well ahead of possible pursuit, and he trusted Crewe to maintain the lead.

But now that he had a few moments of quiet, the consequences of his choice weighed on him. Ash had made an irreparable mistake. He was sure of it. By leaving with Nora, he damaged his cover, and destroyed any chance of returning to the house. Worse, he alerted Morrison to his true agenda, considering Ash just *stole* Nora, the key to the man's work.

And what of Isabelle Kingfisher? He should have paid more attention to her than he did, but he was so ensnared by Nora. What would Bruce say to that? What could Ash say? I abandoned the one assignment you gave me before it was finished, but look, here's a woman who's already told me what she knows, thus rendering her rescue completely superfluous.

Bruce wouldn't think much of that. Damnation. Every

time he tried to do something right, he was punished for it. When would he learn that God was never going to stop making him miserable?

He wanted to forget it all, to fall into the clouds that the laudanum would summon.

Nora was silent, her inquiring gaze focused outward into the darkness. After the carriage passed the still-burning lighthouse off to their right, the world turned black again. Yet she watched. Ash reminded himself that this was the first time in over a year she'd had a different view.

A while later, she spoke. "Crewe missed the turn onto the London road."

"We don't want that road," he muttered. Then he asked, "How did you know it was the London road? It's too dark to read any signpost."

"I remembered from the time Edmund drove us down here," she said, not looking at him. "So we're not heading to London?"

"That would be the obvious choice, wouldn't it?" Ash responded. Edmund would assume exactly that, and he'd begin the chase on the road to the city. He'd lose time because he'd have to stop along the way, inquiring after them at inns and other likely stopping points. Meanwhile, Ash and Nora would journey ever farther away, hopefully slipping out of Edmund's grasp. It was the least he could do.

"I see," she said. "Where are we going, then?"

"Along the coast road for a few days. We will turn to London, but along a road that no one could possibly guess —after all, even we don't know which one we'll choose yet. Once in the city, I'll contact the Zodiac and then we'll locate your brother."

"A few days…is that too much delay?"

"We have time. Edmund will be wasting the next several days on a wild goose chase, and by then we'll have passed on all the facts to the Zodiac, and they can take the next steps."

"Not you?"

"My part's done," Ash said, his voice flat. "The sooner I'm out of it, the better. Once you're reunited with your family, you'll not have to suffer my company any longer."

"I like your company," Nora said instantly. Then her face clouded. "Though there is the matter of lodging, which could be difficult."

"I have funds," Ash assured her.

"I meant…" Nora blushed. "How will we present ourselves? We're traveling together, but you can hardly tell an innkeeper we're unmarried…"

"Then we'll say we are married," Ash said. "Who's to question it? In any case, until I'm entirely certain that Edmund hasn't picked up our trail, I don't want you out of my sight."

Nora's eyes widened. "You mean…share a room?"

"That's the customary practice, isn't it? If anyone asks, we're husband and wife."

"Should we use another name?" she suggested.

Ash gave a bitter laugh. "Why not? Let's be Mr and Mrs Priestly."

"A false name may not be enough to hide from Edmund," she said. "He'll share a description of me, won't he?"

"Possible, but to be honest, I don't have much in the way of disguises for you." He looked at her more carefully. "You're not even wearing shoes. Lord. Well, we'll do our best to be circumspect. You can keep the hood of the cloak up till we reach the room, and that will hide your hair, and your excuse for a gown. Even if Edmund does take this road eventually, he won't get much information other than that a couple of similar description stayed the night. He'll have to chalk it up to coincidence."

"Isn't that a gamble?"

"One thing I'm very good at is gambling."

He sighed and sat back, unable to pretend all was well. All he wanted was oblivion. He was relieved beyond measure to find that the bag at his feet contained the precious wooden case—he would find a moment of solitude and take a dose. *Then* he could face the ramifications of his mistake.

They reached a large inn about an hour later. It was busy enough that the arrival of one more couple would not attract much attention.

"You'll do all the talking, I suppose," Nora said.

"Safer that way. You just keep that hood up, hide your bare feet under the hem, and embody the ideal of a quiet, retiring wife."

She rolled her eyes but did as he said.

Ash walked in and got the innkeeper's attention right away, no doubt aided in that by the clink of a coin on the counter. "Dinner, and a room for the night. One facing the road, if possible. I like to watch the people come and go."

"Certainly, sir. We have just such a room. Would you like dinner served upstairs?"

Nora nodded from beneath her hood, and Ash said, "Yes. The common room is too busy for my wife."

Ash arranged for Crewe to stay in the servants' loft, and paid for the feed for the horses. At the end, he dropped another coin in the innkeeper's palm, and then led Nora upstairs.

The room was probably the best one the inn had to offer. It was fairly large, and clean. The furnishings were simple but high-quality—no castoffs or broken items here.

Nora pulled her hood off as soon as the door closed. "Well," she said. "So far, so good. They seemed to believe you."

"They're paid to believe their customers," Ash said. "And now we've got a whole evening before we can move again."

"I don't mind." Nora was prowling around the room, looking at everything, opening the few drawers and cabinets. "It's not Grasmere House, so it will be better."

Food was brought up by a maid soon after, and Ash took charge, hiding Nora from the maid's sight.

Nora tucked into the food quite happily. Ash ate a little, but he was so focused on the idea of the laudanum that food had no appeal.

"After you eat, you should sleep," he said. "You're not used to all this."

"I'm not sleepy."

"Sleep anyway," he grunted as he rooted around in his small bag. When his fingers brushed the top of the wooden box, he glanced up at a Nora.

He was disturbed to see that she was watching him. "What is it?"

"Have I done something wrong?" she asked.

"What? No."

"You've been upset since we left the house. I am sorry I didn't have time to warn you of my escape, but I couldn't wait, and the fire was the best distraction I could hope for."

"I'm not angry." Not at her, not exactly. But he was ready to snap. The wooden box was right there at his feet and he couldn't open it; he couldn't remove it from the bag until Nora looked away. She was far too inquisitive for his comfort just now.

Thankfully, Nora chose to build up the fire in the grate and then sink into one of the curved wood chairs. She sat back and closed her eyes. "I suppose I should enjoy my liberty while I have it," she murmured. "Who knows what will happen next?"

Ash knelt down and eased the box out of his bag. Nora seemed to be either dozing or relaxing—in any case, she wasn't watching him. He opened the lid and began to pull out the bottle of laudanum, being as silent as he could. His nerves were screaming at him now, in a way he'd rarely experienced before. Everything had gone wrong, and he couldn't fix any of it. All he knew was that the drug would deaden his feelings, and slow the endless cycle of thoughts in his brain. The sooner he could get it in his body, the better off he'd be.

"What are you doing?" Nora asked from where she sat. He shot a look over at her, but she was still leaning back, her eyes closed.

"Nothing you need to be concerned about."

"No? Whenever Mrs Lloyd gave me laudanum, I'd spit it out when she turned her back."

Ash went still. "What?"

"That's what's in the bottle," Nora said. She sat up and twisted to watch him. Silhouetted against the fire, she was all darkness, and Ash didn't like it at all. "That's what you're about to drink down."

"It's none of your business what I do or don't choose to drink."

"We're traveling together, staying in a room together, running from the same person together. So I'd say your mental state is my business." Nora rose from the seat and walked over to him. "Wouldn't it be better to keep your head clear? I hated the laudanum, when I couldn't avoid it. It clouded my head and made thinking impossible."

"That's my goal," he muttered.

"Why?"

"There's such a thing as thinking too much. Too much remembering."

"What are you remembering?" she asked, one eyebrow raised.

"Things I'd rather forget," he snapped. "God, Nora. Why does it matter?"

"I should tell you this," she said quietly. "I remember everything."

"Yes, I'm sure you've got plenty of horrible memories from the past year." He got an idea. "Take a dose with me. We'll both forget everything we need to forget, at least for tonight."

She shook her head. "I won't. I always remember everything."

"This is stronger than the syrup you were given. Trust me, you'll soon forget the whole ordeal."

Nora knelt down to Ash's level. "Ash, I remember *everything*," she repeated, her eyes locked on his. "I always have."

"Everything…as in…"

"We missed the turn for the road to London," she said. "I saw that turn once, over a year ago. Never again. But I knew it in the dark."

Ash stared at her, the precious drug momentarily left aside.

"The inscription on your gun case, which I saw once when I was sneaking around your room: *For A, from your ever faithful second. R.*"

"So you remembered a phrase…"

She began to recite the words of a letter Ash knew very well, word for word. It had been hidden in his case.

"How did you know that?"

"I saw the letter. Once. I remember, Ash. I remember things that I see written down. I remember everything Edmund was ever said to me, every time he laughed at me. I remember which tiles on the roof of Grasmere House are broken…that's why I don't slip. I remember which baseboards creak, that's how I can get around with no one hearing. I remember. Do you understand what I'm saying?"

"I think so."

She took his hands in hers. "Then you should understand that I know exactly what it's like to be stuck inside one's own head, to be lost in a loop of memories, over and over, and it never changes and there's nothing you can do about it. All the opium in the world won't change your past, or your memories of it."

"I need this," he said, clutching the cool glass bottle.

"You need to keep your head," Nora said firmly. "It's too dangerous for you to drift off."

"Thank you for the warning," he said, trying to keep his temper in check, "but nothing is going to happen tonight. If I don't do *some*thing, I'm going to go out of my mind."

"Ah. In that case, I have a solution."

And Nora leaned over and kissed him.

Chapter 19

NORA KISSED HIM BEFORE SHE lost her nerve. At the touch of her lips, he made a low, satisfied sound in his throat, and Nora's interest sharpened. She put her hands on his shoulders, cautiously, wondering how long it was acceptable to kiss a man one wasn't married to. She hoped he'd not get bored and push her away.

She'd kissed him before, but it was different this time. Now they were alone, with no risk of discovery or disruption.

Ash reached for her and drew her close. He kept her tight against him even after she ended the kiss. "What was that for, Nora?"

"If we're going to pretend to be married, playing Mr and Mrs Allen, why stop at merely sharing a room?"

"It's Allander," he said quietly. "My real name is Allander, not Allen." His eyes flicked over her face.

"Oh. That's hardly different, is it?"

"Different enough. I should have told you earlier."

"Well, I can understand why you wouldn't."

"You can?" He sounded so wary.

"Of course. A spy needs to be careful who he trusts.

But you can trust me, Ashley Allander."

"Thank you." Ash brushed her cheek with his lips, then said, "As for the pretense, it's for others. I never intended to take advantage of the situation."

"Perhaps I *do* want to take advantage of the situation," she said, sounding rather more prim than the topic warranted. "Besides," she hurried on, "you said you need a distraction."

He took a deeper breath. "I see. So it's a mutual benefit?"

"Or mutual selfishness. Would it serve as a replacement, if we…?"

He took a ragged breath. "Yes." The way he looked at her now made it clear that he definitely wanted to indulge in something.

Nora smiled. "So will you…would you be willing to indulge in me, I mean indulge me, just for a night?"

"Yes." His hands slid down from her waist to her hips, and his expression was wondering, as if he didn't really believe this was happening. "Yes, if that's what you want."

"It is."

He smiled at last, then moved to kiss her again.

"First put the bottle away," she said, forestalling him. "You don't need it tonight."

Ash nodded and reluctantly stepped away to follow her instruction. Once the laudanum was safely back in the box he said, "Done. Any more requests? Or may I now seduce you with wild, reckless abandon?"

Nora burst out laughing at the deadpan way he said it, which meant that she was not prepared when he got her in his arms and kissed her neck, his mouth hot on her skin.

She went from amused to aroused in the space of a breath. "Oh," she gasped.

He laughed now, the sound vibrating against her. Then she felt a quick nibble and a flick of his tongue.

"You taste good," he murmured. "Better than opium."

"Mmm." Between his touch and his unexpected words, she seemed to have lost all power to form sentences.

"I'm going to taste a lot more of you," he went on, proving it by giving her another quick bite at the base of her neck. "All of you, actually."

"All?" she echoed. Lord, Nora, you know words in English. Use them! "Um, how will you do that?"

"Any way you want me to, darling," he said. "What do you like in bed?"

"I…don't know." She swallowed nervously, suddenly realizing the full meaning of what she'd just suggested doing with him tonight.

"Nora." Ash's eyes were suddenly dark with concern. "What is it?"

"I don't know anything," she admitted. "I've been married and widowed, but I'm so ignorant."

"Then let me remove your ignorance," he said. Then that smile flashed again. "Along with your clothes, which are, if I haven't said already, not suitable for a lady traveling anywhere, especially to London."

"What do you propose to do about it?" she asked. "I have no other outfit."

"Well, get this one off first, and worry about the rest later."

"I…don't have a nightgown, either."

"Trust me, you won't need one."

"But, when I…I mean, during my marriage, I never…" She ducked her head, confounded by explaining the details of her most intimate experiences.

"He never took your clothing off?"

"No. He never said he wanted to. I don't think it was proper. Or he didn't think it was proper. In a marriage, that is. "

"Just as well I never married," Ash muttered. "Nora, tonight you need to forget proper, or what you think other people want." His gaze was intent, and far too perceptive. "It's been far too long since you've got what you want, Nora. You should indulge your own needs, starting tonight."

At his words, tension flowed out of her body. He not only understood her deepest desire, he'd articulated it in a way she'd been afraid to, even to herself.

She took a nervous breath. "Could you show me something I might like?"

"I could." He walked them both to the bed.

"Should I lie down?" she asked.

"Why not just sit for now." He set her on the edge of the bed, and knelt in front of her.

He took her hands in his and began to kiss her palms, gently, teasingly. Nora inhaled. Why should that particular act feel as daring as it did? He was only kissing her hands. And yet she still felt shivers of pleasure shooting through her.

"Would you like more?" he asked.

Yes, she would like more. She couldn't complete the thought out loud. The sensations rippling across her body were overwhelming.

No longer kneeling, Ash moved up her bare arm, pulling her toward him as he laid more kisses onto her skin.

He moved from the delicate skin on her inner arm to the even more delicate skin of her breast, the top generously exposed by the inadequate dress she wore. Nora inhaled deeply in reaction. He took it as an invitation, pulled the fabric down slightly, revealing most of her breasts.

"You're not wearing stays," he noted, very casually.

"I…didn't know I was leaving the house today," she said, and then was interrupted by Ash's tongue on her skin.

Nora felt her body catch fire. The man before her was treating her in a way that she had never experienced before, and the pleasure of it was undeniable. She couldn't stop a moan of satisfaction slipping past her lips.

"So, there's something you like," he whispered, his breath hot on her breast.

"Yes," she breathed. She was startled to realize that she was lying on her back now, with Ash over her.

"You're a beauty," he said, looking her over.

"You need not lie to me. Flattery isn't what I'm looking for."

"I'm not lying. You are a beauty, and I've been wanting you like this since I saw you that first night."

"Just because I appeared in your room half-dressed?" she asked wryly.

"Hardly. Though you made an impression, I admit. No, I like the way you look at me."

"How do I look at you?"

"As if I'm someone worth saving." The darkness in Ash's eyes was at odds with his joking tone, and Nora frowned.

"What do you mean? How can you possibly be so… condemned? After all, you do good work, for a good cause. And you've been kind to me."

"Maybe I've got very selfish motives," he said roughly, his hands tightening on her waist.

Nora gasped, but not because she was scared. No, she was aroused. Being so close to Ash was intoxicating, alluring. She reached to kiss him again.

"Ash," she breathed, between kisses, "what should I do?"

"You asking me for moral guidance?" he returned. "I've got a bit of conflict of interest, darling." He pulled her tighter against him, rocking her hips against his.

"Oh," she gasped. "No. I meant…show me how to please you."

He shook his head. "Not tonight. You offered yourself as a distraction, remember? So I am going to distract myself with every inch of you."

"Oh. When do we begin?"

"We already have. Do you like this? How we are right now?"

If he meant the way he was kissing her, and touching her body, then she liked it very much, and said so.

"Then we continue," he said. "We've got all night, and I like to take my time."

"That's…yes," she said, once again losing her ability to form basic phrases.

Ash smiled when he heard her, obviously aware of her confusion. "Before," he said, "when your husband came to your room, did you ever keep the light on?"

"Of course not!" Nora said, shocked.

"And of course, you weren't naked in bed."

"No!"

"Well," he said with a smile. "Then those are two more things which you can find out if you like, just to begin. Oh, and if you want, you can help me get these clothes off."

"Ash! You can't just ask a woman to do that."

"Why not? You've already seen me naked," he pointed out.

"Yes, but I wasn't the cause of it."

"You will be now," he said. He could hardly stop himself from laughing. Nora shook her head, but still reached out to grab the hem of his shirt, because the truth was that she did want to see him naked again.

A few moments later, she got her wish. "You're by far the most handsome man I've ever seen," she said. "Clothed or not."

"Then you can't have got out much," Ash said. "I'm not that extraordinary."

"Yes, you are."

He smiled. "Well, all right, I am. Not that it means much."

"Beautiful people never think it means much to be beautiful," Nora said. "You probably have women throwing themselves at you."

Ash ducked his head to kiss her neck once again, so she couldn't see his expression. But then he murmured, "The only woman I want to throw herself at me right now is you."

"That's lucky," she said, laughing, "since I'm here."

"You're cynical, Nora," he accused. Then his hands found the edge of her skirt, and he made quick work of her clothing, discarding it somewhere on the floor. Or possibly in the fireplace. Nora didn't know or care.

He surveyed her body, his gaze intent.

"What is it?" she asked nervously.

"If you were mine," he said, his voice low and hot, "I wouldn't ever lock you away. I'd dress you in something extravagant and take you out and show you off and let the whole world know that not only are you brilliant, you're also beautiful and everyone should be wildly jealous of me, for somehow having got your attention."

Nora's breath caught in her throat. The image of her as the center of attention was enticing, especially as described by Ash, who probably would buy her a gown expressly so he could enjoy taking it off. "I'm...I'm not sure I'd be good at that."

"At what?"

"Being noticed."

"You get used to it," he said. "I did."

"You're noticed?" she asked, curious.

"More than I like," he replied. "But it doesn't matter. They only see what I want them to see."

Nora couldn't ask him more about what he meant, because he distracted her with a string of kisses that left her unable to breathe, let alone think.

Ash cupped her breasts in his hands, teasing each bud under his thumbs.

Nora sighed. "Do you...like to do that?" she whispered.

"Love it," he confessed. "Love feeling your skin, your whole body. Love seeing you go pink when I stroke you, love feeling your nipples grow hard—I want to taste them."

"You do?"

"Let me," he begged.

She nodded, and gasped at the feel of his mouth on her breast, a barrage of new feelings brought on by the entirely novel feeling of his tongue lapping her nipple, his teeth scraping her flesh so gently. Nora suddenly gasped, feeling a bloom of pleasure lower in her body, as if there was some invisible string between her breast and her belly.

"Ash," she whispered. "That feels very...good."

He released her nipple from his mouth and did the same to the other, till Nora was breathing fast, her body growing hot.

She felt Ash's hand on her thigh, dangerously close to, well, everything. He inched upward, going slowly enough that she could tell him to stop. She didn't.

"How did he touch you?" Ash asked.

"He…didn't. Not more than he had to, I mean, to get my nightgown out of the way."

"Never?"

"Why? Is it necessary?"

"Who cares about necessary? It's fun."

"Is this supposed to be fun?"

"What else? What's the point of sin if it doesn't feel good? Let me touch you."

"Yes," she breathed.

He eased one finger into her. Nora moaned, feeling so sensitive that every little shift made her want to scream.

"God damn," he said, his voice tight. "You're exquisite. So responsive. How do you feel?"

"I…" She had no words. Her marriage never yielded anything like this. Her body felt on fire, and the man above her seemed very intent on stoking the flames.

He watched her as he explored her most intimate places, listening to her breath, smiling as she succumbed to his touch. She told him how much she liked it, though words were terribly difficult. Ash told her he'd touch her as long as she wanted him to.

"In that case, forever," she murmured. Then Nora cried out once as her whole body reacted to his attentions. His fingers slowed, drawing out the pleasure. Nora rocked her center against the palm of his hand, sighing as she pressed herself to him. "Oh," she said, as something just like warm sunlight seeped through her muscles from her center out to her limbs and her fingers and toes.

"You'll remember this?" Ash asked.

"Yes." She closed her eyes, smiling as she felt her body ease and relax. Then she realized something. "Wait. You only…you haven't…" He hadn't actually used her in the way a husband did. "You don't mean to *stop* now," she said, disbelieving.

He laughed softly. "I did say that my aim was to please you tonight. And you seem pleased."

"But I'm not!" she protested. "That is, I am. But I don't want to end…if there's more…" she broke off, feeling utterly embarrassed.

"Don't do that, Nora. There's nothing to be ashamed of."

"I don't know *any*thing," she complained. "I don't even know how to ask you for what I want."

"What do you want?"

"You."

Ash's expression was both amused and longing. "You're certain?" he asked.

"After all, it's not as if I'm a virgin." Did he need convincing at this point? She reached to touch him, just as he'd done to her.

"Christ, Nora," he hissed. "That feels good."

He was big and heavy in her hand, and she could tell that even the touch of her fingers made him more excited. Nora closed her fingers around him instinctively, suddenly very curious. And she knew exactly where curiosity would lead her.

Ash pushed her back on the bed, and then moved over her, covering her body with his own. She ran her hands up and down his sides, then his back, delighting in how warm his skin was, how a very light sheen of sweat made her fingers slide over the contours of his body.

She spread her legs to allow him to settle between her thighs. He braced himself on his arms, and bent his head to kiss her on the mouth, a long, slow kiss that paradoxically made her more frantic.

"Ash, please," she said.

"I want to watch your face, love," he said quietly. "I like to see what I do to you."

Nora nodded, tense with desire again, as if he'd not just pleasured her and brought her to completion already.

He eased himself into her, going gloriously slowly. Nora felt him fill her up, inch by inch, his hard length sliding into the slick heat of her body. She opened her mouth in astonishment, both at the sensation, and the feeling that he fit her so perfectly.

Ash's eyes never left her face, though he too looked surprised for a moment. Then he let out a long sigh of relief. "You're so lovely, Nora," he breathed.

She merely nodded, too overwhelmed to say anything. Anyway, what could she say? He was the one with the experience, the knowledge, not her.

He used his knowledge then, showing her that he knew exactly how to please her. He took his time, watching her react and moving in response to her excited gasps. Nora kept her hands on him, running eager fingers along his chest, his shoulders, his arms.

"Ash," she kept saying, as if his name had power. "Ash."

He bent to lay kisses along her neck and chest, his lips hovering where her pulse beat close to the surface.

"You are more intoxicating than any drug I've had, and I've had a lot," he confessed.

Hearing that, Nora curled her fingers, tightening her grip on him.

"Ash," she moaned at last. Her body contracted again, sending cascades of pleasure through her, somehow deeper and darker than before. She shuddered with desire, and Ash slipped one arm under her shoulders to hold her close to him.

His kiss became a bite, his teeth sinking into her

shoulder as he let out a moan. He suddenly withdrew from her and laid his body tight against hers. He pressed closer, and stiffened as he came. Nora felt the warm wetness of his seed against her skin.

"What's wrong? You didn't wish to finish inside me?" she asked. Her husband always had.

He took a moment to answer. She listened to his breathing slow to a more normal rate. At last he said, "Nora, I'm not that heartless."

"Why heartless? Why would I mind, if you wanted—"

"You'd mind if you got with child," he said quietly. "Or did you forget that little possibility?"

"Oh. Yes, of course." She knew that was a risk, but she hadn't even thought about such consequences until he mentioned it. How very dangerous passion could be, after all. Yet, she wasn't sure she *would* mind.

"I don't want to hurt you, darling. Not in any way, tonight or in the future," he said, shifting to move off her. He got up, found a piece of soft flannel by the wash basin, and moistened it in clean water. Returning to the bed, he washed her clean as simply and as unaffectedly as he'd done everything before. Even in the aftermath, he was a considerate lover. Her husband had simply left her room with a sincere and slightly embarrassed goodnight. He never stayed with her afterwards, and he certainly never touched her or acknowledged her body after he was done with it.

Ash still seemed intensely interested in her. When he'd tidied them both up to his satisfaction, he lay back down by her, pulling her into his arms.

Nora went very willingly. She assumed she'd feel shy or awkward after the exchange they'd just had, where she'd literally bared her whole body and psyche to him. Yet now she felt only a glow of contentment.

She laid her head on his chest, and with her one hand, she absent-mindedly traced lines on his body.

He in turn played with her hair, just as absently.

Neither of them spoke for several moments, but Nora didn't feel the silence was awkward. Indeed, she couldn't recall ever being so peaceful. Odd that she felt so at ease with a man she hardly knew.

After a while, Ash leaned in to kiss her forehead. "I hope tonight will be counted as a good memory."

"It will," she assured him, shyness sweeping over her at last.

"You'll remember everything? As in, *everything*?"

"Yes."

"Will you tell me what that means, Nora? I promise I've got my mind back now, thanks to you. And if I'm right, you didn't tell me about your gift by accident."

* * * *

As he spoke, Ash watched with concern as the joy drained out of Nora's face. "It's not a gift," she mumbled.

"Are you sure? It's a rare skill—not even a skill. You can't learn memory."

She shook her head. "No. I was born with it. I don't mean I remember being in the cradle," she added. "Just that all my memories are crystal. They don't fade, and I can recall any of them, at any time, whether I want to or not."

"Edmund knew about your talent?"

"He depended on it. Edmund doesn't like to have the messages written down. Or anything written down, in fact. His explicit orders were for me to keep it all in my head. He gave me some paper for working things out with the codes, but he checked everything. I couldn't even sneak one piece to write a letter to someone—not that I could have posted it anyway."

"You kept everything in your head?" If so, that was astonishing to Ash.

"Yes. The symbols for the code, the messages that were sent, even the names of the few people he spoke to. He used me as a secretary. My duty was to remember all the signals and tell him how to translate words into the code and send it back. In truth, Edmund never liked being a signaler, though it would have been easier if he made himself a reference book."

"But he didn't, because he thought it might fall into the wrong hands."

"I always thought he was being overcautious. He did get more stringent about it once Mrs Kingfisher came to the house. Perhaps he was more worried about her leaving with the information than *me* leaving with the information."

"How did Edmund learn of your memory, if he never met you until after your husband passed?"

Nora took a deep breath. "Albert must have told him. There's no other way."

Ash tilted her head up so he could look at her face. "You're angry about that."

"I don't think he did it deliberately."

"But you're still angry."

She said in a frustrated tone, "He wanted to reconcile with Edmund, and told him too much. If he just kept quiet about it all, about my invention and the payment and my memory, none of this would have happened! I would never have been taken away, and locked up, and made to follow Edmund's every stupid order. I wouldn't have had to plead with servants who just shook their heads and told me that I had to be mad to even argue that I was sane..."

Ash pulled her closer. "Enough. You don't have to say anything more."

But Nora clearly wanted to say more. She'd been kept silent for too long. "I spent whole nights not able to sleep up there in the attic. I'd talk to Albert—as if he could hear me—and ask why he had to tell his brother anything. Why he couldn't have just stopped talking and come home to me. Instead he died there. He left me without any warning."

"I'm sorry it happened that way."

Nora confessed, "I hated him sometimes. My own husband. I just lay there alone at night and cursed him for leaving me behind."

After several moments, Nora wiped her eyes. "This is not the usual topic for pillow talk."

"You're not the usual sort of woman."

"You must be bored silly," she mumbled.

"No."

She heaved a breath, then unexpectedly punched a little fist into his chest. It didn't hurt at all, but he gave an *oof* anyway. "What was that for?" he asked.

"Why are you so...horribly...*kind*?"

Ash chuckled at that. "I'm not kind. It's just that I'll do anything to get you to stay in bed with me."

She shook her head, but now she was smiling again, making him feel better. "I'm not exactly a seductress," she said. "Anyway, where else would I sleep?"

"Nowhere, I hope. I'm not done with you yet." He kissed the spot on her cheek where the dimple showed.

"You're not?" she asked. "What else do you plan to do with me?"

He offered several suggestions, most of which made her blush bright pink, which was adorable to watch.

"Any of those appeal to you?" he asked.

"All of them."

Ash instantly tightened his hands, as if this maddening woman might get away. "Did you just say all of them?"

"Of course," she said. "I've done none of them, and if I'm to understand what I'm getting into, I need to experiment. That's the key to perfecting any process." Her eyes sparkled as she spoke.

"You *are* a seductress." Ash laughed. Nora was his first lover in years who actually made him laugh.

"No," she said. "I'm just very happy to be free of that place. How better to celebrate than to do several things that have been forbidden to me? As soon as I get to London, I'm going to buy all new clothes, drink champagne until I get sick, and race a horse down the middle of a busy street. All before noon the first day."

He laughed quietly. "I believe you."

"You shouldn't," she said. "I don't have any money, I don't drink, and I've never had much luck at riding. I'm not very good at being bad."

"You'd learn quickly enough if you put your mind to it. But in fact, I like you as you are." Ash drew her to him, and kissed her deeply.

* * * *

Ash awoke much later, with Nora still in his arms. She lay asleep, her mouth parted, her fine hair in disarray. He took a long moment to gaze at her, frankly taking advantage of the chance to see her naked. Nora was a beautifully made woman. She was blessed with gorgeous coloring, from her blond hair touched with red to her creamy, prone-to-blushing skin. And her figure was just as alluring. He ran a finger lightly along her arm up to her shoulder, then down the edge of one breast, to her stomach, then to her hip. He loved her hips. Just thinking about her hips aroused him. Ash always appreciated women, but this was an unusual obsession, his need for Nora and her body.

"Good morning?" she asked.

He must have woken her up with his explorations. Ash squeezed her hip slightly. "A very good morning, if it starts with you."

"You intend to start with me?" she echoed, her eyebrow raised.

"Would you like me to?" he asked, his arousal increasing.

She ran her hand up his chest. "If you don't mind."

He didn't mind teasing her to an arousal as sharp as his own. He didn't mind covering her breasts with kisses until she was moaning, and he didn't mind hearing her breathing grow ragged when he entered her.

In fact, that only thing he minded was withdrawing before he came, because spending himself on the bedsheets wasn't nearly as satisfying as it would be in her body, when he could enjoy every second of it with her.

"God damn," he hissed, when he was done.

Nora ran her fingers lightly down his back, a sensation that both soothed him and made him want to take her again, immediately.

"That feels good," he sighed. "It all felt good, darling. You're intoxicating."

"Like your drug of choice?"

"Far better."

She said, "If you feel the need again, I could distract you…again."

He smiled and shook his head. "That is entirely too appealing, Nora. How would you know whether I was truly suffering or just wanted you?"

"I wouldn't," she said. "So I'd have to rely on you being honest."

"Honest," Ash echoed. "Well, to be honest, I want to keep you here until you're entirely bored of me. But I can't. We have to return to London eventually."

She looked a little put out at the reminder. "I suppose you're right. But we don't have to travel *too* directly, do we?"

Ash kissed her again before getting out of the bed. "No, I think we ought to confuse any pursuers by taking an odd route. That might require another night or two of travel."

Nora bit her lower lip. "I can live with that."

He could too.

Chapter 20

A FEW DAYS LATER, NORA found herself in the carriage once more. Ash sat with her, and outside, Crewe drove along a route of his choosing. Some of the roads were narrow and winding, but every time he turned, they got closer to London.

The past few days had been fatiguing, for travel by carriage quickly lost its allure. The nights, however, more than made up for it. Nora's education in the bedroom was proceeding rapidly, and both she and Ash were delighted with her progress.

Though she tried not to think too deeply on it, she knew that she was wading into very dangerous waters. If she wasn't careful, this chance affair might become troublesome. Ash never hinted at his own expectations, but Nora thought it very unlikely that any private relationship between them would last beyond his involvement in the matter of the light signaling. Once they spoke to his group, the Zodiac, and sorted out the ownership of the invention to the government's satisfaction, Ash would be off on another secret task. Or so Nora imagined. She was a practical woman…she just wasn't feeling entirely practical about Ash at the moment. She'd sort out her feelings soon enough.

On the bright side, she now wore an outfit suitable for a lady. Crewe had procured it at some point during the first night on the road. Nora didn't know how or where he got a gown that fit her, and it seemed impolite to ask. She dressed in it with Ash's assistance—he was adept with ladies' clothing, she thought, suffering a little twinge of suspicion.

Then she smoothed down the fabric of the gown, a lovely, soft cotton lawn. She stifled her darker thoughts. Ash and Crewe had already done far more to rescue her than anyone else.

Eventually, after the light began to fail that day, they rode into the heart of the city. The spirit of London surrounded Nora, embraced her with its noise and chaos and its smells and its complete disregard for who she was. The sheer mass of the city and its people was a comforting veil for her. No one walking these streets knew who she was, and no one cared.

The other side of that coin was that Nora also had nowhere to go. She leaned toward Ash.

"I don't have a home anymore," Nora confessed. "Albert and I only let it from a landlord, and I know Edmund never paid more rent after Albert died. So I'm not sure where…"

"Nora, you're staying with me."

"I can't stay with you," she objected. "That's not proper at all."

"This isn't an ordinary situation," Ash said. "You don't know where your brother is, and if Edmund isn't in London already, he will be soon. It's not safe for you to stay alone. At my home, you'll be protected."

"From Edmund, perhaps. But what about my reputation? I'm a widow…though you can bet Edmund will dispute that! I can't stay at your house."

"My people are very discreet," Ash assured her. "Trust me."

"Even so." Nora threaded her gloved fingers together in her lap. Being a preternaturally gifted valet, Crewe had managed to find perfectly-sized gloves in addition to everything else. "We…we must not appear to have an intimate relationship."

"Nora." Ash shot her a look. "I said you can trust me."

She nodded slowly. "Very well then. Where do you live?"

"You'll soon see. We're almost there."

Within ten minutes, the carriage stopped at a tall brick house set a bit back from the street. The neighborhood wasn't one Nora had ever been in before, but it seemed quiet and respectable, though certainly not grand.

Ash helped her down from the carriage and walked her up the path, just as he might with any female relative.

"Mr Allander," said the man who opened the door. "Very good to see you home, sir."

Ash nodded as he stepped inside. "I shall have a guest staying with me for a while. Please see that a room is prepared for Mrs Morrison."

"I'll inform the maids, sir. Did you…"

"Ash!" a new voice interrupted from above. "You're back! How wonderful."

Nora looked up the stairway at the same moment as Ash. A stunningly dressed lady stood at the top, a smile lighting her face. Nora felt like a little mouse in comparison, with her borrowed outfit.

Ash too seemed flummoxed for a moment, watching the lady descend the steps. The folds of her gold skirts caught the candlelight in the sconces along the stairs, giving her an otherworldly glamor. Nora understood his reaction—she too was struck by the lady's beautiful clothes and mass of carefully curled dark hair.

By the time she reached the bottom of the stairs, he recovered. "Reggie."

"As ever," the lady replied, with a little smile that rounded her cheeks. She cast a curious glance at Nora. "And your traveling companion?"

"Ah. Yes. May I present Mrs Morrison." He turned to Nora, saying, "This is my…Aunt Regina. She's staying here. As well."

Nora wondered at Ash's flustered speech, which was so unlike him. Even the lady looked surprised. Nora said, "How do you do, ma'am."

"How do you do, Mrs Morrison. I am Miss Fox, since Ash seems to have forgot my full name."

"We've been on the road since very early this morning," Nora said in explanation.

"My dear, you must be exhausted," said Miss Fox, her manner warming. She gestured to someone unseen. "Show Mrs Morrison to her room. She will doubtless want to refresh herself before coming down again."

"Yes, ma'am." A maid emerged from the shadows. Regina murmured something in the maid's ear as she passed, and she nodded.

"If you'll follow me, ma'am," the maid said to Nora.

Nora climbed the steps, glancing back once to see the gold-gowned Regina directing Ash imperiously into a side parlor. Ash went, rather like a dog after his owner. Perhaps that was the way in larger families. Nora never really had a chance to find out. She was learning more in the past few days than she ever expected.

Upstairs, Nora was shown to a cheerful, blue-wallpapered room in the back of the house. The maid brought fresh, hot water to wash, and then left her to her own devices. Nora brushed her hair out slowly, thinking of the change in her circumstances and, more particularly, her changed status with Ash. Perhaps she had been foolish to sleep with him, but surely a woman was allowed to be foolish once in her life?

Nora's husband had been a good husband, in that he was kind and affectionate, rather than merely polite. He kissed her when he came home and when he left. He had enjoyed taking her out, showing her off to their small circle of friends. "My lovely little Nora," he'd called her, with pride.

He didn't come to her bedroom very often, particularly not after the first few months of their marriage. When he had come, it was always after he asked—very delicately—if she would allow him to. She nearly always said yes, save for when it was her time of the month or when she felt ill. He never pressed her, never made her feel bad for refusing him.

The times he did come to her bedroom, he treated her kindly, with affection and with apologies. She was never entirely sure what he was apologizing for, besides what was assumed to be a woman's natural distaste for the act, it being so carnal and messy and foreign.

In truth, Nora didn't mind it, despite the mess and the strangeness. She saw how much he enjoyed it, and liked that she could offer him some pleasure in her body, though it was clear that whatever connection they had, it was limited by his reticence and his respect for her ladylike upbringing. Passion was not something he offered, and it was clear that it was not something she should want.

Yet she did. Meeting Ash had sharpened her long

dormant desire, and when offered the chance, Nora acted on it. But now she was in his house. Granted, it was a house full of servants, not to mention his glamorous aunt. She would surely expect decorum, and her mere presence would prevent any bad behavior on Ash's part. Aunt Regina seemed rather a dominant force in Ash's life.

* * * *

Downstairs in the small parlor, Reggie shut the door behind her. "*Aunt?*"

"I panicked," Ash said. "I completely forgot you were staying here, and I had no idea what to say."

"Evidently. So I take it this respectable young lady has never even heard of you or me. To get straight to the point, why in God's name did you bring such a woman here? Who is she?"

"She's important," Ash said. "I met her while working on Bruce's assignment, and circumstances forced me to leave with her. For her safety," he added.

"Will she be safe here, in *this* house?"

"She's a widow, so her reputation shouldn't be completely in tatters. Especially as you're here."

"I'm hardly a suitable chaperone."

"Nora doesn't know that."

"So it's *Nora*, is it?" she asked, with an eloquent arch of her eyebrow. "How close you've grown in a short time. Are you mixing pleasure with business?"

Reggie was no fool, and she knew him well enough to read him like a book. Still, a little discretion was necessary.

"It's not what you think. Nora...Mrs Morrison, she's an inventor, and someone was exploiting her for that invention, because it's potentially very valuable. Her life would have been in danger if she'd stayed behind. I couldn't let that happen. This was the best choice."

"Oh." Reggie's pique disappeared, replaced with sympathy. "The poor woman."

"Taking her along was the best choice," Ash repeated, hearing the defensiveness in his tone. "Bruce will want to talk to her anyway, so it made sense to keep her here. She's got no family. Well, she does, but they have to be located. Until then, can you be Aunt Regina? Please?"

She sighed. "What choice have I got, since you've already named me such? You must tell your household, though, or someone may let the ugly truth slip."

"I'll take care of it. Thanks, Reggie."

"I suppose I do have to repay you for the hospitality. And this could be amusing."

"Just be kind to her. She's been through quite a bit, even if she doesn't look it. Oh, and she's literally only got the clothes on her back. Do you think…"

"Say no more." Reggie assured him. "I'll remedy that very quickly."

"Are you going out?" Ash asked, surveying her attire. "You look as though you intend to."

"I was," Reggie said. "Though perhaps Aunt Regina should stay in, like a good chaperone."

"Would you?" Ash asked. "Just for supper, and you can go out afterward. Nora would feel more comfortable with another lady in the house."

"I'm hardly a lady."

"You are to me."

Reggie smiled at that. "Very well. I'll inform your kitchen that supper for three will be needed."

Ash went to his own room to wash and change for dinner. His longtime valet Sullivan was horrified by the state of Ash's luggage. No doubt he'd chastise Crewe for it later—the Disreputable said he'd remain in Ash's house because he would likely still be needed. However, he demoted himself to footman and hostler-at-large.

"I'd have packed these things better," Sullivan groused. "Look at the wrinkles in this vest. And where's the rest of it?"

"We were in a bit of a hurry," Ash said. "Some of it's lost, I'm afraid. Doesn't matter. Not sure I want to wear those things again anyway." In fact, most of the clothes he'd taken weren't his style—they'd been selected to fulfill his government clerk persona.

Once dressed in his usual clothing, Ash felt much better. "Excellent, Sullivan. Now I've got to go collect my guest for supper."

Nora's room was on the same floor, but in the opposite corner. The door was open, and Nora was there, of course dressed in the same outfit as before.

Ash looked in the doorway. "Comfortable?"

Nora was perched on the edge of the bed, looking toward the window. She looked back over her shoulder and beamed at him. "This is a lovely room. Thank you."

"It's all yours, for as long as you need," he said. "Supper will be served shortly. Are you hungry? "

"Yes, but I haven't got anything to wear for a meal downstairs."

"We can forego the formalities just this once."

Ash walked Nora downstairs, which allowed him to be close to her only as much as the rules of civility allowed—her hand curled around his arm. He wanted more than that. But he'd promised to betray no hint of their more intimate relationship.

"Is your aunt joining us for supper?" Nora asked.

"Yes. I believe she wants to know all about you," Ash said.

"You call her Reggie?"

"Always have," he said, with complete honesty. "Or Reg, sometimes. She's...not a stickler for rules and convention." Not in the least.

"That must be why you get along with her."

"One of the reasons."

"I wish I had someone like that," Nora said wistfully. "You're very lucky."

Reggie appeared for supper in all her glory, and applied herself to being as charming as ever. One of Reggie's greatest gifts was an ability to set anyone at ease— man or woman, rich or poor. The magic worked on Nora as well. She was soon chatting away with Reggie, relating many anecdotes of her earlier life that Ash hadn't yet heard.

Nora did skip over some of the more difficult episodes, giving only a brief account of how she ended up at Grasmere House. Reggie heard much of what was left unsaid, though, and shot Nora a look of deep empathy when Nora's attention was elsewhere.

Ash mostly kept quiet, more interested in watching these two very different women interact. He was relieved that both of them seemed to like each other. He had no idea what he'd do if that wasn't the case.

On a more practical level, the supper also cemented the role of *Aunt* Regina in Nora's mind. She had no difficulty accepting Reg as an idiosyncratic but loving relative whose relationship with Ash was merely one of platonic affection. Which was true, Ash reminded himself. It had been true for years.

After dessert, Reggie excused herself to go out for the evening. "Rest tonight, dears," she said. "After travel, there's nothing better than a bed." She gave Ash a sly wink, which fortunately only he could see.

"Good advice," he said to Nora. "Shall we both go up?"

She nodded. "Yes, thank you."

He walked her to her room. At her door, Nora turned to say goodnight. Ash caught her by the waist and kissed her before she could say anything.

Her lips still had a trace of sugar from dessert on them, and she responded to the kiss instantly, her fingers curling around the lapels of his jacket as she drew him closer.

She parted her lips. Lord, he needed her. This wasn't enough. "Nora, invite me in. Please."

Her breath was hot, her interest high. But she murmured, "We agreed that no one could know about us."

"No one will," he promised. "We'll be quiet. I won't stay."

"What if I want you to stay?" Nora's eyes were wide in the dim light. Ash could barely stand to look into them, he felt so raw with need.

"Your choice," he said.

Nora's slow smile made everything worth it. "Then come in," she said.

A hour or so later, Ash held a sleepy, satisfied Nora in his arms.

One thing about sleeping with an inventor was that she was very *inventive*, and she certainly had a strong commitment to experimentation. Considering how innocent she'd been at first, her progress was astonishing. And extremely fun to be on the receiving end of.

Ash drifted in and out of sleep that night. He could count on one hand—with fingers to spare—the number of times he'd been so enamored with a woman that he couldn't bear to leave her to sleep alone. Each of those times paled in comparison to this.

You're exaggerating because this is new, he warned himself. Yet even as he tried to rationalize his feelings, he knew that Nora was different from all the rest. Every time he saw her, he wanted to be closer to her, to have her smile at him, to have her look at him in that way that made him feel human.

With Nora at his side, Ash could step out of the world he'd felt so caught in. He'd have a reason to try, and he'd have an anchor to stop him from drifting back.

Obviously, he couldn't just propose to her. Not with all the madness they were currently embroiled in. They had to inform the Zodiac, catch her false husband, find her family, and resolve her legal status as a widow. Not to mention that Ash would surely need to prove himself reformed in the eyes of the world, and more specifically Nora's older brother, whenever they found him. All that would take time.

Ash didn't want to think of all that tonight, however. Now, he only wanted to be with Nora, and forget all the things that brought them together. Nora lay half-draped across him, her head on his chest. He looked down at her face, the features smooth with sleep.

Well, not quite smooth. He frowned, noticing her eyelids twitching, as if she were caught in an upsetting dream. Ash pushed her hair back and bent to kiss her forehead.

She half-woke. "Ash? Where are we?"

"Home. Together."

"Ah. Good." She closed her eyes again.

Ash held her a little tighter. He was lost. He wasn't quite sure when it happened, but he was now long past any point where he could walk away from Nora.

Chapter 21

DISCRETION FORCED ASH TO LEAVE Nora's room in the dead of night. He returned to his own room, where the bed was horribly cold and lonely. He fell asleep wishing he'd remained with Nora.

The next morning, Ash was woken by a dour-faced Sullivan, who announced that his brother waited downstairs.

"What time is it?" Ash asked.

"Half past eight, sir." The valet didn't bother to hide his disapproval over the absurd hour. No one called on anyone so early in the day, even family.

"Dear God." Ash blinked the sleep out of his eyes. "Well, he won't go away. Help me get ready."

A quarter hour later, Ash was dressed and ambulatory, though his head still felt clogged due to the short time he'd actually slept.

Bruce was waiting impatiently in the parlor, accompanied by a young woman Ash had never seen before. August sunlight streamed in through the east-facing windows, filtered by the green leaves of the trees directly outside. The shifting, dappled greenish light made the room look as if it was underwater for a moment, and Ash simply stood there, struck by the fancy.

"What's wrong with you?" Bruce asked, on hearing him enter.

"Never go in here at this hour," Ash said. "Looks completely different in the morning."

Bruce shook his head. "I'm surprised you know what morning is."

"Oh, please," Ash said. "Don't act as though I'm a complete libertine. I've seen several mornings, usually when I don't sleep the night before."

"How does that disprove the libertine theory?"

"It doesn't. I just don't want you to *act* as though I am. How did you know I was back in London?"

"Your Disreputable sent word immediately. I came as soon as I could."

"Damn Crewe." Ash then looked over to the young lady. "I don't believe I've had the pleasure."

"I am Miss Chattan," she said. "Please think of me as a simple amanuensis for the Zodiac."

The girl had eyes sharp as a cat, and didn't look like a simple anything, but Ash knew better than to argue the point.

Instead, he gave a brief account of what he'd discovered while at Grasmere House. He explained the basics of the light signaling, the tangle of the twin brothers, and the added confusion of Isabelle Kingfisher.

He finished with high praise for the inventor of the whole thing, pointing out that even if Edmund Morrison got clean away, the Zodiac would still be able to bring the details of a much-needed communication method that could possibly save thousands of lives during the course of a war.

The two others listened carefully, sometimes asking questions. Miss Chattan recorded most of what Ash said in a little notebook.

He also described watching the messages being sent with light. That got both Chattan and Bruce excited.

"What sort of messages?" Chattan asked. "What subjects were they on? Any numbers? Were they coded?"

"I don't know," Ash told her. "Please remember that I'm not one of you."

"Crewe said you brought a witness along," Bruce said at the end. "Who is he?"

"She. Elanora Morrison. She knows all the details of the work, and she has a remarkable memory for details. For everything, in fact. She'll know all the messages. "

"Wait." Bruce said, "You kidnapped the wife of the man you were sent to investigate?"

Ash snapped, "Christ, she was in danger. What should I have done? Leave her?"

"Yes."

Ash stared at his brother for a long moment. "You're serious? You'd have left someone to die?"

"The idea of clandestine work is to keep agents hidden, Ash. That's common sense. You should have known better."

Ash reminded his brother, "If you wanted a trained spy to do your spying, then you should have found one. I'm sorry I'm not as much of a selfish, cold-hearted bastard as you seem to think I am. The lady was in danger, and I wasn't going to leave her."

"How noble."

"Even I can occasionally act like a gentleman. Speaking of that, don't talk about me or my past. Particularly not in front of Mrs Morrison."

"She doesn't know your reputation?"

"You crafted me a new identity, remember? She knows my real name now, but it means nothing to her. I aim to keep it that way."

"Wise. Well, let's find out what she knows."

"Now?" Ash frowned, but he knew when Bruce got in a mood, he was implacable until he attained whatever it was he wanted. "It's nine in the morning."

"Wake her up."

"Not likely." The voice was Regina's. She strolled into the room. Her day dress, while technically appropriate, was little more than a wrapper, and Ash suspected she chose it deliberately to make the guests uncomfortable.

"My lord," Reggie said to Bruce. Her tone sounded much more sarcastic than usual. "What brings you here at such a scandalous hour? The lady you're so interested in is surely unconscious."

Bruce actually took a step back. "What is this? Has she made you into her watchdogs?"

Reggie didn't budge. She was likely the only woman in all of London who could stand toe to toe with Lord Forester and not back down. "Never mind my motives, my lord. You can wait to meet her."

"It is a matter of some importance, Miss Fox." The young lady spoke for the first time in a while.

"How do you know her name?" Ash asked Chattan.

"I know many things, Mr Allander, including how to keep a secret. So the sooner your brother and I can speak to the witness, the sooner we can determine if we ever need to speak to her again. You do want us out of your life, correct?" As she spoke, Chattan stared at him, unblinking. "It's not as if you're interested in continuing your association with the Zodiac. You were quite clear you had no desire to actually join us as an agent."

Before Ash could respond to that, a new voice broke in.

"I don't understand."

He turned to see Nora there, looking perfect and puzzled. She scanned each of them in turn, her gaze falling on Ash last.

Her eyes narrowed. "You told me I could trust you."

Chapter 22

NORA WOKE UP ON HEARING voices in the corridor—first a servant, then Ash, and later Regina. She got up and dressed hurriedly, tucking her hair into a knot. Her wardrobe still consisted of only the one gown. Luckily, the simple style was in vogue, and she thought she looked presentable. Then Nora went downstairs, following the sound of people talking, thinking that any commotion must somehow involve her presence in the house.

In the sunlit parlor, no fewer than four people were arguing. And the subject indeed seemed to be Nora. She was about to step in and announce herself when she heard the unfamiliar female voice say quite clearly that Ash wasn't a member of the Zodiac.

A little chill ran down her spine. Had Ash lied to her? Who were these people discussing her situation?

"I don't understand," she said out loud. She walked into the parlor, studying each person. Regina looked upset, possibly just because she was awake at this hour. Nora surveyed the other woman next. She was unassuming, and rather messily attired, with equally unkempt ash blonde hair. Perhaps she too had been hounded out of bed. The man next to her was both taller and broader than Ash, and gave the air of someone who always got what he wanted. Nora distrusted him on sight.

Then there was Ash, staring at her in chagrin.

"You told me I could trust you," Nora said. "You said you were part of this organization. Are you an agent of this group or not?"

"Yes," said the tall man, just as the messy-haired woman said, "No."

Ash glanced at the pair, clearly annoyed. "At least agree among yourselves, would you?" He turned back to Nora. "It's a bit complicated. I was requested to go to Grasmere House, just as I told you. And it was the Zodiac that sent me. But I'm not a regular agent—it was more in the way of a favor."

"A favor? You became a spy as a *favor*? To who?"

The tall man bowed slightly. "Lord Forester, at your service."

Nora blinked. This hulk of a man was a lord? Well, that explained the air of privilege about him. "My lord," she responded, with formulaic politeness. "I am Elanora Wells Morrison."

"Mrs Morrison." He gave a nod, then gestured to the other woman. "This is Miss Chattan. She is…" He trailed off.

"I assist in the running of the Zodiac," the young lady said crisply. "A group of which your host Mr Allander is not formally a part, though he did act on our behalf. We regret imposing on you so early in the day."

"Do you," Nora said quietly, watching her. They were likely around the same age and station. Miss Chattan's clothing was well made, but rather plain. She didn't dress like a servant, but neither was she gowned like a lady. The closest comparison Nora could make was that of a schoolmistress, or perhaps a governess. There was something no-nonsense about Miss Chattan.

"We do," Miss Chattan said. "But you can understand that we'd like to hear the details of your story."

"Has Mr Allander not shared that already? I told him how the light signaling works."

"But you did not tell him the content of the messages."

"The content of the messages?" Nora asked warily.

"He says you have a gift for memory."

Nora looked at Ash, whose expression turned distinctly guilty.

"You told them." A familiar feeling of betrayal knifed through her.

"I mentioned it," he muttered. "Purely to explain… never mind." He turned away and walked toward the window.

"He explained about your memory, and your confinement for madness," Chattan went on.

"I was confined because someone wished to confine me," she said hotly, "not because I was mad."

"No one here could think that, dear," Regina said. Her tone was confident, but Nora noticed the glance between Chattan and Forester and knew that her sanity was certainly in question.

"Can you remember any of the messages?" Lord Forester asked at last.

"Of course." Nora closed her eyes briefly, summoning the memory of the latest one sent before Ash came to the house. "I remember all of them."

"Excellent. Can you share them?"

"I could, but I'm not at all sure I wish to."

"Beg pardon?" Miss Chattan asked.

"I don't know very much about the Zodiac, and it seems I know even less than I thought. I don't care for sharing my secrets unwisely, which I suppose I've already done." She shot another look at Ash.

She felt the anxiety tightening her muscles, speeding her heart. She didn't know any of these people, and Ash, by his own admission, was hardly connected to them. All Nora knew of spies was that the work was considered dirty and brutal, something the upper classes generally disdained. So who were these people, truly? Who was to say they would let her go once she told them what she knew? Wouldn't it be prudent, from their perspective, to silence her after she shared her knowledge?

"If Morrison was sending messages to unknown ships, as Ashley described," Lord Forester said, "then we have to assume it wasn't just a test. He had a reason for sending those particular messages."

"That's a large assumption, my lord," Nora said slowly. "Edmund told me that the messages he came up with were deliberately pointless. He was extremely concerned that someone would notice the signals and start to pay attention. So perhaps what I would tell you would simply be a waste of time."

"Tell us, and we'll decide if the information is valuable or not." Lord Forester stepped up to her. "There are enough sane people in the Zodiac to do that."

"Watch your language," Ash snapped. "She's not insane."

"Then she'll understand that the most intelligent course of action is to share what she knows," Forester countered.

"Convenient that the most intelligent course of action is the one that benefits you," Ash said.

"It benefits everyone," Forester said. "Or at least

everyone in Britain who wants the country to remain British."

"Don't drag patriotism into this discussion. All of us here want the same thing."

"Then let the lady prove it by cooperating." Forester pointed to Nora, but didn't look at her. "It's a simple decision."

Ash rolled his eyes. "So if she refuses to do as you order, it's a sign of either insanity or defection?"

"What other reason could there be?"

Nora raised her hand to get the men's attention, but both were too involved to notice.

"Not everything is as simple as you seem to think, *my lord*." Ash spat the last two words out with particular vitriol. "But then, not everyone lives with your advantages."

Forester narrowed his eyes. "You chose your life."

"Keep my life out of this," Ash hissed. "This discussion is about Mrs Morrison."

"Then let's hear what she knows."

"No!" Nora burst out. "Are none of you listening? You seem to think I'm some sort of pit to be mined, shovel by shovel till you've got your gold. But it's not so simple as that. Nor do I see the wisdom in offering up the one piece of useful information I still have."

"You don't have to tell them now," Ash said to her. "Or ever."

"Yes she does," the taller man said. "That's why we're here, and I don't have time to coddle the lady. The sooner we hear about these messages, the sooner we decide if we need to take action."

"And what of me?" Nora asked. She didn't look directly at the man, fearing his response. "What of me once I say what I know? That doesn't much matter, does it?"

"You're free to do as you like afterward," Forester

responded indifferently.

"No. I'm not, and that's the problem." Nora shook her head. "If you'll excuse me, I'll be upstairs in the guest room. You all can do what you like, but I don't know you, and I *don't* trust you. Any of you!"

With that declaration, she fled upstairs.

* * * *

Ash watched Nora run from the room. He wanted nothing more than to run after her, to explain what had happened. But he couldn't. Not while Bruce was occupying his house.

"Well, that was a stunning example of persuasion," Ash said to his brother. "I know why I'm not a member of the Zodiac, but perhaps Miss Chattan and her superiors should review your credentials, too."

Bruce shook his head, rubbing the back of his neck with one hand. "All I wanted is the lady's information. You had to go play devil's advocate, and make a simple conversation into something else entirely."

"You can't just storm into a situation and take over, Bruce!" Ash said. "You barely met her before you began to interrogate her."

"Your account suggests that she knows something important. We need to hear what it is. Also, why was this Mrs Kingfisher woman at the house? If she set a fire to destroy evidence of Morrison's work, it implies she has a motive. If she's a spy, who is she working for?"

"Do regimes hire women as professional spies?"

"It's happened before." An odd little smile crossed Bruce's face.

"I'm not saying it would be a bad idea," Ash clarified. "I just don't picture government bureaucrats as that forward thinking."

"Espionage is a very practical discipline. People do what's necessary, regardless of social convention."

"So by that logic, I was right to take Mrs Morrison away," Ash pointed out.

"Very well," his brother admitted. "You were right to do as you did."

"Your trust in my judgment is so reassuring," Ash muttered. He pictured the bottle of laudanum in his room upstairs. He could just walk up, drink some down, and none of this would matter…

"I thought you spirited her away for personal reasons," Bruce was saying. "But now that I have seen her, I apologize. She's not your sort at all."

"My sort?" asked Ash. "You mean the bored wife of a lord, looking for a dalliance to pad out her dull life?"

"Isn't that your type?"

Ash said, "For a spy, you certainly rely too much on old gossip." And Bruce was blind for thinking that Nora was somehow not desirable. Granted, she wasn't exactly turned out for show, but how could anyone look at her and think she was plain, or dull?

"Can we get back to the main issue?" Reggie interjected. "Your primary objective ought to be regaining the trust of Elanora Morrison."

Ash looked over at Miss Chattan. "You should have recruited Reggie."

"What makes you think we didn't try?" Chattan replied.

"I want nothing to do with all that," Reggie said. "I've enough excitement in my life. As a friend, however, I do suggest you three work out your next steps to convince our Nora to cooperate, *after* she has a few moments of peace and quiet. From what little I've seen, she's an intelligent woman. She'll keep her secret to herself unless you offer something she needs."

Reggie looked at Ash as she spoke, and he looked at the floor. If only he could offer Nora something she needed.

The group discussed the situation again, this time with Bruce and Chattan asking many more details of Ash's experience.

"This is all damned confusing," Bruce muttered at last. "Everyone's got another name they're using, or a family they're exploiting, or a sibling they're hiding. Why can't anyone in this mess be an only child?"

"I'm an orphan," Reggie said coolly. "Does that in any way simplify things for you, my lord?"

"Apologies, Miss Fox." Bruce had the grace to look abashed. "That's not what I meant."

Ash happened to glance over at Miss Chattan. Suddenly curious, he asked, "Have you got hidden siblings?"

Chattan raised one eyebrow. "I'd prefer to leave my family out of this, and I'm quite certain my family would prefer it as well."

An interesting evasion, Ash thought. But his real concern was Nora, sitting upstairs somewhere, probably convinced she was being used just as she was before.

"I should go talk to her," he said suddenly.

The others looked at him. His words had nothing to do with whatever they'd been discussing.

"Mrs Morrison, you mean," Reggie said at last. "Let her be for a little while, Ash. When she's ready, she'll return."

* * * *

Nora fled to her room and locked the door behind her.

How ironic! She spent a year trying to escape confinement, yet now the first thing she did was confine herself. What was it in human nature that made people do exactly the thing they proclaimed to never want to do again?

She was too disturbed to think properly at first, but the conversation downstairs made her consider the messages once more. Nora summoned them all up in her mind—it was easy to line them up in her brain, all one after another, just like notes on a clerk's desk.

As she told Ash before, the most recent ones were the oddest:

GIRL TOY WORTH SEA BAIT

SEABIRD FOUND NEST WATCH TOY WAIT

BIRD SEE TOY MARKINGS KNOWN

GET HER SON TOOL SOON FIREBIRD FLY NORTH

SHIP GO EMPTY BIRD WILL STAY NEST TWO MISS ONE

RECEIVED ALLE

BIRD WATCH AT PAUL WORTH PATH DAWN BIRD BREAK TOY END

She puzzled over them, trying to make sense of any word or phrase. The *BIRD* seemed important, but what was the *TOY*? And was *BAIT* correct? Or did Morrison signal that one wrongly, considering *WAIT* was also a word in the next message?

"There's a seabird, and a firebird, and someone's bird-watching with Paul," she whispered. "Who's Paul?" Morrison never mentioned anyone by that name.

Then a knock sounded at the door, breaking her concentration.

"Ma'am?" a voice called. "I work here in the house. May I enter?"

"Are you alone?" Nora called.

"Yes, ma'am."

Nora opened the door.

A maid in a freshly starched uniform curtsied to her. "Name of Judith Markby, ma'am. Apologies for not being here yesterday evening, but your arrival was unexpected and I was out of the house. I'm to assist you in whatever way you need."

"Am I to call you Markby?"

"Oh, I'm not a lady's maid," the other demurred. "Judith will do."

"Very well, Judith. What I need at the moment is something to eat. I missed breakfast and I don't want to encounter anyone downstairs at the moment. I'm not feeling sociable."

"Easily managed, ma'am."

Judith left and soon appeared again, bearing a tray laden with enough food for several days of confinement. Nora attacked the plates of raisin buns, creamy cheese, and cut fruit, and drank her tea as though she'd gone thirsty for days.

While she ate, Judith moved around the room, unpacking a trunk that appeared as if from nowhere. It contained several gowns in Nora's size, along with all the accoutrements to go with them. Nora watched with growing surprise at the number of gloves and shoes and ribbons and stockings that spilled out of the trunk. "Who is responsible for all this?"

"Mr Allander ordered these to be gathered for you last night, ma'am. And his…aunt offered more precise instructions as to your needs. There's only one evening gown, and a few day dresses, a nightrail, and some pieces

I could employ any time of day. These two white gowns could do for afternoon, I think, with the right accessories."

"This is far too extravagant," Nora said nervously. "I can't repay this."

"Gifts need not be paid for, ma'am," Judith said. "Mr Allander and Miss Fox were clear on that point."

Nora sighed. How could she object to kindness? Even if she wasn't sure exactly what Ash was when it came to the Zodiac, Nora had to admit that he'd always been good to her. Her pique softened considerably, and by the time she was brave enough to leave the room and seek out an explanation, her curiosity was once again in the forefront.

However, she didn't find Ash. When she got to the parlor, only Regina was there.

"I'm sorry for running out earlier," Nora said. "I made a bad impression."

"Don't apologize. Who could be prepared for such a conversation?" The other woman rose from her seat and moved through the room. Regina Fox possessed a liquid grace, making every step and gesture look elegant and refined.

"You picked out my dresses, didn't you?" Nora asked. "The ones Judith brought up. They're all perfect."

"I'm glad to hear it, dear. No woman should be without a suitable wardrobe. It is our primary shield and weapon in this war we call society."

"Thank you doubly, then. And Ash…that is, Mr Allander, too. Is he here?"

"The house has emptied, except for me," Reggie said. "Would you care for a turn in the garden? I expect you don't like looking at walls for hours on end."

No, she did not. "Yes, that sounds lovely."

The garden behind the house was not extensive, but it

was suitable for a "turn," and the two ladies walked along a white gravel path dividing well-tended beds of flowers and blowsy, late summer greenery.

"I suppose he's given up on me, after my behavior this morning," Nora commented, thinking of Ash's expression from earlier in the day. "Though he could have warned me!"

"You're being a little hard on Ash," Reggie said. "He was just as surprised by the early visit as you were. I'm quite certain they didn't mean to ask you for your help in the way they did—everything got a bit heated."

"That's one word for it. Do you know about all this? This Zodiac?"

"Just enough to wish I'd never heard of it. But Bruce is deep into it, and he dragged Ash in as well…with the best of intentions, I'm sure."

"Who's Bruce?"

Regina said, "Lord Forester's given name is Bruce."

"Why would he drag Mr Allander into it? What hold has he got over him?"

"They're brothers." She sighed.

"Brothers?" Nora gasped. "Ash is really brothers with that horrid man from this morning? Wait, doesn't that make Lord Forester your nephew as well?"

Regina winced. "Oh, mercy."

"Sorry. Perhaps you don't like to think of it. He was very rude, lord or not!"

"He's not the most polished of men," Regina admitted. "Bruce is…Bruce. Ash got all the charm."

"He is charming," Nora admitted, with a blush. "I'm surprised he never married." In fact, Nora was intensely curious as to what other women were in his life. "Do you happen to know why?"

Reggie glanced sideways at her. "Did Ash ever tell

you that he was once a seminary student?"

"Very briefly. He didn't seem happy about it."

"Second sons often aim for the clergy, but Ash wasn't just looking for a career. He had a vocation. He was deeply interested in matters of the spirit, and the nature of the divine."

"He's never….well, he doesn't seem like he'd be…"

"He doesn't look like the typical country vicar, I grant you, and of course, he didn't follow that path in the end. Fate often chooses our paths for us. But he was sincere in his interest. It takes a certain type of woman to truly capture his attention. One who is as passionate and inquisitive as he is."

"Oh," Nora said. The image of such a woman came to her mind….but it didn't resemble anything she saw in the mirror. Ash's ideal would have to be as beautiful as he was handsome, perhaps some glamorous creature with raven hair. "He'll find her one day."

"When he finds her," Reggie said, "he certainly will do his best to pursue her. She will likely come to see things his way—Ash understands women. More than most men."

"Is it because he was in training for the church that he's so understanding?"

Regina coughed, then said, "Ah…perhaps. I couldn't say."

"Was he like that before? You're his aunt, so you must have known him before and after."

The other lady stood still for a long moment. "I really only got to know him after he'd ended his studies. He seemed so young then," she added, her voice faraway and wistful. "But so…"

"What was he?"

"Hungry. Hungry for everything that most people

don't think about. Knowledge. Wisdom. An understanding of how the world truly works."

"Like a natural scientist."

Regina smiled. "Not exactly. Not like you, dear. His gifts lie elsewhere."

"As a spy?" Nora said.

Regina stopped walking and turned to face Nora. "You have been dancing around your real question, Nora. What do you wish to know?"

Nora bit her lip. "May I ask it plainly, with no offense taken?"

"Please."

"Can I trust him?"

Reggie sighed. "I do not pretend to know Ash's motives. No one can truly see into the soul of another, no matter how many poets would like us to believe so. But Ash means well. Whatever he may do, he means well. If you remember anything about Ash, remember that."

"I shall. Thank you."

"You'll get your chance to speak to him directly very soon." Reggie nodded toward the French doors to the house. Ash stood, framed by the doorway. He lifted one hand in greeting.

"Would you ask him to join me?" Nora asked. "I want to stay outside for a little while."

"Certainly, dear."

Nora sank to a nearby bench that was strategically placed below a birch tree, near some aromatic herbs that were growing rampant in the summer heat. She noted again Regina's graceful movements as she walked toward Ash. The two conferred in voices too low for Nora to hear at that distance. Regina put a hand on his shoulder for a moment, then disappeared into the dimness of the house, while Ash strode to Nora.

If he was upset by that morning, it didn't show in his appearance. He was dressed simply, like any other gentleman, but on him, the clothes all seemed to fit better than usual, and to convey something of Ash's insouciant attitude.

When he reached her, he bowed. "I'm glad to see you out here," he said. There was a seriousness underlying his easy words. Had he thought she'd still be locked in her room?

Nora recalled one thing that Ash should be contrite about. "You told them about my memory."

He winced a bit, then nodded. "It came up as I was telling the basics of my experiences with Edmund Morrison and the house and you. I didn't set out to do it. But you never said it was more secret than anything else."

"I didn't think I had to! Don't you remember where we were when I told you? Did you think that was a casual conversation? What *else* did you tell them? Did you mention that we slept together?"

"No." Ash sat next to her on the bench, leaning over to take her hand. "No, Nora. Of course not. Christ."

"Don't swear like that. I believe you."

"Thank you."

"I was upset," she said, in explanation. "I didn't know what to think."

"Forester is perennially brusque. If you thought this morning was bad, you don't want to catch him when he's truly annoyed."

"I assume you've seen that, since he's your brother."

"Ah. Reggie told you. Yes, we're brothers. Hard to picture, isn't it?"

Nora looked more carefully at Ash, trying to compare his face to the man she met that morning. "Your coloring is like his, and there's something around the eyes. But no one would guess it if they weren't told to look for a resemblance."

"Definitely not twins," Ash said. "Bruce is five years older, and as unlike me in personality as in looks. And of course, I'm far more handsome," he added, reverting to humor.

"Yet you both have the same ideals," Nora ventured, "because you both undertake work for the Zodiac."

"*He* does so. I only did a favor for him." Ash looked at her, his expression clouded. "I should have told you, but I needed you to trust me. Would you have confided anything in me if I'd told you I'd virtually no experience of gathering intelligence, or of rescuing very lovely maidens?" He added the last with a little smile, one that begged her forgiveness.

"I don't know what I would have done, Ash. But in the future, will you please not conceal such things? It's important."

He looked down at the ground for a long moment, then said, in a different tone, "What's important, Nora, is your memory. Not me, or anything about me. You're the one with the gift."

"That's not a *gift*," she said. "You think I want to remember some of the things I've got in my head? Do you know what I'd do to forget them? But I can't. I've tried. But they're all still there. Maybe if I took a dose of your particular indulgence…"

"No, don't do that," Ash said hurriedly.

"You said it takes you away."

"Only for a while. And you can never be sure if the *away* it takes you to is a place you want to be. Don't muddle up your mind, Nora."

"You do it to your mind."

"I regret it afterward. Every time."

"Then why don't you stop?"

"Because I'm not strong enough," he said bitterly.

Remorse struck her. "I didn't mean to…"

"What? Speak the truth? At least someone is. Not that anyone really knows about my little habit. Just you, actually."

"Why don't you go to your brother? Wouldn't he help you?"

"I'd rather die," Ash said. "Bruce has no weaknesses, and therefore no tolerance for those who do."

Nora leaned over to catch his gaze. "I'd like to help you, then."

"It's my problem, Nora. Not yours. I'll solve it in time."

"Ash, you can't solve a problem if you don't understand its origins. If you talk to me, tell me about your life…"

He cut her off with a kiss. Nora gasped when his lips touched hers, suddenly lost in the purely physical sensations.

When he pulled back, Ash said, "The fact that you offered is enough. But it doesn't matter now. What matters is your mind. Your knowledge of those messages."

"You're going to convince me that I should share them with the Zodiac?" Nora asked, still experiencing the aftereffects of his touch.

He shook his head. "You have your reasons not to, and they're sound. No one has the right to invade your mind, or pry something out of you. I'm sorry that the Zodiac asked for your knowledge that way. I swear I didn't know they would."

"You don't blame me?"

"No, I don't blame you at all. But I do think they're correct—the messages might be more important than you think. If you don't want to share them, though, I'll simply get them another way."

She frowned. "How?"

"I'll find Morrison. Or Isabelle Kingfisher. They know the content of the messages too, and I have no compunction about getting the information from them." Ash added, "I have flexible morals."

"Be careful," Nora said, anxious for him. "I know Mrs Kingfisher set those fires, when it meant people could have died. Who knows what else she's capable of?"

"I'm capable of quite a lot myself."

Nora said, "This is surely different. What if it comes to violence?"

"I'm good with a gun and better with a blade. Don't worry about me."

"Oh, indeed. When was the last time you picked up a sword?" Nora asked skeptically.

"A few weeks, my Lady Doubt. I've been busy, remember. But as it happens, I'm going to meet my fencing master tomorrow. I like to stay sharp…so to speak."

Nora sighed. "I hope you're a better fencer than comedian."

"Much better. And while I'm out, you should relax. Take Judith with you if you want to go for a ride or a stroll—you're not a prisoner here. Promise me you'll be careful."

"I promise, if you do the same."

"Done." Ash took her hand up to his lips and kissed her fingers. "You give me a reason to make promises, love."

Nora felt warm down to her toes.

Chapter 23

AS HE SAID, ASH DID go to pay a long overdue visit the fencing master Salvator Caizo, an Italian who had set up his own *salle* in London, having decided that the island of Britain was woefully lacking in quality education. Now somewhere around fifty years old, with iron-grey hair, Caizo himself had dozens of exploits attached to his name, some of which were very dark indeed and spoken of only in hushed tones—well outside his earshot. Caizo never confirmed or denied such stories, including an accusation of a duel that was in essence a murder, because Caizo was so much more skilled than the one he challenged. The otherwise voluble, affable Italian maintained a strict silence regarding his past. That was one of the reasons Ash chose him as a teacher. He felt a certain kinship with anyone who had so many rumors attached to his name.

The *salle* was nearly empty that day. Caizo greeted Ash with his customary exuberance. "Allander, I have not seen you in weeks! I feared the worst for you, though I've heard nothing, nothing of a duel involving you. And I hear of them all."

Ash grinned as he returned the master's bone crushing embrace. "Not to worry, maestro. No duels. I was called away from the city unexpectedly, that's all."

"Ah, that's all? You do not say what called you away. A lady, I think. You show her your *botta segreta*, eh?" Caizo laughed at his own innuendo, already waving a hand to prevent Ash from retorting. "No, no. A man says nothing when it is about *la donna della sua vita*. That is good."

Ash shook his head. "Are we going to talk about not talking about women? Or are you going to teach me something?"

"Teach you what? You are my best student. So many of these young men, they think they come here a dozen times and they know everything. Fools. Practice. Practice. Practice. That is the way." Caizo huffed in frustration at such students, though he never refused their money.

"Then let's practice," Ash said. "You can show me how rusty I've grown."

A little while later, Ash was dressed in his usual fencing uniform of plain pants and a white shirt closely tailored to his body, since billows could easily catch a blade and make one of the fencers stumble. He pulled his own practice sword off the wall where he stored it.

Caizo did not go easy on him. Though it left Ash tired, sweating, and profusely apologetic that he neglected his lessons, he was grateful. He needed the structured action of the *salle*. He liked the give and take of a bout, and the exertion was tiring but not exhausting. It was probably not a coincidence that the days Ash attended the *salle* were followed by nights when he rarely felt the need for laudanum.

Caizo kept him moving and on his toes through the practice session. He was a stringent but fair master, always striving to improve his students' performance. It was good business, too. Ash won duels, and everyone knew Caizo was his teacher. The Italian had every interest in making sure Ash was in top form.

The practice of fencing always helped Ash focus his mind—an important skill when an opponent was trying to impale you. The foils used in practice were buttoned, and therefore not dangerously sharp. Still, no fencer wanted to be touched by one. It was a matter of pride.

A couple hours later, they finally halted.

"Not bad," Caizo declared, which was high praise from him. "You didn't go soft while you were away. Now, listen, Allander. You stay away from evil women, hear? They steal your strength."

"What about good women?" Ash asked.

"Ah, you find a good woman, you keep her, for they are rarer than diamonds, better than gold! Speaking of gold, by the way, how is she, your darling Signorina Volpe?"

"Miss Fox is quite well. She's staying with me, as a matter of fact."

Caizo sighed rapturously. "What a creature! You tell her I ask after her. She has my heart, you know. And my sword. I will die for her, just to know she would lay a flower on my tomb."

"I'll tell her," Ash promised, amused. Caizo was yet another of Reggie's conquests, and Caizo had never done more than dance with her a few times. He always swore he would defend her name in any duel someone dared to call—and no one ever had.

Ash promised once again that he would be back soon. Caizo might forgive one lapse, but Ash knew that the master valued consistent practice about all else.

* * * *

Ash returned home in the afternoon, feeling somewhat more himself. He got as far as his foyer when Crewe came through the passageway from the kitchen and the servants' area.

"Sir, we've found the doctor who signed the certificate that Edmund Morrison wanted."

"Already? That was fast."

"He has a practice here in London." Crewe led Ash to a small room on the ground floor, where a paper sat on a table. Crewe offered it for inspection, adding, "This is a copy of the doctor's copy. He remembers the conversation with Mr Morrison and is confident in his diagnosis."

Ash frowned, looking the paper over. "How could he ever think Nora is mad? Eccentric, maybe, but she's as sane as anyone else. No one could speak to her and think she's otherwise."

"Well, that's the thing, sir. The doctor never spoke to her."

"What?"

"He made the diagnosis and filled out the certificate based on the testimony of her husband."

Ash was appalled. "How is that valid?"

"It's not uncommon," Crewe said. "At least, according to what I hear. The family is assumed to know the situation best. A doctor is a stranger."

"Wait," Ash said, tapping a name written at the top. "He used the word of the husband, written here as Albert Morrison. But if it was Edmund who actually spoke to him, the certificate can't be worth anything."

"How would the doctor know?" Crewe shrugged. "It not his responsibility to ascertain whether a person is who they claim to be. The certificate is dated, though. Last

August."

"Nora was confined in the house by then. So it *was* Edmund Morrison. Her real husband was already dead."

"Hard to prove without a body. The evidence of a madwoman won't get heard in court."

"The evidence of a wife against her supposed husband won't get heard either," Ash said. "Damn. Edmund's been clever. He's got what he needs to win a legal battle, and *I* can't counter the claim. I have no standing. Nora has no legal recourse unless she can *prove* he's not Albert Morrison beforehand."

"What if she gets him to say it…in a place with witnesses?" Crewe suggested.

"He'll never admit to it. His whole scheme depends on him stepping into his brother's place." Ash frowned. "We have to find Nora's brother. He is family, and does have standing."

Crewe said, "He could have a doctor pronounce Nora sane. That would at least make a judge consider, right?"

Ash shook his head. "Unless we got the doctor to falsify the date, the other certificate is older. So a judge might still conclude that Nora was incapacitated at that time, and therefore her testimony would be unreliable."

The servant took a few energetic steps around the room. "Sounds to me as if another approach would be more effective. Find where Edmund's hiding and send a few Disreputables to scare him into behaving."

"A tempting thought," Ash said. "But this business is already shadowy enough. We can't add more threats to it. Nora needs to end this in an above board and legally correct way."

"So we keep looking for the brother's whereabouts," Crewe said, accepting the unspoken request. "Yes, sir."

"Good luck," Ash said. "And good work so far. I've

no doubt you'll track him down."

He let Crewe go, and soon found Reggie in a sunny sitting room on the second floor. She was reading a book, but put it aside when he entered.

"Good afternoon, nephew," she said, with a little smirk. "How did you spend your day?"

"Little fencing earlier. Caizo sends his regards," he added slyly.

"That man!" Reggie laughed. "Don't ever tell him I secretly find him adorable."

"Not the word I'd use," Ash said, ruefully rubbing at one shoulder. "He was not pleased at my extended absence."

"You can't have fenced all day. What else?"

"Some investigation into Mr Morrison."

"For the benefit of the Zodiac?" she asked. "Or Nora?"

He frowned. "Couldn't it be for both?"

"It could, but one of those things motivates you more than the other. Which is it? Or should I say, who is it?"

Ash sat down beside Reggie. "Say what you're thinking, Reg."

"She's in love with you."

"Blunt enough," he muttered. "What makes you think that?"

"I can read a woman's face as well as anyone." Reggie shot him a look. "She may not even tell herself yet, but it's true. You need to take care. Don't hurt her."

"I've no intention of hurting anyone," Ash said. "Least of all Nora."

"Intentions are all well and good, but people do tend to get hurt around you, Ash. You ruin women. It's your special gift."

"Nora is different."

Before Reggie could press him further, Crewe knocked and stepped into the room. "Excuse me, but there's a caller in the foyer. Looks…rather out of place."

Ash was instantly suspicious. "How out of place?" Had Edmund discovered that Nora was staying in his house? "Does he sound like trouble?"

The servant made a face. "He sounds American—judge that how you will. He would know how to handle himself in a fight, I'd wager. But I don't think he's part of the business on the coast."

"Why not?"

"He's asking to speak with Miss Fox."

"You should have opened with that, Crewe," Reggie said. "What's his name?"

"He didn't have a card, but he gave his name as Philemon Greene," Crewe said, very precisely.

"You know him?" Ash asked her.

She shook her head. "A mystery to me. Perhaps an admirer, seeking closer acquaintance." She had plenty of those.

"If that's so, why the hell would he call at *my* home?" Ash asked. He was still suspicious that the stranger was involved with Nora's enemies.

"Maybe he couldn't wait any longer. After all, I have been raiding your sideboard here for weeks."

"Will you see him, ma'am?" Crewe asked. "I've put him in the parlor to wait."

"Let me join you," Ash said to her.

"You think I'm unable to handle myself?" Reggie shot him a look, saucy and confident.

"Humor me, Reg. As a friend."

"Well, in that case I accept."

They went down together to the parlor.

The stranger was standing at the bookcase, his head

tilted nearly sideways as he read the spines of Ash's books. He did look out of place, from his wardrobe alone. There was something odd about the cut of the clothing, from the hem of the pant to the short collar of the jacket, both of which were unornamented rusty black. He turned on hearing footsteps, revealing a crisp white shirt under the plain vest and jacket. Then Ash blinked, recognizing at least one thing about the man. He was a Quaker.

"Good morning, Mr Greene," Ash said pleasantly. "We heard you wished to speak with my houseguest."

"Indeed," said Greene. He offered a hand for Ash to shake and then bowed his head to Regina. "Miss Fox, I have come a ways to speak with thee—you."

"Don't tell me my fame has spread to the New World," Reggie drawled, putting a bit of extra insinuation in her comment.

The man looked uneasy. "Not precisely."

"So you're not an admirer," she said. "Have you come to save my soul, or am I beyond redemption?" Reggie asked.

"No one is beyond redemption," he returned, speaking with a quiet dignity. "As for why I'm here, it's a personal matter." He looked at Ash, obviously hoping he would leave.

"How can it be personal when we've never met?" Reggie asked.

"I can elaborate, ma'am, but it is a…delicate matter."

"I'm not a delicate woman, Mr Greene. Say on."

Ash held up a hand. Something in Greene's demeanor made Ash nervous, as if he was about to trespass on something. "Reggie, if you'd like to hear this in private…"

"No," Reggie said sharply, before deliberately softening her tone. "I'd like you to stay, Ash." She kept her gaze on the stranger, not bothering to hide the familiarity with which they addressed each other.

Reggie sat down and invited the men to do the same. "Speak your business, Mr Greene."

"Miss Fox," he began. "I sailed from Philadelphia in April in order to locate you. It's taken longer than I'd like, but I had very little information to go on. I assure you that I am confident the message I carry is for you, Regina Fox, of St Stephen's convent."

Reggie's chin came up, her mouth open in surprise. "St Stephen's!"

"You were raised there, then," he said. "Good. I am glad to hear it confirmed."

"How do you even know of that?"

He waved it off as unimportant. "The point is why you were left at St Stephen's."

"The usual reason," Reggie said. "My mother didn't want me. The nuns who raised us took me aside one day and told me how I'd been left on the doorstep, in an old fruit box. Said it still smelled of apples. There was a little money at the bottom of the box, which they took in pay-ment. There was also a note with my name—though not my mother's."

"Nothing else?" he asked intently.

Reggie paused for a long moment, but then simply said, "Nothing of consequence."

"You resent your mother's choice," Greene guessed.

"No." Reggie sighed. "I am well aware of the difficul-ties women face when they find themselves burdened with a child. She made the choice for herself, rather than for me. God knows I've made a career of self-interest. Who am I to condemn another for it?"

"You came all the way from the States to ask Reggie about her past?" Ash asked.

Greene shook his head. "No. In fact, I am here to ask about her future. Miss Fox, I have been sent by Eulalia Fox Greene. Your mother. She asks you to come home."

Reggie stared at him, her face going white in shock.

Ash stood up, angry on Reggie's behalf. "You expect Regina to get on a ship with you simply based on your statement that you're taking her to her long-lost mother? There are easier ways to kidnap people."

"And cheaper," Greene agreed.

Reggie said, in a low, tight voice, "I don't know what your game is, Mr Greene, but I'm not an innocent lamb to be fleeced."

"It's no game, but I apologize if I've offended you in any way, ma'am." Greene stood up. "I'll leave now."

"Thank you."

"I am staying with an acquaintance until my ship sails." Greene supplied a street direction. "Should you wish to contact me before then, send a message there."

"Don't expect me to," Reggie said.

"Good day, ma'am, sir." Greene bowed stiffly. He turned at the door. "You're quite sure there was nothing else in the box? Perhaps folded into the letter stating your name?"

Reggie frowned. "Go away. I am quite done with you."

"Your mother hoped it had been saved, but it's possible that it was taken as part of the payment." Greene reached into his coat pocket and withdrew a folded handkerchief. "In the event that it will help convince you, I will leave this, though your mother was quite adamant that I should only do so if you could first produce its twin."

"Twin?" Ash asked sharply.

"The other half of the pair," Greene said. "Your mother left one earring with you and kept the other. She always hoped she'd be able to return to you, bearing the proof of your relationship. What has been separated must be rejoined."

"Who *are* you?" Reggie asked, staring at him.

"As I've said. Philemon Greene." He handed her the folded cloth.

"Why does my mother trust you to come after me? Did she pay you?"

"She has paid for my expenses, but I'd do anything she asks."

"Why?"

"Because I'm her son."

Reggie's eyes widened. "You're my *brother*?"

"Half brother," he clarified. "She married my father in America several years after she emigrated. She was born Eulalia Fox, but she is now Eulalia Greene."

"Dear God," Reggie said softly. "How terrible."

"Why should it be terrible?" Greene asked.

"For you to come all this way for nothing."

"Nothing? I've discovered you, have I not?"

"You can't seriously expect the offer to stand. Not after you've learned what I am. No wonder you didn't make our shared parentage known on your introduction!"

"It was the less important revelation."

"You shouldn't tell her you found me," Reggie said. "I doubt my mother wants to learn that her daughter became a whore."

Greene said, "I believe she wishes to see her daughter again in this life, and all other considerations are secondary."

"She will regret seeking me out."

Greene gave her a long look, and repeated, "That which has been separated must be rejoined."

Then he left.

After a moment, Reggie unfolded the cloth to reveal a pretty pearl drop earring. She looked pale as a ghost.

Ash said, "Reggie, you should lie down."

"No." But she remained sitting on the long chaise by the window. "I might want some strong tea."

"I'll order some. But Reggie, talk to me."

"Ring for a maid," she said quietly.

A maid was summoned to run to Reggie's room, where she extracted a small box from Reggie's personal cache of valuables. She returned shortly after, presenting the box to Regina, as if it were some sacred relic.

Reggie took it and slowly removed the lid.

Inside was a single gold and pearl drop earring, the exact match to the one Greene had given over.

"He was telling the truth," Ash said.

"Oh, God," Reggie whispered. "I have a mother."

For the first time in years, Ash saw his friend cry.

Chapter 24

THAT AFTERNOON, NORA HAD BEEN tinkering around in the sitting room provided for her use. She played with a few water glasses and candles, trying to resurrect an old idea for an experiment. The project occupied her quite happily for a while, but when she heard the front door open and close a few times, she decided to find out what was happening. She was about to enter the front parlor when she heard an out-of-place noise. A sob?

"Reggie, you don't have to go. Even if he's telling the truth, you don't owe these people anything!"

"I just don't know!" Another half-stifled sob reached Nora's ears. She stopped short at the doorway, peeping in at the scene of Regina sitting on the long couch, with Ash leaning over the back, his arm around her shoulders, his head close to hers.

Ash was speaking, trying to soothe the distraught Regina. Nora was about to step in and offer to help, when something in their pose kept her feet still. Why was Ash so close to her? Why did she cling to him like that? Surely that was not how family behaved.

"Ma'am?"

The new voice startled her. Nora turned to find a maid bearing a tray with tea.

"I…I was going in the parlor," she began to explain. She felt like an eavesdropper.

"Best not to, ma'am," the maid said in a practical tone. "Miss Fox is in a state."

"Oh. Yes, of course." Nora backed away.

She backed all the way to her room, where she grabbed a straw hat and rang for Judith.

"I have to get out. I have to walk," she announced, once Judith appeared.

Nora walked out of the house with Judith following dutifully, no more intrusive than a shadow.

She tried to focus on the quiet streets, and the green trees in the park, where the summer heat was less.

Despite her effort to forget, the image flashed against her eyes again. Ash consoling Regina. But how close they were, how strangely intimate they seemed. Ash had her close in his arms, like a lover.

Or was Nora giving into jealousy for no reason at all? Perhaps she really was out of her mind, and everything before was just a fantasy she dreamed up.

Nora took a deep breath to steady herself. "No. It's nothing." But the way Ash's lips were at Regina's cheek, the way he had his fingers entwined with hers.

"I'm imagining it." But Nora didn't imagine things. She saw them.

And then, when she looked up, she saw something else.

A familiar shape darted between two trees a few hundred yards ahead. Nora would know him anywhere. It was Edmund Morrison.

She stopped in her tracks. Judith nearly bumped into her.

"Ma'am?" the maid asked, confused.

"That man." Nora nodded in Edmund's direction. "The tall blond one in the grey jacket. Do you see him?"

"The one walking the dog?" Judith asked.

"Yes. We need to follow him, but he can't see me! Not once. Understand?"

"Ah, why must he be followed, ma'am?"

"I can't explain now. Just come with me."

Nora kept a healthy distance between her and Edmund, but she never let him out of her sight. She watched as he exercised Tippo on the lawn of the park, and then as he and the dog walked out a gate onto the busy thoroughfare.

She hoped to see where he was living or if he was going to meet someone. He walked slowly, often stopping to watch some woman or other who happened to be passing by or standing by a shop. The dog constantly sniffed the air.

Edmund was looking for her, Nora realized. He must be walking likely neighborhoods in the hopes of catching her. Even in a city the size of London, with many thousands of people, it might not be that difficult. The classes sorted themselves out, and there were places Nora would never be found, because they were either too high or too low for a lady of her standing. Edmund could cross those places off his list.

Nora suddenly felt the comforting anonymity of London crumble. Edmund was already closer to her than she ever wanted him to be. Why was she practically daring fate to expose her?

Just then, Tippo sniffed something in the air and snorted, turning his head toward Nora and Judith.

"Oh, Lord!" Nora gasped. "We've got to hide! Get away!"

"This way, ma'am." Without further ado, Judith practically pushed Nora into the doorway of a spice shop, redolent with smells and much darker than the street outside.

"Ladies, what are you in need of for your kitchen? Binsley's has it all!" the proprietress said cheerfully, dusting her hands on her apron. A cloud of cinnamon scent surrounded her as she walked toward them. "Pepper? Anise? What are you looking for?"

"A back door," Nora gasped out.

"Excuse me?" The proprietress's eyebrows rose an inch.

"A man has been following my mistress," Judith said. "Very unpleasant man, and she'd rather avoid him than suffer his acquaintance."

"I know the type," said Mrs Binsley, wrinkling her nose. "Say no more."

She pointed to a narrow pathway between two towering stacks of crates. "Through there, if you please. The door opens onto Grape Alley. Mind your skirts and shoes! And noses, for it stinks to high heaven."

Nora murmured her thanks and the two women slipped out into an alley every bit as nasty as advertised.

They both managed to avoid the worst of the refuse piles, and then to escape Edmund and Tippo's possible pursuit. By the time Nora returned to the house, she was tired from walking far longer than she intended, and tense from thinking of Edmund so close by. When she saw Ash approaching, her first instinct was to reach out to him.

"Where were you?" he asked. "I was worried."

"A walk. And while I was out, I saw him!"

"Who?"

"Wait...what happened this afternoon?" she asked, remembering what drove her out of the house. "Why was

Regina crying?"

Ash shook his head. "News…a relative she never thought to hear from again."

"She got word of a death? Oh, I am so sorry."

"Not a death. It's complicated, and not my story to tell," Ash said. "I've never seen her so upset. Not ever. Reggie's always been unshakable…"

Nora felt horrible for suspecting an illicit relationship between them, especially when Ash was so clearly distressed on Regina's behalf. "At least she had you there. That must have helped."

"I hope so." Ash seemed lost for a moment. Then he blinked. "Forgive me. You said something happened while you were out, and I cut you off. Tell me."

"I saw Edmund. "

"Where? When?"

"On the street, while I was walking."

"You were walking alone?"

"No, Judith was with me. She saw him too."

Ash looked at the maid, a question in his eyes.

Judith said, "There was a man that distressed Mrs Morrison, and she asked me to help her follow him. Whether it was Mr Morrison or not, I couldn't say," Judith added, a bit reluctantly, "since I've never seen him."

"If it was Edmund, why did you follow him?" Ash asked Nora. "That was dangerous."

"To see where he went, of course! If we knew where he was staying, wouldn't that help?"

"You risked a lot, Nora. Judith, you should have known better than to allow it."

"Am I a maid or a nanny?" Judith responded. "I did as instructed."

Ash sighed. "So you did. You are excused."

Judith gave a little curtsey that might have had some

mockery in it. Then she retreated toward the servants' wing.

Ash turned back to Nora. "Next time, I'd prefer it if you told me before you go somewhere." He took her by the arm, leading her into the drawing room, where things were already prepared for the meal of afternoon tea. She had been gone longer than she thought.

"You were occupied," she said, remembering the scene, all too vividly.

"Even so. It would not have been an interruption."

"Your Aunt Regina might disagree."

"She'd say your safety is more important than some misplaced sense of politeness."

He escorted her to a seat, then sat himself. Nora looked to the door. "Will Regina join us?"

"She's lying down in her room after the shock she received," Ash said, after pouring Nora some tea. "I'll have something brought up to her."

"It *was* Edmund," Nora said suddenly, her mind still occupied by the afternoon's event. "I'm not mad. He was really there, and I didn't dream him up."

"I believe you."

"I can't prove it," Nora went on, miserably. "I know Judith thought it strange when I insisted we shadow him. But it *was* him. He had his dog, Tippo! Of course no one in London knows the dog either..."

"Nora." Ash took her hand. "I believe you."

She took a deep breath and closed her eyes. "You do?"

"Yes. It makes sense that he's come to London. But if he is here, you need to be extra circumspect. Don't go anywhere you used to go when you lived with your husband. Edmund is probably watching for you there."

"Should I stay in the house?"

He made a face. "I hate to insist on that. You were

locked up long enough."

"It's different this time."

"Well, that's a relief." Ash gave her a little smile. "I'd feel better if you stayed. Just for a few days, or until we learn where Edmund Morrison is staying. Agreed?"

"Agreed."

* * * *

For the next several days, Nora did remain in the house, except for a few daily walks in Judith's or Ash's company. For those walks, Nora wore a fancy straw hat that obscured much of her face. A lady ought to wear a hat out of doors anyway, so it was not unusual except for its slightly exaggerated brim.

"Does it look as if I'm hiding?" Nora asked the first time Judith offered it to her.

"No, ma'am. It looks very glamorous, with all those feathers along the band. Miss Fox said so, and she would know."

Apart from the walks, she didn't have much opportunity for diversion, so she was delighted when Ash asked her to join him that evening for a supper: "Here at the house," he said, "but still a little surprise. Will you come?"

Of course she would. In preparation, Judith laid out a gown Nora had never seen before. "What's this?" she asked. The gown was silk—a lovely mossy green color— with jet beads sewn at the neckline, adding a subtle sparkle. The sleeves and bottom hem were lined with delicate black lace.

"Mr Allander thought it would suit you, ma'am. Do try it on. Hurry now."

A few moments later, Nora was staring at herself in a

mirror, astonished. The deep tone of the dress made her pale skin glow, and her light hair seemed more vibrant. The whole effect was elegant and refined, yet Nora still felt like herself. She smoothed her hands down the silk layers. "Oh."

"Perfect, ma'am," Judith said approvingly. "Just let me tend to your hair."

Tending to her hair meant sweeping the red-blonde waves up into a twist, with a few strands left loose to frame her face. Nora couldn't wait to see Ash.

Ash smiled when he saw her descend the stairs. "You're wearing it."

"Of course," she said. "It's perfect. Thank you."

"You look perfect in it," he said. "I hoped you would like it."

"I do…though you should not have given me any-thing."

"Then you'll simply have to not mention that it was a gift from me." He stepped closer and slid his hand down her back. He added, very quietly, "When you wear it, though, I'd like you to remember it's from me. And know that I want to be as close to you as this fabric is."

"Ash," she cautioned, though her whole body reacted to his words. "Behave."

"I am behaving," he protested, with a wicked smile. "I've behaved for days, and it's a trial, believe me. Now let me escort you to supper."

Supper was served not in Ash's dining room, but out-side in the garden. A table and chairs had been placed out on the lawn specially, and the space was illuminated with many candles.

"Oh, this is lovely!" she exclaimed.

"I know you'd like to be outside more than you have been, darling. This is the best I can do at the moment."

He seated her and then sat opposite. Only two chairs were at the table, so they were obviously dining alone. Nora loved the atmosphere of the gardens at night, but the intimacy of the setting was inescapable. Ash had promised to hide the extent of their relationship. Yet he bought her an expensive gown and offered an unquestionably romantic setting for a simple meal—no one would look at them and think they weren't intimately involved. His household, at minimum, must suspect the truth.

Yet, did it matter so much? Nora hadn't been so happy in ages. She loved being with Ash. They talked about everything: what she was working on, what news he brought back from his excursions into the city, silly stories of childhood friends, idle comments about the stars. By unspoken agreement, they avoided discussion of Edmund Morrison or the Zodiac. Tonight was an escape, and only after the very last course did she admit it had to end.

"Thank you for a lovely evening," she said. "I should go up to my room now, though. It's later than I thought."

"I'll walk you up," he said, rising to help her out of her seat.

He escorted her upstairs, and with every step, Nora wished she didn't have to end the evening at her door.

Ash seemed to have the same thought, for he turned to her, and murmured, "I don't want to say goodnight, darling."

Nora bit her lip, then said, "You could come in. Just for a moment."

He opened the door without looking. Nora stepped inside, finding that Judith had left one candle burning, so that the room was bathed in a faint glow.

Ash lost no time, and shut the door behind him. A moment later, Nora was in his arms. He kissed her in a slow and leisurely way, his mouth trailing along her neck and chest. Nora sighed. An intoxicating mixture of calm and arousal swirled within her. If only they had all night.

He paused his attentions for a moment, surveying her with pleasure. "You're so beautiful, Nora."

"It's the gown."

"It's not. Let me take it off, and I'll prove you're still beautiful."

"Ash, you shouldn't," she chided, though she sounded rather too entranced to be effective.

"It's not just looks, though I do love the way you look. Your beauty is your spirit. You never give in, even when most people would have lost hope long before. And you never lost that curiosity of a child—that's why you're so brilliant. You look at the world, you ask questions about it. Do you even know how rare you are?"

She blushed.

"God, I want to kiss every inch of you."

"We…agreed…and we already violated that once…"

"I know. But I want you to know that I want you anyway. It's probably for the best that we've agreed to behave. I know that you'll remember everything I do, so I can't offer a poor effort. It's rather intimidating, Nora, to know that every little move is being recorded."

"By this point, you must know that you've already proved yourself." Nora said. She loved the way Ash spoke, never far from humor, even when things got very serious between them.

But now, he looked more serious than ever.

"Nora," he said, "there's something I need to confess."

"Confess? Is it a sin, then?"

"Some think so." He took her hands in his.

Nora waited for him to speak, but he said nothing.

"What do you want to say?" she prompted.

"I'm trying to decide where to start," he explained.

"It's…rather convoluted."

She frowned. "Could you begin at the beginning?"

"I don't know where the beginning truly is." He took a deeper breath, then said, "All right. I think I can tell this properly. Please listen, Nora. What you think at the end is up to you, but at least listen."

"Of course." Why did he look distressed? What sin could require such a preamble?

"When I was younger, about nineteen, I was a student of theology," he began.

She nodded.

"I was living in a country parish at the time, and that autumn—"

There was a knock at the door. Nora jumped in surprise and disentangled herself from his hands.

Ash shook his head in frustration and stalked to the door, yanking it open. "What?"

"Sir," Crewe said, very carefully not noticing anything improper about the fact that Ash and Nora were alone in a closed, candlelit bedroom together. "I'm afraid you have a visitor downstairs."

"At this hour? Tell whoever it is I'm not home," Ash growled.

"It's Mr Wells."

Nora gasped. "Daniel! He's here?"

"Lord," Ash muttered.

"How could he possibly be here?" Nora asked, bewildered.

"I requested that Crewe try to track your brother down. He found a street direction yesterday and I sent a letter this morning. I thought we'd be lucky if we got any response at all. Then I'd find out if it was the correct Daniel Wells. I certainly didn't expect anyone to show up at the doorstep." To Crewe, he said, with an edge of anger,

"I'll be down in a moment."

"With me!" Nora added.

"No," Ash corrected. "Mrs Morrison will be summoned after I speak with her brother. No questions, Nora. Trust me on this."

She wondered exactly what required trust, and then belatedly realized exactly how bad it would look for Ash and Nora to traipse down the stairs together. "I'll stay here for a few moments," she whispered, heat rising in her cheeks.

"Thank you," Ash said, squeezing her hand. "It won't be long."

No, it wouldn't be long at all. Not long before she saw her family for the first time in years, and not long before she would be whisked away from Ash...possibly forever.

Chapter 25

ASH TOOK A DEEP BREATH before he left the room to go downstairs. An uncharacteristic nervousness—and also, to be honest, unconsummated desire—made him shaky. Now Ash was about to meet the man who might control Nora's future. He put on an expression of what he hoped passed for respectable concern. Then he entered the parlor where the newcomer waited.

"Good evening, Mr Wells," Ash said, striding in. "Thank you for answering my letter in person. We haven't met yet, of course. I'm Ashley Allander."

"Where is my sister?" Wells asked bluntly. He didn't smile, didn't nod. He only stared at Ash coldly.

"Mrs Morrison is upstairs in a guest room. I believe she was resting—she's had a difficult time lately."

"Send for her."

"Already done. She'll be pleased to see you. She's been adamant about contacting you."

"Has she?" Wells asked suspiciously.

"Of course. She is your sister, correct?"

"She is. And now I learn she is here, at your…residence." Wells looked around Ash's home with distaste. "Where she has had no female companionship."

"Not true. Miss Fox, who is also staying here, is most concerned with Mrs Morrison's welfare."

Wells looked barely mollified by that information. "And who else knows my sister is staying in this house?"

Ash had to step carefully here. "My household knows, obviously. Miss Fox. My own brother…Lord Forester." Ash left out Miss Chattan, for obvious reasons—in any case, Ash suspected the Empire would fall before Chattan spoke out of turn. "If your concern is discretion, I assure you no one would mention Mrs Morrison's presence."

"Thank God."

"Have I offended you, Wells?" Ash asked.

"I've heard about you…from Mr Morrison." Wells's voice was very correct, just this side of cold. "Via a letter to my place of business. He said Nora had suffered some mental break. He took her to the sea to recover, but while there, she grew worse, and set the house on fire just before a visitor spirited her away."

"That is his version? You'll find Mrs Morrison's story is quite different…and I for one think her the more credible witness."

"I've met her husband. He is an honorable man."

"That's true," said Nora, from the doorway. "But the man who wrote to you isn't my husband."

Both Mr Wells and Ash looked over. Ash was struck by the change in Nora's appearance. Gone was the green gown he had got for her. Now she was clad in a very modest, even drab outfit that seemed to beg to be overlooked. Her hair was still up, though, and whatever she wore, Ash found her completely beautiful.

"Nora!" Wells rushed over to her just as she stepped inside the room. The embrace between the siblings was obviously as heartfelt as it was awkward.

"Daniel," she said, her voice choked. "I'm so happy to see you again."

"Nora, just what is going on?" he asked, moving to

take her by the shoulders and look her over. "What happened to you?"

With remarkable calm, Nora explained the main points of her story. Sometimes she paused, looking to Ash for help—particularly when the truth would have forced her to mention the Zodiac or Ash's exploits. He jumped in where he could, and smoothed over a few incidents. He could tell that Wells was not entirely convinced, but then, it was a difficult story to believe.

"I haven't known her very long," Ash said quietly, toward the end. "But Mrs Morrison strikes me as a woman with a very logical and analytical mind. She doesn't seem fanciful or likely to suffer hallucinations. Moreover, I'd trust her memory, which is uncommonly sharp…as I'm sure you know."

Wells nodded at that, at last becoming less certain of his stance. "Nora, you never forgot a thing, that's true."

"So believe me now," said Nora. "Albert Morrison is dead, and I am a widow. Edmund seized what he saw as an opportunity for gain. I would never do something like set fire to a home! You know me better than that. *He* is lying, not me."

Her brother gave an unhappy sigh. "This is going to be a difficult problem to solve."

"Did Morrison communicate through a solicitor?" Ash asked.

"No. He said he wished to keep the matter private."

"That means he couldn't afford a solicitor," Nora said. "Trust me, Edmund Morrison is barely able to pay for his meals. He's terribly deep in debt."

"You suggest I buy him off?"

Ash shook his head. "If you try, he'll never go away. He'll make your lives miserable. You need to prove his claim is false. Publicly, whether in the courts or in the press."

Wells looked appalled at the idea of floating family business in the press. Like most people, he regarded newspapers with deep ambivalence. "I don't know. I just don't know what to do."

"There's no rush," Ash said. "I promise you that Mrs Morrison is perfectly safe here—"

"No," Wells said abruptly. "While I am grateful, I think that it is in Nora's best interests if you do not see her again. As Nora's closest relative, it is my responsibility to keep her from all manner of harm…even the appearance of harm."

"I see," Ash managed, knowing that, painful as it was to admit, Wells was correct.

Nora didn't look pleased either. "You want me to leave *now*? Tonight?" she asked.

"Naturally. The sooner the better."

"But…" She trailed off when she saw Wells's expression. "Very well."

A few moments later, Nora was hustled into a carriage, with only a small bag packed by Judith, who promised to see the rest of her things packed and delivered the next day.

She looked back at the house as the carriage departed. Ash stood in the entrance, watching her go. The ache in his chest hurt more than anything he had experienced for years. He hated to see Nora leave home…and he vowed to do everything necessary to get her back where she belonged.

* * * *

Once they were alone in the carriage, Daniel sat back and regarded Nora.

Nora looked back warily. He was her brother and her only family, yet in many ways they were nearly strangers after several years apart. She searched for signs of his more youthful self, and found few. He was older, more tired, and more aloof.

"It was very good of you to search me out so quickly," Nora said. "When had you heard from Edmund? You must have been worried."

"The letter was sent to the family's solicitors several days ago—it is the best place to reach me, in fact, since I've been abroad so much."

The Wells family had used the same solicitor's firm for three generations, so anyone who knew the family at all would start a search there. That also meant Edmund might not know where Daniel actually lived. Nora was relieved by that thought—the last thing she wanted was for Edmund to appear in front of her again.

"When did you get back to England?" she asked.

"Several months ago. I had written to you before I left India, though from the sound of it, the old street direction will be useless."

She nodded sadly. "I wasn't able to take anything. The pictures, the books, even my clothing and the household things…Edmund forced me to leave them behind. They're lost or sold off. All I currently own was provided by Mr Allander."

"Very generous."

Something in Daniel's tone made her look more closely at him. "It was generous. Why does it offend you?"

"A man who is not your husband buys you gifts, installs you in his house…"

"Gifts? He and his *aunt* provided much needed clothing, for I had nothing more than I was wearing when I fled from Edmund. As for staying in his house, where else was I to stay? I was sure of no one, half my old friends will be out of the city for the summer, and I didn't know what continent you were on. Should I have gone to a hotel?"

"Lord, no."

"Mr Allander has been..." She paused. A savior? A true friend? Wonderful? Everything she wanted to say was too revealing, too personal. "...very generous."

Daniel looked directly at her. "Be honest, Nora. Did he mistreat you in any way? Did he take advantage of you?"

"No!" Not by the logic that she *wanted* him to do everything he did.

"Are you certain? The state you were in..."

"Daniel, you must understand. What Ash...Allander did was all for my benefit. He went out of his way to help me, when he certainly had no obligation to do so. You ought to be grateful to him. If he hadn't helped me..." Nora broke off. She was no actress, but the very real tears that threatened to fall were perfectly timed to elicit her brother's contrition.

"Oh, Nora," he said, reaching over and putting a hand on hers. "Don't cry."

"It was unimaginable," she said, crying despite his words. "You have no idea what it was like in that house, with that horrible man using my brain for his own ends. Every day felt like a year. I tried to get out again and again. But I couldn't do it alone. I was so close to despair..."

"Nora, Nora," Daniel said. "It's over."

"It's *not* over. Not till Edmund is stopped. He's still claiming to be his brother, to be my husband. He could have me thrown in an asylum, just on his word! Do you understand that?"

"I do, and I'll take steps," Daniel swore.

"Thank you. But don't criticize me for how I escaped. And please don't insult the one man who actually helped me."

Daniel said, "I admit he seems to have served you well. But it is best you do not see him or correspond with him again, at least not until this situation is dealt with."

Daniel obviously expected her to accede, but Nora didn't respond.

"You're still my little sister," he went on, "and you're still my responsibility. Do you understand?"

"I do."

Daniel looked hard at her for a moment. "Good. I have enough on my mind. While you stay with me, you can keep the house, and behave just as a good woman should. We'll get it sorted."

Nora spent a sleepless night in a small room scantily furnished with a narrow bed, a stand with a washbowl, and a spindly little desk upon which a Bible lay. That was all. She blew out her candle, and wondered about this abrupt end to her ordeal…and her adventure.

In the morning, she woke up when some nearby sounds filtered into her consciousness. She opened her eyes to find Judith at the foot of the bed, unpacking a small trunk.

"Judith! Are you in the wrong house?" Nora asked. "Surely your duties end at Mr Allander's doorstep."

Judith gave a little smile. "Good morning, ma'am. My instructions are to attend to you, and that is what I shall do. Unless you object to my work?"

"No," Nora said. "I couldn't find a better maid, I'm sure."

"That's settled, then. Now, would you like the blue gown for dinner? I'll see that it's pressed in time. And would you like breakfast here, or in the dining room? Your brother has gone to work for the day."

"Then here will do."

* * * *

A week passed by, very slowly, and Nora's new routine hardly varied. She read, she kept the house, she talked to Judith. Sunday was church, which Daniel insisted she attend, because all good women attended church. Then it all began again.

Living in Edmund's house had been a nightmare. Living in Ash's house had been a beautiful dream. Daniel's house was hard, dull reality.

Judith, bless her, managed to get letters from Ash past Daniel's gaze—not that difficult, for he was distracted with his own business—and into Nora's hands. Nearly every day, a folded letter was slipped to her, a bright spot in the long stretches of cloudy days. None of them were very long, and mostly seemed to be written for the purpose of keeping her spirits up. Nora read the latest missive.

Home is very quiet without you. Reggie sends affectionate regards. Still looking for M and K's whereabouts. Will send word as soon as there's any news. Yours, A.

Nora smiled to herself.

"Good news?" Judith asked, in her mild tone.

"No news, really. But that's better than bad news." Nora added somewhat hastily, "It's not a love letter, you know. He only wants to keep me apprised of some events."

"Not my concern either way, ma'am," Judith said. "I am asked to see that you receive a note, and so you shall."

"And you post my letters back to him," Nora added.

"Thank you."

"Just doing my duty, ma'am."

Nora didn't know what she would do without Judith. She seemed to always be ready at a moment's notice, and only rarely did she let Nora out of her sight. Nora suspected that Ash gave the maid instructions to that effect, and the maid took his words very seriously.

Judith could sit quietly and sew for hours, no more obtrusive than a shadow on the wall. She would read to Nora when asked. She was a good reader, though she much preferred a novel to the newspaper articles Nora usually requested.

"Ma'am, must you be so interested in the politics of the Continent?" Judith asked after reading a column about Napoleon's recent fortunes in war, a topic of immense interest to most Londoners. "Wouldn't you like a bit of a gothic novel instead? All those misty moors and dread dark pits in the basements of manors, and the haunted heroes with their brooding!"

"That holds little appeal for me," said Nora, who'd lived in a setting a little too like the novels to wish to revisit it. "Do you like such stories?"

"I like excitement," Judith confessed, as if it were a sin. "So I was happy to find work in London."

"I wonder, Judith, what led you to leave your former employer. They must have appreciated your calm."

"I like to think so, ma'am. The fact of the matter is that I previously worked in Cheshire, in a very quiet setting. But I was raised in London."

"So you wished to return to your family?" Nora guessed.

Judith gave a little smile. "Family is important, ma'am. Both the family you're born to and the family you find along the way."

Chapter 26

Though Edmund Morrison had contacted Nora's brother, the man himself was lying low. No one could discover exactly where he was staying, including the Disreputables, who prided themselves in their ability to find anything. Similarly, Isabelle Kingfisher hadn't been seen in the city either, so far as Ash could tell, but something told him that she was there too. She had to be.

Ash decided he might be the best person to find her. He had connections none of the others in the Zodiac could have. He knew gamblers and bookies, con artists and criminals, aristocrats and professional beggars. One of those people knew Mrs Kingfisher, and where she was. All Ash had to do was find that person.

Easier said than done, of course. It meant returning to his old world, to the late nights and parties and endless carousing. But that was where his sort of people were.

Night after night, Ash went out. He nodded and greeted everyone he knew, though he wasn't interested in the mass of humanity surrounding him. Ever since returning to London, Ash was feeling distinctly unsocial. Still, he chased the phantom of Mrs Kingfisher through the gaming hells and private salons and hidden houses that comprised London's underground world. A woman such as her, with shady intentions and striking looks, had to know *someone.*

So Ash asked. Sometimes he asked for her by the name he knew her by—Isabelle Kingfisher—sometimes he just described her, and sometimes he merely listened to the swirls of gossip being exchanged around him. Night after night, he returned home empty-handed. And night after night, he increased his dosage of the laudanum to carry him away from all the memories his activities were bringing back. Five hundred drops, then six hundred, then seven. His dreams grew tangled and his temper grew short.

Still he persevered. Tonight, he entered one of the newest gaming hells in town. He played a few rounds for appearances' sake, won twenty pounds, lost fifteen pounds, and then moved on to his real business.

"I want to find a man," he told the circle of men who were either playing or watching. "Name of Kingfisher. Ring any bells?"

The others shook their heads, one saying, "No. Can't say that it does. Why?"

"Well, it's actually about his wife, Isabelle Kingfisher."

"Ah. Is he going to call you out?"

"Hope not," Ash said with an easy grin. "But I'd rather see him before he sees me, if you take my meaning."

During the round of laughter that greeted his words, Ash felt as if he was looking at himself from outside his own body, watching the actions of a stranger. Ash had lived in this world for years, and the smoke-filled, candlelit rooms of these sorts of places were very familiar to him, just as the clientele was familiar: rich members of the moneyed classes and everyone else who hoped to make a profit on them. Some were young lords, out for excitement and a taste of the underworld they only heard stories about. Some were older, men who either enjoyed the diversions offered here, or had become addicted to them—gambling, women, drink. Then there were the others. The professional gamblers, who lived at the card tables. The courtesans seeking their next patron, and the more common prostitutes seeking their next customer. All were gowned in sumptuous satin and lace, their faces expertly touched with the cosmetics forbidden to proper young ladies. Only the dim lighting preserved the illusion of beauty—bright daylight would expose the rips and stains on the gowns, the poor fit of secondhand finery, not to mention the pockmarks of disease and the wrinkles of premature aging. But in the night, they were all angels. The presence of women, with their light voices and laughter, created the impression of a party. Ash knew it was a marketplace.

Secretly, he'd always felt distaste for the city's underworld and the way its inhabitants preyed on the weaknesses of most of the visitors. True, some were there of their own choice and knew exactly what they were getting into. Most of the well-born men would suffer few consequences from their adventures. But that didn't hide the desperation of so many, or the bitter unhappiness of many more.

Ash had endured it for so long because he had no choice in the matter. Reggie thrived in this world, and he knew he could too. Still, he had always dreamed of getting out, somehow restoring his name, and returning to the world he left. But life didn't operate that way—one could never go back.

He'd more or less resigned himself to his fate…until Bruce dangled the offer of the Zodiac in front of him, and until he met Nora. If Ash could manage to prove himself, both to the Zodiac as a dependable agent, and to Nora as a worthy partner, Ash could finally escape.

The possibility was so tantalizing he sometimes forgot to breathe. But he actually had to *do* it. He had to locate Isabelle Kingfisher or Edmund Morrison, and find out exactly what they planned to do with Nora's invention. Then he had to tell Nora the truth about his own past, and hope that she'd give him a chance to show he wasn't the man the rumors claimed he was.

Then, somewhere, he heard something that tickled a memory. The voice of one of the gamblers came more clearly through the din.

"…they say the Princess Amelia is weakening again. She returned to the sea, though if the sea could cure her, would it not have done so by now? Poor creature."

Ash reflected for a moment on the irony of a man who normally cared not a fig for any woman in his sight, yet who worried about the fate of a girl he'd never met. Royalty was a different breed, as far as most people were concerned.

The man was still talking. "The king himself went to visit, and I feared that meant it was the end. Yet they say he's coming back tomorrow. Folk are already lining up along the road to the palace to cheer him."

Ash closed his eyes, picturing the scene. Mrs Kingfisher had shown unusual interest in the plight of the royal family. Would she be one to stand on the side of the road as the king passed? He hoped the answer was yes.

It was now three in the morning, which meant he had several hours before the king could reasonably be expected to pass by. So he had that long to deduce where a single individual would choose to stand. Where in God's name would Mrs Kingfisher be likely to watch from? The city was far too large to simply guess.

"Think," Ash muttered to himself. "Think like a snobbish, royalty obsessed social climber."

He pictured Isabelle Kingfisher's face, her clothes, her comments about the king. Then the image came to him. Of course. Where else would she watch from but from the gates of the royal residence itself? The logical end of the route, and the place where the king would appear most impressive.

He hurried home, and pressed Crewe into helping him search. "We'll start looking as soon as it gets light and people begin to take their places. I'll work from one side, and you from the other. Keep an eye out for anyone close to Mrs Kingfisher's appearance. You remember her?"

"How could I forget?" Crewe asked. "You don't think Morrison will be with her?"

"Not sure. If you see either of them, be careful. Just keep them in sight. The goal is to find out where they go afterwards."

Crewe nodded. "We need a runner, someone who recognizes us both and can move through a crowd fast."

"You know someone like that?"

"As it happens, I have just the Disreputable for the job."

Crewe sent word, and before dawn, a skinny boy appeared at the kitchen entrance. Crewe showed him in. Over a mug of tea, the boy studied Ash's face, committing it to memory.

"Rook here can run messages back and forth, or even contact the Zodiac if needed," Crewe explained.

"Rook, is it?" Ash asked. "You know the streets in the area around the royal residence?"

"Yes, sir. Used to pick pockets there, back when I was a young lad," the still-young lad explained. "Got all the alleys and side streets up here." He tapped his head confidently.

* * * *

The trio left Ash's home soon after, before the full light of day burst out over the city.

The streets around the palace were always busy, but this particular morning it was even more chaotic. Residents had heard the news of the princess's health via the newspapers, and many followed the developments quite breathlessly, for the young Amelia was known to be a sweet young lady doted on by her father.

However, the mood was festive, not somber. Vendors sold snacks and flowers, or colorful ribbons with the princess's name printed upon them. The crowd chattered amiably to each other, anticipating the arrival of the king, hopefully with good news.

Ash moved through the crowd as best he could, always on the lookout for Mrs Kingfisher. It was a near impossible task, especially since he and Crewe were the only two men who had seen her face. More eyes would have helped, but there was nothing for it.

He kept moving ever so slightly closer to the palace gates, as the crowd increased. Then, about a half-hour later, he saw her.

She stood on a small box, and a burly male servant stood below her, shoving some other spectators away when they threatened to obstruct the view. The lady herself wouldn't slip away from Ash's sight now. Not in her vivid red gown, her coppery hair, and the spyglass she held in one hand. She was peering through the glass down the street to where the king was expected to come from.

Just then, Rook tugged at his jacket. "Sir! Crewe is still looking, but he says he hasn't seen anyone like her."

"Never mind, Rook," Ash said. "I've got her here. Across the street, in that bright red dress."

The boy glanced to the side, and then nodded. "Got it. If you say that's her, then what should Crewe do now?"

"I'm going to keep her in view, and follow her until I can't anymore. With luck she'll lead me to wherever she's staying. Have Crewe go on home. If I'm not back in a few hours after the king passes by, he should go to the Zodiac and let them know what's happened."

Rook nodded and then dashed off.

Ash found a good spot to keep an eye on Mrs Kingfisher. He didn't think she'd notice him in the crowd, but she did have that spyglass. He lowered his hat slightly on his forehead.

A ripple of noise made everyone turn their heads. The king was approaching.

Within moments, chattering people passed the news down in a wave. The princess still lived! The crowd, naturally, roared into a joyous clamor. Even Ash, who was thoroughly jaded, felt a little better on hearing it.

The king's entourage advanced slowly up the road. Ash kept his attention on Mrs Kingfisher, only glancing occasionally at the spectacle.

She, however, was riveted. She followed the passage of the king's carriage, holding the spyglass to her eye as she slowly rotated to keep the king in view. She didn't cheer with the others. She never even cracked a smile.

When she lowered the glass, she took out a little notebook and jotted something down with the stub of a pencil. Then she climbed off the box she'd been using as a perch. Ash saw her and the servant turn to leave. He dashed across the street and started to follow. Luckily, Mrs Kingfisher's bright clothing made his task a little easier.

The lady hailed a carriage; so did he.

The lady left her carriage a while later; so did he.

The lady walked down a shaded residential lane; so did he.

He trailed Mrs Kingfisher—at a discreet distance—until she turned at the gates of a rather large house and walked confidently up the short drive to the main doors. From the way the servants all reacted, from the footman to the housemaid inside, this was definitely Mrs Kingfisher's home.

Ash waited until the doors closed, and then took a stroll around the perimeter of the property. When he saw another housemaid working by a smaller outbuilding, he knew what to do.

He approached her quite directly, and let her see him coming. She had been scrubbing at a particularly large stain on a blanket, and she left off the work to survey him. Ash was dressed like most other gentlemen in the city today—he deliberately avoided anything too noticeable.

"Good morning, Miss…" he said.

"Clara," she supplied, automatically.

"Miss Clara. Good day to you."

"You selling something?" she asked, puzzled. Ash had nothing with him, unlike most salesmen, who carried samples of their wares. "You can go to the side door and ask for Mr Peters, but he'll say no. He always says no."

"I'm not a salesman," Ash said. "And I think my business would be with the master of the house. Or the mistress? I saw a lady in a red dress just a moment ago. Who was she?"

"You mean Miss Wren," the maid said. "This is her house."

"Is it?" Kingfisher, Wren...the lady had a pattern in her false names. That could be useful.

Clara was looking him over. "Still haven't said what your business is."

"I'm a tutor," Ash said, giving the girl his most charming smile. "Many subjects. Philosophy, history. Or languages, including French and German. Perhaps the lady of the house has children who need instruction?"

"No children," the girl said. "She's unmarried."

That was interesting. Either Isabelle Kingfisher lied to this girl, or she lied to Edmund Morrison. Ash said, "Then the lady herself. Perhaps she wishes to perfect her French?"

The girl laughed at that. "Small chance, for she *is* French. Born there, and only came here a year or two ago. Speaks French half the day, and then gets angry when I don't know what she's rattling on about. If she wanted all French maids, though, it'd cost more. So she's only got Lisette. Listen to *them* go on, would you. Why move to England if you're not going to speak proper English? That's what I want to know!"

"French isn't so bad," Ash said, then said, "Vous êtes une belle fille, intelligente, avec de beaux yeux."

"What did you just say?" she demanded.

"I said you're a fine, intelligent girl with beautiful eyes. And it's just a statement of fact. You must have some young man hoping to catch your attention. You won't work in this house forever."

"Oh. Well, then." She ducked her head. "True enough, that last part. We're all to be let go next quarter."

"All of you?"

"Except Lisette. She'll stay on, naturally. The lady hasn't said anything yet, but we've all heard the talk. She's packing up and moving somewhere. Not going to rent this house much longer."

"Why move?"

"Because she's only living here until one of her relatives passes away…Uncle Royce, or something like that. She says his time is short. Not that she looks sad about it. I expect it's about an inheritance, and she must dance attendance on the old man to get what she wants. That's why she's hardly ever home."

"So your job is not overtaxing, at least. When it's over, you'll find a new place, Miss Clara, never fear."

"Just hope she doesn't write her letter of reference in French," the maid muttered. "Wouldn't that be just like her. Nothing is as good as her birthplace! She even admires the Emperor. She talks about him like he's the Savior himself."

"And how does she like our earthly king?"

"Can't repeat what that lady says about His Majesty!" the maid snapped. "Horrible stuff. But for all that, she can't stop talking about him, can she? Goes to the places he goes, follows all the parades and processions and such. Once met the Princess Amelia, if you can believe it! Bet Miss Wren never told the princess what she thinks of her father. All fawning and smiles then, in her fancy gowns and jewels. I think she's jealous, is what."

"You're likely correct, Miss Clara," Ash said. "Not much gets past you." He looked around, about to take his leave. Then something caught his eye.

"What's that?" he asked, moving into the little building to pick up the object of interest. It was a large piece of curved, colored glass. He lifted it up to the sunlight, where it took on a ruby glow.

"Ah, that. One of Miss Wren's obsessions, I guess. She bought so much glass a few weeks ago, and she was playing with the pieces night after night. But a few days ago, she had it all carted down here. It's just rubbish now."

"I'll pay you for this piece," Ash said. "It's interesting, isn't it?"

Clara's eyes brightened. "You can buy them all, if you're serious."

"I just want one." He put a coin in Clara's hand, wet and soapy from her work.

The maid tucked the coin away in her shoe. "Thank you kindly, sir."

"Pleasure, Miss Clara. Best of luck to you."

Ash walked off, having learned more than he expected. Yet he now had more questions than ever. Who was the woman who called herself Mrs Kingfisher in one place and Miss Wren in another? The only thing that was certain was her whole past was a fabrication.

Chapter 27

"You seem a bit at odds, ma'am."

Judith offered the observation in a quiet, even tone, as if she was only noting a change in the weather.

"I feel too cloistered," Nora said. A few weeks ago, she thought finding her brother would end all her difficulties. Yet, now that they were reunited, Nora had to face the reality that Daniel was unable to change very much about her circumstances without considerable effort. And he seemed too preoccupied to think of Nora much at all. "My brother expects me to be a mannequin, I think, rather than a person."

"It has been some time since you lived with him. He'll get used to it soon enough."

"And until then, am I to go to church and the back garden and nowhere else?"

"Why are you so restricted? Go shopping, or call on a friend."

"My friends are few, and not in London till summer closes." Nora held up a letter. "My old acquaintance Lydia Farley, now Mrs Mumford, wrote to convey her condolences that I had to endure London's heat. She did say she was coming back to town soon, though she was never one for punctuality."

"Well, then strike out on your own. A museum, perhaps. So long as you avoid your old haunts, the risk of Mr Morrison encountering you is low."

"It's too late today, and anyway, Mr Wells will want to approve of it. I'll ask him over supper."

Nora laid her groundwork carefully. She told Daniel that she needed to go shopping, and even asked him for spending money.

"It would be better if you did not go out, Nora. Give me a list and I'll see that they're purchased for you."

"Some of the items are specifically feminine," she said. "Undergarments and the like."

Daniel colored briefly. Even the hint of transgression into a uniquely female realm made him uncomfortable. "Your maid can go on your behalf."

"I need to go myself," she said, keeping her tone reasonable. "For fittings, you see." That wasn't strictly true, but Nora gambled on Daniel's ignorance of how ladies handled matters of shopping for intimate things. "And anyway, I thought I'd visit the art galleries at New Somerset House afterwards. I need to get out."

"Your maid must accompany you, then," he said. "Take a carriage to and from. I won't have you overtaxing yourself. You always liked to wander."

The next afternoon, Nora walked through the art galleries, admiring the walls, each covered top to bottom with art. Portraits of men and women from ages past looked out at her. Kings and dukes and earls, all dressed in sumptuous velvets and furs, or standing triumphantly in military garb. Princesses and high-born ladies showed off gowns and jewels that may have bankrupted whole towns, and now the images glimmered for all time, just so ordinary people like Nora could gaze upon them in wonder.

As she moved through the rooms, Nora felt a wonderful sense of aloneness. She wasn't lonely at all, rather she felt anonymous and free. When was the last time she'd been unsupervised in a public place? She couldn't remember. Possibly she never had been.

In the long gallery, Nora suddenly spotted the figure of Miss Chattan, who stood contemplating a portrait of George III, done at the beginning of his reign, when he was a much younger man. In the portrait, the king stood in front of an unoccupied throne, his stance confident. He held one arm akimbo, the hand on his hip. The other was placed over his heart, a signal by the artist that the king pledged his fidelity to his people above all.

Perhaps unconsciously, Miss Chattan had mimicked the king's stance, and the result was a curious mirroring— on one side, a young king decked out in the trappings of power, and on the other, a young woman dressed in common, unremarkable clothing that proclaimed nothing at all about her status. Yet there was something in her expression very like the king's. Despite all the differences between the subject and the viewer, here was a woman who understood power.

Then Chattan turned and looked toward Nora. "Why, Mrs Morrison. What a coincidence."

"Good afternoon," Nora said, quite certain that coincidence had nothing to do with it.

"May we talk?" Chattan asked, taking it as a given that Nora would agree.

They walked on, and found a smaller gallery that contained only still-lifes by lesser-known Flemish painters. The room was deserted. In the center, a single bench was placed, which would allow visitors to sit and view any painting in the room.

"This will serve our purpose admirably," Chattan said. She sat on one end of the bench, facing the door. Nora walked around to sit opposite, her back to the door. Thus the women could look at each other without the conversation appearing too furtive, should anyone wander in.

"And what," Nora asked, "is our purpose?"

"To establish a rapport, Mrs Morrison. Our previous conversation was not the best showing, I admit. But we are on the same side, are we not?"

Nora frowned. "I have no side. I'm nobody."

"You're somebody who has seen more than most people. Rather like Mr Allander. He's been busy since you departed his home, you know."

"Has he?"

"Yes. He's been quite active in looking for Mrs Kingfisher. She is more dangerous than the average mistress. Allander reported his findings to me last night, and I did a little more work based on what he discovered. It seems she's actually French, but is masquerading as an Englishwoman. She struck up an acquaintance with Edmund for a particular purpose…but we don't know precisely what her goal is. Not yet. The messages you remember could help us learn it."

"I don't think so."

"Let me be the judge," Miss Chattan said.

"What makes you better placed for that role than I am?" Nora asked.

"You'll simply have to trust me on that."

"If I'm to give up my knowledge, I'll want something in return."

"What?" Chattan's eyes narrowed.

"Tell me about Ashley Allander. There's more to his past than anyone has told me. Why is his relationship with his brother so strained? Why were you so quick to say he's not part of your little group?"

"He's not," Chattan said. "I was merely stating a fact."

"One his brother contradicted. Mr Allander did perform an assignment, and he did just discover more about Mrs Kingfisher. So what holds him back from a full invitation?"

Chattan looked extremely uncomfortable. "It's not my place to say."

"Yet it's your place to hear anything I'd say to you!" Nora said. "You ask much of me, but offer nothing in return. How is that a fair exchange?"

"Life is rarely fair."

"A fact I know well, Miss Chattan." Nora said. "But in this case, I do not think it out of line to request some simple facts."

"There is nothing simple about facts. They are as chimerical as rumors…perhaps more so. They change their appearance and their weight depending on who views them."

"That's no reason to keep people in the dark," Nora said.

"Mrs Morrison, you are very naïve."

"And you wish to keep me so?"

"Frankly, yes. You are on the edge of something far more complicated than you could dream of. Don't fall further into it. You'd be far happier if you walked away."

"After telling you all I know, of course."

"My intentions are noble, Mrs Morrison. So are those of everyone in the Zodiac. Let us deal with Edmund Morrison and Kingfisher and whatever they're up to. You are not suited to the task."

"Everyone is so confident in deciding what I'm suited to! Doctors I've never met declare me mad or sane. My own brother confers with solicitors about my marital state, because my word is not enough. Complete strangers decide I'm suitable as a source of information, yet I'm not prepared to learn anything *from* them. It's a wonder I'm allowed to choose my own gown." Nora looked down at her outfit. "Strike that. My maid pulled this one out."

Chattan's brow furrowed through Nora's recitation. "I am sorry for your difficulties, Mrs Morrison. But I am telling you the truth when I say it's important to know what those messages were. Think it over, and send me word when you are ready to share."

"What of my request?"

"If you want to know about Mr Allander, you should ask him," Chattan said. "Though you'll wish you didn't."

Nora frowned, not sure whether Chattan was trying to intimidate her.

Chattan tugged her gloves on a little tighter. The fingertips were stained with ink. "Good day, Mrs Morrison. I hope you consider what I've said. All of it."

The lady left, striding out of the room, the hard soles of her shoes clicking on the parquet floor.

Nora sat for a long moment, not sure of anything. Then she made her way through the galleries until she came to the entryway, where Judith sat primly on a chair in the corner, her back straight. She rose as soon as Nora approached. "I trust you enjoyed your excursion, ma'am. But we should be returning home."

"Yes, indeed," Nora said.

Her conversation with Miss Chattan was thoroughly vexing. Nora hated the suspicion that everyone around her knew something she didn't. Was that one reason why she was so reluctant to share the messages? At least she had a secret of her own.

She closed her eyes, and let her mind take her back. Every night that Edmund used her to send a message, all the little flashes and pauses, the click of the glass panels in the lantern, and Edmund muttering letters and words and phrases under his breath. Nora remembered it all, just as she remembered the smell of the sea and the way the cobwebs in the corners of the lighthouse room puffed in the breezes. She could retrace every step, repeat every line spoken. She turned over a few of them once more.

GIRL TOY WORTH SEA BAIT

SEABIRD FOUND NEST WATCH TOY WAIT

*BIRD WATCH AT PAUL WORTH PATH DAWN
BIRD BREAK TOY END*

She could recite the words but the meaning eluded her. Why bird? Why toy? What path led to dawn? She wondered if Ash would be able to shed any light on it. She didn't dare write to him—she didn't want to put the lines on paper.

What she did was far simpler. She wrote Ash a short note, asking him to meet her on an upcoming evening, in the safely public yet rambling Covent Gardens. She was sure she'd convince Daniel that it was healthy for her to attend a musical concert there, and she'd be able to talk with Ash for a few precious moments among the crowd. He was clever. Perhaps he'd see meaning where she missed it. He was right about one thing—Nora had been relying on herself for too long. She needed to trust him, and the Zodiac, to help her.

She sent the note off with Judith, who promised to see it delivered.

Chapter 28

IT DIDN'T TAKE LONG TO receive word back from Ash, telling her he'd find her at the Gardens on the appointed evening.

Nora put on her new gown for the occasion. The green silk caressed her skin as she moved, and she remembered Ash's flirtatious comment about how he wanted to touch her just as the silk did. Memories of their few nights of passion surfaced, and Nora wondered if they'd ever repeat that experience. Not likely, considering the current situation. When would they ever find themselves together, yet alone?

Nora sighed. She pulled on long gloves and twirled a light, wispy wrap around her shoulders. At least she would see him, talk to him. That was enough.

Late summer in the city was often dull, for many of the ton fled the heat to reside in the country until the Season started in a few more months. Worse, the hot weather could make the buildings feel like steam baths. A night at the Gardens, with the relatively open setting and mishmash of classes all attending, made the best of the situation.

Nora wandered the paths for a little while, simply taking in the magic of the scene. The evening sky was deepest blue, displaying the last hint of light before night claimed it. Stars were already coming out above, little glimmers that could hardly compete with the spectacle below. The Gardens were alight. Candles in pierced metal containers dotted the pathways so people could walk more safely, and colored paper lanterns were strung above the lawns and hung in the tree branches. Nora heard that later in the evening fireworks would be set off near a pond. The whole scene was like a fairyland, and so different from the usual that it attracted crowds of people night after night.

There were concerts some nights, and entertainers such as magicians and acrobats who set up little spots, hoping to dazzle the passing guests into dropping a few coins in their boxes. Elsewhere, one could find a table and order food and drink, dining among the dancing lights.

Nora smiled as she walked, delighted with all she saw. Everywhere she looked, she hoped to see Ash. She didn't yet, but that was to be expected, considering the crowd. Nora kept on, drawn forward by the sound of music.

She hovered at the edge of the area where people had gathered to dance, lining up with men on one side, women on the other. Nora surveyed the bright-colored gowns all lined up, and made a game of choosing which one she'd pick out for herself.

Just as she settled on a dress in a china blue, something in the corner of her eye made her turn her head. Uneasiness threaded through her veins. A certain shape had just crossed her vision, but she couldn't find it again.

She took a few steps to the right, slipping among the observers. There it was again, the shape that was both familiar and wrong.

Then she saw it—the outline of a man she knew all too well. For one unnerving moment that made her question her sanity, she actually thought it was Albert. That he'd somehow come to find her and explain that he was alive once more, and the past year had been a terrible misunderstanding.

But after a few seconds where Nora could feel her heart thumping oddly against her ribcage, the man turned a little to the side, and logic reasserted itself.

She looked again, through the dim, many-colored lights. She was absolutely certain the man she saw was Edmund Morrison. What she couldn't know was whether Edmund had sighted her in the crowd.

She ducked behind a small group of people all chattering with each other and heaved a breath. She had to get away from here, from the whole Gardens. Nora took one step, then remembered that Ash was also here. Edmund would also recognize him! Nora had to warn him.

But she couldn't be seen herself! Conflicted and confused, Nora moved erratically through the crowd for a few moments.

Once, she was sure she saw Edmund looming behind her, and she almost stumbled.

"I say, are you all right?" an older gentleman asked her.

Nora looked at him, registering only that he was a man she didn't know, and therefore dangerous. "Let me be," she said, backing away and then dashing back among the shifting tide of revelers.

She kept going, not certain of what direction she was even heading. The hundreds of colored lanterns bobbed in the breeze, and Nora had a sudden fancy of being adrift among clouds and stars with no one to hang onto. She whirled in a state of panic, and ran directly into someone.

Strong hands took her by the shoulders, keeping her still. "Nora."

She took a deep breath. "Ash." The one person she most wanted to see. In this chaotic place of all places, he'd found her. "You're really here?"

"Of course I am. You asked me to meet you. Nora, what's wrong? Tell me."

"Edmund was here! Just now!"

"Did he see you?"

"I don't know. I think so. He must have. Don't you think? It can't be coincidence he was here tonight."

"There are a lot of people here tonight. Perhaps he was here for another reason."

"Not the music! He's a philistine."

"Then perhaps he wanted to meet someone else. It's a public venue. No one can stop him."

"You believe me, that I saw him?"

"Yes. Why wouldn't I?" He looked around. "Let's move to somewhere a little less visible."

He led her down one of the narrower paths, one that headed into woods. A few lanterns pointed the path out, but otherwise, it was much darker here.

A little line of lanterns showed a side path to an out-of-the-way place, where a stone bench sat under a massive, spreading oak. As they walked, Ash kicked each little lantern on its side, the flame drowning in wax every time, obscuring their passage.

Finally, only the little lantern on the end of the bench itself was left burning.

"This is better," Ash said after a few moments. "With your dark gown, no one will pick you out in the trees. Not like the first time I saw you, in your white dress." He laid a kiss on her forehead. "Have I said you made an impression? I thought you might have been a ghost, if I believed in ghosts."

"Or you thought me mad," Nora said, still anxious, still certain Edmund was following.

"No, love. I thought that I'd never seen such a strange, striking woman, and I wanted to find you, learn all about you, and prove you were real."

"I was on the roof. You didn't think I was unhinged?"

"Not for a second."

"Everyone else does. They don't say it, but they wonder if I really am mad. My brother says he believes me, but he never looks as if he does."

"Nora, that's not true. You're perfectly sane, and brilliant. I'm sure your brother knows that. But listen, I'm glad you decided to talk about the messages. Keeping what you know to yourself is only hurting you. Then you won't be so anxious when you see Edmund next—not to mention that he'll have less reason to take any sort of action against you."

"I'm sorry it took me so long to come around to it."

"Understandable. But you know, it's good to have allies."

"Is that what you are? An ally?"

"No." He bent to kiss her neck.

Nora sighed, in relief as much as arousal. Lord, she had missed his touch.

"Ash," she murmured. "Is this wise?"

"No," he admitted. "But it's what you want. What I want too."

"What if someone notices I've been gone?"

"Who will see? If you need to, say you got lost in the crowd. No one will question it."

"What if someone sees us here?"

He knocked the last little lantern over, and the circle of light collapsed. "Solved, love. If you object to being ravished in the middle of the woods, now's the time to say so."

She kissed him hungrily, no longer willing to wait.

Ash wrapped his arms around her, pulling her close. "The last time I saw you in this dress, I was ready to beg you to let me take it off."

"We can't do that. Not here." But she wanted him to.

He shrugged out of his jacket, then pulled her in an embrace. He sat on the bench and told her to straddle him. "This way," he said, "your pretty hairstyle at least stands a chance."

She wanted to laugh, but was afraid the sound would carry. Ash lifted her skirts as she knelt over him, settling her knees on either side of his hips. A few moments later, all the fabric and clothing barriers were shoved aside.

"Are you sure?" Nora asked, hoping he was.

His erection brushed between her legs, and he cupped her bottom in his hands. "I need you," he hissed. "I haven't been able to *breathe* properly without you."

"Yes." Nora knew exactly what he meant. She felt the tip of him nudge her center and slid down along the length of him.

They both exhaled silently, long sighs of relief after being apart for too long.

"I love you," she said without knowing that was what she was thinking.

Ash paused, his expression caught between surprise and delight. He moved one hand to her neck, then drew her down, her face to his. "Nora. Kiss me."

She kissed him, putting all her emotion into her touch, hoping to show what she couldn't explain.

She gasped as he moved within her, the sensations spreading through her body, from her core to her fingers and toes.

"Oh," she whispered. "Oh."

"You're wonderful, Nora. I love hearing you, seeing you."

She felt the same way about him. Seeing Ash, with his strong, virile body beneath her, feeling how he reacted to her touch, made Nora flush with pleasure. She lost herself in the sensation of having him so close, and just as she stifled a little cry of completion, Ash gripped her very tightly and smothered his own voice, his mouth at her neck.

Ash held her to him for a long moment, his breathing fast. Nora wrapped her arms around his shoulders, her hand pillowing his head on her chest.

He'd done what he always avoided before. He finished inside her. Nora knew it, just as she knew it was unintentional. But being with him was worth the risk to her.

He finally withdrew from her with a low, strangled curse. "Nora. Christ, what did we just do?"

"I'm sorry."

"Don't you dare apologize to me, love. It's not your fault that I lose all sense as soon as I touch you. God, that was stupid of me. I completely lost my mind."

"So did I," she confessed. She had no idea how likely or unlikely a pregnancy would be. "I didn't care."

"That's the problem, isn't it?" he murmured. "Not caring until it's too late."

"Let's not get ahead of ourselves. Quite possibly nothing will happen."

He kissed her softly. "Nora, if something does happen, I'll do whatever you ask."

"I know." Then she sighed. "This is not at all what I intended to do tonight. I meant to speak to you about the messages."

"Those messages," he said, helping her to stand up. "I'll listen to what you want to tell me, but I'm not sure I can help much on my own. I hate to say it, but the Zodiac doubtless has better resources." As he spoke, he got himself back to a respectable appearance.

She brushed off her gown and shook her wrap free of leaves. "I'll speak to your associates, then. Could we go tonight, do you think? Or should I come to your house tomorrow and we can speak there? Chattan contacted me, you know. She'll come running if I send word." Nora smoothed her hands over the gown, checking that all was restored. "Shall we return to civilization? Are you ready?"

"Nora, I…" He looked stricken. "There's something I want to tell you. Well, there's a lot I want to tell you. But something very particular. Something you need to know."

"Then say it."

"It will take a while to explain. More time than we have now. But it's important. Can I…arrange to meet you? Somewhere safe. To talk. Just to talk."

"Of course. You can call on me at home."

"I may not be able to do that." Ash sounded frustrated, nervous. Very unlike Ash. "I'll think of something."

"Well, whatever it is, you can tell me after we've gone to your friends in the Zodiac."

"Yes. That takes precedence." He took her hand. "Nora…"

"What's the matter?"

He tried to say something, then stopped. "Christ, I can't even speak anymore. Meeting you changed everything."

"I hope what I know will help."

"Not that. I don't care about the messages or Edmund's plan or the Zodiac. I mean you. You and me."

"Ash, you have me. Listen. We'll contact the Zodiac

right now, tonight. I'll tell them about the messages, and after that, you can say what's on your mind. Agreed?"

His expression was difficult to see in the dark, but he said, "Agreed. I am ruled by you."

She laughed, though she felt a little nervous now, wondering what he intended to tell her. "Come with me, then. We have a lot to do."

* * * *

Nora and Ash slowly made their way back to the more populated area of the gardens. Ash didn't speak much, but he kept his hand on hers—which rested on his arm—as he escorted her back, a subtle, unnecessary gesture that warmed her heart. She was still aglow with the feeling of bliss that being reunited with him brought her. If some of his talk had been a little odd…well, perhaps he'd been as shocked as she was by what they'd just done. Nora was never so impulsive, and yet she didn't regret it at all. Being with Ash felt right.

He leaned a little closer to her then, his side nudging hers. "We don't have to go back, you know," he murmured. "We could just run away. No one would stop us."

"Tempting." She turned to smile at him, but just as she was about to speak, someone called her name.

"Mrs Morrison! Miss Wells! Nora!"

Nora looked to the sound, first alarmed, but then overjoyed. "Oh, my," she said. "It's Lydia!" She raised her voice. "Mrs Mumford! Hello!"

"Friend of yours?" Ash asked. Something in his tone was so strange that Nora looked at him in complete confusion.

"Yes. A longtime friend. You should meet her. I'll introduce you."

"Bad idea," he said shortly.

Within moments, Nora was being greeted enthusiastically by Lydia who, despite being a married woman, still giggled like a schoolgirl.

Then Lydia looked over toward Ash. "It's Allander, isn't it? I had no idea you were acquainted with Mrs Morrison."

"I'm not," Ash declared.

Nora was so surprised by his response that she could say nothing at all.

Ash smiled charmingly. "I merely saw a lady in need of an arm for a few paces. Parts of the path are muddy," he added, in explanation. "Well, my duties as knight errant are surely concluded for the evening. Good night, ladies."

"Good night!" Lydia turned to her, and virtually dragged her away.

Nora cast one confused glance back at Ash, who was already lost in the darkness and shifting crowd of the Gardens.

"Muddy path, was it?" Lydia asked. "You do look a bit rustic. Is that a twig in your hair?"

"I was attacked by a…a rogue elm," Nora said quickly, reaching up to find the offending twig.

"My goodness. A rogue elm. Well, don't tell the French. They'll get ideas."

"I just stumbled once, in the darkness."

"Nora, you poor dear. No wonder Mr Allander took pity on you. They say that he does have a good-natured side, though of course you're lucky he took no deeper interest in you." Lydia said meaningfully.

"Deeper interest?"

"Don't tell me you've never heard of Ashley Allander."

"No. What should I have heard?"

"Oh, my word. What scandal hasn't he got himself into over the years? You do hide away with your books and instruments, though. I suppose you would not have heard it all."

"None." Nora felt faint.

"Come with me. I'll take you home in my carriage, and tell you every last detail."

Lydia hooked her arm companionably though Nora's, just as if they were young girls again. She chattered away amiably on a host of subjects that Nora cared nothing about. But she knew Lydia wouldn't divulge the truly salacious gossip until they were alone.

Finally, after what seemed years, they were inside Lydia's carriage. Nora sat on the edge of her seat, too nervous to relax.

"So Mr Allander has a reputation?" she asked bluntly.

"Reputation! Dear, he attracts scandal like a flame attracts moths. His name is one of the worst in London."

"But he seemed so kind," Nora ventured. Perhaps there was a mistake. There was another Mr Allander who Ash got confused for.

"Kind? Perhaps. Charming is a better word. Allander is a rake of the worst sort. Many ladies' lives have been ruined by him—he's known as the Fallen Angel. He's got no conscience or scruples. I have no idea what game he was playing with you, dear, but you may be sure that it was some sort of game. No matter how charming you find him—and by all accounts, charm is his main weapon—you cannot trust him."

"What exactly has he done?"

"What hasn't he done?" Lydia laughed. "His exploits are mostly…romantic…in nature. Of course, what makes it worse is that he's one step away from a title. His brother is the Viscount Forester, if you please! Can you imagine if the title ever went to Allander? That sort of man gadding about with lords and ladies of quality! It's not to be thought of. Thankfully, Forester is a proper gentleman, and hardly associates with his brother. Only the minimum that blood demands."

Nora closed her eyes. Well, that sealed it. She couldn't pretend that there was some case of similar names.

"Now, where to begin…" Lydia mused. "Ashley Allander is the second son of the late Viscount Forester, the title his older brother now holds. He was a very clever boy—learned languages with ease, understood philosophic arguments that grown men struggle with, and more importantly, displayed a true affinity for spiritual matters. He was allowed to continue his studies, and entered a seminary to prepare for a career in the church."

"How long was he there?"

"Three years, or thereabouts," Lydia guessed. "At the time he was kicked out, he was eighteen or nineteen years old. Very mature and handsome, with a quick wit and a beguiling nature. Everyone seemed charmed by him."

"Women, you mean."

"No, everyone. His charm at that point wasn't sensual in nature. He truly impressed his teachers, his patrons… and those who encountered him as parishioners. He was on track for a brilliant career."

"What went wrong?"

"There was an important lady in the parish. Her husband was a military officer—rather a distinguished one. She took pride in the reflected glory of his sacrifice, while enjoying the freedom that came from living away from a watchful husband's gaze."

"Go on."

"The lady became pregnant. With her husband gone,

the two possibilities were either something divine...or quite profane."

"I take it that an immaculate conception was ruled out."

"Once her condition could no longer be hidden, she named the man who had—in her words—seduced her and taken advantage of his position."

"Ashley Allander."

"Yes."

"She accused a theological student of seducing her?"

"Yes. She said he seduced not only her, but also her daughter."

Nora blinked. "What?"

"The daughter was also with child, though she was not as far along. As you might imagine, the scandal was unprecedented. The young Allander was removed immediately, and disavowed."

"He wasn't allowed to defend himself?"

"My dear, he never tried," Lydia explained simply. "Not once did he contradict the ladies' accounts of the events. Indeed, in the succeeding months, he seemed to relish the celebrity the scandal brought him, and he *earned* the title of Fallen Angel. He fled to London and behaved in as debased a manner as his old way of life had been austere. He drank, he gambled, he caroused. He was a most popular companion to be seen with, for both men and women. Who doesn't love to be close to the flames? But in truth, even such a scandal as that would not have ensured his enduring notoriety if he had not begun another, even more shocking affair."

"More shocking than simultaneously ruining a mother and her daughter?"

"In its way, yes. He took up with a woman widely agreed to be the most alluring in all of London. She was sought after by many, and very expensive to keep. She's often called the Lady in Gold—none other than Regina Fox!" Lydia sighed, obviously delighting in the pleasure of revealing a juicy story to fresh ears.

Nora swallowed. So much for *Aunt* Regina. She'd known there was something odd between them, but hearing it confirmed hurt more than she could have thought. She struggled to maintain her composure, lest she show far too much emotion to Lydia.

"If she was so…golden," she stumbled over the words, trying to put a thought together, "how could he afford her?"

"Ah, good question. He's also known as an inveterate gambler, though smarter or luckier than most. So perhaps he earned the fee that way. Or perhaps even Miss Fox was so enamored of him that she pursued him out of pure lust. They say he was perfectly gorgeous as a youth. An angel to look at, a devil to sleep with."

Nora winced at that.

"Oh, dear," Lydia said, hastily. "I forget how sheltered you are. But if what I told you makes your cheeks burn like that, I promise there are far worse stories. Husbands call him out for duels over what he's done with their wives. One father tried to shoot him on a city street! He's a dangerous man to be around."

"I'll never see him again," Nora muttered.

"Very wise, dear."

Lydia saw Nora to her door, and then left, promising to meet her again soon. Nora used her own key, and walked into the darkened foyer of her house. Her house? She felt like a stranger, as if there was no home for her anywhere. She trusted Ash. Worse, she loved him.

She stumbled into the unlit sitting room and sank onto a chair.

Nora wanted to wail in rage. How could she have been so blind? She tripped blithely into Ash's trap, and worse, she'd done it more than once! He must think her such a simpleton, for believing his words and falling for his seduction. Not that she had much of a chance. From the sound of it, he had years of experience in ruining women, many surely far more worldly than Nora. How could she have known better?

Yet it stung. She always thought of herself as no-nonsense, a woman who might not control her surroundings, but at least understood them. But Ash confounded her better sense. She truly thought she'd found some sort of... *connection* with him. How he must have laughed at her when she confessed her feelings.

She rammed her hand into a fist and punched down on the thin seat cushion, hitting the hard wooden panel beneath. The violence did nothing to relieve her turmoil, but her knuckles ached, and tears sprang to her eyes.

She took a heaving breath, struggled for a moment, but then simply gave up. She let the tears fall freely, spattering into her lap and marring her gown, which was likely already destroyed from her last encounter with Ash, when he seduced her yet again, with only a few words and some well-placed kisses.

"God damn it," she muttered, unconsciously echoing Ash's tendency to swear. More tears fell onto the silk. She hated this gown, hated the man who gave it to her. She had to get it off.

Nora stood up abruptly, and yanked the offending fabric from her body. The green silk ripped under her fingers and the folds of the skirts sighed as they fell into a puddle at her feet. She kicked the dark pool of fabric away, as if it was poisonous.

She wiped at her cheeks with the back of her hand.

What a fool she was, sobbing and tearing at her clothes like some flighty figure in a gothic novel. Nora couldn't stop though, and her choked sob sounded loud in the darkness.

Just then, the door to the little side garden squeaked on its hinges. Nora looked over, alarmed.

Someone was slipping though the door into the room.

Ash. The Fallen Angel.

Chapter 29

PUBLICLY DENYING HE KNEW NORA was the most difficult thing Ash had ever done. His instinct was to step even closer to her, to put his arm around her and tell everyone that he adored her. That he intended to be with her for life.

But that was the last thing he could proclaim, because his name and reputation were deplorable, and any public association would only hurt Nora.

So he pulled the familiar mask back on, the image of the careless rake who would never bother with a woman like Nora. He pretended she meant nothing to him, even though she meant everything.

The confusion in Nora's eyes was just the beginning. It would get worse.

When Ash watched the other woman take Nora away from him at the Gardens, he knew he was done for. Whoever she was, she'd tell Nora all the very basest of the rumors, because that was what everybody did when Ash's name came up. Ten years of experience taught him that.

But Nora was different. Maybe she'd hold her judgment until he could defend himself, or at least explain himself.

He couldn't wait until the next morning, so he hired a cab to Nora's home and snuck around to the side. The place was silent and dark—had he reached it first?

Ash opened the door carefully and slipped in. He hoped to find Nora before anyone else found him.

Then he saw Nora standing the darkness, clad only in a thin white chemise. One strap had ripped, leaving her shoulder bare. She looked remarkably like she had the very first time he saw her, except for her expression, which was one of pure disgust.

"You. How did you get in here?" she asked, her voice cold. "Never mind. I expect you're quite good at sneaking into ladies' homes, and not because you're a spy. You're a fallen angel."

At the hated nickname, he clenched his hands into fists and then deliberately relaxed them. "Nora, I need to talk to you."

"I don't need to talk to you," Nora said. "Go away."

"You're only half dressed," he said. "What happened?"

"What happened? I took off the gown you gave me because I hate it. And I hate you."

"Nora, please. Please let me explain."

"There's no need. I heard the story of your life from my friend. At least someone decided to reveal the truth."

"I can guess what she told you, but what you heard wasn't the truth."

She let out a short, angry laugh. "How idiotic do you think I am? Granted, I was a naive little idiot before, but I have the facts now. You won't be able to talk sweetly to me any longer, and you certainly won't tumble me into bed...or anywhere else!" she added.

"I should have been honest with you, Nora," he said, "but I never meant to hurt you. And for God's sake, stop calling yourself an idiot," he added. "It's not what you are."

"Shut up! Stop pretending you've got the slightest

interest in me. I gave you what you wanted—more than once. Now kindly leave me alone."

"That's not what I want from you," he said.

"Of course. You want my brain as well. My memories."

"I told you over and over that the decision to share what you know is your own. The Zodiac wants the information, I admit, but I told them they couldn't rush you."

"Well, you would say that, since you had me in your keeping. Very convenient for the occasional seduction. I apologize, by the way. I must have been a bitter disappointment after the Golden Lady."

"Oh, Jesus Christ," he muttered.

"Did you joke about it when I wasn't in the room? Did *dear Reggie* laugh?"

"It wasn't like that."

"Do you deny you had an affair with her?"

Ash sighed. "No."

"Well." Nora's voice broke a little, as though the answer hurt more than the others.

"It happened a long time ago."

"Then why is she living in your house now?" Nora asked.

"It's complicated. It's all complicated. I did try to tell you. More than once, but the time was never right, or we were interrupted."

"If the truth mattered, you would have found the time, Ash!"

"I know. I know. I'm sorry you found out about my reputation the way you did. But for Christ's sake, Nora, please let me explain. Give me one more chance."

Nora stared at him, unmoved. "You led me along just until you got caught. And now you want to mend things? Make them just as they were before? No. You've used all your chances up."

"Nora—"

"Get out of my house. Get out of my life."

He walked to the door, but then turned back, hoping to get though to her in some small way. "What of the Zodiac?"

"You think I'd go to them after this? After they kept back the truth of your past, too? They were so careful, so eager to keep me in the dark. Because I'd be more useful that way. Well, I'm done being useful to you or to the Zodiac or to Edmund or to anyone. You can go to hell, Ash. And if you happen to see anyone from the Zodiac, you can tell them to go to hell, too."

With those words, Nora drove him out the door into the night. While he stood there in the garden, the latch on the door snapped. The message was clear. He would never be welcome in Nora's presence again.

He made his way to the street, moving without thought. He chose a direction at random, and just kept walking. He was far too disturbed to think about something as pointless as where he should go.

Where could he go? Ash knew hundreds of people in London, and yet the list of names of those he could rely on was depressingly short.

Reggie came to mind first. Reggie, who had always been there for him. He couldn't go to Reggie now though. She was off entertaining a potential new patron, some visiting aristocrat from Hungary. There was no way for Ash to intrude on that tête-à-tête, unless the gentleman was considerably more open-minded than usual. And besides, scotching Reggie's chances for security was hardly the way to repay her friendship. He'd find her in the morning. If he made it that far.

Caizo? He was a teacher, not a confidante, and Ash

couldn't imagine dragging anyone dealing with his own rumors into yet another quagmire.

He thought of Crewe next. He hadn't known the man very long, but he seemed as steady and dependable as they came. But it was one thing to trust a Disreputable with aid on an assignment. It was quite another to confide his worst personal failings. Anyway, what could Crewe possibly do to help? He worked for the Zodiac, at the end of the day. With Ash's luck, the servant would just report all the news directly to Bruce.

Bruce. His only brother. His only real family. But now, they were practically strangers. Ash was nothing more than a disappointment to Bruce. Imagine asking him for any help now… Ash would rather walk through the door-way of hell.

Instead, he walked straight through the half-hidden doorway of the nearest dive he could remember, a place that would certainly have a ready supply of the laudanum supposedly only available through an apothecary. While his mind roiled with anxious, angry thoughts, his body knew exactly what it wanted. Oblivion. Without con-scious design, he'd come to the sort of place he'd always be welcome, so long as he could pay.

Ash descended into a dim, hazy world where red-stained lanterns barely illuminated the number of name-less bodies indulging in any vice they could afford. The smells of gin and sweat assailed him.

He actually smiled. Here was where he belonged. Per-haps he'd never leave.

Chapter 30

Ash woke up in an unfamiliar bed. That in itself wasn't particularly remarkable, though he usually knew *whose* bed it was. Ash looked around the room, or what he could see of it. The curtains were drawn mostly shut, and no lamp or candle was lit.

The sheets and bedclothes felt marvelously soft and clean. For some reason, Ash expected them to be grimy. He rapped experimentally on one poster of the bed. Solid oak. In all, the room was well appointed, if rather dull. His opium-laced dreams were never this bland, so he assumed he was awake.

"Hello?" he called. His voice came out as a croak. It startled him so badly that he shut up. What the hell had he been doing?

Scraps of memories floated back toward him. He'd done something stupid, something involving a woman. And not the usual sort of thing. No, this was more important.

Ash turned over, and promptly fell off the bed onto the floor.

He groaned in pain. Perhaps he hadn't walked in a

while.

Moments later the door opened, and a voice called out, "Sir?"

"Over here," Ash said, from the floor.

A servant's feet entered his vision. "Sir?" the young man asked. "Why are you on the floor?"

"I was curious about the carpet," Ash said, saying the first thing that came to his tongue. "It's quite fine. Whose carpet is this, by the way?"

"Lord Forester's."

Ash groaned again. That was worse than he feared. "Damn. Don't tell him I'm awake."

"Certainly not, sir."

The servant left, undoubtedly to tell Bruce that Ash was awake and ready to be berated. The minimal light filtering through the curtains seemed ungodly harsh. Ash closed his eyes.

"Ash. *Ash.*"

He opened his eyes again. Bruce towered over him.

"Stop that," Ash muttered.

"Stop what?"

"Towering. You're always towering."

"I'm tall, and you're literally sprawled on the ground. What do you expect?"

"Exactly that. You standing tall. Me on the ground. It's always been that way."

"No, it hasn't," Bruce said. "You were doing perfectly well until you managed to offend half of society. Even then, you made the best of it. What finally drove you to opium?"

"Finally? I've been using it ever since seminary."

Bruce was incredulous. "You can't hide that sort of thing for so long."

"You'd be amazed at what a person can hide when no

one cares. I started taking laudanum at the recommendation of a professor. Said it would open my mind to the divine. Which it did."

"Nothing is very divine about lying in some filthy sub-basement for days. You're lucky we found you."

"Why did you bother looking?"

"You're my brother."

"Ah. It would look bad if the younger brother of Lord Forester died in a gutter somewhere."

"I don't care how it looks, Ash! I searched for you because you're my brother. You were missing for eight days!"

"That long?" Ash tried to hide it, but he was a little alarmed by the news. "Where exactly was I? How'd you find me?"

"You moved around for the first few days, apparently. But we found you at last. Crewe had a few ideas of where to search, once we understood what we were searching for. You don't look like an opium addict."

"I'm not an addict," Ash snapped.

Bruce tossed something on the floor next to Ash.

He picked up a crumpled paper. Smoothing it out, he recognized it as the wrapping of the little cake of opium he swore he'd never actually need to touch. If the wrapping was all that was left…Ash shuddered. "I'm not an addict," he repeated.

"You admitted you'd been using it for over a decade, and you were in some disgusting hovel or another for over a week. Yes, you *are* an addict. While we're on the subject, what caused this fiasco? What could possibly have driven you this low?"

Nora.

Ash closed his eyes, because he suddenly remembered everything that happened, and his first instinct was to, yes, find some opium. All the opium.

"You may have a point," he muttered.

Bruce leaned over and hooked his hands under Ash's shoulders, dragging him upward. Ash stood briefly, then sat back on the bed when standing took too much effort. "I may have…overindulged this time."

"That's what you're calling it?" Bruce asked. "Well, it doesn't matter. Don't do it again."

"It's not as if I've anyone left to hurt."

"I disagree. Reggie would disagree."

Ash said, "Reggie doesn't have to know this happened."

"She already knows, because she helped us look for you."

"Damn." Ash shook his head, trying to clear it. "Who else?"

"Crewe. A few more Disreputables. They know the streets and the underworld well. You're lucky they do."

"All that effort for me? You didn't even want to hand me that assignment. You were desperate…obviously."

Bruce inhaled. "No. The Zodiac was desperate, and I recommended you."

"Wait." Ash must have heard that wrong. "You were the person who gave them my name?"

"Who else? I know what you're capable of doing. You have many of the skills they look for in an agent. You're intelligent, you speak multiple languages, you understand people. You even have a ready-made cover—you spent over ten years perfecting it. You could make an outstanding agent, *if* you put your mind to the task. But not if you're in thrall to a drug that makes you lose yourself for days on end."

Ash winced. "Too late. You've already seen what happened. It will undoubtedly happen again."

"You could change, if you wanted to. You don't have to continue living like this."

"You think I want to live like this?" Ash glared at his brother. "You think I've enjoyed the past ten years?"

"Rumors suggest you thoroughly enjoyed every aspect of your life."

"The rumors are bloody lies."

Bruce crossed his arms, looking disturbingly like their late father. "All you have to do is try," he said, with the confidence of someone who had never experienced what Ash had.

"I have tried," Ash explained, trying to regain his calm. "I fail. Repeatedly. If my life has a story, that's it. Failed our father as a child. Failed in my vocation. Failed the family name. Failed to defend myself. Failed to get out of the hole I fell in. Failed my friends. Failed Nora."

"Who?" his brother asked, puzzled.

"Elanora Morrison," Ash said. "*Nora.*"

A flicker of something showed in Bruce's eyes. Pity, probably. He asked, "How did you fail Mrs Morrison? You got her out, didn't you?"

"Got her out of a house. Didn't get her out of trouble. Either way, it doesn't matter, because she won't ever speak to me again."

"Why not?"

"She's heard everything now. All the rumors. Or, enough of them. She kicked me out of her house before I could begin to tell her the truth."

"What truth?"

"*The* truth." Ash sighed in frustration. "What really happened all those years ago. My side of the scandal."

"Your side isn't terribly flattering."

"Shut your mouth, Bruce. You don't know my side, because I've never told it! You think you've got the whole dossier on me, when in fact you're peddling in the same lies that all the gossips of London are."

Bruce stared at him for a long moment, then said, "Ten years is a long time to wait to tell your version of the story."

Ash shrugged, then fell back on the bed. "It was too late for me ten minutes after the first rumor started flying." He pulled the blanket back over him, and deliberately turned over on his side, away from Bruce. "I'm tired." A childish move, but the only one he had the strength to make. He couldn't deal with Bruce or the world.

He expected more protest from his brother, more pressure to reveal the promised truth. Instead, all he heard was the sound of Bruce's footsteps retreating.

He was alone again. Ash heaved a sigh of relief, and then fell back into sleep.

* * * *

A day later, Ash was on his feet again. Under the illusion that he was a grown man who could be trusted, Bruce and the household left him to his own devices. A mistake, as it turned out. In his wanderings, Ash discovered a medicine cabinet that contained a nearly full bottle of laudanum. A single dose for an ordinary person was a teaspoon. Ash took half the bottle, rather proud of himself for his restraint. He's save the rest for later.

But for now, peace.

He woke up in the same, slightly more familiar bed. He blinked several times, trying to clear the strange trails of light from his vision. He must still be experiencing some of the opium's effects. This time, he avoided falling out of the bed and instead rang for a servant.

The maid who came in kept her distance. "Awake now, sir?"

"Seems so. Listen, I had a bottle of some medicine. Where is it?"

The maid rolled her eyes. "Night stand."

He looked to the left, seeing an empty bottle. "That's not the one. Mine was half full."

"You drank the rest of it, sir. While you were dancing."

"I was dancing last night?"

"Yesterday afternoon, sir. On the dining room table."

"Oh."

"His lordship was rather vexed. You broke a piece of Lady Forester's favorite crystal. And you knocked Miss Fox to the ground when she tried to help you walk."

"Reggie was here?"

"Miss Fox is still here. In fact, she asked to be notified when you woke."

"I'm not ready to speak to anyone."

"Unfortunately for you, sir, Lord Forester's orders were to ignore your wishes in all matters. She'll be up shortly." The maid walked out.

Ash waited in dread until Reggie opened the door. She didn't look at him, but strode to the windows and flung the curtains open.

Ash winced automatically until he realized it was night outside. "What time is it?"

"Does it even matter?" Reggie asked. "You seem intent on ruining every day of your life." Then she turned and faced him. In her shimmering gold silk gown, which glowed in the reflected light of the fireplace and the candles, she looked rather like an avenging angel. "You lied to me," she accused him.

"I didn't," he protested.

"You hid the truth then, which is the same. You dabbled in opium years ago, I knew that. But you said you had stopped!"

"I did! Mostly."

"Then what in God's name were you doing for the past week and a half? Yesterday? Last night? Why bother to go through the effort of pulling you out of hell when you just go plunging back into it?"

"I just…needed…a little."

"You can't even say the name of your addiction, can you? A *little* does not cause a man to pontificate on the virtues of sacred aviaries while climbing on the furniture!"

"What the hell is a sacred aviary?"

"I don't know, Ash!" She threw up her hands. "*You* were the one raving about them in some drug-induced madness. You scared me! I thought you completely lost your mind. I didn't know if I would ever see you rational again. You collapsed, did you know that? Fell head first off the table. Bruce nearly didn't catch you in time."

"I'm sorry, Reg. I didn't know you were there."

"You didn't know anything at all. You still don't. Why are you doing this? After all these years?"

He took a deep breath. Swallowed. "It helps me forget my life."

"You don't like your life? Change it."

"I don't think I can."

She shook her head, and spun around, putting her back to him. Ash stared at her, at a loss. What did it mean when his dearest friend turned her back on him?

"Reggie, would you do me a favor?"

"What?" she asked dully, still not facing him.

"Get me a dog, would you? Any old dog will do."

That made her turn. "What do you need a *dog* for?"

"I need to know there's one creature in the world that doesn't hate me."

Reggie glared at him through narrowed eyes for a minute. Then she laughed, and not in a pleasant way. "I'll get you your damn dog, Ash. I'm not going to be your watchdog for much longer anyway."

He blinked, upset at the change in her tone. "What's that supposed to mean?"

"While you've been lost in your haze of smoke, I've been talking with Philemon Greene."

Ash sat up, the last rags of fog clearing from his brain. "What? The Quaker?"

"My half-brother, yes."

"You're not seriously considering going with him." Ash looked at Reggie, trying to read whether she was teasing him. "You'd sail to America on a whim?"

"It's not a whim, Ash." Reggie didn't smile. "Look at me. What do you see?"

"My friend."

She sat on the edge of the bed. Her expression softened for an instant. "Be less loyal. What do you see?"

"A beautiful woman. A clever woman. A woman too intelligent to be taken in by a…a fantasy."

She nodded slowly. "You're right. But the fantasy isn't Mr Greene's story." She stood up, crossed the room to the looking glass. "The fantasy is the idea that nothing changes. You called me beautiful, but your view is biased."

"No, no, no, Reg. You're ravishing. You always have been."

She tapped the glass with one knuckle. "But I won't always remain so. You think I'm beautiful, because you knew me when I was younger, and because your eyes are tainted with affection. The truth is that I'm getting old.

I'm losing my charms little by little."

"No."

She looked back to him. "Oh, I'm plenty charming still. Wit and experience are not to be discounted. I daresay I've pulled many a man out of the arms of some young, bland beauty who wasn't interesting enough to compete. But there's a limit to anything, Ash. My career is nearing its close."

"You've got that Hungarian count, haven't you? You have admirers lined up."

"A shorter line every year. Older gentlemen, who prefer my appeal…for now. It won't last. I don't begrudge it. But neither will I deny it. I'm not going to be the fool who stands in the middle of a ballroom, convinced that I haven't aged a day in all my years. I won't be laughed at when a man turns me down for another, younger woman."

"So you'll just up and leave?"

Reggie chuckled as she walked back to the bedside. "What better exit could I make? To sail off into the sunset, still admired, and not pitied. What better capstone to my legacy could there be, but a wildly romantic, redemptive end to my scandalous career? They'll talk about it for months."

"Reggie." Ash took her hand. "They'll talk about it for years."

She smiled, more gently. "See? It's not so bad a plan after all."

"What if…all does not go well in America?"

"I have funds. If I don't like what I see in one place, I'll go elsewhere. I've already conquered this island. Perhaps a continent is the logical stepping stone."

"They've got no idea what's coming to them."

"Neither do I," she admitted. "I haven't been surprised in a long, long time, Ash. I'd almost forgotten what it was like, to feel like I'm about to step off a precipice. It's exciting. That's what I've been dying for. Novelty. Hope. At last, all these things are being offered to me…and perhaps even a family."

"I'll miss you."

"You'll have your dog," she said slyly.

"Don't listen to me ramble on. I don't need a dog."

"What about Nora then? Do you need her?"

"Ruined any chance of that. She won't see me."

"Probably for the best, if you care for her." Reggie leaned to kiss his forehead in a sympathetic way.

His brief lift in spirit collapsed again. "I know it, Reg. I knew it when I first saw her, that I would eventually hurt her. I did it anyway." He'd been so selfish, keeping Nora close simply because that's where he wanted her, and not even with the guts to tell her that he was last man in London a lady like her should be near. "I can't fix this, Reg. I don't know what to do." He looked up. "You want company on the way to the States?"

Reggie sighed. "You ran away once, Ash. Ten years ago. You can't do it again. You have to find a way through."

"Through to what?"

"To reconciling with your brother. To asking Nora's forgiveness. To not craving opium every waking moment."

"I can't do any of those things." Ash pulled his hand from his friend's. "You'd better book passage soon, Reg. I'd prefer you to be gone when everything truly falls apart."

She slapped him. Not very hard, but it got his attention. "Ashley Allander! You are not dying, and you're not getting out of your mess the easy way. But if this is how you see things now, I don't want to be here the next time you make a fool of yourself!"

With that, she turned on her heel and stalked out of the room.

* * * *

Ash wasn't alone for long. Crewe threw the door open less than an hour later.

"Word downstairs is that you're so far gone in the head that your one request was a dog. Is that true?"

He shrugged. "I've long since stopped worrying about what's true or not regarding stories about me."

Crewe glared at him. "What is wrong with you? People who care about you are throwing second chances at you, and you're throwing them all away."

"What does it matter to you?" Ash sat up in the bed. "A month ago, I didn't know you. I don't even pay your wages. The Zodiac takes care of that."

"For now."

"What's that supposed to mean?"

"The Disreputables are a creation of the Zodiac. We survive because the Zodiac needs people like me, people who can't step into a ballroom on our own, but who know all the alleys in London. We're useful to the Zodiac."

"I know that."

"But you never stopped to think about what it means," Crewe went on. "If we're *not* useful, just how long do you think all the high-born Signs will want people like us around? If you fail, I fail. If I fail, the Disreputables fail. If the Disreputables fail, then that's one fewer way out for people like me. People who've got criminal histories, or a price on their heads. People who don't have any honest way to make a living because no decent folk would trust them. So *that's* why I'm still here, Mr Allander. I'm here until *you* succeed or until I'm dead. Understand?"

Ash just stared at Crewe for a long moment. Then he said, uncertainly, "They won't blame you for my mistakes. I'm not part of the Zodiac."

"If you know what the Zodiac is, you *are* a part of it. You might not be a Sign, but you're involved."

"Involved in what? It's over now. The Zodiac knows the details of Nora's invention, and what does it matter if she won't divulge the specific messages she happened to see? And anyway, she's living with her brother again, and was quite adamant that all she wanted was to return to a normal life. There's no more assignment. It's over."

Crewe held up a folded letter, just out of Ash's reach. "No, it's not over. Not yet."

"Is that for me?" Ash asked. He'd only got a glimpse of the handwriting on the outside, but he recognized Nora's style.

"Do you care, sir? Thought the assignment was over."

"Give me that." Ash snatched the letter from Crewe and unfolded it. What did Nora have to say?

Chapter 31

AFTER SENDING ASH AWAY FROM her house, Nora indulged in another fit of tears, and then a night and a day where she refused to even get out of bed. The subsequent days were not much better. Judith brought her tea and toast and naturally said nothing about Nora's mood—it wasn't a maid's place, particularly a maid so briefly in a woman's service. Daniel said nothing either, because he was scarcely there. His work kept him at the office for long hours, and he frequently dined elsewhere, so Nora could retire for the night before he even came home.

Thus, she had very little sense of what was happening in her life. Daniel offered some very brief updates on the matter of her martial status.

"Got another letter from Morrison," Daniel said one night, about a week later. "He says he won't give up his claim and that he'll bring in the doctor who wrote the diagnosis of madness should you try to argue your case. I'm afraid that a judge will not look kindly on a madwoman's word versus a husband's and a doctor's."

"But you know I'm not mad."

"Yes," Daniel said, "However, I can't be a witness if I

wasn't there to see it."

Nora sighed. "What if I could contact our old neighbors? Or locate our housekeeper Mary Bridger? She lived with us. She could vouch for my sanity."

"You may try," Daniel said, with no evident hope. "Write some letters to your old neighbors. Or find old acquaintances. What was the name of your friend…Lydia Farley?"

"Mrs Mumford now. I've already spoken to her," Nora said. A sour taste rose in her mouth, as she remembered Lydia's innocently given but devastating gossip. "She would vouch for me, I'm sure."

"It would help if one of your supporters was a man. Close to you, but with an unimpeachable reputation, and known for good judgment."

"The only man who would qualify is dead," she said hotly. "That's why I'm *in* this mess."

Daniel frowned. "Don't raise your voice to me, Nora. I'm not the architect of your troubles."

"I apologize," she said, bowing her head.

He looked mollified. "Very well. I have to travel to Portsmouth for a few days on business for the company. Perhaps when I return, the situation will have changed."

Nora said nothing. She couldn't help feeling that Daniel wished the situation, and Nora, would simply disappear. Only blood and a need to honor the family name guaranteed his support.

So she spent hours virtually alone, with little to do other than relive all the worst scenes of her past, from the loss of Albert, to the indignities Edmund inflicted on her, to the horribly sharp memories of Ash. She brushed her hand against her bedsheet one morning, and the sensation abruptly triggered memories of the night at the inn. Just the thought of what they'd done made her flush. She sat down on the bed, putting her face in her hands.

"Such a fool," she muttered. *Why* had she trusted him? Just because he seemed so intriguing, and kind, and deeply interested in her, plain little Nora.

"Just an act." Nora told herself that every time, and every time she struggled to convince herself Ash was so talented an actor.

In any case, he honored her last wish. Since he left her house, she hadn't seen him or heard from him again. It had been over a week of complete silence—for all she knew he'd fallen into a hole somewhere and never climbed out. She worried, a little bit, and then told herself to ignore the pangs of doubt. Ash didn't need her, didn't want her.

Instead, she tried to work. She sent Judith out to fetch various types of glass, and then spent hours attempting to regain her interest in the experiments she once found so fascinating.

But now, she could hardly be bothered. She merely fiddled with the glass, propping pieces up in front of candles and mirrors to create rainbows throughout the room. The effect was pretty, and at times mesmerizing. But it was nothing more than a diversion. She learned nothing, advancing not a step toward improving her communication method.

"*Bird see toy markings known,*" she muttered. It was one of the messages that Edmund sent. "*Bird see toy.*"

She was certain it was a code, but she'd always shrugged it off. She told herself that it didn't concern her, that someone else would sort it out. But now, here she was, alone with her secret knowledge. The only person who could sort it out was her.

Nora spent the rest of the day, and the night, and the day after that trying various methods to decipher the words, but nothing worked. Nora had only a rudimentary background in such matters, and all she knew was that the code was either much more complex than it seemed, or it relied on a specific key she didn't have access to.

Perhaps someone did, however. Nora recalled an old colleague of her husband's, who took an interest in codes and ciphers. She wrote a letter to Mr Windigate, sending it to the club where both he and Albert had been members. The letter gave no details of the messages—Nora didn't trust anyone at this point—but merely stated that she had encountered a sticky problem in a code and could they meet to discuss it, if he had time?

Then, because she was forced to wait for a reply, Nora went back to fiddling with her glass panes all night. She was tense and irate, but at three in the morning discovered how layering two or more panels could create an intensely bright beam against the wall. The effect delighted her so much that she simply started to laugh out loud, which brought Judith rushing up to the room.

"Ma'am, what is going on?" the maid asked.

Nora stifled her giggles. "Look!" She aimed the glass panels carefully, and then lit the candle. A bright spot of light appeared on the wall. "It's as bright as daylight!"

"Yes, ma'am." Judith didn't seem nearly as impressed. "Shouldn't you get to sleep? It's very late."

"I'm not sleepy. Anyway, my back aches," she said petulantly.

"Then I could bring you a tisane."

"I don't want a tisane."

"What do you want?"

Ash. Nora wrinkled her nose, disgusted with herself for still thinking like that. "Nothing," she said, her voice now dull. "I suppose I should sleep after all."

Judith remained to put out the lights and close the

door. Nora pulled the covers up high, wondering whether she'd made a fool of herself. If her goal was to present a sane and sensible face, she probably should not remain up until the small hours, playing with fire and glass and laughing to herself.

Nora woke the next morning to find that she had bled, signaling her monthly course. Well, that accounted for her pain yesterday. She was simultaneously relieved, because she was in no position to have a child, and disappointed, because if she was bearing Ash's child, she'd have a reason to contact him. She hated herself for it, but she missed him. Despite everything, she longed to be near him again. Every day, she thought of things, nearly said them aloud, and then remembered only Ash would find them funny.

Judith was attentive and good-natured, but she was a closed book. She reacted to nearly everything with a quiet calm that never hinted of her feelings. In contrast, Nora felt that her heart lay exposed for all to see. How could anyone look at her and not know that she felt shredded?

"Letter for you, ma'am."

Judith's timely intrusion snapped her out of her miserable thoughts. She picked up the letter on the tray, pleased to see that Mr Windigate had replied already. After she read through the note, she said, "He requests that I meet him at his club this afternoon at two. One room permits ladies as guests, and we can talk there."

At half past one, Nora and Judith rode in a hired carriage toward Mr Windigate's club. Nora sat with her hands in her lap, tugging the fingers of her gloves. Judith sat opposite, looking starched and prim in her maid's uniform.

"You hope this gentleman can help you with your experiments?" Judith asked.

"Not my own experiments, but rather a puzzle that's

been bothering me," Nora said carefully. While Judith knew the gist of Nora's recent experiences, Nora never told her about the messages. "I only want a little information, and I don't want to get anyone else involved in my troubles if I can avoid it. So a quick interview, and then—"

Without warning, the carriage lurched to a halt. Nora nearly tumbled to the floor, and Judith threw her hands out as her back was pushed against the front wall of the cab.

"What's the matter?" the maid shouted to the driver.

The was no reply. Nora peeked out the side window. "He's gone! I see him running away!"

"Stay here, ma'am. I'll be back." Judith pushed open the door and bounded out of the carriage in the wake of the disappearing driver.

Nora barely had time to take a breath before the other door was flung open and a man appeared, holding a knife tight by his side. "Get out," he ordered shortly.

"Excuse me?" Nora asked, too surprised to think clearly.

"Get out, or I'll pin you right to the seat where you're sitting."

He jiggled the knife to make his point. Nora nodded slowly. "Did Morrison hire you?"

"Never mind who hired me. Get out."

Nora could see he was serious, so she slid down the seat to the open door. The man stepped back to let her descend.

"Quick now," he muttered.

Once she had her feet on the ground, the man pushed the tip of the blade into her lower back. "Walk forward," he said. "Down this alley. Don't be clever. Just walk."

Nora took a step down the alley where the carriage

had stopped. Everything must have been planned carefully. The carriage blocked the view of passersby, making it unlikely anyone would notice a man escorting a lady down the alleyway.

"Where are we going?" Nora asked.

"You'll find out."

"I'd rather know in advance."

"I'd rather you didn't ask so many questions." He prodded the knife a bit. "Understand?"

"I understand that if you want to take me to someone you can't puncture me!"

"Then cooperate. Give me the papers."

"What papers?"

"The ones you're taking to the man. Windigate."

"There are no papers!"

"Then what are you asking him to decode? Don't be clever, lady, just hand the papers over. Whatever you got the stuff written on."

"There's nothing, I swear!"

"Don't try to play me—"

An *oof* from behind interrupted him. Nora was shoved forward, and when she scrambled to look around, she was astonished to see Judith attacking the man. The unarmed maid moved fearlessly, moving her body in ways Nora didn't even recognize. Short, fast punches and kicks made short work of the equally flummoxed mugger. Judith kicked the knife away in one instant, and in the next, knocked the man off his feet.

He groaned, putting a hand to his head. "Who in blazes are you?"

Judith ignored him, asking Nora, "How are you, ma'am? I thought the driver might have been a distraction, so I came back quick as I could."

"I'm in one piece, thank you."

"Good. Stay there, if you please."

Then Judith swooped down on the man, straddling him in a way that made Nora blush. Judith's intentions were anything but romantic, though. She grabbed the man by the hair. "Who hired you? What do you want?"

"He thinks I've written down some information," Nora said. "But I don't have anything."

"Who's behind this?" Judith asked again.

A shout came from the end of the all by the street.

"Someone has seen us!" Nora said, relieved.

Judith sighed, then slammed the man's head onto the cobblestones. He went limp.

"What did you do that for?" Nora squeaked out.

"Just let me manage this, ma'am." Judith quickly rose to her feet, and then screamed. "Help! Help, please!"

The cry sounded helpless and panicked—not at all in keeping with the actions Judith performed. Yet her expression was now one of terror, and she moved to stand very close to Nora.

By that point, several people had come running toward them. Some were gawkers eager for a spectacle, a few were genuinely concerned for the safety of what appeared to be two helpless women, and one was an actual Bow Street Runner who happened to be nearby and followed the commotion hoping to expedite the reporting of a crime—usually Runners weren't summoned until a messenger asked for them at Bow Street.

Judith played the role of dutiful servant, giving the Runner a false but plausible story about an attempted mugging.

"He was about to take my mistress's reticule when he slipped on a rock and lost his balance. Hit his head when he fell—that's Providence at work," Judith finished, with a pious nod.

Several members of the gathered crowd murmured agreement. The Runner offered to haul the still-unconscious man away and see that he was confined until he came to and could answer some questions. "Not least being his name," the Runner said. "We like to know who's misbehaving."

Nora simply stood there, still in shock at the revelation that her maid was not what she seemed to be. Judith politely refused further aid from anyone, other than for a gentleman to hail another carriage for them to return home—he also insisted on paying the fare. Judith led Nora to the carriage, keeping one hand on Nora's shoulder, as if she were far more shaken and delicate than she was.

Once in the carriage, however, Nora pulled herself out of her haze. "Judith Markby! Who are you and what is going on?"

"I'm a good servant, ma'am. To your other question, it was thought that considering the situation, it would be beneficial if someone could watch over you, at least until the matter of Mr Morrison is resolved."

"You're...with the Zodiac?"

Judith smiled deprecatingly. "Only in a manner of speaking. Remember Crewe? We are all servants, providing necessary service, albeit to unusual people. Like Crewe, I have some skills that were not learned in my education as a maid. We're called the Disreputables due to our disreputable pasts. But in all ways that matter, ma'am, you may rely on me as your humble servant. "

"You might have told me before."

"Apologies for the delay, but it's so often an awkward subject to raise."

"I imagine so," Nora conceded. "You sound as if you've done this sort of thing quite a lot."

"A fair bit, though every job is different."

"That attack just now," said Nora. "Why didn't you tell them what really happened? You wouldn't have got in trouble for defending me against him."

"They never would have believed me, and if they did, then there would have been many more questions. It's better this way. People see what they expect to see. They saw a lady and her maid nearly accosted and saved by Providence. The authorities get to haul away a criminal, and everyone feels that the natural order is restored."

"But you deserve the credit for stopping him."

"Which you have very kindly acknowledged, ma'am. What the world thinks of me is of no concern."

"If you say so." Nora was doubtful.

"What is a concern, ma'am, is the fact that the letter sent from Mr Windigate was intercepted, allowing an ambush to be set up while you were en route to your legitimate appointment. It means your enemy knows where you are."

"But I should have no more enemies! Edmund gains nothing by trying to kidnap me again."

"Does he know that? If he wishes to silence you…"

"Oh." That sounded just like Edmund, in fact. "You mean I should tell the Zodiac what I know."

"Certainly, you should tell someone what just occurred. Mr Allander perhaps."

"That I cannot do."

"Why ever not?" Judith asked.

"He's not trustworthy," Nora explained. "I learned the truth about him via a friend, who shared some news she happened to know.'

"News?"

"Rumors, I suppose. It was news only to me!"

"As you say, ma'am." Judith added, cautiously, "I will

note that I myself am suspicious of rumors, having started a fair number myself for various purposes. You should not believe all you hear."

Nora sighed unhappily. "I don't know what to believe."

"He has the confidence of his brother, for what that's worth."

"I told him I would not see him again. My own brother does not wish me to see him or correspond with him in any way."

"Ah," said Judith. "Much as you were once forbidden from climbing on rooftops and running away to freedom?"

"It's not the same at all," Nora said.

"No?"

"Of course not. My brother has my interests at heart."

"Family so often thinks so," Judith agreed. "Of course, he doesn't know about the Zodiac, or the implications of your invention. Might his advice change if he did?"

"If Daniel knew all that, he'd have heart failure," Nora said.

Judith simply waited with what Nora could only describe as an air of polite yet bullying expectation.

"Oh, very well," Nora said at last. "I shall write to Mr Allander. Though only because it is in my interests, not his," she added hastily.

"Yes, ma'am."

Chapter 32

NORA DID WRITE TO ASH, and within hours, she received a response. Ash was at his brother's London home, for some reason, and Nora was welcome to call there that evening for a private conversation. Nora didn't care what Ash thought of her, but she did spend an inordinate amount of time choosing what to wear and how to dress her hair. One dress seemed too gaudy, another too plain. One was far too light in color—it would remind Ash of the summer gown she was wearing the first time he saw her. Another was too dark—it would remind her of the dress she was wearing the last time Ash saw her. Judith tolerated all the indecision for a while, then pointed out that Nora was expected to be there in one hour. "You've gone through all your gowns, ma'am. Twice. What are you looking for that isn't there?"

"I don't know. An *appropriate* look."

"It's a private meeting, isn't it? No one will judge you for what you wear."

"*He* will."

"Mr Allander's focus will surely be on what news you bring. Now, I suggest the plum-colored gown with the cap sleeves. You can wear that black cropped jacket on top—

the air is cool tonight. And your leather walking boots will be quite suitable. It's not as if you'll be dancing with the gentleman."

"Certainly not," Nora said, though of course the idea of dancing with Ash sent her into a little daydream straightaway.

A half-hour later, Judith managed to get Nora presentable and into a carriage. Judith rode with her, unwilling to let Nora be alone for any amount of time.

When they arrived, Nora was shown immediately into a small parlor, and told that Mr Allander would be informed of her arrival. Judith disappeared in that way only well-trained servants can.

Nora stood by the mantle, too nervous to sit. When she heard a floorboard creak, she spun around to see Ash.

He was just as devilishly handsome as ever, in an understated outfit that was tailored perfectly. He could have been about to leave for some late evening entertainment. Perhaps he would do just that after Nora left. In their time apart, Nora had half-convinced herself that she'd somehow exaggerated his charm. She hadn't—Nora's memory was precise, even when she would rather be wrong. He had the same exquisite face, same dark eyes. The only change from her recollections was that he looked a bit thinner, as if he'd been ill.

Ash had stopped short, just looking at her. He seemed about to say something, then stopped once more. He held up the letter she had sent. "You were attacked today."

"Yes. Judith took care of it."

"Good," Ash said, then fell silent again.

Looking closer, Nora saw that his face was actually haggard. "Are you well?" she asked, before realizing the question was too intimate for their supposed level of acquaintance and too caring for their actual relationship...

which was beyond repair.

He shook his head, pushing the question aside. "That's not why you're here, is it?"

"No. I've come about the messages. Someone attacked me for them…they must be important. But I can't decipher them alone."

"You could have contacted Chattan."

"I…thought it should be you."

He gazed steadily at her. There was a challenge in his expression. "Why?"

"Don't you want to finish this?" Nora asked. "I hate leaving a puzzle half-done."

"What do you care if I'm left puzzled or not? Anyway, as we both know, I'm not in the Zodiac."

Nora bit her lip. It had been a mistake to come here. "I'll go. You're right, I should have simply contacted Miss Chattan. I'm sorry to have intruded on your time."

She got three steps toward the door when Ash blocked her way. "No. I want to hear it. All of it." He added earnestly, "Please."

Nora couldn't look him in the eye when he was so close. "Very well. Shall we sit?" She retreated to a chair on one side of the fireplace.

Ash sat down in the identical one on the other side. "I'm listening."

"First, read the messages as I write them. Then we can discuss what they mean." Nora listed them, in order, from the first one to the last on a page Ash provided. Ash read them, then sat back, barely moving other than to tap his fingertips, over and over, soundlessly against each other.

"The last one was sent only a day before we had to leave the house," she said.

"Those messages are…"

"Weird. Nonsensical. Random." Nora nodded. "Edmund told me they were deliberately so, to do the tests properly. A person might guess the end of a well-known quote and thus a mistake in signaling could be overlooked."

"But you don't think they're random now?"

"No," Nora said. "I always thought they were a bit funny, but I never thought they were important enough to have someone attack me in an alley. There must a code in the messages—beyond the code used to send them, I mean. Edmund wasn't just testing my invention. He was already using it."

"You're probably right."

"I've tried to decipher it," she said, "but I'm better at thinking up patterns than uncovering someone else's."

Nora looked over the page again, focusing on the last several messages.

GIRL TOY WORTH SEA BAIT

SEABIRD FOUND NEST WATCH TOY WAIT

BIRD SEE TOY MARKINGS KNOWN

GET HER SON TOOL SOON FIREBIRD FLY NORTH

SHIP GO EMPTY BIRD STAY NEST TWO MISS ONE

RECEIVED ALLE

BIRDWATCH AT PAUL WORTH PATH DAWN BIRD BREAK TOY END

"I know these words are correct in the sense that they are what was sent via the flashing," said Nora. "But I've thought and thought and I still don't know what any of the messages *mean*."

Ash said, "We need to focus on one of these words to

begin. *BIRD*. That appears in almost all of them. So it's important. And there are variations—seabird, firebird." He paused, frowning. "Toy. Nest. It's all so...I don't know."

"Try. It's also what?" Nora asked.

"I said 'all so'. Two words."

Nora blinked in realization, then studied the paper again. "Two words. What if these compound words should be split? My system doesn't make spaces very clear...it relies on context for the receiver to sort it out."

"*FIRE* then *BIRD*," Ash said speculatively.

"*SOON* there will be a *FIRE*, then the *BIRD* flies *NORTH*. Isn't that what happened? There was a fire, and we fled north to London."

"So you're the *BIRD*?" Ash looked skeptical.

"No, I don't think that's me. But a *kingfisher* is a bird," Nora said.

"I thought of that too," Ash agreed. "Especially because Isabelle Kingfisher uses the last name Wren here in London. She was there in the house, so Edmund could have been referring to her in these messages, but why? What's the significance?"

"What if Edmund didn't create these messages? What if he was told to flash them by Isabelle? He'd take credit if he could. That's Edmund's usual practice, remember."

"Why would she feed him messages?" Ash asked.

"Because it was a good way to communicate with a contact of hers, all while keeping Edmund unaware of what was happening. He was entranced by her, so he'd do virtually anything she asked."

"But why did she need him?" Ash mused. "She was after the process, considering that I saw glass lenses like yours in her shed. She knew how it worked, more or less. She could have left at any time."

"She must have had a reason for staying in England. A reason why she couldn't just up and leave. A mission of some sort."

"*TWO MISS ONE*," Ash read out. "Two missions in one?"

"Perhaps she told the ship to go, because she was staying in the nest—Grasmere House. One mission was to steal my invention," said Nora. "Then what was the other?"

"I don't know. Something that made her stick close to Worthing, and also to live in London. What does she do all day?"

"Act like a snob?" Nora suggested. "If her mission was to be an irritating social climber, she did well enough, even if she never actually met Princess Amelia in Worthing."

"Princess…" Ash echoed. "In London, I saw her at the parade when the king traveled back from Worthing. She was watching him very closely, but I wouldn't say she looked at him in adoration."

"She's watching the royal family?"

"*BIRD SEE TOY MARKINGS KNOWN*." Ash pointed to one message. "How about this? Toy rhymes with *roi*, French for king. *Markings known*…she was studying the carriage, what it looked like, what horses were pulling it, maybe even the route the king uses."

"Based on a rhyme?" Nora asked uncertainly.

"I know it sounds far-fetched, but doesn't it also make a certain sense?"

"Maybe. You said you know where she's living?"

"Yes." Ash nodded. "We'll go to Isabelle Kingfisher and make her tell us what we want to know." Ash stood up.

"Wait, now? It's going to be well after midnight by the

time we get there!"

Ash gave her a little smile. "You truly don't spend much time in society, do you? Midnight is when the interesting things start."

"I suppose there's only one way to be sure of her. All right, let's go to her house and see."

Once decided, it didn't take long to get ready to leave. Ash gave some instructions, and then directed one of the footmen to pack two boxes in the carriage, one long and one short.

"What are you bringing?" Nora asked.

"Sword. Pistols. Some extra shot."

"Isn't that a bit…extreme?"

"When we're searching for a foreign spy who likes to set houses on fire with people still in them? No, I don't think so." Ash walked to the open door of the carriage and held out his hand, ready to help her inside.

Nora took a breath before putting her hand in his. It would mark the first time they touched since their falling-out. She wore gloves, but she was still unprepared for the effect, which was to make her want to throw herself at him and never let go. Instead, she raised her chin higher and pretended he didn't exist.

Thankfully, Ash let go as soon as she stepped up into the cab. He got in and sat opposite, looking entirely at ease. He didn't seem to be affected by Nora's proximity.

A moment later, the horses started trotting down the street.

He said, "With luck, we'll be able to surprise Mrs Kingfisher into revealing Edmund's whereabouts. Then, once he's detained, you can wrest the full meaning of the messages from him."

"What if he won't talk?" Nora asked.

Ash shrugged. "Then I move to the sword and

pistols."

"Let's hope it doesn't come to that."

They arrived at the place where Ash said he'd found Mrs Kingfisher. Despite the hour, several windows of the house were still lit up. But she was not there, according to the servant who opened the door.

"She's not here, or she's not receiving?" Nora asked, refusing to give up at this point. "We only have one question to ask her."

"She's not here, ma'am," the servant said more firmly. "She has gone out for the evening and I don't know when she'll return."

Ash had been peering into the home, where the furniture visible in the other rooms was getting covered with sheets. "Looks like you're not done readying the house after your mistress returned to the city after the summer."

"The sheets are going *on*, sir," the man said, exasperated. "The lady of the house and her guest may be away for some time. If you'd like to leave a card…"

"Who's the guest?" Ash asked.

"Excuse me?" the man replied. A polite gentleman did not inquire as to whom a stranger might be hosting, especially not of a servant.

"You again!" A new voice rang out. Nora looked further down the hallway, seeing a maid with a stack of blankets in her arms.

At the moment, the maid was fixated on Ash. "You must be *very* keen on tutoring, sir."

"Not exactly, Miss Clara," he responded, with the same sort of smile that once charmed Nora. "Do you happen to know where she went, and who she went with? Was it a man called Morrison?"

"Why yes, sir. He was staying here."

Ash cursed very softy, and this time Nora sympathized

with him. She should have guessed that the two would be with each other in London! Isabelle must have told Edmund that Nora set the fire—and he believed it.

"I don't know that they're coming back, though," the maid went on. "My mistress directed me to pack all of Mr Morrison's things. She said she'd know where to send them after she was done at St Paul's."

"St Paul's?" Nora asked. *PAUL* was one of the words in the messages.

"That's what she said." Clara gave a little shrug. "Afraid I don't know more than that."

"No matter," Ash said. "You've helped quite a bit already, Miss Clara."

A moment later, Ash had hustled Nora out the door and back to the carriage. "We've got to get to St Paul's Cathedral," he muttered. "Quarter of an hour, I think."

Nora was thinking hard, and thus forgot to hate Ash's hand on her back. "It's not the cathedral."

"How do you know?" Ash asked in a low voice, as he helped her inside.

"Intuition?" Nora frowned. "Something about that last message. *PAUL WORTH PATH.* A path is like a road. If we know it's a St Paul, then what if it's a church on a road? Think of the message like this: *St Paul's on the Worthing Road.* It must be a church along the highway to Worthing. You said she was watching the king's progress in the city earlier, and I remember how she'd always ask about his travel plans to the coast. Why would she need that?"

"*BIRD BREAK TOY.* If we're right about the meanings, she's the bird, the king is the toy. She is going to break the toy? She intends to assassinate him." Ash hit the roof with his knuckles. "Crewe, get on to the Worthing Road. Drive until you see a church called St Paul's. And drive fast!"

"Yes, sir!"

The carriage lurched forward. Just then, Nora realized Ash had been holding her hand. She jerked hers away, and caught Ash's hurt expression before he hid it.

"How long will it take to get there?" she asked.

"An hour or two, perhaps, depending on the state of the road. It's well outside the city."

"That's too much time! Can't we get help?"

"And lose more time? We can't fly, Nora. Neither can anyone else. It has to be us, now. You'll have to endure me a little longer."

"That's not what I meant," she demurred. "I just don't want to choose wrong."

"A feeling I know very well," Ash said, "despite choosing wrong nearly every time."

"What are we supposed to do? Just *sit* here? I'll go mad…at last."

Ash offered, "I could tell you a story, if you like."

"What kind of story?"

"The kind that's true."

Chapter 33

ASH KNEW THIS CONFESSION WASN'T going to be easy, but at least Nora couldn't run away—unless she jumped out of the carriage.

Instead, Nora turned to the window. "I already know the truth about you."

He tried again. "Listen to me, Nora. No one but me knows the real truth, because I've never actually told all of it to anyone before."

"So you deny the rumors?" she asked.

"List them, and I'll tell you which ones I deny."

That got her to look at him, though her expression was forbidding. "You *want* me to repeat your scandals back to you?"

"A lot of those scandals aren't mine. Some of them, yes. I'm no saint…haven't tried to be one since I was nineteen years old. But don't believe everything you hear. My name gets attached to a lot of rumors to add spice to the stories. Lord, if I actually seduced a tenth of the women who've claimed I did, I wouldn't have time to gamble away all the money I supposedly get from swindling my various lovers."

Nora shook her head. "You expect me to believe you over the rest of the world?" she asked.

"Well, I am the best-placed person to recount events," he said, "considering it's my life."

"They can't all be lying," she said, more uncertainly than before.

"People are uninterested in the truth when something else sounds better. The more lascivious the story, the more it's repeated in whispers, as all those proper ladies gossip with each other. Everyone enjoys scandal at arm's length...just like your friend from that other night. She told you all the stories quickly enough, and I expect she loved telling them."

Nora pursed her lips, unable to refute it.

"Let me tell you what really happened, Nora."

She wouldn't meet his gaze, but she muttered, "Very well."

So he told her. Told her every stage of his scandal, from the beginnings when he was an eager, naive student hoping to impress his superiors in the church as well as the people in the village. He described how he fell into what he thought was love...when he met Susan, and accidentally set up his own downfall after her mother Mrs Goulding tricked him and then accused him of such scandalous things he couldn't even respond. Instead, he got lost in the furor and lost the battle for his reputation before he even fully realized it was a battle. And by then it was too late. He'd been kicked out, essentially disowned, and was left without any support. He got his education—it just wasn't in the subject he expected.

As he talked, Ash felt some of the old anger boiling up, remembering his frustrations at his own ineptitude and the conventions of society that made it so difficult for him to speak clearly on what did—and didn't—happen. Yet, telling the whole story out loud to another person didn't sting quite as much as he feared. Perhaps because he was finally more worried about something else, namely Nora's reaction.

For the most part, she remained unnervingly quiet. Once or twice, she asked for another detail or a forgotten fact. But she never said a word of what she thought. And she let him keep speaking.

He sped up his account when he reached the part of the story where he moved to London. From that point on, the private and public versions of his life grew much closer. There were details, naturally, that the gossips got wrong. And there was the issue of his need for the laudanum, which he'd managed to hide from everybody until the end. But the essence was true: Ash became an immoderate, immoral scoundrel out to please no one but himself…and the string of women who insisted on joining him in bed. Ash became what people assumed he already was, and he wasn't going to deny that.

Nora sat in silence for a moment, pondering what he'd told her so far.

"There's something I need to know. When you were cast off by everyone, and made your way to London," Nora said at last, "you met Miss Fox."

"True. I met her very soon after moving to the city. Probably one of the luckiest moments of my life, though I didn't know it at the time."

"Lucky. Because you met a courtesan."

"We did have an affair. It started a long time ago," he said, his voice gentle. "And it ended quite a while ago, too. Years ago."

"How can you say that when you're obviously still so close to her?"

"We're close because we understand each other, in

ways that few other people can, or would want to. My relationship with Reggie has changed…just as I've changed. Yes, we began as lovers. But it didn't remain that way, for all sorts of reasons. But I do still love her. I hope I always will. I'm proud to call her a friend."

"What do you call me, then? A diversion?"

Anger flashed through Ash. "Who told you that?"

"No one told me. But what else can you expect me to think, after hearing—"

"Unless someone told you that I adore you, they don't know a thing."

Nora's eyes widened.

"I adore you," he repeated. "I've been in love before. I know what I'm saying. Just because I've had a number of relationships where love had nothing to do with it doesn't mean I'm incapable of loving."

"So the last time you were in love…"

"Was when I had just come to London. Regina was older, of course. She had entered her trade at fourteen, and was notorious by twenty, which was long before I met her. That she let me start an affair with her, Regina Fox, the woman in gold…I became more infamous for catching her eye than for what had caused my scandalous state in the first place. And I never looked back."

"But you still love her."

"Yes, but not in the way you think." Ash ran a hand through his hair. "Reggie's been a lot of things to me since I first met her, and yes, she is a courtesan, and yes, we had a relationship. But now it's different."

"How can it be? She's still a courtesan. She's beautiful and glamorous. She's everything I'm not. How can you pretend you're not in love with her?"

"Because people change. Love isn't the same day to day, Nora. It grows, or it shifts. Sometimes it dies. What I feel for Reggie doesn't have anything to do with how I feel about you."

Nora closed her eyes, and he could guess at her thoughts.

"Nora?" he asked after a moment. "Does it matter that much? That Reggie and I are friends?"

"Not if you're only friends, but…"

"That is all we are. Reggie will tell you the same thing."

"Because she knows what I want to hear!"

"God, Nora, if you won't believe anyone, how can anyone convince you? The last thing in the world I want is to hurt you."

"Then what do you want first in the world? What do you think of me?"

"I think you're far too good for me."

"Do you wish we hadn't met?"

"No," Ash said instantly. "I'd do it again, Nora. I'd steal you over and over."

She tried to take a breath, but it caught in her throat, and her eyes shifted, focused on something too distant for him to follow.

"Nora, Nora, listen to me." Ash reached to put his hands on her shoulders. "What happened? You were lost, darling."

"I was…remembering," she whispered.

"Us? You were remembering us?" he asked, hungry for any hint that she wanted the memories.

"Yes."

Ash really couldn't stand it anymore. He kissed Nora, fully aware that her response might be a slap in the face.

Her mouth was softer than he remembered, and instead of slapping him or pushing him away, she actually reached for him and kept him close. He didn't press her beyond a kiss, and he ended it before she might change her mind.

When he pulled away, she sighed and shifted a little, resting her head on his shoulder. The bliss he felt from that was stronger than any dose of laudanum he'd ever taken in his life.

"I wish you'd told me," she whispered.

"I know. I should have told you earlier. I did try, more than once. But we either got interrupted, or I lost my nerve, or I couldn't stand the idea of you hating me."

"I tried to hate you," Nora said. "I couldn't seem to get the knack for it."

Her words gave him even more hope. "You know, one of the reasons I fell in love with you is how you treated me. You trusted me, and you wanted my help. I forgot how that felt. And that's why I kept putting off the truth. I didn't want to lose that. It reminded me of who I'd rather be."

"Ash…"

"I'm not asking you for anything," he said. "I have no right to ask. But I wanted you to know the truth. What you do with it is up to you, love."

"I want—"

The carriage lurched to a halt. Ash looked out the window. "St Paul's. We've arrived."

* * * *

Nora stopped Ash as he was about to get out of the carriage.

"Wait. I want to begin again," she blurted out. Part of her was still wary, still wounded. But she could also sense that everything Ash had told her was unvarnished truth. It was so utterly different from society's view of him, and yet exactly in line with the man she knew. Nora recognized at last that Ash took a chance in being honest with her—from the very beginning, he'd acted as he felt he should, not how society or his public persona predicted he would. That was why he helped her at first, and why she fell in love with him so very quickly. Ash's deepest secret was that he was good. So she repeated, "I want to begin again. If you might forgive me."

"If I'd forgive *you*?" he said incredulously.

"I should have listened earlier."

"I should have talked earlier."

Nora reached for his hand. "Truce?"

"Truce." He took her hand, held it tightly, then let go. "First though, we have some business to complete." Ash pulled one of his ornate dueling pistols from their makeshift case below the seat. He handed it to Nora. "Hold this, please."

She took it nervously. "I don't know how to fire a gun."

"I've no intention of letting you get that close to danger. I'll take one pistol and Crewe will have the other," Ash explained as he retrieved the second.

The two stepped out of the carriage and started walking. They had been riding for nearly two hours—Crewe had made one brief stop at a tavern near the edge of the city, where he knew a Disreputable happened to be. A message would be taken as fast as possible to the Zodiac.

Crewe stopped the carriage just after passing St Paul's church, which sat very close to the road on the eastern side. He joined them, and Nora handed off the pistol with a feeling of relief.

Nora looked around. There was a hint of light in the east. It would be dawn in an hour, but for now all the trees were cloaked in blackness, with shadows below. The church was a darker, geometric bulk ahead of them.

"I don't see anyone," Nora said.

A second later, a clump of earth exploded near Nora's feet. Ash grabbed her and pulled her several feet away, into the shade of an oak. He stopped only when they reached the trunk, which blocked the view of the church. A man's indistinct shout followed, and Nora recognized Edmund's tone, though not the words.

"Gunshot," Ash said in a low voice. "Are you hurt?"

"No." She was feeling shaky though. "Did he just *shoot* at me?"

"Stay here," Ash warned. "Crewe, circle around the church grounds and then return to Mrs Morrison. We need to know if there's someone else around."

"Yes, sir." Crewe moved off, gun in hand.

Ash turned back to Nora. "Stay here, *please*. I'm going to go into the church to find Edmund."

"You can't do that. It's too dangerous. He'll see you coming!"

Ash smiled at her. "This is where I prove that my past studies weren't completely irrelevant. I know all the ways into and around a church. Don't worry about me."

"Say a prayer while you're at it," Nora said, feeling that he was being too cavalier about the whole process.

He dashed off, moving parallel to the long side of the church.

She leaned against the side of the tree trunk, peering around the edge, hoping to catch a glimpse of what was happening. A few moments later, she saw a figure walking through the churchyard toward the road. It was unmistakably Edmund. Furthermore, he didn't seem to be armed. He walked a little closer toward her as he got to the road. He was looking around, and then behind him, tense and alert.

She waited until he passed her tree, then stepped out to follow him.

"Edmund," she said, loud enough so he could hear her, but no one beyond could.

He whirled, saw her, and heaved a great breath. "Elanora! It is you. Were you hit?"

She held out her arms to prove her mobility, and to show she was empty-handed. "Does it look as if I was?"

"I couldn't be sure. I tried to stop…I was worried you were shot."

"Why would you care?" she asked, incredulous.

"I never wanted to actually hurt you, Elanora! I swear." In fact, he did look distressed. "It's Isabelle! She's up there, in the bell tower, and as soon as she saw someone moving about on the ground, she aimed and shot. I only saw that it was you a moment later, when you ran away."

"You're telling me that it's your mistress who's up there with a gun?" Nora asked, disbelieving.

"A rifle," he confirmed, even as he looked up and down the road, then back to the church tower. "She's an excellent shot. She's been planning this."

"Planning what, exactly?"

"The king sometimes travels this road to Worthing when he visits his daughter there. One of many routes. Isabelle has been studying them all. The roads, the timing, even the decorations on the carriages and what color horses are used." Edmund looked more and more panicked as he spoke.

Lord, she and Ash were mostly correct about the content of the messages. Nora pointed to the lantern he gripped in one hand. "Is that for a signal?" she asked.

"I'm to send the message towards the tower, where she'll see it. As soon as I spot the king's party at the end of the road there, by the bend."

"So she can be ready to kill him."

"Not kill!" Edmund protested. "It's a ruse, that's all. She'll shoot near him, but he'll live, of course!"

Nora just stared at him for a moment. Then she spoke. "Edmund Morrison. How dare you stand there on two feet and say such nonsense when you're the one who sought to have *me* declared mad?"

"It was only to keep hold of you," he said. "I was going to let you go. I was, I promise. I just wanted the invention, and the money from it. And then I was going to let you go, and just keep Albert's name. Who would have known? I intended to leave London anyway. Oh, this has all gone wrong," he said, with all the remorse of a bully who has met a larger bully.

"It started out wrong, Edmund. The moment you assumed your brother's identity, it was wrong. The moment you used me, it was wrong. But, by God, now you're in a plot to kill the king!"

"No! Isabelle said there would be no killing. She said we'd just stage an attempt, then we were to pretend to flush out the assassin, who we'd say got away. But the king would thank me! He'd be grateful and call me a hero. That's what Isabelle said…" He trailed off, perhaps realizing how utterly naive he sounded when he spoke the words out loud.

"You fool," Nora said, feeling a little sorry for him. "From the moment she met you, she's been using you for her own ends. You were flattered by her, and you told her about the invention—but you passed it off as yours. Then she came to the house, and you were completely ensnared. Did you never see it? Not even when she set the house on fire?"

"An accident," he whispered.

"No accident." Nora was merciless now—she had to get through to him. "Isabelle set that fire very deliberately. The lighthouse too. She was covering her tracks because she's a spy. A spy for the French."

Edmund shook his head. "It can't be."

"Her cover as Mrs Kingfisher probably worked on most people. But she speaks French perfectly well, and she lied about much of her past. You had to know something was off. You ignored it all because you wanted to believe her."

"She said we were natural partners," Edmund said. "With the invention and the money we'd make from selling it to the right people, we could do anything. She said she wanted me to make connections among the elite. But I had to be noticed…and what's more noticeable than saving the life of a king?"

"That was what she told you?" Nora asked. "She worked for months on all these details, and the minutiae, just to make *you* look good? You know what would have made you look good? Showing the signaling process to the government, just as Albert and I intended to do!"

"Don't rub my nose in it," Edmund said miserably. "I'm not my brother, and I never will be."

"Why would you want to be him?"

"Because he was better!" Edmund burst out. "He made a life for himself. Everyone who met him liked him, ever since we were boys. Identical twins, yet one was beloved and one was despised! It's not fair."

"The solution is to improve yourself, not steal another's life."

"Too late. It's too late."

Nora saw him look back to the church, and knew he was teetering on the edge of desperation.

"Edmund, look at me," she ordered. "It's never too

late. You can stop this madness."

"How? She controls everything."

"She does not," Nora snapped. "She's only one person. Even now, Mr Allander is probably dealing with her."

"That man," Edmund grumbled. "He stole you and your invention right from under my nose."

"He didn't steal me—I was running away. He just happened to be going the same direction."

"How fortunate for you."

"I think so," Nora said quietly.

"And what do you need me for, when you have someone such as him on your side?"

"It's not about sides! I need you to help us," she said.

"How?"

"Don't signal," Nora said. "All you have to do is *not* signal. The king will pass by before she's ready to shoot. He'll be safe. You don't have to continue the path you're on. You can choose differently."

"I don't know. I don't know." He looked back again. "If she suspects me of deserting her, she'll shoot me…"

"Then stay out of range." Nora shook her head, exasperated. How had such a man mastered her for so long? Then she remembered how broken by grief and shock she'd been, out of her mind with misery. It took her that long to come back to herself…with a little aid from Ash at the end.

"Come along," she said, pulling him toward her. "We'll move off into the trees, and she won't even know."

"You stay that, but she's got very good eyes…"

"No one can see through stone," Nora said. "Come. Give me the lantern. Keep walking."

Edmund offered her the lantern, too distracted to protest.

Nora took it by the iron ring at the top, feeling the

weight of the contraption. All that iron and glass did made it cumbersome. She'd have to refine that in the next phase of her work.

Edmund was shuffling along in the undergrowth, muttering about all women being false. Nora bit her tongue rather than point out that he used a false name for over a year. Edmund, she realized, was simply one of those people so wedded to his own view of the world that nothing and no one could sway him from it.

Suddenly, there was a rustling ahead, and Crewe rushed out into their path to intercept Edmund. "Stop there!" the servant warned Edmund. Crewe held the pistol in one hand, and he looked as if he was well acquainted with how to use it.

Edmund stopped, but then whirled around to face Nora. "This is a trap! You want to kill me!"

"No!" Nora said quickly. "Calm down, Edmund. Crewe won't hurt you."

The Disreputable said, "He's the one behind all this, isn't he?"

"Wait, Crewe," Nora said, hoping to diffuse the situation.

But Edmund turned once again, remembering the pistol. He glared at Crewe, who was a much smaller and slighter man. Nora could tell that Edmund was sizing him up, deciding that he'd win a fight even though his opponent was armed.

"You think you can trap me," he growled. "You should have brought an army. I'll beat both of you unconscious and then go after anyone else in my way."

"Bad idea, sir," Crewe said. "There are more people in your way than you can see."

"Eh?" Edmund looked quickly to the left and to the right, interpreting Crewe literally. Then he simply growled and bunched his shoulders, preparing for a brawl.

Nora recognized that look from Edmund, and couldn't let it come to blows. She took a breath, aimed, and swung the heavy lantern in an arc toward Edmund's head.

Edmund saw it too late to dodge or even block it with an arm. He slid to the ground, unconscious.

Crewe sighed and put the pistol down. "Guess you had the situation in hand, ma'am. I saw you both coming and wasn't sure what was happening. Jumped in too quick."

"No harm done," Nora said. "Well, he'll have a headache. But at least no one was killed."

Crewe nodded in approval. "He said your invention would be important in a war. I can see why."

Nora put the lantern down. "It's not the intended use."

"Handy all the same. Well, Morrison's nothing to worry about now, and if Mr Allander is in his usual form, he'll be improvising his way into a spider's web."

"Oh, Lord," she gasped. "We can't wait here. We have to help him."

"Course we do," Crewe said cheerfully. "That's the point, isn't it? Help each other, or else we're all just bumbling around in the dark."

Without another word, they left the snoring Edmund and made their way toward the church, where both her love and her enemy waited.

Chapter 34

ASH WASN'T LYING—HE REALLY did know his way around church buildings. It was not only his studies in seminary that gave him such knowledge. It was also a childhood in which he was small and insignificant, always on the lookout for hiding places and escape routes from older boys who tended to chase him. The refuge of a quiet church appealed to him long before he had any spiritual ambitions.

This church had its hiding places too. Ash found a small door toward the back, no doubt built to make it more convenient to walk between the church and the separate vicarage, which was set further back and showed no signs of life. Ash hoped that whoever lived there was a heavy sleeper—the last thing he needed was an innocent person wandering into this situation.

He entered the church itself and let his eyes adjust to the deeper darkness inside. He reasoned that the shooter was somewhere above, because any shooter wanted a good vantage point. There was a narrow, winding staircase in one corner. It wasn't meant for the public, but rather for servicing the bell tower and gaining access to the roof. Ash took a deep breath and reminded himself that it was all indoors, all confined space. He couldn't fall. So he climbed one step and then another, over and over. He was grateful that he could actually fit through the narrow passage. It was a tight squeeze—Bruce never would have made it with his bulky frame. At the highest level, when the stairs ended, Ash slowly, silently pushed open the door at the top.

He was at a small landing. One side of the landing accessed the bell tower itself, the ropes and chains visible through the opening. Ash's heart dropped, just thinking about the distance to the ground. He could fall after all.

Somewhere above, those ropes connected to the massive church bells. In another direction, the landing touched the front wall of the church, the one facing the road. There was a small round opening in the wall. It wasn't quite a window, but rather a vent, with wooden slats across it to allow air but block rain. A few of the slats had been ripped off to give enough space to poke the barrel of a rifle through.

Standing in front of the round vent was the woman he knew as Isabelle Kingfisher. Dressed very practically in men's clothing, she now held a rifle by the barrel, the butt end of it resting on the floorboards. She peered intently through the gap.

"Anything of interest down there...such as a king?" Ash asked.

She whirled around, putting a hand to her side, as if to draw a weapon. "How did you get up here?" she hissed.

Then she saw Ash's face, and frowned. "You. The auditor? Mr Allen."

"That's not exactly my profession, or my name," he said. He kept his pistol concealed behind his back, just as she was undoubtedly concealing something deadly behind her back. He went on, "But then, you're not Mrs King-fisher. Or Miss Wren. You like birds, though. I know that."

"You don't know who or what I am."

"I know you're an assassin. When is the king expected to come by?" he asked casually.

"Within an hour or two. My partner will signal when the entourage is sighted. I chose this place because he likes to take this road when he leaves the palace in the early morning."

"And how do you know he'll leave it this morning?"

"Because one of his people rode back from Worthing last night with a message. I have done my work. I recognize all the people close to the king and to the Princess Amelia. I know what carriages they use. And I pay to keep eyes on the gates so I know when news is delivered."

"No one thinks to hide news of the princess," Ash agreed. "It isn't guarded in the way that military information is."

"Yet it governs King George's movements, because he cares about her, and fears to be separated from her." She shrugged. "Compassion drives him. Compassion is a weakness."

"I'm sorry," he said.

"For what?"

"For you. It must be a sort of hell to think like that."

"You're a spy as well," she said. "So you must believe it too. Don't pretend to be a gentleman, concerned for my soul."

"Well, we are in a church," he said. "Does that bother you? To use a church to commit murder?" It bothered Ash. The whole idea violated the notion of a sanctuary, and Ash realized just how much he still cared about it.

"Not in the least. I told you—you know nothing about me."

"Let me guess who you are," Ash said, deliberately giving her a smile.

She rolled her eyes. "Why not."

"Your given name isn't very important, but your true name, the one that matters…L'Oiseau?" Ash asked.

She gave a tight smile, and he knew he guessed right. Her soubriquet was the French word for bird. She used the variations as throwaway names whenever she needed them.

"How?" she asked.

"The messages you told Morrison to send via the lantern signals," he explained. "You're the *bird* that's mentioned in several of them."

"Morrison told you? Or were you watching the lighthouse?" She frowned. "No. You weren't at the house that long…"

Keep her talking, Ash said to himself. Keep her distracted. "It wasn't Morrison, and I only saw a couple of the messages. It was Mrs Morrison who told me."

"Ah." L'Oiseau nodded. "She was your target all along? You took her away that night."

"I did," he confirmed.

"There was something about you…"

"My charm, you mean?"

She snorted. "You were too observant for a typical man. I couldn't be sure, though," she said. "Your description wasn't in any of my dossiers. We've infiltrated quite a few of your branches, you know. Who are you with? Navy? No. Are you one of Grayling's men?"

"I'm not a member of any group," Ash said, honestly enough. He had no idea what other groups she was talking about—he was just glad she didn't say Zodiac.

She raised an eyebrow. "An independent agent. How interesting. You heard about the lady's invention, didn't you? You knew the Emperor would pay for a communications system like hers, if someone brought it to him."

"How much would he pay?" Ash asked curiously.

"Thousands. It's worth more on the Continent anyway. Imagine towers everywhere, manned by signalers who can relay messages from Paris and back for hundreds of miles at any time of day or night." She seemed genuinely motivated by the prospect. In a way, her expression reminded him of Nora's—that same excitement and curiosity. But L'Oiseau turned her enthusiasm to rather horrid ends.

"Valuable indeed," Ash said out loud, hoping to keep her focused on the money.

She said, "There's no need to make a scene. I'll cut you in on the reward. After all, you got the inventor herself. Good work. That's worth a payment. She must have more ideas where that came from. We'll take her to France when I'm done here, and I'll manage the exchange."

"She's not leaving England. Neither are you."

L'Oiseau laughed. "You can't stop me."

"I think I can."

"Because you're a better agent than I am?" she asked in disdain.

"Truth is," Ash said, "I'm not an agent."

"What?" She blinked in surprise. "You have to be."

"I'm not. Just an ordinary person."

"If that's true—and I don't believe you—then why are you here?"

"Because I have to be. If I left it to others, it would be too late. Trust me, I never dreamed I'd be involved in anything like this. But I am...and I will certainly try to stop you killing the king."

Her expression went cold. She moved fast, whipping out a previously concealed knife. She lunged forward, ready to stab him.

Ash pulled his arm around, preparing to aim for her. Then she threw her knife, and he had to duck the whizzing blade.

The second of surprise was enough to let her pounce. Screaming, she fell on him and wrested the pistol from his grasp.

Ash pushed her hard, reaching for the weapon. L'Oiseau flung it away to prevent him from regaining it. It slid into a corner, lost in darkness.

Then she whirled backwards, and when Ash could straighten up and see her clearly, she held another knife in her hand.

"You're an arsenal all by yourself, aren't you?" he asked.

"I'm here to kill a king," she retorted. "What did you think I'd have…a book?" Then, without waiting for an answer, she lurched again, the knife gleaming in her hand.

Ash sidestepped just as she shifted her balance. His fencing lessons were ingrained in him, and even without a weapon, he could still defend himself effectively. He used the split second in which she'd already committed to a move and struck her arm at the elbow.

She gave a short scream of pain and reflexively opened her hand. The knife fell to the ground. Ash kicked it away, in the opposite direction the gun had gone. It skittered toward the opening of the bell tower and slid over the edge. There was a moment of silence, then a faint clatter far below.

"Long way down," Ash commented as he stepped back to the stairway door.

"That's how you'll go down," L'Oiseau snarled, even as she glanced out the round vent again.

Ash took a cautious breath. The lady's attention was in too many places. Once the signal was flashed to her, she only had a brief moment to carry out her plan and couldn't be distracted.

"Are you being paid to assassinate the king? Or is it a matter of patriotism?" Ash asked.

"Both," she said. "I'm being compensated, but it will also be a pleasure."

"What did an English king ever do to you?"

"Nothing. It's simply that we are at war. I am an enemy to everyone in this country. Even though I may smile and speak the language and laugh at bad jokes and pretend that I'm happy to be here…you're all enemies. A true agent never forgets what side she is on. I was given a task. I will complete it."

"No, you won't!" another voice proclaimed.

Those words were uttered by a breathless Nora, who had climbed the steps with the stealthiness she had perfected over the last year. Even Ash hadn't heard a thing.

He looked back at the doorway to see Nora offering the second pistol. "Take this!" she said.

"Ah, thank you." Ash took it, his hand sliding over the familiar grip. "That's better."

"No!" L'Oiseau had picked up the rifle and was aiming it directly at Ash.

"Nora, down the stairs," he shouted, moving to block L'Oiseau's sightline to Nora through the doorway. If the spy was going to shoot someone, he'd make sure it was him.

She shot, the sound from the rifle bursting through the enclosed space, just as Ash moved forward while ducking his head. Stone shattered behind Ash. Dimly, he was aware of his ears ringing in the aftermath of the shot, but he was still in motion, headed directly for L'Oiseau.

The drawback of her particular rifle was that it could only be fired once before it needed to be reloaded. She pulled back, preparing to use it as a bludgeon. But she was petite, and her fury wasn't well matched to Ash's years of training with Salvator Caizo, who frequently made him practice defending himself unarmed.

Ash put all those practice sessions to work. He grabbed her right arm and forced her to step back. He was too close for her to effectively swing the gun at him, and he kept pushing her backwards. Too late, she realized that she was teetering on the edge of the bell tower opening. She gasped, ducked hard, and slipped under Ash's arm. He grabbed the gun barrel as she did so, and pried the weapon from her.

Without thinking twice, he hurled it into the opening.

"No!" L'Oiseau's shout echoed off the stones.

"You're welcome to go after it." Ash scrambled away from the opening, his heartbeat tripling at the thought of stepping anywhere near it again.

She stared at him in absolute hatred, then looked toward the stairway, a calculating glint in her eye.

Ash knew exactly what she was thinking. She wanted to get Nora.

He lifted his pistol again. "Move to the vent, where you were before."

"You only have one shot," she said.

"Yes, but I won't miss. Move."

She took a sliding step backwards, obviously trying to think of some way to turn this to her advantage. She glanced to the corner, where the first gun had been lost.

"Don't try." Ash refused to look away and kept forcing her back step by step.

When one ankle ran into the wall, she stopped. "What now? Will you kill me?"

"Seems unsporting, I admit," said Ash. "I've got a gun and you haven't. Not a fair fight at all."

"Throw it away then," L'Oiseau said, with a sly smile. "We can fight again, hand to hand. I'll push you right off that ledge, I swear. You don't care for heights, do you?"

He ignored that. "I have no intention of shooting you. I'm not a murderer. Just walk down the stairs ahead of me, and I'll see you're detained for trial."

L'Oiseau curled a lip in disdain. "As if that's better. Just shoot me."

"No."

From the stairs, an unseen Nora shouted upward, "Ash, this is no time to be chivalrous!"

"The point of chivalry, Nora," Ash said, raising his voice and half-turning his head, "is that it's constant. One doesn't discard it simply because—"

He was interrupted by L'Oiseau hurling herself toward him, taking advantage of his distraction.

But unlike the beginning of their fight, this time his distraction was just a ploy. Ash never lost sight of his target. He aimed and shot.

She fell down heavily, her beautiful face etched with shock.

Ash expected her to offer a final insult, but as the moment of silence lengthened, he realized that she was already dead, and that everything was over at last.

"Nora," he said. "Where are you?"

"I'm not hurt," she replied, still unseen, answering his real question. "Edmund is unconscious outside. All is well...I think."

"Stay where you are. You don't want to see this." He turned away from the corpse and took the first flight of steps down to where Nora was waiting on the landing. "Let's get out of here. I'm quite done saving the realm."

Once on the ground floor of the church, he saw Crewe, who had set himself up to watch both the bell tower door and the way outside.

"Good to see you, sir! The lady told me to stay here below," Crewe said. "Just in case something else happened while you were both up there."

"Thank you, Crewe." Ash was conscious of feeling completely drained. It would be a long time before he forgot the face of the person he'd been forced to kill.

Nora slipped her hand into his, and Ash gripped it tightly. He had no words for Nora, not now. But he didn't let her go.

They walked outside. Crewe was ahead of them by several paces, and in the slowly strengthening light, they could see that Edmund was stirring. He sat up, holding his head.

Ash walked directly to Edmund. "Crewe, hold him."

Crewe nodded and did so, though it appeared that Edmund Morrison was no longer a threat.

"I won't hurt you, any of you," the man said. "What do you want from me?"

Ash held out one hand, indicating that Nora had the first say.

Nora crossed her arms. "Here's what I want. I want you to publicly declare that my husband, Albert Morrison, died over a year ago, in your presence. You'll give up any claim of any kind to his inheritance and to his wife."

Edmund nodded.

"If you don't, just remember that if you're put on trial for conspiracy to assassinate the king, you'll hang for your part in the plan."

He nodded again.

"And after that, I never want to see you or hear from you again. Understood?"

"I never thought it would go so far," he said, defending himself.

"You never thought at all," Nora said. "That's your problem. You assumed that to get something, all you had to do was want it. But such achievements take effort. And time. And the willingness to work for them, even when no one is praising you and there's no promise of a reward. Albert understood that. If you really want to be like him, you have to understand it too."

"I *am* sorry," he said.

"I accept your apology," she said. "But you're at a beginning, Edmund, not an end."

Ash nodded in wholehearted agreement. "Well said. Start walking, please. Crewe, see that Mr Morrison doesn't wander off. He looks a bit unsteady on his feet."

Crewe nodded, and took Edmund by the arm. "This way, sir."

Ash turned to Nora. "How are you?" She was trembling after a long night and a violent last hour.

Then Crewe pointed down the road. "Sir!"

A closed coach was coming down the road, moving at a speed much faster than was expected or safe.

"Is it the king?" Nora asked, fatigue making her voice quaver.

"Only one carriage, and no other riders," Ash replied, squinting to see better. "It may not have anything to do with us."

As it happened, though, it did have to do with them, because the carriage belonged to Bruce.

Before the vehicle came to a halt, Bruce, looking taller and more raw-boned than ever, pushed the door open and jumped out. He took a long look at everyone, then said, "I got the message. But it looks as though I arrived too late."

"Too late for the action," Ash said, sensing the reversal of roles. "But you're welcome all the same, brother."

Chapter 35

A FEW DAYS LATER, ASH walked outside the main house at Old Harrow, the ancestral home of the Allander family, specifically the Viscount Forester. He hadn't been there since before his father died, and he never thought he'd return. But after hearing Ash's account of what happened, Bruce insisted that he had to come *home*, just as Nora needed to go to her own home. Both Ash and Nora were overthrown by the weeks of tension, and both needed complete rest. Bruce didn't say it, but Ash knew that his brother also feared Ash would turn back to the laudanum at the first opportunity if he was left alone.

Ash had no desire for the drug. The only desire he had was for Nora to be as close to him as possible. Unfortunately, she had agreed she needed to return to her own brother's house. Ash feared the fragile truce they formed would break again, once Nora reconsidered everything.

He'd started half a dozen letters, and finished none of them. Though he'd spent a good part of his life knowing exactly what to say to women, when it came to Nora, words failed him.

The sky was just transforming from night to dawn.

The last few stars in the west winked out, and the eastern sky turned violet. He found a chair on the white gravel veranda. Despite the odd hour, he was fully dressed, and *not* in the outfit from the previous night. Ash used to get up early to watch the sunrise when he was very young. He decided to resume the practice, at least while he was in the old house. In a few days, no doubt, he'd be back to London. For now though, it was pleasant to ignore the future.

He was still sitting there an hour later, when it was full daylight and the household stirred with life.

Bruce found him there and took the opposite chair. "Morning. Could you not sleep?"

"I slept well. I just decided to wake up early—mostly to prove I could do it."

"There's no need to prove anything."

Ash nodded, but he didn't quite believe his brother. In many ways, Ash would spend the rest of his life proving himself to people.

"Do you have mornings like this?" Ash asked his brother. "I mean to say, we stopped an assassination attempt a week ago, and the sun is just there, rising in the east, as if it's an ordinary day."

Bruce laughed once. "I never thought of it like that. Yes. I suppose I have. Mornings where everything goes on as usual, because we can't say what happened the night before. That's an important element of the Zodiac—discretion."

"Pride of a job well done," Ash said. "Still, one might like a medal for valor. Not for me, of course. I despise ceremony. No one would believe it anyway."

"The right people know what's been done for the nation," Bruce assured him. "That's enough for any sign of the Zodiac. We don't seek glory."

Ash nodded, thinking that was rather what he'd been taught while he was studying theology. Glory wasn't a thing to be sought.

"Any word from Miss Fox?" Bruce asked after a moment.

"Letter arrived yesterday. She's pleased everyone is still alive."

"Tell her she's welcome to come out here to see you recuperate from your…difficulty with laudanum." Considering Bruce's and Reggie's respective positions in society, the offer was generous. Bruce was less tradition-bound than Ash had assumed.

But Ash shook his head. "She has to remain in London to take care of her business affairs. There's only a few weeks before her ship sails. She's decided to travel to America."

"For certain?"

"Yes. She's accepted her mother's invitation to go to Philadelphia. I believe the idea is that she'll meet the family she didn't know she had, and they'll all find out if they like each other. In any case, her passage has been booked, and within a few months she will dazzle a new continent."

"England will miss her."

"You mean I will." Ash sighed. "Reg did say she was sending a remembrance, whatever that means. Knowing Reggie, something unique. And very likely awkward."

"She does have a sense of humor," Bruce said. "I always liked that about her."

"Liked what about who?"

Ash looked around to see that Bruce's wife Sophie had joined them. He got up to offer his chair while he found another. "Morning, my lady," he said.

"Barely morning," the slender, pretty woman replied. Sophie sat down, arranged her skirts to her satisfaction, and then fixed her husband with a stare. "Liked what about who?"

"We were talking about Regina Fox," Ash said, a little maliciously. It wasn't every day that one got the chance to bring up a courtesan's name in front of his brother's wife.

Sophie merely smiled. "I only met her once, but she struck me as a most remarkable woman."

Ash glanced at her, surprised at her reaction. The Viscountess Forester looked a perfect lady, but Ash guessed she was not everything she seemed—for instance, when the hell had the proper Sophie met the scandalous Miss Fox? He wondered how deep her involvement with Bruce's activities went.

Sophie, however, moved swiftly on to other topics. "It's been some time since you've lived here at Old Harrow, Ashley."

"Well over a decade."

"What do you think?" She spread one arm in a gesture meant to encompass the whole estate.

He nodded to Bruce, knowing he was the one responsible for all the improvements of the land and the house. "I'm impressed. It looks better now than it ever did while we were growing up."

"Well, I've worked at it enough," Bruce said.

Ash nodded. "Fate knew what she was doing when she made you the eldest. Thank God the title went to you. You were meant to be here."

"And you? Do you wish to continue to live in London?" Sophie asked Ash.

"I suppose." Ash shrugged. "But I need a change of scenery for a while, at least until I find a way to deal with my less appealing habits."

Bruce and Sophie exchanged a glance. Then Bruce said, "Speaking of a change of scenery, Ash, join me for a ride. You've barely seen most of the estate since you got here."

Not long after, the two brothers were riding away from the main house, along a route of Bruce's choosing. The brightening day was clear, with only a few clouds in the west. A perfect day to ride. Ash was content to let his brother set the pace and direction. He was too occupied in looking around at the painfully familiar scenery. He was surprised to discover that not all his memories were bad ones.

"It's that tree," he said once, pointing to a massive oak in the distance. "The one I got stuck in the one time I actually climbed it!"

"I used how much rope to get you down from there?" Bruce asked, laughing. "You were prepared to camp on a branch overnight rather than trust my knot tying skills.

"Well, the way down looked far more terrifying when I got up to the top."

"As I recall, the promise of sticky pudding was the only thing that made you come down at all."

"Mrs Wilmore made the best sticky pudding."

"None better," said Bruce.

They entered a small, densely packed grove of birch. "This is the path to that old cottage, isn't it?" Ash asked.

Bruce nodded. "It is indeed."

"What was it called? Hawthorne Lodge? It must have crumbled to dust by now."

"Not quite. You'll see."

They rode through the fields and then a little copse of trees, emerging though the other side into a small valley. At one end of the clearing stood a modest home. Newly stuccoed walls shone bright white against the ancient, dark timber beams. The roof was new, as were most of the windows. A small garden flourished in the front of the house, growing rampant in the final warmth of the year.

"Look at that!" Ash said, feeling as if he'd slipped back in time.

"It *was* nearly a ruin before I had the funds to restore it." Bruce looked the cottage over with a critical eye. "Took a few years, but it's in better condition now than ever."

Ash saw the flap of a curtain through an open window. "Amazing. Who lives here now?"

"Well, no one. But it would do very well for a couple. For example, a newlywed couple, looking for a change of scenery."

"You're serious?"

"Neither you nor she have had much of a normal life lately. Perhaps it's worth a try."

"There are too many rumors…"

"So counter them with cold, dull facts. Counter them by showing the world that you too can be boring and domestic and respectable. Mr and Mrs Allander can do that, can't they?"

Ash took a breath. "There is no Mrs Allander. Not yet."

"You haven't asked her?"

"We were a bit busy the last time we were together. And I'm not sure how to go about it," Ash admitted. "Never done it before. Proposing, that is."

"You know, I scotched it when I first asked Sophie," Bruce said. "She more or less turned me down flat."

"Well, that's encouraging," Ash said sarcastically. "If a woman has to think twice before saying yes to a viscount, what will a woman say to me?"

"You won't know until you ask the woman," Bruce pointed out.

"Then I have some time."

"Less than you think. She's coming here."

"What?"

"I thought she'd have an interest in your recovery, so I invited her. She accepted. Should be arriving by coach tomorrow."

"You could have warned me!"

"I am warning you. You have a full day."

Ash turned his horse around, but then glanced back at the cottage. The appeal was undeniable, but he knew he wouldn't be happy there alone. "I'll have to ask Nora," he murmured.

"Good idea."

Chapter 36

ALMOST A WEEK HAD PASSED since the fateful night at the church. In London, Nora was finally free of the legal entanglements Edmund Morrison threatened her with. She was officially the widow of Albert Morrison, and as such, was able to accept the payment for "Albert's" invention of light signaling, the final version of which had been passed onto the proper authorities. After receiving payment for it, she would be a woman of independent, if modest, means. Nora could do whatever she chose to do.

Unfortunately, she wasn't at all sure what she did want to do. Living with her brother permanently was out of the question. Nora could never fit the mold of womanhood that he expected. She wanted to pursue her studies and her experiments. She wanted to travel. And she wanted to be with Ash.

But Ash was not in London, and Nora didn't know if he was having second thoughts about her—he sent no letters, a sign she regarded as foreboding.

When the letter from Lord Forester arrived, Nora scrutinized it as if it were in code. Was the invitation to visit a mere formality, an offer not meant to be accepted? Why did Ash not write to her himself? Why did she want to start packing *immediately*?

When Nora arrived at the estate of Old Harrow, both Allander brothers were there to meet her. Lord Forester, though still very tall and intimidating, clearly tried to put her at ease, unlike the last time they spoke.

"Welcome to Old Harrow," he said. "We've been expecting you."

"Thank you," Nora replied, with a little curtsey. "I'm glad to be here, because I have a difficulty."

"What difficulty?" Ash stepped up, his expression worried.

Nora opened the door of the carriage again. A small puppy with a reddish gold coat bounded out and promptly began running in circles around the trio. "*This* is my difficulty. He's very energetic. And likes to chew."

"You have a dog?" Ash asked.

"No. *You* have a dog, courtesy of Reggie. She arranged for me to bring him along. She says her final patron—that Hungarian count—raises them. Reggie begged one puppy from the last litter. Apparently, they're very loyal. And good hunting dogs."

"I don't hunt," Ash said, already bending down to the ground to greet the newcomer. The dog sniffed curiously, then leaned into Ash, with a happy whuffling noise. "But I suppose I could learn. He'll need a name."

"Think about that later," Lord Forester said, scooping up the tiny, wriggling dog as though he did that sort of thing every day. "Why not let our guest get settled?"

Nora was shown to a bedroom, and then set upon by the vivacious Lady Forester, who gave her a tour of the house that culminated in a turn around the gardens. At the end, Ash stood there, waiting for Nora.

Lady Forester handed Nora off to him with a beatific smile. "I imagine you both would like some time to yourselves. Dinner is at seven!"

Ash offered an arm to Nora, who took it instantly. "I wasn't sure if I was really meant to come here," she confided. "But I wanted to see you."

"You're meant to be here, love," Ash said, leaning over to give her a quick kiss on the cheek, regardless of who might be watching.

Nora ducked her head, feeling shy. "I suppose our relationship is not exactly a secret now."

"I hope not. I want the whole world to know that I adore you."

Hearing Ash say those words out loud made her heart race. "Well. That's bold enough."

"I'll probably always be a little scandalous," he admitted. "Though I'm trying to be more proper."

"Not trying too hard, I hope," Nora said. "I like the Ash I know."

"The scandalous one?" He gave her another kiss, this one considerably less proper than the one before.

"Ash!" she scolded him...once she got her breath back.

"Liked it?"

"Yes! But that doesn't mean you can just kiss me anywhere or anytime!"

"Tell me where and when, love," he said, his grin positively rakish. "I'll be there. I've missed you," he added, his voice changing to a more somber note. "I've missed you more than you can guess."

"I'm here now," Nora said. "And so are you."

Ash nodded. "Not a bad place, is it? Old Harrow. Thought I'd never set foot on the estate again. Now that I'm back, I feel like I could stay. You know, there's a little cottage on the estate."

"Would your brother approve of that?" Nora asked curiously.

"He made the offer."

"Oh." Nora looked over the land. "I can see the appeal. It's beautiful here. So peaceful."

"Yes."

"Do you want a peaceful life?" she asked.

"What do you mean?"

"You did well as a spy," she said. "They want you to keep working for them. They don't say it, but I saw how Miss Chattan acted before, and how your brother acts now. They'll ask you to join the Zodiac. I suspect your brother wants you close for that reason."

"Perhaps it's you they want, you and your gift for memory."

"I've thought of that," Nora said calmly.

"Would you ever be interested in…such work?" Ash asked hesitantly. "Not that you need to. With the income from your invention, you can do what you like."

"I'd like to invent something else," she said. "Many things. Something that will help win the war, or better yet, avert the next war. I can't do that if I'm all on my own. Lone genius sounds well and good, but most advances are the result of cooperation."

"So you would be interested in working with the Zodiac?"

Nora smiled at him. "Perhaps. It depends, of course, on my situation. I haven't quite yet decided what I'll do or where I'll live."

"Ah." He looked at the ground. "As to that…I should state, um, that is, I have intentions."

She bit her lip to avoid laughing at his sudden bashfulness. "Have you? Tell me."

"My first intention is to sever most of my old associations, and to recover from my past habits, the laudanum above all."

"That's wise."

"My second intention is…when I'm better, I will ask you to be my wife."

"No," she said, very gently.

Ash looked stricken. "No?"

"No." Nora took his hand. "I'm not willing to wait that long, and I don't want to be the prize for your good behavior. I want to be with you *now*. Now is when you need me, when you need to be with people who love you. I approve both your intentions, Ash, but not the order of them."

He took a deep breath, his expression caught between hope and fear. "What if I fail again? I'd hurt you as well. I can't do that to you."

"Love isn't for perfect people. If you fail, all the better for me to be there to help you get back up." Nora turned so she was facing him fully. "I don't ask for you to be a perfect husband or a perfect man. All I want is for you to try, and to be honest with me. That's my offer, Ash. Take it now, or leave it forever."

"Did you just propose to me?" Ash asked.

"Yes." Nora smiled at him. "Interested?"

He had her in his arms so fast she almost didn't get a breath in before he kissed her. Then he let her go just long enough to say, "Will you stay with me, Nora? I can't promise I'll be perfect. But I'll try. Marry me, and hold me to my promise."

"I will," she murmured. "I'll hold you to your promise, and you just hold me."

ABOUT THE AUTHOR

Elizabeth Cole is a romance writer with a penchant for history. Her stories draw upon her deep affection for the British Isles, action movies, medieval fantasies, and even science fiction. She now lives in a small house in a big city with a cat, a snake, and a rather charming gentleman. When not writing, she is usually curled in a corner reading...or watching costume dramas or things that explode. And yes, she believes in love at first sight.